Vonda N. McIntyre is a multiple Nebula Award–winning author of more than a dozen novels of science fiction including *The Moon and the Sun*, the *Starfarers* series, and books set in the *Star Trek* and *Star Wars* universes.

NEBULA AWARDS

AWARDS

SHOWCASE

2004

EDITED BY

Vonda N. McIntyre

A ROC BOOK

ROC
Published by New American Library, a division of
Penguin Group (USA) Inc., 375 Hudson Street,
New York, New York 10014, U.S.A.
Penguin Books Ltd, 80 Strand,
London WC2R 0RL, England
Penguin Books Australia Ltd, 250 Camberwell Road,
Camberwell, Victoria 3124, Australia
Penguin Books Canada Ltd, 10 Alcorn Avenue,
Toronto, Ontario, Canada M4V 3B2
Penguin Books (N.Z.) Ltd, Cnr Rosedale and Airborne Roads,
Albany, Auckland 1310, New Zealand

Penguin Books Ltd, Registered Offices:
80 Strand, London WC2R 0RL, England

First published by Roc, an imprint of New American Library,
a division of Penguin Group (USA) Inc.

First Printing, March 2004
10 9 8 7 6 5 4 3 2 1

Copyright © Science Fiction and Fantasy Writers of America, 2004
Additional copyright notices can be found on page 281.
All rights reserved

Set in Bembo
Designed by Ginger Legato

REGISTERED TRADEMARK—MARCA REGISTRADA

Roc trade paperback ISBN: 0-451-45957-1

Printed in the United States of America

CONTENTS

INTRODUCTION: THE HEART OF THE NEBULA

In 1965, Damon Knight had the brainstorm of starting Science Fiction Writers of America (now Science Fiction and Fantasy Writers of America), SFWA. Persuading a group of writers to agree on anything is often compared to herding cats. Even contentious people can see the benefit of banding together to share information and work for better conditions for writers, so Damon succeeded. He founded the organization, served as SFWA's first president, and chaired the contracts committee for many years. Today, almost forty years later, the publishing climate is increasingly difficult for writers and SFWA's work even more important.

I recently tracked down SFWA's charter membership list (you might find it in the SFWA history section—now in the planning stage—of the SFWA Web site, *http://www.sfwa.org/*. The charter members included many of the best-known names in the field, as well as a number of newer just-hitting-their-stride writers. The established writers included Poul Anderson, Isaac Asimov, Leigh Brackett, Rosel George Brown, Robert A. Heinlein, Fritz Leiber, Edgar Pangborn, Frederik Pohl, Edward E. Smith (E. E. "Doc" Smith), Theodore Sturgeon, A. E. Van Vogt, and Jack Williamson: the authors whose work enthralled those of us in the baby boom generation and influenced the people who created the American space program. They are writers whose stories are still in print, still vital.

The newer writers on the charter membership list included Ursula K. Le Guin, Joanna Russ, Robert Silverberg, and Kate Wilhelm, writers who blazed new trails for science fiction and fantasy, and who opened doors for those of us who started publishing in the next few years.

Many of the writers on that original list are still writing—Grand Master Jack Williamson won a Nebula in 2001 for his novella, "The Ultimate Earth." A number of years ago when Jack got his first computer and enthused about it in Old High Martian like any teenage computer geek, I treasured putting that incident together in my mind with the story that he emigrated to New Mexico, in a covered wagon, in 1912. (If the story is apocryphal or even only exaggerated, I don't want to know. As a wise friend once told me, "A story isn't worth telling if it isn't worth exaggerating." However, I've found over the years that amazing stories about sf writers tend to be . . . true.)

Several of SFWA's charter members have stories or articles in this book. One of the new writers on that first membership list, Ursula K. Le Guin, received the Grand Master award this year, as well as publishing a new collection of short stories. Though she writes in many fields and many forms, she always describes herself first and foremost as a science fiction writer.

This anthology's table of contents resembles the original SFWA charter membership list; it's about equally divided between established writers, and writers who are just hitting their stride. I expect that in another forty years, many of those established writers will still be working, expanding our universe with their imaginations. In forty years, the newer writers will include Grand Masters.

But some of the charter members are gone, now. In 2002, Damon Knight died. His colleagues have written about him, in his many incarnations—writer, artist, critic, colleague, teacher, mentor. I'm sad at his passing, but glad to be able to celebrate his life.

My earliest memories are of science fiction and fantasy. I think I dreamed science fiction in my playpen. I started writing before I knew how to read. And there were always dinosaurs close by (the first film I ever saw was called *King Dinosaur*).

But I made a marvelous discovery in 1965, when I bought my very first issue of *The Magazine of Fantasy & Science Fiction*: whole worlds beyond my reading of Wells, Verne, and the Heinlein and Asimov juveniles.

Sometime around 1971 I bought a copy of the Ted White–edited *Amazing Stories* and the crazy notion came to me that I might sell a story or two to them. A mere twenty years later I accomplished that. Thirteen years after that, "Bronte's Egg" gets a Nebula. On a geologic scale my rise has been incredibly swift, though my output is still slow enough to make Howard Waldrop look like Lester Dent or Walter Gibson in comparison.

About "Bronte's Egg": I know a shrink who thinks all my stories are an effort to find or create the family I never had (as compared to the family I did have). He's probably right, but I think that observation describes an entire, plentiful class of writers. What's interesting to me is how far that simple need can take a writer into realms that she or he would never have ventured. What does one make of a "family" that consists almost entirely of discarded, abandoned, misused toys? There were several times while writing "Bronte's Egg" that I stopped myself and said, "No one is ever going to stand for this!" For some odd, compulsive reason, instead of giving up I just worked all the harder. I couldn't give up because somewhere in this preposterous story situation I perceived something that was really worth saying—but that's true with everything one writes, isn't it?

The response to "Bronte's Egg" has been a complete surprise but extremely gratifying. Readers are good people, and I trust them to know when I've given them something worth their time and effort. I hope I can continue to keep doing that, and I thank them for having followed my madness this far.

Richard's Web site is http://www.sfwa.org/members/chwedyk/.

RICHARD CHWEDYK

There is an old house at the edge of the woods about sixty kilometers out from the extremes of the nearest megalopolis. It was built in another century and resembles the architecture of the century before that one. In some ways it evokes the end of many things: the end of the road, the end of a time, the end of a search (which the house has been, and on occasion it still is). But it is also a good place for beginnings, a good place to begin a story about beginnings—as good as any and better than most.

And it began at dawn.

As the first hint of daylight entered the large second floor bedroom where the saurs slept in a great pile, Axel opened his eyes and whispered, "Yeah!"

There was *stuff* to do and he was ready.

He pulled himself out from under Agnes' spiked tail and Rosie's bony crest and horns, then over Charlie's big rear end, almost stepping into Pierrot's gaping mouth. He pressed, prodded and pushed his way until he could lift up the blanket and make a straight dash to the window. He hopped onto a wooden stool and from there climbed up another step to the box-seated window ledge. His little blue head moved left to right like a rolling turret as he stared out at the wall of trees past the yard, silhouetted against the brightening sky.

The *sun* is coming! And the sun is a *star*! And it's spinning through *space*! And *we're* spinning through space around the sun! And—there's *stuff* to do!

"Stuff to do!" he whispered, hopped back to the stool and then to the floor.

Axel looked back at the sleep-pile. It was a great, blanket-covered mound. Except for the breathing, a few grumbled syllables and occasional twitches, none of the other saurs stirred. They were good sleepers for the most part—all but Axel. Axel could run about all day long from one end of the old Victorian house to the other, and when sleep time came and the saurs gathered themselves into a pile, he would shut his eyes—but nothing happened. His *mind* kept running. Even when he did manage to drift off, his dreams were of running, of traveling in speeding vehicles, like interstellar cruisers. And even if *he* wasn't moving, he dreamed of motion, of stars and planets and asteroids, of winds and birds and leaves in autumn. The whole universe was whirling and spinning like an enormous amusement park ride.

He'd been to an amusement park once, so long ago he couldn't distinguish it anymore from the rest of life.

He had no need to creep out of the room. The thump-thump-thump of his big padded feet disturbed no one. His tail in the air didn't make a sound. He ran past the room of the big human, Tom Groverton. The human ran and ran all day long too, cleaning and feeding and keeping the saurs out of trouble—but he got tired and slept almost as hard as the saurs.

Axel headed down to the first floor. Descending human stairs should have been difficult for a bipedal creature only forty centimeters tall, but he flew down them with ease. There were *so* many things to do today! The universe was so big—that is, *sooooo* big! How could anyone just lie about when the sky was already lighting up the world?

No way! Axel thumped the floor with his tail. Space and Time and Time and Space! The Universe is one big place!

He'd learned that from the computer.

The computer was on a desk in the dining room, or what had been the dining room when the house was just a place for humans, before it became a shelter for the saurs. The desk was over by the east-facing window. The computer was old in many respects, but the old computers were often more easily upgraded, and as long as they were linked to all the marvelous systems out there in the world past the porch and the yard, there was nothing this old model couldn't do.

"Yeah!"

Axel rolled a set of plastic steps up to the desk and dashed straight up until he stood before the huge gray monitor—huge to Axel, at least.

"Hey! Reggie!" Axel addressed the computer by name.

The computer could be voice-activated and voice-actuated. The brain box chirped at Axel's greeting and the screen came to life. Icons were displayed in the corners and along the top, one of them being the Reggiesystems icon: "Reggie" himself, the light green seahorse-or-baby-sea-serpent thing, with its round black eyes and orange wattle that drooped down his jaw like a handlebar mustache.

The icon dropped to the center of the screen and grew until it was almost half the height of the screen. The figure of Reggie rotated from profile to head-on and in a smooth, slightly androgynous voice he spoke:

"Reggie is ready."

"Hiya!" Axel waved a forepaw and smiled, mouth opened wide, revealing all his tiny, thorn-like teeth.

"Good morning, Axel," said Reggie. "What can Reggie do for you today?" Reggie always referred to himself in the third person.

"A whole bunch of stuff!" Axel stretched his forepaws far apart. "Important stuff! Fate of the universe stuff! Really truly big important stuff!" His head bobbed with each exclamation.

"Where would you like to begin?" Reggie said with patience.

Axel looked sharply to one side, then the other. "Don't know! I forgot. Wait!" He nodded vigorously. "The screensaver! Show me the screensaver!"

The icon's head seemed to jiggle slightly, affirmatively, as if acknowledging the request. Reggie disappeared and the screen darkened to black. Axel drew his paws together in anticipation.

A bright speck appeared in the center of the darkness. It grew until it flickered gently, like a star, then grew some more until it looked as big as the sun.

It *was* the sun—as it might look if you were flying through space, directly toward it. It filled the screen until it seemed you were in imminent danger of crashing right into it.

"Aaaaaaaahh!" Axel screamed with delight.

The sun moved off to the right corner of the screen, as if you were veering away and passing it by. Darkness again. Another bright speck started to grow in the screen's center: Mercury, the closest planet to the sun. It was followed by Venus, then the Earth, and Mars, and Jupiter—all the way through the solar system until a pudgy oblong bump rolled past odd-wise and all that was left on the screen were hundreds, thousands of bright specks, changing their positions at differing speeds, as you might see them if you were flying through space.

"Yeah!" cried Axel. *"Yeah!!"*

Through the haze of the Oort Cloud, then out past the solar system, the stars kept coming and coming until you could make out a bright little smudge, like a smeared thumbprint in luminous paint.

It was a galaxy! Another galaxy!

"Yeah!" shouted Axel. "Yeah yeah-yeah-yeah-yeah YEAH!"

The galaxy grew in size until you could just about make out some of the more individuated members of the star cluster. Axel cheered them on.

"Yes! Galaxies! Let's *go!*"

The screensaver cycle was over and it was back to the beginning: the little speck grows into the sun, then the planets, then the far off galaxy—

Axel watched it all again, and then one more time before Reggie interrupted his reverie.

"There was something else you wished Reggie to do?"

"Ohhhh. That's-right that's-right that's-right!" Axel kept his eyes on the moving stars. He remembered someone from the dream he'd had during his brief sleep: he couldn't remember who, but it was someone he wanted to talk to. "I gotta send a message!"

"And where do you wish to send the message?"

Still looking at the screensaver, he said, "To *space!*"

Reggie took an instant longer than usual to reply. "Space, as an address, is not very specific. Are there any particular coordinates in space to which you wish your message directed?"

"What are coordinates?" Axel kept looking at the stars.

The screensaver blinked away. In its place appeared numbers from top to bottom: numbers with decimal points and superscripted degree signs—

"Coordinates," Reggie said, "are a way to divide space by increments, so that one can more accurately determine which part of space one is looking at or to which section one might want to direct a message."

"Ohhhhh."

Reggie scrolled the numbers upward. Axel gaped at them, partly perplexed at the notion of numbers as directions, partly in awe at the sheer volume of them. Numbers, decimal points, degree signs—space was threatening to become an impenetrable wall of numbers. If he thought about it any more his head would heat up and explode.

"That one!" Axel pointed with his left forepaw. "I'll take that one!"

The numbers stopped scrolling. "Which one?" asked Reggie.

"*That* one!" He pressed the forepaw to the glass screen, then tapped against it adamantly.

The numbers were so small—and his forepaw so big in comparison—that Reggie could still not discern which coordinate Axel had chosen. Reggie highlighted one of the numbers in bright red.

"This one?"

"Yeah! That's it!" In truth it wasn't. But the red highlighting was so distracting to Axel, whose choice of number was already purely arbitrary. Facing a wall of numbers, one seemed as good as another. "Send it there!"

"What kind of message?" Reggie asked. "Vocal? Alphabetical characters? Equations?"

"Like, maybe radio," Axel said. "Or whatever you've got that's faster, like micro-tachy-tot waves, or super-hydro-electro-neutrinos."

"One moment," said Reggie. "At what frequency?"

"Frequency? Just once is okay." He rubbed a little spot just under his jaw.

A machine, even one as sophisticated as this Reggiesystems model, is not given to sighing, though one might imagine this model had many occasions to do so. What Reggie did was increase his pauses and slow down his speech delivery.

"What is meant by 'frequency,' Axel—" Reggie explained it all carefully. Axel faced another wall of numbers and made another choice—exactly the same way he'd made the first.

The numbers disappeared and the screensaver images returned. Axel watched it as avidly as if he'd never seen them before.

"Reggie has reserved time on the radio telescope at Mount Herrmann. The message can be sent at 13:47 our time this afternoon, when their first shift team breaks for lunch."

"Wow!" Axel's head reared back. "Thank you, Reggie. Thank-you-thank-you-thank-you!"

"Reggie still needs one more piece of information."

"What's that?"

Very slowly, Reggie said, "The *message*, please."

"Oh, right!" Axel tried to remember the message he'd worked out during the night, as he'd peeked out from under the blankets and stared out through the window—at the rectangle of indigo speckled with pinpoints of light—and imagined all the "space guys" out there. Space and Time and Time and Space—They might look like Axel:

blue theropods with coal-black eyes, tiny forepaws and clumpy feet—but without the long scar down his back; or they might look like one of the other saurs—miniature tyrannosaurs or ceratopsians or long-necked sauropods or crested hadrosaurs. Or they might look like human guys, or birds, or jellyfish, or clouds—

"What is the message?" Reggie asked.

"Okay-okay-okay. The message—" Axel held out the last syllable as long as he could to buy a little more time. "—is—it's—'Hiya!'"

"That is the message?"

"Yeah."

"The *complete* message?" Reggie didn't often emphasize his adjectives that way.

"I don't know. Is that enough? What else should I say?"

Reggie paused long enough to formulate an appropriate answer. "You may say as much or as little as you like, but it is customary to tell the recipient of a message who you are."

"Why?"

It may just have been a function of the old hard drive (technology had long since moved past the use of them), but Axel heard a strange, almost nervous, clicking coming from inside the brain box.

"Because the recipient might possibly—for some reason completely unknown to Reggie—want to send a message back to you, in reply."

"Heyyy—" Axel imagined the screensaver running backward—you could do that if you looked at it hard enough—back through space the other way. "Space guys! Yeah!"

"You may also want to tell them a little about yourself," Reggie suggested. "Where you live. What you do. Where you come from—just to be friendly."

"Ohhh! Yes! Got it! Yes! I can say—'Hiya! I'm Axel, and I live in this big house and I'm here with all my friends. We're saurs, you know, all of us except for the human who brings us food and cleans up stuff. His name is Tom. But we're saurs!

"'Saurs are like dinosaurs. They were these really big guys who lived a long time ago and went extinct. We're supposed to look like them except we're smaller and we don't have the scary parts.

"'We came from a factory that was like a laboratory too, and we were made out of living stuff—you know, biology.

"'They made millions of us and sold us to humans as toys. All these human guys who made us made big, big money and drove around in giant bankmobiles and wore top hats and had houses a *thousand* times bigger than this place. But then they had to stop selling us.

" 'Turned out we were smarter than we were supposed to be, and lived longer. This lady from the Atherton Foundation said we weren't toys at all but real-real-*real* things that were alive and they shouldn't be selling us.

" 'But we kept getting cut up and run over, or the kids who owned us stepped on us or threw us out of windows. Or the parents who bought us drove us to the woods and left us there—or they stopped feeding us and stuff like that. So after a while there weren't many of us left.

" 'People started to believe the Atherton lady. They set up a bunch of houses for us and that's how we got to live here.

" 'We do all sorts of stuff the guys who made us didn't think we could do, like think and feel and live longer than three years. My buddy Preston writes books. My other buddy Diogenes reads all the stuff in the library. And the Five Wise Buddhasaurs, who don't say anything but they play this stuff that sounds like music sometimes. And Agnes is this stegosaur with plates on her back and spikes on her tail and she knows all about humans and what's wrong with them. She's twenty-five years old, so she must know *everything*. Doc is smart too, but he's nice!

" 'The guys who made us said we couldn't make eggs because we don't have the right parts and stuff, but we can do *that* too! Not me, but like Bronte and Kara—female guys. The humans aren't supposed to know, except for Tom and Dr. Margaret—she's the lady who comes every week to make sure we're not sick or dead. I'm not supposed to know either because they think I can't keep a secret, so don't tell the other space guys about this, okay?

" 'And when I finish this message, I'm gonna build Rotomotoman. He's this cool robot I dreamed about last night. Reggie's gonna help me, because Reggie's the very-best-smartest whole computer in the world. Then I'm gonna get on a starship and travel all through time and space and save the universe and crash into supernovas and get sucked into wormholes.' "

Axel took a long, necessary breath, then said to Reggie, "Is that okay?"

"Under the circumstances," Reggie said, "Your message is— exceptional."

"Wow!"

"It is, however, customary to ask after the well-being of the recipient of the message, and to close the message—"

"Oh, oh, I know! I know! So I'll say, 'Hope you're okay. Your friend, Axel.' Like that, right?"

"The message will be sent as you dictated it," Reggie replied, "with a few grammatical corrections."

"All *right!*" Axel leapt up. "A message to space! Thank you, Reggie! Oh, thank-you-thank-you-thank-you-thank-you!"

"You are very welcome, Axel," said Reggie. Then, with what one might interpret as a trepidatious pause—and with careful attention to pronunciation—he asked, "Now, please explain to Reggie, what is a Ro-to-mo-to-man?"

■

Tom Groverton stood at the door of the room where the saurs slept. Eyes half open, hair still mussed, a middle button of his shirt undone, he said the word "breakfast" clearly but not too loudly and stepped back as the little ones ran past him.

The bigger saurs rose slowly: grunting, grumbling and stretching. The triceratops named Charlie always had a little trouble righting himself. He braced up against his mate, Rosie, until his hind legs were reasonably straight. The two gray stegosaurs, Agnes and Sluggo, went through a ritual that resembled push-ups—hind legs first, then forelegs up slowly with a sliding sort of motion.

Hubert and Diogenes, the two biggest theropods—each over a meter and a half tall—helped the other big guys, like Sam and Dr. David Norman. Tails really do help.

Diogenes lent a forepaw to Doc, the light brown tyrannosaur with a "tricky" left leg.

"Thank you, my friend," Doc said, his eyes barely visible under his thick lids. "Each day it seems to get a little harder."

"It does for everyone," said Tom Groverton from the doorway.

Doc nodded. "But not quite the same way for everyone. You were a little one once, who grew into an adult. We saurs were engineered. We were 'born' with our eyes open. What growth we experienced is beyond memory. The little ones stay little and the big ones were always big."

"Either way, we grow old," Tom insisted.

"Until we grow cold." Doc smiled serenely. "Or perhaps you can say we wear out instead."

"So do we."

As Hubert and Diogenes folded up the blankets and covers, Tom walked over to the wheeled, bassinet-sized hospital bed in the center of the room. Upon it was a figure who was recognizably a saurian and recognizably a theropod, but whose limbs—all of them—were missing and whose tail was a crushed-looking stump. Several long-healed scars criss-crossed his abdomen and where his eyes should have been were empty sockets.

"Good morning, Hetman," Tom said to the figure on the bed. "How are you feeling?"

"Not so bad." Hetman's voice was faint and raspy, always a little more so in the morning. "I had an odd dream. Odd, but pleasant."

"What was it?" Doc asked, resting his forepaws on the bed railing.

"Very odd. Very odd indeed." Hetman turned his head toward the voices. "Can you imagine me riding on a horse's back?"

"I can, old friend." Doc closed his eyes. "Like Zagloba, the Cos-sack—rebellious, reckless, full of life—riding with incomparable skill." He opened his eyes again and smiled. "It must have been a splendid dream."

Hubert and Diogenes stood at the bed railing, ready to move Hetman downstairs to breakfast.

"Like some help?" Tom offered.

"They can manage." Doc spoke for them. Hubert and Diogenes were quite literate and articulate but spoke only when necessity dictated. "Thank you all the same, but you better get downstairs before Jean-Claude and Pierrot get impatient. You remember yesterday."

The day before, Jean-Claude and Pierrot chanted "Meat! Meat! Breakfast *Meat!*" until even the little ones who ate nothing but soy pellets and oatmeal shouted along.

Tom nodded. He looked at the other saurs who had still not gone down to breakfast: Agnes, Sluggo, Kara, Preston and Bronte. All of them were looking up at Tom except for Bronte. The bright green apatosaur was gazing in the direction of Hetman's bed.

Tom gave them an asymmetrical grin before leaving the room. "Well, don't wait *too* long."

When he was gone, Hetman whispered, "Check the egg! I twisted in my sleep last night. I'm afraid I may have hurt it!"

Hubert turned Hetman gently on his side and lifted his pillow as Doc watched. Under the pillow was a pale yellow egg, no more than a few centimeters long.

"It's fine," said Doc.

"Don't let Doc pick it up," said Agnes. "The clumsy oaf."

"My dear Agnes, I had no intention."

Sluggo had already run over to retrieve a tiny cardboard box stuffed with cotton, hidden behind the chest near the window, where the blankets and covers were kept. He pushed it back along the floor with his snout. Diogenes picked up the egg and carefully placed it in the little box.

Agnes nudged past Sluggo and examined it, almost sniffing it, in search of the slightest possible fracture. "I guess it looks okay."

Kara butted Agnes with her head. She was an apatosaur, but her head was big—and hard. "Let Bronte see. It's *her* egg, after all."

"Oh. Right." Agnes stepped back and let Bronte timidly press in.

As Bronte stared, a set of three tiny furrows took their place on her forehead. She worried, she pitied, she pondered, all at once as she took in the egg's contours and slightly rough surface. She held her breath and stared.

They all did, gathered around the cardboard box, except for Hetman, who listened as carefully as the others watched.

"The shell looks so frail," whispered Sluggo.

"Are you an idiot?" said Agnes. "Have you touched it? It's like granite. She won't have the strength to break through that shell."

"Or he," Doc suggested.

"What do *you* know?" Agnes grumbled.

"What do any of us know?"

Agnes grumbled again, but left it at that.

None of them knew if the time was soon for the first hairline cracks to form on the shell—for the little creature who might be within to break through the calcium walls of her prison and her protection—or his. Now. Later. Or ever.

Agnes' egg had had a yolk and a fetal sac, but no infant. So had Kara's. Bronte's first egg had contained a tiny, almost shapeless thing that never moved and never showed any signs that it could have moved, like some little plastic charm in the center of a bar of soap. The saurs had sealed that one carefully in a little plastic box and buried it in the garden.

In the past few months they had combed every database they could find with any bit of information about egg-laying creatures. They knew about ostriches and cobras, platypuses and echidnas. They even read about dinosaurs—the "real" ones, the ones who had lived millions of years before. It helped them guess at what might—or what *should*—happen, if anyone could have guessed that this *could* happen at all, which no one had.

Bronte had even practiced with bird eggs Sluggo had found out in the yard, eggs that had fallen out of nests in the trees. They hatched successfully, but who knew if the egg of a saur was anything like the egg of a sparrow?

"It needs heat," said Bronte, who spoke rarely, and then only in a whisper.

"Sit on it," said Agnes. "Gently."

"It's too frail," said Sluggo.

"Put it by the window, in the sun," said Kara.

"Too much," Agnes replied. "You might boil it. Then, what if it clouds up in the afternoon?"

"We might ask Tom," Sluggo suggested meekly. "Or Dr. Margaret."

"No!" Agnes thumped her tail on the floor. "It's not their business! It's *our* business! Besides, they won't know any better than we do. And *besides* that besides, if it gets out that we're producing eggs the humans out there will go into a panic. They'll stick us in labs again and examine us and try to work out what went wrong. Or they'll just round us up and exterminate the whole lot of us."

"They—they wouldn't do that," said Sluggo. The words didn't come out with quite the certainty he intended.

Agnes sailed on the energy of her own bleak visions. "They might even decide they like the eggs and make us sit in pens and lay them like chickens! They'll boil, scramble and fry them!"

"No!" Bronte and Sluggo gasped almost in unison.

Kara simply butted Agnes again. "Shut up!"

"Mark my words!" Agnes gave each syllable blunt, apocalyptic emphasis. "You can't trust humans! They say one thing then do the other. They want the whole damn place for themselves. They want everything. Everything! They're greedy and sneaky and creepy and they kill things for pleasure! They screw up everything then go around and look for more things to screw up!"

"That's true," said Preston, who for all the thousands of words he'd written, bent over a keyboard, tapping away with his four digits, rarely spoke more than a dozen words in a month. "After all, they made *us*."

"What kind of a joke is *that*?" Agnes' spiked tail swept the air in a short arc.

"Tom isn't like that," said Sluggo. "Dr. Margaret isn't like that."

"They aren't *now*." Agnes lowered her tail. "But they can turn on you just like that! It's all that *meat*. It poisons their brains and they go crazy. That's why you always have to keep your eyes on them."

"Dr. Margaret doesn't eat meat," Sluggo reminded her. "She's an herbivore."

"A vegetarian, you mean," said Doc.

"Oh, shut up! Who asked you anyway?" Agnes sneered at Doc.

"Who asked *you*?" said Kara. "We were talking about the egg."

"What we need," said Doc, resting a forepaw on Bronte's back, "is patience. We must be careful and observant. This egg may not hatch, my dear. But if it doesn't we will learn more and know better next time."

"Someday," Kara whispered, "one will hatch."

"I hope so." Doc patted her consolingly. "But as much as I hate to say this, it may also be possible that—in our genetic idiosyncrasies— we may be only capable of performing half the job."

"Oh, who died and made *you* king?" Agnes turned away in disgust—or perhaps to hide her pained expression momentarily.

Doc smiled and gently said, "Sweet Agnes, pay no attention to me, then. I am just a lame old fool who knows nothing except that he loves all his good friends here assembled."

"You old windbag!" Agnes backed away. "As if I trusted carnosaurs any better than humans! You're all filled with baloney!"

"Nevertheless," said Hetman, his weak voice belying his proximity, "I have a feeling this one will hatch. Just a feeling, but they're about all I have left."

"Hetman," Agnes said after an embarrassed pause, "I didn't mean *you* when I said that about carnosaurs. I—I get carried away sometimes."

"*Do* you?" Kara snorted.

"If you didn't get carried away," said Hetman, "I'd fear I'd been spirited off to another house in the night. Don't apologize for being Agnes, Agnes."

She responded with a rumble—this time from her stomach. A moment later, Doc's stomach made a stuttered purr, like the starting up of an old internal combustion engine.

"Breakfast," said Kara.

Hubert and Diogenes nodded and pushed Hetman's bed toward the door, where they nearly collided with the blue blur of a breathless theropod.

"Preston! Hey! Preston!"

Axel slowed himself just long enough to shout a hurried "Hiya!" to Hetman, Hubert and Diogenes, then he charged on, coming to a halt as he slid broadside into Agnes.

"Uff! Will you watch it!" Agnes barked. "Isn't it enough—"

"Sorry-sorry, Agnes. Preston! Preston! Can I have—"

His attention was drawn to the cardboard box, and its contents.

"Heyyy!" Axel took a careful look inside. "There it is!"

Doc nodded. "There it is."

He looked around at the others and pointed to the box. "That's the egg!" he said, as if they might not know yet.

"Indeed," said Doc.

"Know what that means?" Axel continued.

"No," Agnes sighed impatiently. "What *does* that mean?"

"Someone's been having *SEX*!"

"Oh, shut up!" Agnes shouted. "You don't know a thing about it!"

"Yes-yes-yes-*yes*! I learned all about it from the Reggie! I saw 'Animal Mating Practices and Habits,' 'Barnyard Babies,' 'From Sperm to Germ'—or something like that, and—and I saw 'Angelique Blows Her Birthday Candles.'"

"Shut up! *Shut up!*" Agnes' back plates clicked with the tremor of her tail smacking the floor. "Are you completely—"

"Axel," said Doc, "not that I want to distract you, but you came up here to ask Preston something, didn't you?"

"Yes! Right! Yes!" Axel stepped over to Preston. "Can I have five thousand dollars?"

Agnes gasped. *"What!"*

"Five thousand dollars. That's all. And, and then they'll *build* him! They really will! They already made up the diagrams and ski-mats and stuff! Reggie showed them what I wanted!"

"And what's that?" asked Agnes. "A working brain?"

"I'll show you! Come on!" He took a few inaugural steps toward the door. "Come on!"

"'Him,'" Doc said with his best deliberation, in an effort to get Axel to slow down and explain. "You said 'him.' And 'they.' You said 'they' too. Who is 'him'? And who are 'they'?"

"Rotomotoman, Doc! It's Rotomotoman! Rotomotoman!" Axel beckoned with his forepaw. "Come on!"

Doc wasn't sure if this was supposed to be an answer to one question, or two, or to no questions at all. The more he tried to decipher what Axel said the more his stomach rumbled.

Agnes shut her eyes and raised her back as far as it would go. "Why? Why *us*?"

"I—I think we better go along with him," Doc said, "if we're ever going to find out what this 'Roto-man' thing is."

"Roto-*moto*-man!" Axel corrected him, then said it again more quickly, as if the mere saying of the name was a kind of sheer delight.

"He's flipped," Agnes said. "What hold he's had on sanity—"

"It hurts nothing to see what's got the little fellow so excited." Doc took a step toward the door.

"Little *fellow*," Agnes spat the words out and turned to Bronte. "Little *fellow*!"

"Come-on-come-on-come-on!" Axel shouted from the doorway.

Preston picked up the box with the egg and, hearing no objections from the others, followed Axel. Bronte kept to Preston's side, as close to the egg as possible, with Kara on the other side. Doc limped along with Sluggo while Agnes, furiously reluctant, brought up the rear.

By the time the entourage reached the stairs Axel was already at the bottom. Looking up and waving.

"Hurry up!" he shouted, as if they were missing the last total solar eclipse for the next fifty years.

"Patience," said Doc, as he and the others boarded the lift. "Patience. We're coming."

The lift was an adaptation from the "human days" of the house and was originally built to carry a wheelchair up and down the stairs. Now it was a simple flatbed platform that transported the saurs who were too small, too lame or too tired to climb up or down between the two floors. Speed was never part of its design or of its renovation. To Axel, it was agony watching the others come down on the lift, like being forced to watch the tide go out.

When the lift came to a halt, Doc and the others had barely gotten off before Axel raced on to the dining room and up the plastic stairs to the computer.

"Come-on-come-on-come-on!"

"We can see the screen from here," Doc said, as the group settled a meter or so back from the desk. "Show us whatever it is you want us to see."

"Reggie," Axel said to the screen, "display Rotomotoman."

The monitor screen displayed a gray background and light blue grid lines. A snatch of music played, something with a bouncy tempo and a lot of horns. A metallic gray figure appeared on the screen—a cylinder topped with a hemisphere. Just above the line where the cylinder met the hemisphere were two white circles with two smaller black circles inside them, like cartoon eyes. The cylinder rested on four small circles that one could suppose were wheels or casters, and attached at its sides were two articulated rods that one could imagine were arms. At the end of each rod was a flat, rectangular plate, out of which sprung five digits, one set off thumb-like from the others. The retinas of the presumed eyes shifted slightly from left to right, as if the figure were surveying the scene around itself.

"Go!" cried Axel.

The figure rolled off to the left of the screen, followed by horizontal "speed" lines and a cartoon dust cloud left behind. It reappeared, this time rolling in from the left and disappearing to the right side of the screen. It rolled from left to right, right to left, left to right again, as Axel chanted:

"Ro-toh Moto-*Man*! Ro-toh Moto *Man*!
Ro-toh Moto-*Man*! Ro-toh Moto *Man*!"

Before the saurs became completely dizzy watching this relentless back and forth motion, the grid lines were replaced on the screen by a simple cartoon street scene, with houses, sidewalks, trees, bushes, lawns and fences. Rotomotoman remained still now while the speed lines and changing background lent him the illusion of motion.

A chorus of voices joined the musical accompaniment.

The melody was simple enough, like a theme from an old television program from the middle of the last century, cannily synthesized by Reggie:

"*He's our man! Ro-to-moto Man—*"

Axel sang along, staring at the screen, completely enthralled.

"*He's our man! He's not from Japan—*"

Doc looked at Preston. Kara looked at Bronte. Sluggo looked at Agnes.

"Japan?" he asked.

Agnes shook her head. She stood in front of the box with Bronte's egg where Preston had placed it on the floor, as if to shield the egg from the sight.

The "theme song" continued:

> "*Whaa-at a man!*
> *It's none other than that Ro-to Moto Man!*"

"But," Bronte whispered to Doc, "it's not a man at all."

"It's not even—" but Doc couldn't go on.

The verse repeated, while Rotomotoman, up on the screen, crashed through a brick wall. He raced down a busy street while a flashing red light rose out of the top of his hemisphere-head. He extended himself on thin metal legs. His cylindrical body also extended, something like a telescope, until Rotomotoman could see through second- and third-floor windows. By the end of the second verse, little flashes of flame were shooting from one of the digits of his right "hand," as if it had turned into a machine gun.

By end of the song, Rotomotoman was holding at bay a group of "bad guys" who wore traditional snap-brim caps and black masks over their eyes. Their arms were raised in surrender. Round, bulging bags with dollar signs printed on them lay on the floor where the bad guys had dropped them. A policeman with the appropriate badge, gun and club saluted Rotomotoman before taking custody of the villains. Rotomotoman modestly returned the salute. A man in a dark suit, a monocle and top hat—presumably a bank president— shook Rotomotoman's metal hand—the same one from which bullets had been firing earlier.

The screen faded.

The saurs stood there, gaping in silence, wide-eyed, stunned and dumbfounded.

"See?" Axel trotted down the plastic steps. "Wasn't that great? Wasn't that the neatest-greatest thing you've ever seen?"

Doc, struggling for a politic response, was the first to speak. "Axel," he asked sympathetically, "have you been getting enough sleep?"

"Axel," Agnes said quietly but firmly, "are you nuts?"

"I saw it in a *dream*!" Axel insisted. "If I dreamed it, I was sleeping!"

"I wish *I* were dreaming," said Kara.

"But these guys can make a *real* one!" Axel continued. "A

real-real-real Rotomotoman! I asked Reggie and he found a company that makes—what did he call them? Prototypes!"

Bronte, in her whispering voice, said "Roto-prototypes."

"Proto-motoman," Preston mumbled.

"We should disconnect Reggie," Agnes said. "Right away."

"So—they can *build* him!" Axel turned to Preston. "And they can
send him *here*! And—and it costs five thousand dollars. So can I have
it, Preston, please? Please-please-please?"

Agnes made a sound that started like a cough and ended like a
gag. "Five thousand dollars for a trashcan on wheels! A trashcan on
wheels *that crashes through walls*! A trashcan that'll run around and *crush*
us until we're flat as pancakes! A trashcan with a revolving red light
flashing on his head and *bullets* shooting *out of his fingers*!"

"Yeah!" said Axel. "Isn't he neat?"

"Axel—" Doc started, but Agnes cut him off.

"Axel, look around. Do you see any walls around here that need
to be *smashed* through? Do you see any saurs that need to be *flattened*
out? Do you see *anyone* that needs to be *riddled with bullets*?"

"Won't do that! Won't do that!" Axel raised his forepaws. "Reggie
said we shouldn't ask for that. No bullets, no smashing. He's gonna
have sense—like, a sensing system so he won't squash anybody!"

"In other words," Agnes said, "a trashcan that rolls back and forth,
endlessly and uselessly. For *five thousand dollars*!"

"Not a garbage can!" Axel admonished her. "Rotomotoman!
He'll be mine! I made him up! Reggie helped but *I* made him up!"
His voice took on a pleading tone. "He won't smash anything! He'll
be our *friend*!"

"He won't shoot anything?" Sluggo asked.

Axel shook his head. "Rotomotoman is *good*."

"It's good you made Rotomotoman," Bronte said. "That was
very clever of you. But—"

"You did a very nice job," Kara added. "Very well done. But—"

"You are a deranged idiot and probably insane," said Agnes.

"Thank-you-thank-you-thank-you." Axel bowed to each of
them.

"But perhaps," Doc ventured, "it would be better for everyone—"
Axel turned to him.

Doc pointed to the computer. "—if your Rotomotoman limited
his activities just to that screen." His stomach rumbled—another call to
breakfast. "You can still play with him as you wish. Rotomotoman can

smash through whatever he likes as long as he remains on the screen." His stomach now made an "urrrr" sound, distinct from the other noise.

Axel looked carefully at Doc.

He continued. "You can assuage the rancor of sweet Agnes here and relieve the apprehensions of the rest of us."

Axel kept staring, saying nothing.

"Axel? Are you listening?"

"Yes." Axel nodded. "Do it again."

Doc cleared his throat. "Do *what* again?"

"Make your stomach go 'urrrrrr' like that."

Doc took a deep breath. "I meant, did you listen to what I *said*?"

"Sure. What was it?"

Agnes thumped her tail against the floor. "He said that there's no way in hell that we're ever going to agree to have that metal trashcan in this house!"

Axel's jaw dropped and his eyes grew wide. One could almost feel the theropod's heart sinking. "But, but—I made him up! *I* did!"

He looked at Kara, Bronte and Sluggo—he couldn't bear to look at Agnes. "It's not what Rotomotoman *does*! It's that he *is*! Do you see? I've *got* to make Rotomotoman!"

"*I* see that Preston would have to have lost his mind to waste five thousand dollars on a useless, dangerous piece of junk!" said Agnes.

"Axel," Doc said with great sympathy, "Preston here writes books all about great star captains, mighty armies and flying cities, but he doesn't have to build prototypes of them or march them through the halls of our little abode." He patted Axel on the head. "We can't build everything we imagine."

Axel stepped away, head lowered, and turned to Preston.

"Is that true, Preston? Is that how you feel?"

It was always difficult to gauge Preston's feelings. He spoke so little, and what he wrote in his books presented so many points of view it was difficult to figure which ones might be his own. He smiled at his companions, a little more to one side of his mouth than the other.

"I think what Axel has done is creative and—amusing," he said in his soft tenor voice.

"Amusing?" Agnes replied. "I suppose a direct hit from a missile would have you in hysterics!"

Preston put his hand on Axel's head and led him to the plastic stairs, up to the computer. The other saurs, with the exception of Agnes, were speechless.

"Preston!" she cried. "What are you doing?"

Axel and Preston kept going without reply.

"Preston, you're not—you wouldn't *dare!*"

At the top of the stairs, standing before the computer, Preston said, "Reggie?"

"Reggie is ready," the computer replied.

"Please connect me to my bank."

"Preston!" Agnes wailed. "You've gone nuts too? Preston!"

"What will Tom say?" Sluggo asked Doc.

"I suppose Tom will have to deal with it. As we all will."

Preston leaned over and said right into Axel's ear, to make sure he heard, "Remember, no machine guns. No death rays. No crashing through walls. No squashing little ones. No speeding."

"Yes-yes-yes-yes-YES!" Axel wrapped his forepaws around Preston's leg. "Whatever you say! Oh, thank-you-thank-you Preston!"

The transfer of funds to the prototype company went smoothly. It had long ago ceased to be strange for non-humans to hold bank accounts. The idea that banks thought in terms of anything but accounts and their activities belongs to the generation of our foreparents. Preston's financial holdings were hardly remarkable except for their size, as were the accounts held by some other saurs—like Alphonse, who often won money on radio quiz programs—and Doc, who had a trust fund from a former "owner."

Axel's excitement set the plastic stairs wobbling as the two came down from the desk.

"Oh, thank you, Preston! Thank-you-thank-you-thank-you-thank-you! You are the best-best, most wonderful perfect greatest friend in the whole complete universe! Thank you thank you *you YOU!*"

"Is *anyone* in here planning to have breakfast?" Tom Groverton stood behind them, arms folded and head tilted. "Now that everyone else has finished?"

"Breakfast-breakfast-breakfast!" Axel dashed out past Tom. "Come on, Preston! My best-best friend! Let's have breakfast!"

"Sorry for the delay," Doc said to Tom, "but we had a little business to take care of."

"Business?"

"I'll explain later," Doc said. "I think it will take a little time."

"Don't ask me," Agnes shook her head wearily, "I don't think I ever want to eat breakfast again."

Bronte carefully covered up the egg with a swath of cotton before Preston picked up the box and headed for the kitchen.

"What's that? Another egg?" Tom asked.

Agnes raised her tail and stared severely at Bronte.

"Y-yes," Bronte said nervously, looking from Kara to Agnes. "Sluggo found it the other day. A crow's egg, I think. It-it's rather big."

"Well," Tom said, bending down and rubbing Bronte just above the little furrows on her brow, "best of luck. You're a first-rate egg-hatcher. You'll do a fine job."

"Thank you." the words came out as a rasp, as if her mouth was very dry.

She followed Preston out of the room, just behind Kara and Sluggo, slowly heading for the kitchen. Doc walked with his head down, attempting the difficult gesture of rubbing his head with one of his short forepaws. His stomach rumbled again.

"After breakfast." He sighed. "After breakfast."

Agnes narrowed her eyes and stared up at Tom.

"You just mind your own damn business!" she said, and followed the others out of the room.

■

At dawn the next day, when Axel crawled out from the sleep pile and ran downstairs, he heard muffled sounds coming from the living room and noticed that the big video screen was still on.

Hubert had turned off the video just before sleep-time—Axel distinctly remembered. Maybe the video had gone on by itself—or was there another saur who decided to get up even earlier than Axel? He hurried over to investigate.

In the middle of the living room, about the same place where the saurs sat when they watched the video, was a lone frog—a *frog*!—about the size of a softball; pale green with a pattern of gray, blotty spots all over.

Next to the frog was the remote control pad the saurs used to change programs. He, or perhaps she, sat very still, head turned to the screen. But the frog must have heard Axel approaching. Before he could get any closer the amphibian slapped the remote pad with his left forepaw. The video clicked off and the frog hopped over to the couch by the window, then up onto the cushions.

"Hey! Where ya goin'? Hey!"

Axel ran after the frog, but not fast enough. In seconds the frog was up on the back of the couch, onto the window ledge and—flooop!—out the window and out of sight.

Axel climbed up after him—or her. He looked out into the yard, still dark in the early morning shadows, then back at the video screen.

"Wow!" he whispered. "A frog who can watch TV!"

■

After breakfast—and after most of the saurs had made their morning visit to the litter room—Doc found a spot of sunlight near the big window in the dining room and pushed the plastic box he used as a stool there. It was a good place to sit and feel a little warmth, and it still afforded him a view of the video screen, where he could see a fat man and a thin man, both in ill-fitting bowler hats, trying to move a piano up a ridiculously long flight of stairs. The piano movers monopolized his attention until the hats started to remind him of the head of Rotomotoman and he looked elsewhere for contemplation.

Little saurs were grouped in front of the Reggiesystem computer. Doc could hear them learning what the principal exports of Ghana were. On the other side of the room, the Five Wise Buddhasaurs were sitting on the couch, running their plastic horns through a synthesizer, playing something fast and wildly rhythmical that they referred to as "Chinese" or "Dizz" music. To his left, Kara was sitting with Hetman, reading to him from *A Connecticut Yankee in King Arthur's Court*. She had the book propped up against the back of a straight wooden chair and she carefully turned the pages with her snout.

Other little ones were using the small, battery-powered wheeled platforms called skates to get from one end of the house to the other. On the far end of the living room, the stegosaur pair, Zack and Kip, were playing with Jean-Claude and Pierrot, the theropod tyrannosaurs, a game using checker pieces whipped across the floor with their tails, like hockey pucks. The game was called "Hit 'Em Hard" until a red stegosaur named Veronica got hit a little too hard by a stray checker. Then Agnes declared the game should be changed to "Not So Hard."

In the library, Diogenes and Hubert busied themselves shelving and re-shelving books for the saurs who perused them, whether they could read them or not—fascinated by pictures, colophons, shapes and even the smell of the paper and binding.

Over the noise of the "Dizz" music and the tinny accompaniment of the hapless piano movers on the video, Doc could hear Agnes shouting to someone on a skate, "Hey! Slow that down! What d'you think you're doing? Racing?"

The world was in order—for the moment. Doc closed his eyes and basked in the warmth. What there was to worry over, he thought, could wait.

"Hey Doc!"

Doc opened his eyes. Axel stood before him.

"Guess what I saw this morning?"

Doc trembled. "*Not* another robot, was it?"

"Nooo!" Axel waved the notion away with his forepaw. "It was a *frog*! In here! He was watching the video!"

"Yes, Axel." Doc tried to smile. "And what was he watching?"

"I didn't see, but I heard news-guy-type voices, like when they talk about stocking markets and underwater volcanoes." He looked up at Doc, who was glancing back at the video screen: the fat man was wailing and the piano was rolling down the stairs.

"You don't believe me, do you?" Axel said.

"My friend, I remember when you warned us of the giant tidal wave bearing down on us. And I remember you telling us that the Army of Northern Virginia was camped outside on the driveway. There were the Saracen hordes riding their horses through the woods—I remember that too. And who can forget the battle-cruisers from Alpha Centauri firing their photon rays at the power lines?"

"But that was *playing*," Axel insisted. "This was a real-real frog-guy!"

"Axel," Doc patted him on the head, "I believe that *you* saw a frog here this morning. But the rest I'd rather leave as a matter of conjecture."

Doc closed his eyes and went back to his basking, but the spot of sunlight had shifted by then. He pushed his stool over a bit to recapture it.

Axel, however, wondering over the meaning of "conjecture," moved on.

Kara and Hetman were close by. She was reading the passage from the novel where Clarence describes to Harry Morgan the trap laid by King Arthur against Sir Launcelot.

"Lancelot?" Axel forgot about the frog for an instant and asked Kara, "Where? Where's Lancelot?"

"*Laun*-celot," Kara said. "The name is Sir Launcelot. He isn't anywhere. He's a character in this book."

"Ohhh." Axel remembered Lancelot, but not *Laun*celot. Lancelot wasn't a character, he was a *saur*—a buddy—long-long-long ago. Axel tried to remember more, but the harder he tried the more he forgot.

"Hey!" he said to Kara, as Lancelot faded back from his memory, "Guess what I saw this morning?"

And he told them all about the frog who watched the video.

He told Bronte, sitting with her egg. He told Tyrone and Alfie and the other saurs gathered around the Reggiesystem computer. He told Hubert, Diogenes, Charlie, Rosie and the Five Wise Buddhasaurs, but none of them believed him.

He even told Tom Groverton, once he finished cleaning up in the kitchen. Tom sat down on the floor and explained to Axel why he couldn't have *really* seen a frog in the living room.

"You know that the house and the grounds are covered by a security system." Tom ran his hand over the blue saur's back. "It's heat and motion sensitive. If anything enters the security zone that's not one of us, it sets off an alarm."

"Like when the cat got in and tried to eat Symphony Syd," Axel said. "Or that raccoon that scratched Agnes."

"Exactly. A long time ago. And since then the system's been improved. So how can a frog enter the grounds without setting off the alarm?"

Axel glanced back at the window where he had seen the frog make his escape. "He must be a really *smart* frog."

Tom showed Axel the security system log on the Reggiesystem, indicating that nothing had even touched the security perimeter the night before, at least nothing bigger than a moth.

"Maybe Reggie knows that he just came here to watch the video and that he wasn't here to hurt anyone."

"I don't think Reggie works that way, Axel."

"Why not?"

Tom opened his mouth as if to speak, then erased the action with a shake of his head and tugged on one end of his droopy mustache.

"Okay. Let's say Reggie did that. Since there seems to be some question about the objective reality of this creature, Reggie figured it was okay for the frog to come in and watch the video."

"So you think the TV frog's not an objectionable reality."

That look came over Tom's face again and again he went for that end of his mustache. "Okay. Let's leave it at that. The frog is not an objectionable reality."

"Then you don't mind TV Frog coming in and watching the video?"

"TV Frog?"

"That's what I'm gonna call him."

"Well," Tom patted Axel on the head, "as long as he's not stealing anything, or hurting anyone, and as long as he shuts off the video before he goes, like you said he did, I don't mind."

A few saurs—some of the little guys, Sluggo, Hetman—believed him, or at least said they did.

And Geraldine came out of the cardboard box she called her "lab" and told Axel that she believed him too.

"He's not a real frog," she said in her soft, tinny voice. "He's from a planet on the other side of the galaxy. He's made a little tunnel through space-time to get here."

Axel took this in without question and concluded: "Wow!"

"Don't pay attention to her," Agnes cautioned him. "She's making fun of you. She makes fun of everyone. She thinks we're all stupid."

"You all *are* stupid." Geraldine said, then returned to her lab. Axel watched the box until the flickering lights coming from inside worried him. Tom put those fire extinguishers nearby for a reason.

"Maybe you need to sleep some more, Axel," Preston counseled him. "Maybe you're dreaming in the daytime because you don't sleep enough."

But that night, Axel stayed behind when the other saurs went upstairs to sleep. He hid behind the couch and waited until the frog hopped through the window onto the back of the couch, then to the seat of the couch, then to the floor. He hopped to the center of the room and slapped the remote pad with his left forepaw.

The screen flickered on, and the frog watched—all night long, occasionally slapping the remote pad to change the program.

He watched old films and talk shows. He looked at nature programs and documentaries about automobiles and the wars of the previous century. He watched a chorus of dancing girls sing the praises of bottled water and a man on a weather program talk for a whole hour about cloud patterns. It put Axel to sleep.

But the frog watched on. He seemed comforted by the images, as if they were relieving him of a great anxiety, or perhaps he was just grateful for the light, for that sense of life moving from moment to moment without threat or danger that the video provided.

"TV Frog" left at dawn, but came back the next night and the night after that.

Axel resolved not to disturb the frog. In the morning, as Axel ran past on his way to the Reggiesystem computer, he would call out, "Hiya, TV Frog!" and leave it at that.

But by the end of the week, as Axel ran past, TV Frog lingered long enough on the window sill so that Axel could see him, in silhouette, raising his left forepaw as if in greeting before hopping out the window to wherever TV Frogs went in the daytime.

■

When the crate containing Rotomotoman finally arrived, all the saurs gathered to watch as Tom Groverton opened it in the center of the living room.

The crate was enormous. Even Diogenes had to get up on his toes to peer inside. Axel climbed up on his shoulders, expecting to see Rotomotoman inside just as he envisioned him, fully charged and ready to go.

What Axel actually saw was about a dozen batches of components wrapped in vinyl bags and cushioned with packing foam.

Along with a copy of the invoice were several sheets of paper filled with very tiny type and headed with big bold letters:

"Some assembly required."

As everyone knows, "some" is a relative word. The creation of the Grand Canyon took "some" time and the formation of matter at the instant of the Big Bang required "some" assembly.

Tom carefully took the components out of the crate. As the pieces slowly collected on the floor, Agnes looked them over, frowning and sniffing.

"Hmph! Looks like they sent you the trash instead of the trashcan!"

"He's all in pieces," Bronte whispered, looking from one component to the next.

"Did he fall apart?" asked Rosie.

"They forgot to put him together," Charlie observed.

Diogenes bent over so that Axel could climb down and survey his unassembled creation. He stood with his mouth agape, looking slightly appalled and definitely overwhelmed.

"We're in luck," Agnes whispered to Doc. "With all these pieces, it'll take months for him to put it together."

"If he manages to put it together at all," Doc replied. "Not that I doubt the little fellow's enthusiasm and determination, but his attention *does* tend to wander."

"Then we'll gather up the pieces and throw them in the cellar, or put them out with the trash, where they belong!"

"Let's not get ahead of ourselves," Doc said in his deep whisper. "I really don't want to see the little fellow despondent or disappointed."

"No, you want that big hunk of metal rolling over your toes every ten minutes!"

Axel wandered around the unassembled Rotomotoman not unlike an accident investigator surveying the wreckage of a train or a jet. He looked up at Tom Groverton.

"What do we do now?"

"That's up to you, Axel."

The other saurs watched silently as Axel took another turn around the components.

Tibor—the brooding, runt-size apatosaur—came up to the crate with a crayon in his mouth and quickly scrawled on it: "Tibor's Imperial Winter Palace—do NOT throw out, by order of Tibor."

Axel pointed to a dome-shaped piece of metal and said to the others, "Look! That's his head! And this other part here—" he slapped the cylinder which was the largest piece taken out of the crate "—that's his body! Those are his wheels in that bag over there! Those rods in that other bag are his arms! And this—" He held up a large white disk which contained a dark, intricate retina in its Plexiglas frame "—this is one of his eyes!" He held it up between his forepaws and against his chest and approached one section of the circle of saurs. The retina rolled around inside the larger disk as if the disembodied eye was scrutinizing the room.

The saurs retreated a few steps. Alfie hid his head against Tyrone's chest.

"Don't be afraid! It's Rotomotoman! Rotomotoman is *good*!"

With the retina rolling back and forth, right to left, along the bottom perimeter of the disk, the smaller saurs were unconvinced.

"You'll see, when I put him together!"

Axel sang the "Rotomotoman Song" and tried to get the other saurs to sing it with him, but as they looked over the pile of parts they appeared justifiably unenthused.

"Beware of any trashcan with its own theme song," Agnes trudged away with the hope that this was the last she would see of Rotomotoman.

■

The contents of the crate were moved into the same workroom upstairs where Preston wrote his novels and Alphonse sent out his quiz and contest entries. It was also where Geraldine kept her cardboard "lab" and, at another desk, Tibor hid in his cardboard "castle."

Axel walked around the still-wrapped components laid out on the floor in a kind of random formation, a kind of "Metal Henge."

In the center of the formation he turned around and around until he was in danger of making himself dizzy.

"Where do I start?"

Preston handed Axel the several pages of tiny type that came in the crate. "Try to read this over all the way through once—*at least once*. Then read each section and do what it tells you and don't go any farther until you finish what it tells you to do."

"Okay. How do you do that?"

Preston shut his eyes and summoned his patience with a great sigh.

"We'll read the instructions together." He sat down next to Axel, took the instructions and held them out where both of them could see. "To paraphrase Aristotle, 'First things first.' "

After reading through the instructions twice together, and after addressing Axel's occasionally pertinent interruptions, Preston arranged the components or sets of components in a circle around Rotomotoman's main cylinder.

"You'll start here," Preston pointed to a little black box that contained a quantity of intricate circuitry. "You put that into the cylinder where the instructions tell you, then you move to the next piece, and the next piece, clockwise. That way you can keep track of what goes first and what goes next. When you get all the way around the circle— and as long as there are no parts left over—Rotomotoman should be completely assembled and ready to go."

"Wow!" Axel walked around the main cylinder and looked at all the surrounding parts. "When do you think we'll be finished?"

Preston shrugged and shook his head. "The sooner you get started the sooner you'll be done." He made sure to stress the "you" in that statement.

"Yeah!" Axel looked up at the ceiling as if he could stare straight through it.

Preston looked at Axel. For the first time in years he took notice of the long scar down his back, then followed Axel's gaze. He gently put his forepaw on Axel's head. He had been looking at the stars through that ceiling for many years himself.

"You'll do fine," he said softly. "Just fine."

■

The discipline of doing one thing at a time was almost too much for Axel to comprehend, but he was undeterred. His energies—which were capable of flying off in a dozen directions at once—were for once singly directed to the task of assembling Rotomotoman.

It wasn't quite high-energy physics, or as the saying went in another century, "rocket science." The most detailed aspects of circuitry and data systems had been assembled at the company that produced the prototype. But each set of components had to be linked to another set, and those to another set. A had to be plugged into B, and B had to be slipped inside C, and so on.

Axel worked until long past sleep-time that first night, and did not join the other saurs when exhaustion finally took him. He curled up next to Rotomotoman's dormant head.

"It won't be long," he said to the polished metal dome, placing his forepaw in the place between where Rotomotoman's eyes would eventually go. "I'll have you all put together in no time."

The next day, he started after breakfast and only stepped away from the work for lunch, dinner, trips to the litter facilities and two times when he asked the Reggiesystem for explanations and advice.

Doc, with great economy, managed to explain to Axel the saurian techniques for manipulating certain tools designed for human hands, specifically the screwdriver and the adjustable wrench.

By the time the other saurs were wrapping up their daily routines and heading up to the sleep room, Axel had made it through the circle of components Preston had laid out from twelve o'clock (the first piece) to three o'clock.

It took all of the following day for Axel to get from three o'clock to five. He didn't go downstairs to eat, but Sluggo brought food up to him.

"He'd finish faster if we helped him," Sluggo told Agnes, as she peeled a strip of rind from an orange.

"So?" she asked. "That's his own damn problem. I didn't ask for that rolling trashcan to be brought here. Besides," she mashed up a piece of orange with her teeth, "the longer he works on that thing, the longer he isn't knocking around here jumping off the couch and screaming about holes in time and space or tidal waves or some damn frog sneaking in and watching the video."

"He might get sick," Sluggo insisted.

"Well, what if he does? We've got more important things to worry about."

She motioned to where Bronte and Kara stared with worried expressions into the little cotton-filled box.

"It's been too long," Bronte whispered. "A bird's egg would have hatched by now."

"It's *not* a bird's egg," Kara said. "It's *your* egg. And we just don't know how long it might take."

"Too long." Bronte bent down and with slightest pressure touched the egg with her snout. "Too long."

■

By sleep-time, Axel had made it to seven o'clock on the circle of parts. The components were joined together, but they had to be placed inside the main cylinder. Together, they weighed much more than Axel could possibly lift, or even drag. And by this time Axel's head was filled with numbers and letters: Bs and Ds and Cs and Qs floated around like tadpoles in a pond; he looked at the joined components, but all he could see was a wall of binary numbers.

Still, he made the effort, grabbing on to one end with his forepaws and pulling mightily.

It wouldn't budge.

He went around to the other side and pushed. The assemblage remained immobile. He kept pushing.

He pushed until Sluggo came by.

"You need to sleep," he said.

"First," Axel said breathlessly, "I have to get this *stuff*," he took several deep breaths and patted the block of components, "into *that* thing—" His voice trailed off as he took more deep breaths and weakly pointed at the cylinder.

They both pushed, but all they could manage to do was polish the floor under their feet.

"Get some rest," Sluggo said when they finally gave up. "We'll think of something in the morning."

"Think," Axel mumbled deliriously. "Think think think! I have to *think*!"

"Sleep first," Sluggo said, and nudged him toward the door.

Axel went along like a prisoner being led back to his cell.

The sleep-pile looked a little like a circus under a collapsed tent. The saurs were already all gathered under the blankets, except for Hetman in his little bed, just next to the pile.

Sluggo lifted the blanket up at one end to look for Agnes and Axel crawled in with him. It was impossible to make his way in without stepping on someone and eliciting responses like, "Hey! Watch it!" "Ooof!" and "Your foot's on my crest!" He climbed around from one end of the pile to the other, paying little attention to the ruckus he caused, but he couldn't find a place that seemed comfortable.

"Think think think!"

He lifted up the blanket, crawled out and headed straight to Hetman's bed, climbing over the railing and getting in next to him.

"Hetman! Hetman!"

"Yes, Axel," Hetman whispered in his raspy voice.

"Okay if I sleep here?"

"You're very welcome to sleep here, Axel."

"I didn't mean to wake you, if I did. Did I wake you?"

"No," said Hetman, who was often haunted by pains old and new, though he refused any strong drugs to help him sleep. "It hasn't been a good night."

"Is the egg under your pillow?"

"Yes it is. Poor fellow," he said, referring to the egg. "I hope he is sleeping better inside his little shell—or she. But perhaps it can't be called sleep if you haven't yet awakened."

"Sluggo said I should sleep, but I have to think too. There's all this *inner* stuff I have to get into Rotomotoman, but it's all put together and too heavy to move." Axel rolled a little closer to Hetman. "Did I tell you yet about Rotomotoman?"

"At least twenty times, Axel, but tell me again. I enjoy hearing you tell me about the wondrous Rotomotoman. Whisper it, though, this time. We needn't wake the others. And maybe it would be best if you left out the Rotomotoman song."

Axel did just as Hetman requested, starting all the way back, from the dream to the "inner stuff," careful to leave out the theme song, though he really-really *did* want to sing it.

As Hetman hoped, Axel fell asleep as he listed the catalog of parts: Motor Assembly A to Relay Systems Response Assembly B, Relay Systems Response Assembly B to Motor Systems Response Assembly C—and so on. Axel's voice trailed off after he mentioned that Thermostat Assembly F attached to Carrier Drawer F1.

Hetman listened. The house was silent except for the occasional grunts and snores from the sleep-pile. He might manage a little sleep too before dawn, if he could just get a little question out of his mind—

What does a Rotomotoman need with a thermostat?

■

Axel slept harder than he had at any time before: he slept past dawn. For once he was not at the window to glimpse the last light of the stars (if it were a clear night) and the first light of the sun (if the day was similarly clear).

Instead, he was lost in a dream of Rotomotoman roaming about the house. The strangest thing about the dream to Axel was that Rotomotoman, with his round head, looked very much like a big soft-boiled egg sitting in a cup. It occurred to Axel that in some ways Rotomotoman was *his* egg—but instead of needing the pieces to come apart, he needed to put them together.

Together!

He sat up, awake. Put them together! He looked around and the room was already filled with sunlight. Hetman lay beside him, asleep at last, but the sleep-pile was gone—everyone was gone, the blankets put away.

He climbed out of Hetman's bed and ran to the workroom just in time to see Diogenes and Hubert lowering the assembled components into the uprighted cylinder.

Not only that, but the wheels were attached to the bottom, the arms attached to the sides: listless, but attached.

Nearby, Doc rested on his little box, screwdriver still held between his forepaws.

A crowd of saurs, mostly little ones, was gathered around them, watching and chattering. The Five Wise Buddhasaurs sat up on the top of a set of plastic stairs, to get the next best view to the ones Geraldine and Tibor had from their respective desktops.

Agnes had the assembly instructions spread out in front of her.

"Okay, next to the motor assembly junk is that other junk."

"The battery pack?" Doc asked.

"That's what I said, you dimwit! You're going to need the gray cable and the two blue cables that are in that little bag."

Tyrone and Alfie opened the bag and brought the cables to Agnes.

"Hey!" Axel said. Everyone stopped and turned to him.

"Don't look at *me*!" said Agnes. "It wasn't *my* idea! I can't help it if everyone in this house has gone completely insane."

"Sluggo mentioned to us this morning the trouble you were having," Doc said, putting the screwdriver down. "We thought a little help might get the project moving along."

"But, but—" Axel moved closer. He couldn't keep his eyes off the cylinder. It was still headless, but it had wheels and arms, and it looked nothing like a soft-boiled egg anymore.

He glanced at the circle of parts: nine o'clock. Three quarters of the parts were gone.

"Guys—I can't—I don't know—"

"Oh, shut up!" said Agnes. "Go down and get your breakfast. Tom's waiting for you. Then get back up here and help us out."

To Diogenes and Hubert, she said, "Now that that thing is loaded and Axel is up, get Hetman downstairs and come straight back. I want the lid put on this trashcan today! Tomorrow at the latest!"

Agnes left nothing else to say. Axel ran downstairs. Diogenes and Hubert left the room looking back over their shoulders. Agnes noticed Doc staring at her with his most serene smile.

"What the hell are you looking at?" she said.

"I am looking at a marvel, my dear—at a kind of brief miracle. I am looking at Agnes in a good mood."

"You'll be looking at a spiked tail meeting your face if you don't move your butt off that box and get to work!"

With that encouragement, Doc picked up the screwdriver and returned to the cylinder without further comment, but unable to remove the grin from his face.

About this time, in the world out past the yard and beyond the trees, a buzz was starting.

As best as anyone could tell, the buzz began in the offices of the radio telescope at Mount Herrmann. Apparently, a message had been sent to certain coordinates from someone who went by the name of

"Axel" and was addressed to "space guys." There was nothing particularly extraordinary in that, as the telescope operators had been accepting messages for many years as part of a promotional and public relations program to aid in the funding of their research, which included a search for extra-terrestrial intelligence.

What started the buzz had to do with the content of the message, of a certain reference to "making eggs." And since the address of the sender was one of the houses operated by the Atherton Foundation for surviving saurs, it presented a rather astounding possibility.

The rumor could have been a prank, a mistake, a misunderstanding. But there were a number of important persons in the bioengineering community that were not sleeping well and would not sleep very well until the mystery was cleared up. And the bioengineering community was an important group of persons who held a great deal of sway in many circles. They did not bear sleeplessness well.

And so a call was made to Ms. Susan Leahy, the grandniece of Hilary Atherton herself, who was then in charge of the foundation.

"They want answers," she said to Tom Groverton over the phone. "Or I should say they want assurance, if you know what I mean."

"They want to send someone over to inspect the house," Tom replied.

"Our charter allows us to legally restrain them, but I'm afraid that would only stir up more controversy. The Office of Bioengineering Standards has never approved of our autonomy and would like nothing better than to challenge it."

"So they're coming," Tom said.

"I'll be with them. And I want Dr. Pagliotti there too," she said, referring to Dr. Margaret. "I won't have them pushing their way around, but I'm afraid they have to search everywhere to their satisfaction to see that the saurs aren't producing their own eggs. If they find anything that makes them think otherwise, they'll file to do further research, and that will get us into a battle I'd much rather avoid."

"I understand," said Tom.

"I know you do. You'll tell the saurs. Let them know we're coming."

"Yes. It'll be good seeing *you* again, at least."

"I only wish it was under less stressful circumstances. You do a wonderful job, Tom. And the saurs never fail to surprise me."

"Then you won't be disappointed this time, Susan. I can assure you."

■

By sleep-time the workroom was empty of everyone but Axel—and Rotomotoman.

The faint traces of moonlight coming through the window endowed everything in the room with a kind of ashen, metallic hue. The circle of components was gone. In their place stood Rotomotoman, just under a meter and a half tall, set upon four sturdy wheels and his narrow, rod-like arms down at his sides. His large, round eyes, set against the curvature of his head, were fixed in an expression perhaps best described as dementedly earnest—a fitting reflection of his creator. When seen in connection with the first horizontal seam of the cylinder, a dozen centimeters below them—a seam that suggested a mouth—those eyes also betrayed a certain perplexity, as if Rotomotoman might be thinking to himself an incomplete expression of surprise in the vein of "What the—!"

A cable connected him to a wall outlet, charging his battery. That was all he needed—with the exception of downloading some delicate software into his brain—before he could come to life.

Axel stood transfixed, staring up at him with undiluted awe.

"It's real," he whispered. "Real-real-real."

"You should get some sleep," said Doc. He'd come into the workroom at Sluggo's request, when Axel could not be found in the sleep-pile. "It won't do to have you falling asleep tomorrow, at the moment of your triumph."

"Look at him!" Axel pointed up at Rotomotoman. "Isn't he the greatest thing you've ever seen? The most stupendous, marvelous, fantastic, *greatest* thing you've ever seen?"

"I've seen quite a lot of him, my friend, in these past few days." Doc's forepaws were still a little sore from handling all the human tools. His foot still hurt a little from when it got wedged under the cylinder while he was attaching the last of the wheels—but it was the foot of his weak leg anyway; the addition to his limp was barely noticeable. "But yes," he put his forepaw on Axel's shoulder, "it is—impressive."

"I couldn't have done it without all you guys helping me. I have the best-greatest friends in the whole universe!"

"It's your creation, don't forget. Without you, your Rotomotoman would not exist, would it?"

"I don't know," Axel said, seriously pondering the question. "It's like now I feel like—like he always *was*, you know? And all I did was, like—"

"Like what?"

"Like, *recognize* him! Like, there's all this real stuff in one place and all this could-be-real stuff in another place, like behind a window. Did you ever see one of those gumball machines that's got stuff other than gumballs in it? Like shrunken heads and rubber spiders and stuff? That's what it's like—like Rotomotoman was in one of those gumball machines and I turned the handle and got him out!"

"Now I *know* you need some sleep, my friend. You're talking like a Platonist. Or even worse: a Jungian."

"What's that?"

Doc patted his head. "It's a kind of person who needs a great deal of sleep. Come along. When Axel sounds profound it's a strong hint that one is either dreaming or should be dreaming."

Doc led Axel out of the workroom with a series of tugs. Only after they turned the corner and entered the hallway would Axel stop looking back at Rotomotoman.

But then Axel stopped in his tracks, struck with an idea.

"Hey!" He gestured to Doc and headed for the staircase. "Now I can show you!"

"It's far too late, little fellow, to show me anything—"

"No-no-no-no! Come on!" Axel trotted a few steps ahead, then looked back at Doc. "But quiet!" He held one digit of his forepaw up. "Ssshh!"

Axel crept down one stair, and then another, and then another. Even at this slow pace, Doc found it hard to follow. His bad leg made it hard for him to take stairs, up or down, at any pace. He held to the round, vertical balusters of the handrail and inched himself along until it occurred to him that he still hadn't been given a good reason for putting himself through this exertion.

"Axel, would you mind—"

"Ssshh! Just a little farther." His whisper was louder than Doc's appeal. "One more step!"

Doc had to put his weight on his bad leg to descend the next step. He winced, but caught himself before he cried out.

"There! See?" Axel whispered. "Can you see?"

Doc could see nothing. He reached for the next baluster, putting himself in an awkward angle, almost hanging over Axel. He raised his tail to counterbalance his weight. If he slipped a mere centimeter he would topple headfirst down the rest of the stairs. But at last he could make out what Axel was pointing to: a light coming from the living room.

The light changed color and intensity with quick little flickers and flashes, as if the video screen was still on.

Not "as if"—it *was* on!

"See?" Axel whispered, more successful this time in keeping his voice down. "It's TV Frog! I told you he was really there! He's really-really-really there!"

"Axel," Doc felt his grip slipping on the baluster. "It's much more likely that someone forgot—" He couldn't finish the sentence, since it was *he* who turned off the video that night.

"Maybe," Doc muttered, "a technical thing. A 'glitch,' as they say. A malfunction in—"

A voice with the range and volume of a train horn sounded above them:

"Hey! What the hell's going on down there!"

In the fraction of a second between Doc hearing Agnes' voice and his forepaws slipping from the baluster, Doc could distinctly see the light go off in the living room, as if someone had slapped the "off" square on the remote pad.

After that, he saw nothing, but distinctly felt himself in gravity's clutches as first he tumbled over Axel, then tumbled again and tumbled again.

He shut his eyes for what seemed like a moment, but when he opened them the lights were on. He was looking up at Axel and several other saurs, including Kara and Sluggo—Tom Groverton was there too—all standing over him with worried expressions. Tom ran his hands over Doc's back and abdomen, checking for broken bones, no doubt.

"I'm all right," Doc said several times, and after Tom examined him carefully he even believed it. Bruises, muscle pains, but nothing worse. Agnes, still at the top of the stairs, kept berating him for "skulking around in the dark like a goddamn idiot!"—which was akin to having a bad ringing in the ears—Doc had lived with that before.

"Ohhh, Doc! I'm sorry-sorry-*sorry*!" Axel repeated it until it became a litany. "I didn't mean—I wanted you to see—that it *was* TV Frog! It really was! I'm soooo sorry-sorry-sorry!"

"I followed along of my own choosing, Axel." Doc tried to reach for Axel's forepaw but, falling short, weakly waved to him. "It must have been funny to watch. A good pratfall, had there been an audience."

As Tom helped him back up the stairs and into the sleep room, Doc couldn't help thinking about the light in the living room. Not that he could believe in TV Frog any more than he had before, but there was something—*something*—very strange about that video screen being on when no one could have turned it on. And as he leaned his head back against the little cushion Kara brought for him, it was that thought, more than any bumps or bruises, that kept him up for the better part of the night.

■

Rotomotoman was ready—almost.

The saurs gathered in the workroom. Most of them were on the floor, surrounding—at what they believed was a safe distance—the figure of Rotomotoman that towered over them. Others were perched on Preston's desk and others yet were on the desk set across from it.

None had ventured up to where Geraldine and Tibor kept their separate abodes, but they too were quite literally out of their boxes to view the great moment. Tibor even wore his "hat," which was really a green piece of concave plastic with a little rim. It looked ridiculous on his head but Tibor insisted it was quite regal and dashing, especially when he wore it at a jaunty tilt.

Rotomotoman was attached by cable to the hard drive of Preston's computer. No one knew how long the download would take, but when it was finished Rotomotoman would come to life. Axel, standing next to his creation, tried to count down the seconds, but he lost his place several times and had to start over.

"Attention!" Agnes called out from her place near the door. "Attention! Keep *back*! When this piece of junk goes berserk there's no telling *who* will be crushed under its wheels! All saurs must *keep back*!"

Only Sluggo paid attention to her, and that was only to get her to stop shouting.

Tom Groverton was there too. No one noticed, though, that he was standing next to the two fire extinguishers he'd placed next to Geraldine's lab.

Axel gave up on the countdown and started to chant: "Go! Go! Go! Rotomotoman! Go! Go! Go! Rotomotoman!"

Some of the other saurs picked it up. "Go! Go! Go! Rotomotoman!"

Others joined in. "Go! Go! Go! Rotomotoman!"

Even the saurs who didn't speak squeaked and chirped to the rhythm of the cheer.

"Go! Go! Go! Rotomotoman! Go! Go! Go! Rotomotoman!"

"Attention all saurs! Keep *back*! *When* the piece of junk goes berserk—"

"Go! Go! Go! Rotomotoman! Go! Go! Go! Rotomotoman!"

"—will be indiscriminately *crushed* under—"

Rotomotoman jerked very slightly, hardly a movement at all. The download was finished. A faint hum and whir emanated from his mechanical innards. His hemisphere head turned slightly to the left and the pupils of his huge eyes followed the same general direction, then started back slowly to the right, taking in the whole scene.

The chanting stopped. Even Agnes held off her shouted warnings.

It is hard to imagine a more startled expression on a piece of machinery, if one can imagine an expression on a piece of machinery at all. The eyes had much to do with it, looking like enormous versions of the eyes that adorned toys and dolls in years long past—but much more active, animated, in fact. Those eyes and the mouth-like seam in his cylinder-torso created an expression: surprise, panic, astonishment.

He surveyed the ninety-odd dinosaur-looking creatures staring up at him—and one human, with arms folded, leaning back against a desk, smiling with apparent admiration.

Rotomotoman raised his arms in a gesture of surrender and recoiled right into Preston's desk.

The liquid-gray display screen on his torso—his only means of communication—filled with exclamation points, question marks and other strange symbols that may even have been incomprehensible to other rotomotomen, if any existed.

"See?" Agnes shouted. "Just as I told you! The monster is ready to pounce! Back away!"

But Rotomotoman just froze in that posture until Axel approached him on the back of the large brown triceratops named Dr. David Norman. Dr. Norman lowered his head and Axel dismounted. He walked straight up to his creation with his left forepaw upraised.

"Hiya! I'm Axel!"

Rotomotoman stared down at the small blue creature. He lowered one of his arms and bent the joint that approximated the elbow of the other. His display screen cleared of symbols, except for five characters of simple, recognizable alphabet and punctuation:

"Hiya!"

Many of the saurs cheered. Tom Groverton put his hands together and applauded.

Agnes nudged Preston and muttered, "You sure there aren't any machine guns in those fingers?"

"Positive."

"No flame throwers or lasers?"

"You saw the instructions yourself. Rotomotoman is weapon-free. He *does* have a rotating red flashing light that comes out of the top of his head, but as you can see he hasn't had cause to use it yet."

Agnes grumbled. "He *still* looks like a trashcan made up for Halloween!"

"Hey! Guys!" Axel said, as if the other saurs might not know yet, "I want you to meet your new friend! This is Rotomotoman!"

Rotomotoman held his metal hand horizontally just above his eyes: a salute to the assembly, with "Hiya!" still on his display screen. More cheers greeted him.

"Come on!" Axel coaxed his metal friend away from the desk. "A little this way! Follow me!"

Words appeared on his display screen: first "Axel," then "follow."

Rotomotoman complied with each direction, if a little tentatively. His software may have overly cautioned him about running over little ones, but he cast his gaze downward and thoroughly surveyed the floor, checking to make sure no one was underfoot. If a meter-and-a-half tall cylinder rolling on four wheels could be described as moving "daintily," it would describe Rotomotoman just then.

Axel led him to the door of the workroom. Rotomotoman—making no sound but an efficient, high-pitched whir—saluted the door. The word "door" appeared on his display screen. He followed Axel down the hallway, holding his salute all the way to the lift platform, where he stopped cold.

Rotomotoman didn't seem confident that he could keep his balance on the flatbed lift, with its guardrails set no more than a few centimeters high. Axel coaxed him on with the assurance that the lift moved so slowly he would be in no danger—*and* with the assistance of Diogenes and Hubert pushing from behind. With "Help!" replacing "Hiya!" on his display screen, Rotomotoman held so tightly to the staircase wall he left a trail of grooves in it, but everyone was too excited to notice them.

As he rolled from the platform to the floor he cast his gaze upward as if in thanks to some heavenly Rotomotogod.

"Look over here, Rotomotoman!" Axel said, pointing to the living room. "That's where the video is."

Rotomotoman saluted the video screen. His own screen alternated the words, "Video" and "Hiya!"

"Over in that room is where we eat!"

Rotomotoman saluted the dining room. "Dining room— Hiya!—Dining room—"

He saluted everything that Axel showed him, including the computer, the plastic stairs, the bookcases and the Five Wise Buddhasaurs' plastic saxophones. And all their names were printed out on his display screen, each punctuated with the same greeting.

"I suppose this question should have come up long ago," Doc asked the ecstatic Axel, while Rotomotoman saluted the lamp table, the couch and a broom Tom had left leaning by the living room window, "but just what exactly is Rotomotoman supposed to *do*?"

"Rotomotoman is here to protect good guys from the bad guys!"

"Well," Doc sighed deeply and patted Axel's head, "may your labors be few."

The notion of "bad guys" was not entirely forgotten by Doc as Tom Groverton gathered all the saurs around in the library later that afternoon. In the back of the room—standing at attention, of course— was Rotomotoman, his creator proudly at his side.

"They'll be here tomorrow, and they'll be looking for eggs," Tom said, his hands folded loosely as he sat on a little stool in the center of the room.

"Tell them to mind their own damn business!" Agnes shouted back.

"That would be fine," Tom said, "if we could. But these folks have rescinded their so-called 'proprietary rights,' based on a certain definition of what you guys are. And as you know they've been looking for loopholes ever since they agreed to the Atherton Foundation's proposal. Your intelligence, your emotional capacity, your longevity— it's baffled them for years. They have the support of a certain portion of the scientific community who'd like very much to make you the subject of study. And they want desperately to find out what they did, well, 'right,' so to speak, when they designed you. Generating eggs might change the deal if they find out. I mean—" Tom cleared his throat, "if they find any."

"Any *what*?" Doc asked in a whisper.

Tom smiled. "That's the spirit. I won't ask any questions and you won't tell me any lies—other than the ones you may already tell me."

"Why, *Tom!*" Doc said, his heavy eyelids raised as far as they would go. "What makes you think we'd tell you any lies?"

Tom ignored the remark. "Remember, I'll be here. Dr. Margaret will be here and even Ms. Leahy will be here to make sure these folks don't do anything out of line. But they *will* be thorough, and we can't really stop them, because we want to show them that we have nothing to hide."

"We *have* nothing to hide," Doc said.

"Exactly." Tom stood up. "Now, I have some things to do upstairs before I start dinner. But there's one more thing: it might be a good idea to keep Rotomotoman in the background when they come. We don't want to hit them with more than they can take."

"What did he mean by that?" Axel asked as Tom left the room.

"He means that our visitors tomorrow are unprepared for your genius," said Doc.

"Genius!" Agnes marched up to Axel. "Spelled the same as 'idiot!' This is all *your* fault! Sending messages to 'space guys!' You're the one who should be locked up! Not Bronte!"

"*Bronte!*" Axel gasped. "Who wants to lock up Bronte?"

"No one said anything about locking up Bronte!" Kara looked over at Bronte, whose concern about her egg had done little to steady her nerves for the meeting. Now she was trembling.

"What do you *think* they'll do?" Agnes continued. "They'll take her off to a laboratory and stick her with needles and cut her up to find out how she did it!"

A cry of alarm rose from the surrounding saurs. Memories of past injuries and dangers became acutely tangible even to the smallest and simplest of them.

"Don't listen to her," Kara said to Bronte. "Agnes is overreacting as usual. No one's going to take you away." She turned angrily to Agnes. "Can't you *ever* keep your mouth shut? We're all in a panic when we need our heads about us!"

"They'll take the egg away, won't they?" Bronte stammered.

"Like the scientists in the video we saw once, climbing into nests and stealing the eggs of rare birds."

"No one's going to do that here," Preston put his hand on Bronte's back. He could feel her shivers. "We'll think of something."

"I'm sorry, Bronte," Axel said. His face never before looked so long and mournful. "I didn't know this would happen."

"It's not your fault," said Bronte, her nubby teeth grinding at her lower lip. "You were just—just being Axel."

"That's the whole damn problem right there!" Agnes said.

"Maybe Rotomotoman can help us now," Axel said in a low voice.

Rotomotoman, in the back of the room, saluted at the mention of his name.

"Listen," Agnes barked at Axel, "I don't want to hear *one more word* about Rotomotoman! Space guys! Electric trashcans! Frogs watching the video! If I hear *anything* more from you—"

Agnes was interrupted by a voice that had so far not entered the discussion. It came back from the little bed over by the window, and in a low, raspy voice.

"Axel is right," said Hetman.

"*What?*" Agnes was ready for verbal battle, and the words "Axel is right" set her back plates upright, but they were spoken by the one saur she would not assail. "*What* did you say?"

"I said, Axel is right. Something Axel told me a few nights ago has kept me up thinking and—I could be wrong, but—Axel, do you still have the assembly directions for your Rotomotoman?"

"They're with Preston's stuff, up by the computer," he said.

"Bring them down here, and hurry! We have *stuff* to do!"

"Stuff to do!" Axel ran upstairs without hesitation.

"The rest of you," Hetman continued, "I want you to look very carefully at the sections on that sheet which refer to the Thermostat Assembly F and Carrier Drawer Assembly F1. Perhaps I'm completely wrong, but I think we've been overlooking something remarkable about that creation of Axel's."

■

When the big car arrived the next morning, Axel was at the window, up on the little lamp table, scouting.

"Huuuu-mans!" He announced to the others. "They're here! And they're in a *bad guys* car!"

The long dark limousine had an official seal from The Office of Bioengineering Standards on the side door. It stopped right in front of the house and out came three strangers, Dr. Margaret and Mrs. Leahy. Of the strangers, there was a young African-American, impeccably dressed in a topcoat and dark suit; a gray-haired Caucasian, much more casually dressed, in an unbuttoned leather jacket and a dark T-shirt; a young Asian-looking woman with very short canary-colored hair, wearing a plaid workshirt and a denim jacket.

Ms. Leahy led the way. Tom met the little group out on the porch.

"I'm really sorry about this," she said as she shook Tom's hand. Susan Leahy was trim and efficient as always, and she was starting to let the gray come into her hair. She was one of those eccentrics who still wore glasses, though hers were rimless. "You've told them what this is all about, didn't you?"

"Yes, they know."

She nodded and turned to the three persons who were to search the house.

"Okay, folks, you know the rules. You can search everything, everywhere, but if anything you do seems to be upsetting or traumatizing the saurs, I or Dr. Pagliotti here will have to ask you to back off. This is Tom Groverton." She put her hand on his shoulder. "Any questions you may have I'm sure he'll be glad to answer. We want to cooperate fully, but you have to understand that we have to act in the best interest of the saurs."

The young African-American, Dr. Phillips, nodded politely to Ms. Leahy. "We've done this kind of work at other houses. I can assure you we'll be as non-disruptive as we possibly can."

Dr. Margaret, who had seen some of the saurs' eggs herself, came up to Tom and gripped his hand. She wore a white jacket that looked a little like a short lab coat, and for once her long brown hair wasn't tied back. She didn't say a word but searched his expression for any sign of what she might expect.

Tom could only shrug. Anything can happen, he seemed to say, but don't get worried yet.

"You know," Ms. Leahy said, "it's nice to have an excuse to come here and visit some old friends."

Axel was still standing at the window, waving to her.

She waved back. "Hiya!"

When the group entered the house, some of the saurs stopped to watch them, cautiously and curiously. The smaller saurs went on with their business, moving from room to room on skates, getting their computer lessons, a brief game of Not So Hard, or watching the video.

"Attention humans!" Agnes announced from atop a lamp table near the door. "Attention all humans! It's time to SHAPE UP!"

"Don't mind Agnes," Ms. Leahy told the officials. "She greets most humans that way."

"Humans!" Agnes continued, "It's time to SHAPE UP! You've been running things stupidly for too long! It's time to STOP BEING STUPID!"

"So here's the little guy who's caused all the ruckus." Ms. Leahy went straight to Axel.

"Miss Lay-hee! Miss Lay-hee! Howya doing? What are you doing with the bad guys?"

Ms. Leahy carefully picked him up and perched him on her shoulder. "Important stuff, Axel. Want to see?"

"Yeah!"

She made sure she had a safe grip on him and that he wouldn't slip, even with all his excited gesticulations. "So what's all this about you sending messages to space?"

"Yeah!" said Axel. "Reggie and me! We sent a message to the space guys and told them all about us!"

The three investigators gathered around to listen to the conversation. The young woman, Dr. Yoon, took out a pocket computer to record it.

"And have you heard anything back from the 'space guys' yet?"

"Yeah! Maybe! At least I think that's why TV Frog is here! He comes at night and watches the video, but no one's seen him but me! Doc almost saw him but he fell down the stairs! He's okay, though. Doc, I mean, but TV Frog's okay too. Anyway, I think TV Frog just wants us to think he's here because he can't sleep. But Geraldine said he was really sent by the space guys, because they know how to drill holes in time and space!"

Ms. Leahy looked at the three investigators.

"Well, here's your source for the egg story."

Dr. Yoon slipped the computer back into her pocket.

"And who's that over there?" Mrs. Leahy pointed to the metal cylinder with the hemisphere head, standing out of the way, just to the left of the video screen.

"That's Rotomotoman! I built him myself! Well, Reggie helped me, and Preston, and Doc, and Agnes, and a lot of the other guys. But I thought him up all by myself!"

Rotomotoman was motionless. His display screen was empty. His left arm was listless at his side but his right arm was raised in a salute. It was hard to say what he might have been saluting—his right eye looked off to his left and his left eye looked off to his right.

The investigators looked over Rotomotoman carefully. They even took his head off and inspected the components. Some of the saurs got very quiet and even Agnes briefly desisted from her shouted exhortations.

"What is it supposed to do?" the man in the leather jacket, Mr. Chase, asked Tom.

"Ask the inventor." He pointed to Axel. "You *can* talk to them, you know."

"He fights bad guys and protects the good guys!" Axel offered without waiting to be asked.

"Doesn't look like he can fight any bad guys in his shape," Dr. Yoon said as she re-secured Rotomotoman's head.

"I—I forgot to plug him in last night!" Axel looked over at Doc, sitting on his little box, nodding almost imperceptibly. Then he looked to Agnes, who waved her tail threateningly.

"I've got to charge him up! He'll be okay tomorrow!"

"The kitchen is this way," Tom said to Dr. Phillips, "but I'm afraid the only eggs you'll find are in the refrigerator."

The investigators looked anyway—very carefully. They looked into every cabinet and along the baseboards and around the ceilings. They went through the cellar and the litter room, the living room, the dining room and the library. They looked behind all the books on the shelves. Dr. Margaret wouldn't let them look under Hetman's pillow, but she took the pillow out herself and let them inspect it.

"If the lady and gentlemen wish to look under the mattress," Hetman said, "they are welcome to do so."

"If I may?" Dr. Phillips said in an apologetic voice and did his work as quickly as possible. Before he moved on, he said "Thank you," to Hetman, came back and added, "Thank you—sir."

"You're very welcome."

They searched all the rooms upstairs and even went up into the attic, where the saurs had their "museum," made up of all the things friends and former "owners" had left them over the years: toys, paintings on construction paper, knick-knacks and little articles of clothing. The investigators found several egg-shaped things, made of glass and plastic, but not one real egg.

Mr. Chase's attention was drawn to a little charm on one of the shelves, a gold-plated Star of David on a slender chain. He picked it up to examine more closely.

"Put it back!" Agnes, who had followed them up into the Museum, shouted at him.

"Is this yours?" Mr. Chase asked her. "It's very pretty."

"None of your damn business! Put it back!"

Agnes harangued the investigators all the way down from the attic.

"Foo! Humans! War mongers! Animal eaters! Planet spoilers! G'wan! Beat it! Scram!"

"Adamant, isn't she?" Mr. Chase said to Dr. Margaret.

"You're upsetting her," Dr. Margaret replied.

"Sounds to me like she's upsetting herself."

"Didya hear?" Axel, still perched on Ms. Leahy's shoulder, whispered to her. "He called Agnes an *ant!*"

Ms. Leahy held her finger up to her lips. "Ssshh. Maybe he meant 'aunt.'"

When the investigators reached the sleep room they were approached by a pale green hadrosaur who, after some deliberation, shouted to them, "Yar-woo?"

"No! No!" Agnes coached the hadrosaur. "That's not what I told you to say!"

The hadrosaur tried again: "Yar-woo!"

"No! 'Foo!' You're supposed to say 'Foo!'" She smacked her tail against the floor.

"Foo?"

"Forget it! Just *forget it!*"

"Foo!" The hadrosaur smiled and walked away.

In the closet of the sleep room, Mr. Chase found a little cardboard box with wadded-up cotton inside. Nestled in the cotton was a tiny egg.

"Here's something," he said to his colleagues, who were searching in other parts of the room.

"Hey! Put that back!" Agnes shouted. "That's not yours!"

Mr. Chase held up the egg and inspected it carefully. It had a blue tint to it, and was no bigger than the first joint of his thumb.

"It's a bird's egg," Bronte walked up to Mr. Chase nervously. "A robin's, probably. Sluggo found it in the yard. Sometimes we try to hatch them—as if they were ours."

She looked up at Dr. Yoon and Dr. Phillips. "If they do hatch, we feed the little bird until it's old enough. Tom can sometimes find another nest in the yard and put it back. Sometimes the older birds accept him." Her voice was trembling now. "It's—it's just sort of a thing we do."

Dr. Phillips took the egg and held it up to the light from the window. "Looks like a robin's egg to me."

"That's what she said!" Agnes stood next to Bronte. "Now beat it! G'wan! Scram!"

"Is this when they pull their guns out?" Axel whispered to Ms. Leahy.

"They don't have guns," she answered.

"I thought they were bad guys!"

"Well, not really. Not *that* kind, at least."

Dr. Yoon, with arms folded, glanced at Agnes and said to her colleagues, "It may be that their eggs and the robin's eggs are almost alike. We better take it in."

"No!" Bronte gasped.

Ms. Leahy bent down and put her hand gently on Bronte's back. "Must you?" She asked the investigators.

"We have to know." Dr. Phillips put the egg back into its box. "I can give you all sorts of reasons, but the answer simply boils down to this: we have to know."

"Hear that?" Agnes shouted to the other saurs. "He said 'boil!' I *told* you they were going to eat them!"

"Please," Kara said to the investigators. "It really *is* a robin's egg. Honest. Don't take it away."

Dr. Phillips bent down and spoke to Bronte, resting the box carefully on his knee. "We won't hurt it. We just need to know what it is. It's a very simple procedure and we can have it back to you in a day or so."

"What if it hatches?" Bronte asked. "You'll take care of the little bird? You won't just—pitch it?"

"If that's what happens, I'll take care of it." He reached out and touched the little furrows on her brow. "I promise."

Dr. Phillips put the cardboard box into a little specimen bag, but left the bag open. Dr. Yoon made some notes with her pocket computer. Saurs filled the room. None of them spoke, not even Agnes, but they all looked at the investigators, who did their work quickly and tried not to look back.

"They may not be bad guys," Ms. Leahy whispered to Axel, "But I'll bet you that right now they don't feel like good guys."

She, along with Tom and Dr. Margaret, followed the investigators back out to the limousine, but in the living room she noticed Doc, still sitting on his plastic box, staring out toward the window as if deep in thought.

She put Axel down and kissed him on the snout. "I'll see you later," she said. "Gotta talk to my old buddy over there."

Ms. Leahy knelt down next to Doc and hugged him. "My old friend. Forgive me for not stopping to talk to you."

"You were busy, I know. There is nothing to forgive."

"I'll come back soon. For a *real* visit. We'll sit on the porch and talk of Cicero and Democritus and St. Augustine."

"Juvenal." Doc smiled. "*'Quis custodiet ipsos custodes'?*" He looked out toward the front door, where the limousine waited. "Not bad for a tiny, manufactured brain, eh?"

"It's not how much brain you've got, but how you use it."

She hugged him again and Doc reciprocated as best he could with his short forearms.

She whispered: "Is there any *real* reason to worry?"

Doc shook his head. "We'll be fine, for now."

When she stood up, Ms. Leahy could see the motionless metal cylinder of Rotomotoman saluting her. She returned his salute, bid farewell to the others and walked out to the limousine.

On the porch, Dr. Margaret asked Tom, "What will you do now?"

"I think I'll sit out here for a while."

She put her hand on his shoulder. "That's not what I meant."

"It's not really my call. It's theirs." He gestured back to the house with his thumb.

"What are they doing in there?"

The horn sounded from the limousine.

Tom walked Dr. Margaret to the limousine. "Come back to-night."

He took her hand and squeezed it gently. She got into the limousine and he watched it until it was out of sight, past the trees. For a few more minutes he sat on the bench on the porch, then got up and looked through the living room window.

Rotomotoman, back in motion again, had rolled out to the center of the room. The saurs were gathered around him in a circle. Tom could hear a faint mechanical buzzing and a high-pitched beep come from the metal cylinder. At the same moment, a section of the odd little robot, defined by nearly imperceptible seams in his cylindrical torso, slid out like the drawer of a desk.

Tom couldn't see what was inside, but he knew what it was. Bronte was the closest to the drawer, peering in with sad, hopeful eyes.

Then she opened her mouth as if to gasp.

She spoke to the others and they all moved in even closer, trying to get a peek inside. Tom couldn't hear a word of it, but he didn't have to.

Axel, perched on Hubert's back to stare into the little drawer, shouted out, "It moved! I saw it move!"

Tom went back to the bench. His coming in now would just create more nervous commotion and probably start Agnes shouting again.

There would be plenty of time later to consider all the implications. The investigators, back-tracking through their information, might request a look at the schematics of Axel's metal friend and discover Rotomotoman's very practical function as an incubator.

But then, Reggie may have anticipated that too, and devised a little camouflage for it. Never underestimate the Reggiesystem, Tom learned long ago.

After all, Reggie too was a kind of human-made life form, and like the saurs had developed in his own way.

For now, though, the moment belonged to the saurs, especially Bronte, the mother-to-be.

■

That night, Axel descended the stairs as stealthily as he could manage, in search of TV Frog. But the living room was dark, the video turned off. For a moment he thought that TV Frog must not have come, but he turned around and saw the illuminated screen of the Reggiesystem computer in the dining room, and before it sat TV Frog, visible in silhouette. The plastic stairs were placed in front of the desk, just behind where TV Frog sat with an old-fashioned clicker mouse, which he slapped with his left paw just as he'd slapped the video's remote pad.

TV Frog seemed to be clicking through a set of files, text on the right side and pictures on the left. Axel couldn't make out any of it, so he crept up the steps to get a closer look.

The pictures weren't very pleasant to look at: emaciated creatures with agonized expressions, bruised, battered, and scarred. Gaping mouths, hollowed eyes, muscles tensed with pain—

They were saurs, all of them.

These were the official files of the Atherton Foundation, all of their cases, with photos taken of the saurs when they were first found or brought to them.

Axel recognized some of them—Zack, Kip, Charlie, Hetman— Oh! Hetman! How did he ever make it? He barely looked alive. He—

The words got all tied up in Axel's head. If he looked at the pictures, at least he didn't have to think about them. But how could he *not* think about them after looking at all the faces, all the pain—

And then he saw a photograph of a small, blue theropod, exhausted, lying on his side, head twisted back as if he could hardly raise it—one black, expressionless eye was visible, staring upward. A second photo showed a long, straight cut down his back, infected and swollen.

The cut was the same length as the scar down Axel's back.

Axel felt as if the desk dropped out from under him—and the floor, the house, everything—as if he was falling through time and space.

"Space and Time and Time and Space—"

Whirling and spinning like an amusement park ride, but only the really, truly scary parts, and no one was there with whom he could share the elation and danger.

A boy, the one he'd been purchased for, had cut him open, goaded on a bet, to see if he had mechanical parts or biological organs. "Not like he's an animal," the boy had said. "Just a thing. Don't matter what anyone does to him."

But the boy said "him," like he *was* someone—

And Lancelot was there! Lancelot, his buddy! The two of them were purchased together, and they lived with the boy and his family. "Buddies forever, Lancelot and Axel, Axel and Lancelot—"

But Lancelot was all cut open, spread out on the floor, screaming, pleading, "Please! Stop! Help me! Kill me! Stop!"

And Axel had shouted too. "Don't! Don't hurt him! Stop it!"

A grown-up interrupted the impromptu dissections. Axel had run, with all his strength. He'd run, hidden himself, bled. With no food, with all his energy and muscle spent, he slipped into a hole on the edge of a construction site and waited to die, like Lancelot.

Axel remembered what that upward-turned eye in the photograph was looking at.

It had been night. The stars were out, and they were everywhere.

"Space—" said Axel. He put his forepaw on TV Frog's smooth back. It shuddered like an unbalanced engine.

"It was all space and big and perfect and endless. And even though I was small, I felt as big as space. I felt as big as the universe."

TV Frog clicked the mouse and the monitor screen went dark.

"That's what I should have asked the space guys about," Axel told him. "What I wanted to ask before I forgot. I wanted to ask if they knew any way to bring Lancelot back, or do something, so that he wouldn't be dead."

TV Frog just sat there. Still shuddering. His eyes looked immeasurably deep and sad.

"I guess they couldn't, huh?"

Whether or not he could answer, TV Frog didn't, which seemed like a kind of answer in itself.

Axel and TV Frog stood in front of the computer, and after a while the monitor clicked on again.

The screen filled with stars.

This time, when the screensaver reached the end of the cycle, with the smeared thumbprint galaxy just in view, it seemed to go a little farther. The galaxy filled the whole screen.

"You know, Reggie says the universe is one big place!"

TV Frog's eyes bobbed down into his head in a kind of affirmative gesture.

"I came down to ask if you wanted to come upstairs and see what's happening. It's the biggest thing that's ever happened here. The biggest thing that's ever happened *anywhere*!"

TV Frog didn't move.

Axel bent down and tugged at TV Frog's forepaw. "It's okay! No one will see you there! They're all looking at the egg!"

Axel kept tugging and urging until TV Frog turned away from the computer.

"We'd better hurry! It's almost ready to hatch!"

But TV Frog propelled himself slowly, one cautious 'flop' at a time.

"Come on! No one will see you! I promise!"

All the way down from the desk, across the floor and up the stairs to the second floor, with Axel leading, TV Frog moved on: flop, pause, flop, pause, flop.

They peered around the doorway into the sleep room. All the saurs were gathered around Rotomotoman, situated in the center of the room. He, like everyone else, was staring into his incubator drawer, his pupils cast at an awkwardly downward angle. Bronte stood closest to the drawer, along with Kara, Agnes, Doc and Preston. The only sounds in the room were the soft purr of Rotomotoman's machinery and the anticipatory breathing of every creature in the room.

Sitting in the back, as far out of the way as they could situate themselves, were Tom Groverton and Dr. Margaret. They were holding hands, which Axel thought especially fascinating. He tapped TV Frog and pointed to them.

"Look at *that*!" he whispered. "I'll bet they're learning how to make eggs too!"

He kept staring at the humans until he heard a kind of chiming sound coming from Rotomotoman. A disk-shaped part at the top of his head slid away and up from the cavity rose a flashing, rotating red light—just as Axel had designed it.

A word flashed on Rotomotoman's display screen: "Ready!"

The little drawer opened.

The quiet sighs of awe and pent up relief from everyone gathered around sounded a little like a low, deep chord from some great church organ.

"Come on! Let's get a closer look!" Axel reached over to tap TV Frog again, but there was no one at his side now.

TV Frog was gone.

"Hey!"

Axel wanted to go look for him, but his curiosity about the egg proved the greater draw. Axel crept up to the incubator drawer and told himself he'd find TV Frog later.

He gently pushed through the thick crowd of saurs. Charlie grouched at him until Rosie reminded him that it was Axel who was responsible for Rotomotoman. They let him through, and Axel climbed up on Hubert's back, where he could easily see into the drawer.

The first few hairline cracks had already appeared on the surface of the shivering egg. A piece of the shell dropped away and from that breach popped a little pink head at the end of a long neck.

No one looked more surprised than Rotomotoman, whose huge disk-eyes implausibly seemed to grow larger at the sight.

The tiny hatchling's eyes were shut at first, but its mouth was open and it made a little sound, a "Gack!" like a clearing of its throat.

Diogenes, who in all his years at the house had never been heard to utter more than a few words, turned to Hetman's bed and whispered, "Did you hear?"

Hetman nodded. "Thank you, that I lived long enough to hear it."

Then he (or she) opened his (or her) eyes.

The small, black, glistening orbs seemed instantly focused. The hatchling looked over the top of the drawer and seemed to see everyone and everything.

Bronte bent down and caressed the little creature with her snout, then tapped away another piece of the shell to free it more.

"It's hard to say," Doc looked at the hatchling, "since he's without precedent, as far as we know, but he looks like a healthy little fellow to me."

"Little *fellow*?" Agnes snapped. "Can't you see it's obviously female? Obviously intelligent? Obviously smarter than any carnosaur could ever *hope* to be?"

"Don't start," said Kara. "It's not the time to fight."

"What will happen now?" Bronte asked Kara. "Will she grow? Will she change and mature? Will she learn to do all the things we do?"

"Who knows?" said Kara. "We'll learn as we go along."

"It won't stay a secret for long," said Charlie, rubbing his nasal horn against the floor. "Those humans in the big car know more than they're saying. They wouldn't have taken Axel's story so seriously if they didn't."

"That they figure it out isn't what matters," Agnes said. "It's what they'll do when they know."

"Which we can't predict," said Preston, smiling at the little pink creature in the incubator drawer. "And this isn't the time to try."

All this time Axel, balanced on Hubert's back, kept trying to get the hatchling's attention, waving excitedly with one forepaw while holding to Hubert's neck with the other.

"Hiya! Hey! Up here! Hey! Hiya!"

The tiny pink sauropod looked up at Axel.

"Gack!"

"Hiya Gack! I'm Axel!"

"That's not her name!" Agnes waved her tail. "Moron!"

Kara nudged her and shook her head. "We'll sort it out later."

When Axel climbed down, Preston put his forepaw on his head and said, "We need to thank you. You—and Reggie."

Axel looked up at Preston. "Don't forget Rotomotoman!"

"Yes, Rotomotoman too."

Rotomotoman stared down and saluted the hatchling, the red light on his head still rotating, as the word "Gack" flashed on his display screen.

Axel looked around the sleep room and noticed that Sluggo was up on the box seat under the window, looking out.

"Hey!" Axel hopped up and joined him. It was his favorite spot, after all. "Whatya doing up here?"

"I—I just wanted to look up at the stars. I don't know why. The egg—and everything—I feel scared and I don't know why. Or I do—but I'm still scared. I just needed to look up at the sky and see the stars."

"Me too." Axel put his forepaws up against the glass. "The moon and the planets and the stars and the galaxies are all spinning through space! And *we're* spinning through space too! It's a fact!"

"When I look up at the stars," Sluggo said, "I feel—I don't know—I feel—"

"As big as the universe!" Axel said.

"Yes. That's it. As big as the universe."

"It's a good night for looking," Axel gazed at the moon, his mouth wide open. "It's the biggest, best universe in the whole world!"

Agnes might have disputed him, and if not there were many others who would, but it wasn't in Sluggo to argue. He had only one universe to judge from, just as he had only one egg to judge from, but the both of them in their different ways seemed pretty remarkable.

And so, in an old house at the edge of the woods, far from the nearest megalopolis, Axel and Sluggo looked out from the window of the sleep room, up at the stars.

"Look at that!" Axel pointed to a luminous streak, razor thin, cutting a diagonal line across the night sky.

"A shooting star!" Axel nudged Sluggo. "Do you see it?"

"Yes," Sluggo answered.

The shooting star was there for a few seconds, then disappeared.

"Wasn't that neat?" Axel said.

"Yes, but—" Sluggo looked over at Axel, then out the window again.

"What?"

"Aren't shooting stars supposed to shoot *down*? That one was going *up*!"

"Heyyyy!" Axel rubbed the spot just under his chin. "That's *right*!"

The two of them kept looking out at the sky—the waiting universe before them and the new world behind, as good as any and better than most—but that was the only upward-shooting star they saw that night.

One of the things I wanted to explore in "Hell Is the Absence of God" was the notion of religion without faith. The lack of definitive evidence allows many of us to reject one religion and choose another based on which one we find most comforting, e.g. "I don't like the judgmental god of religion A, so I'm going to worship the kind and gentle god of religion B." We have that option because neither deity is unambiguously present. But if a judgmental deity were here right now, we'd have to deal with him whether we liked him or not.

Of course, even when the evidence for a deity is ambiguous, not everyone follows the most comforting religion. Many people follow religions that sometimes make them feel terrible about themselves. I suppose such religions offer comfort of a different sort by describing a universe in which there is clarity, and many people find that clarity more valuable than sweeping reassurances. Similar choices would probably exist even after the appearance of a deity: no matter what action a god took, there'd be room for multiple interpretations, and people would still differ on which they preferred.

Ted was born and raised in Port Jefferson, New York, and currently lives outside Seattle, Washington. He has a degree in computer science and makes his living as a technical writer. His short fiction is collected in the volume Stories of Your Life and Others.

Ted's bibliography can be found on the web at http://isfdb. tamu.edu/cgi-bin/p1.cgi?Ted%20Chiang.

TED CHIANG

This is the story of a man named Neil Fisk, and how he came to love God. The pivotal event in Neil's life was an occurrence both terrible and ordinary: the death of his wife Sarah. Neil was consumed with grief after she died, a grief that was excruciating not only because of its intrinsic magnitude, but because it also renewed and emphasized the previous pains of his life. Her death forced him to reexamine his relationship with God, and in doing so he began a journey that would change him forever.

Neil was born with a congenital abnormality that caused his left thigh to be externally rotated and several inches shorter than his right; the medical term for it was proximal femoral focus deficiency. Most people he met assumed God was responsible for this, but Neil's mother hadn't witnessed any visitations while carrying him; his condition was the result of improper limb development during the sixth week of gestation, nothing more. In fact, as far as Neil's mother was concerned, blame rested with his absent father, whose income might have made corrective surgery a possibility, although she never expressed this sentiment aloud.

As a child Neil had occasionally wondered if he was being punished by God, but most of the time he blamed his classmates in school for his unhappiness. Their nonchalant cruelty, their instinctive ability to locate the weaknesses in a victim's emotional armor, the way their own friendships were reinforced by their sadism: he recognized these as examples of human behavior, not divine. And although his classmates often used God's name in their taunts, Neil knew better than to blame Him for their actions.

But while Neil avoided the pitfall of blaming God, he never made the jump to loving Him; nothing in his upbringing or his personality led him to pray to God for strength or for relief. The assorted trials he faced growing up were accidental or human in origin, and he relied on strictly human resources to counter them. He became an adult who—like so many others—viewed God's actions in the abstract until they impinged upon his own life. Angelic visitations were events that befell other people, reaching him only via reports on the nightly news. His own life was entirely mundane; he worked as a superintendent for an upscale apartment building, collecting rent and performing repairs, and as far as he was concerned, circumstances were fully capable of unfolding, happily or not, without intervention from above.

This remained his experience until the death of his wife.

It was an unexceptional visitation, smaller in magnitude than most but no different in kind, bringing blessings to some and disaster to others. In this instance the angel was Nathanael, making an appearance in a downtown shopping district. Four miracle cures were effected: the elimination of carcinomas in two individuals, the regeneration of the spinal cord in a paraplegic, and the restoration of sight to a recently blinded person. There were also two miracles that were not cures: a delivery van, whose driver had fainted at the sight of the angel, was halted before it could overrun a busy sidewalk; another man was caught in a shaft of Heaven's light when the angel departed, erasing his eyes but ensuring his devotion.

Neil's wife Sarah Fisk had been one of the eight casualties. She was hit by flying glass when the angel's billowing curtain of flame shattered the storefront window of the café in which she was eating. She bled to death within minutes, and the other customers in the café—none of whom suffered even superficial injuries—could do nothing but listen to her cries of pain and fear, and eventually witness her soul's ascension toward Heaven.

Nathanael hadn't delivered any specific message; the angel's parting words, which had boomed out across the entire visitation site, were the typical *Behold the power of the Lord*. Of the eight casualties that day, three souls were accepted into Heaven and five were not, a closer ratio than the average for deaths by all causes. Sixty-two people received medical treatment for injuries ranging from slight concussions to ruptured eardrums to burns requiring skin grafts. Total property damage was estimated at $8.1 million, all of it excluded by private insurance companies due to the cause. Scores of people became devout worshippers in the wake of the visitation, either out of gratitude or terror.

Alas, Neil Fisk was not one of them.

■

After a visitation, it's common for all the witnesses to meet as a group and discuss how their common experience has affected their lives. The witnesses of Nathanael's latest visitation arranged such group meetings, and family members of those who had died were welcome, so Neil began attending. The meetings were held once a month in a basement room of a large church downtown; there were metal folding chairs arranged in rows, and in the back of the room was a table holding coffee and doughnuts. Everyone wore adhesive name tags made out in felt-tip pen.

While waiting for the meetings to start, people would stand around, drinking coffee, talking casually. Most people Neil spoke to assumed his leg was a result of the visitation, and he had to explain that he wasn't a witness, but rather the husband of one of the casualties. This didn't bother him particularly; he was used to explaining about his leg. What did bother him was the tone of the meetings themselves, when participants spoke about their reaction to the visitation: most of them talked about their newfound devotion to God, and they tried to persuade the bereaved that they should feel the same.

Neil's reaction to such attempts at persuasion depended on who was making it. When it was an ordinary witness, he found it merely irritating. When someone who'd received a miracle cure told him to love God, he had to restrain an impulse to strangle the person. But what he found most disquieting of all was hearing the same suggestion from a man named Tony Crane; Tony's wife had died in the visitation too, and he now projected an air of groveling with his every movement. In hushed, tearful tones he explained how he had accepted his role as one of God's subjects, and he advised Neil to do likewise.

Neil didn't stop attending the meetings—he felt that he somehow owed it to Sarah to stick with them—but he found another group to go to as well, one more compatible with his own feelings: a support group devoted to those who'd lost a loved one during a visitation, and were angry at God because of it. They met every other week in a room at the local community center, and talked about the grief and rage that boiled inside of them.

All the attendees were generally sympathetic to one another, despite differences in their various attitudes toward God. Of those who'd been devout before their loss, some struggled with the task of remaining so, while others gave up their devotion without a second glance. Of those who'd never been devout, some felt their position had been validated, while others were faced with the near-impossible task of becoming devout now. Neil found himself, to his consternation, in this last category.

Like every other non-devout person, Neil had never expended much energy on where his soul would end up; he'd always assumed his destination was Hell, and he accepted that. That was the way of things, and Hell, after all, was not physically worse than the mortal plane.

It meant permanent exile from God, no more and no less; the truth of this was plain for anyone to see on those occasions when Hell manifested itself. These happened on a regular basis; the ground seemed to become transparent, and you could see Hell as if you were looking through a hole in the floor. The lost souls looked no different than the living, their eternal bodies resembling mortal ones. You couldn't communicate with them—their exile from God meant that they couldn't apprehend the mortal plane where His actions were still felt—but as long as the manifestation lasted you could hear them talk, laugh, or cry, just as they had when they were alive.

People varied widely in their reactions to these manifestations. Most devout people were galvanized, not by the sight of anything frightening, but at being reminded that eternity outside paradise was a possibility. Neil, by contrast, was one of those who were unmoved; as far as he could tell, the lost souls as a group were no unhappier than he was, their existence no worse than his in the mortal plane, and in some ways better: his eternal body would be unhampered by congenital abnormalities.

Of course, everyone knew that Heaven was incomparably superior, but to Neil it had always seemed too remote to consider, like wealth or fame or glamour. For people like him, Hell was where you went when you died, and he saw no point in restructuring his life in hopes of avoiding that. And since God hadn't previously played a role in Neil's life, he wasn't afraid of being exiled from God. The prospect of living without interference, living in a world where windfalls and misfortunes were never by design, held no terror for him.

Now that Sarah was in Heaven, his situation had changed. Neil wanted more than anything to be reunited with her, and the only way to get to Heaven was to love God with all his heart.

■

This is Neil's story, but telling it properly requires telling the stories of two other individuals whose paths became entwined with his. The first of these is Janice Reilly.

What people assumed about Neil had in fact happened to Janice. When Janice's mother was eight months pregnant with her, she lost control of the car she was driving and collided with a telephone pole during a sudden hailstorm, fists of ice dropping out of a clear blue sky and littering the road like a spill of giant ball bearings. She was sitting in her car, shaken but unhurt, when she saw a knot of silver flames— later identified as the angel Bardiel—float across the sky. The sight petrified her, but not so much that she didn't notice the peculiar settling sensation in her womb. A subsequent ultrasound revealed that the unborn Janice Reilly no longer had legs; flipper-like feet grew directly from her hip sockets.

Janice's life might have gone the way of Neil's, if not for what happened two days after the ultrasound. Janice's parents were sitting at their kitchen table, crying and asking what they had done to deserve this, when they received a vision: the saved souls of four deceased relatives appeared before them, suffusing the kitchen with a golden glow. The saved never spoke, but their beatific smiles induced a feeling of serenity in whoever saw them. From that moment on, the Reillys were certain that their daughter's condition was not a punishment.

As a result, Janice grew up thinking of her legless condition as a gift; her parents explained that God had given her a special assignment because He considered her equal to the task, and she vowed that she would not let Him down. Without pride or defiance, she saw it as her responsibility to show others that her condition did not indicate weakness, but rather strength.

As a child, she was fully accepted by her schoolmates; when you're as pretty, confident, and charismatic as she was, children don't even notice that you're in a wheelchair. It was when she was a teenager that she realized that the able-bodied people in her school were not the ones who most needed convincing. It was more important for her to set an example for other handicapped individuals, whether they had been touched by God or not, no matter where they lived. Janice began speaking before audiences, telling those with disabilities that they had the strength God required of them.

Over time she developed a reputation, and a following. She made a living writing and speaking, and established a non-profit organization dedicated to promoting her message. People sent her letters thanking her for changing their lives, and receiving those gave her a sense of fulfillment of a sort that Neil had never experienced.

This was Janice's life up until she herself witnessed a visitation by the angel Rashiel. She was letting herself into her house when the tremors began; at first she thought they were of natural origin, although she didn't live in a geologically active area, and waited in the doorway for them to subside. Several seconds later she caught a glimpse of silver in the sky and realized it was an angel, just before she lost consciousness.

Janice awoke to the biggest surprise of her life: the sight of her two new legs, long, muscular, and fully functional.

She was startled the first time she stood up: she was taller than she expected. Balancing at such a height without the use of her arms was unnerving, and simultaneously feeling the texture of the ground through the soles of her feet made it positively bizarre. Rescue workers, finding her wandering down the street dazedly, thought she was in shock until she—marveling at her ability to face them at eye level—explained to them what had happened.

When statistics were gathered for the visitation, the restoration of Janice's legs was recorded as a blessing, and she was humbly grateful for her good fortune. It was at the first of the support group meetings that a feeling of guilt began to creep in. There Janice met two individuals with cancer who'd witnessed Rashiel's visitation, thought their cure was at hand, and been bitterly disappointed when they realized they'd been passed over. Janice found herself wondering, why had she received a blessing when they had not?

Janice's family and friends considered the restoration of her legs a reward for excelling at the task God had set for her, but for Janice, this interpretation raised another question. Did He intend for her to stop? Surely not; evangelism provided the central direction of her life, and there was no limit to the number of people who needed to hear her message. Her continuing to preach was the best action she could take, both for herself and for others.

Her reservations grew during her first speaking engagement after the visitation, before an audience of people recently paralyzed and now wheelchair-bound. Janice delivered her usual words of inspiration, assuring them that they had the strength needed for the challenges ahead; it was during the Q&A that she was asked if the restoration of her legs meant she had passed her test. Janice didn't know what to say; she could hardly promise them that one day their marks would be erased. In fact, she realized, any implication that she'd been rewarded could be interpreted as criticism of others who remained afflicted, and she didn't want that. All she could tell them was that she didn't know why she'd been cured, but it was obvious they found that an unsatisfying answer.

Janice returned home disquieted. She still believed in her message, but as far as her audiences were concerned, she'd lost her greatest source of credibility. How could she inspire others who were touched by God to see their condition as a badge of strength, when she no longer shared their condition?

She considered whether this might be a challenge, a test of her ability to spread His word. Clearly God had made her task more difficult than it was before; perhaps the restoration of her legs was an obstacle for her to overcome, just as their earlier removal had been.

This interpretation failed her at her next scheduled engagement. The audience was a group of witnesses to a visitation by Nathanael; she was often invited to speak to such groups in the hopes that those who suffered might draw encouragement from her. Rather than sidestep the issue, she began with an account of the visitation she herself had recently experienced. She explained that while it might appear she was a beneficiary, she was in fact facing her own challenge: like them, she was being forced to draw on resources previously untapped.

She realized, too late, that she had said the wrong thing. A man in the audience with a misshapen leg stood up and challenged her: was she seriously suggesting that the restoration of her legs was comparable to the loss of his wife? Could she really be equating her trials with his own?

Janice immediately assured him that she wasn't, and that she couldn't imagine the pain he was experiencing. But, she said, it wasn't God's intention that everyone be subjected to the same kind of trial, but only that each person face his or her own trial, whatever it might be. The difficulty of any trial was subjective, and there was no way to compare two individuals' experiences. And just as those whose suffering seemed greater than his should have compassion for him, so should he have compassion for those whose suffering seemed less.

The man was having none of it. She had received what anyone else would have considered a fantastic blessing, and she was complaining about it. He stormed out of the meeting while Janice was still trying to explain.

That man, of course, was Neil Fisk. Neil had had Janice Reilly's name mentioned to him for much of his life, most often by people who were convinced his misshapen leg was a sign from God. These people cited her as an example he should follow, telling him that her attitude was the proper response to a physical handicap. Neil couldn't deny that her leglessness was a far worse condition than his distorted femur. Unfortunately, he found her attitude so foreign that, even in the best of times, he'd never been able to learn anything from her. Now, in the depths of his grief and mystified as to why she had received a gift she didn't need, Neil found her words offensive.

In the days that followed, Janice found herself more and more plagued by doubts, unable to decide what the restoration of her legs meant. Was she being ungrateful for a gift she'd received? Was it both a blessing and a test? Perhaps it was a punishment, an indication that she had not performed her duty well enough. There were many possibilities, and she didn't know which one to believe.

■

There is one other person who played an important role in Neil's story, even though he and Neil did not meet until Neil's journey was nearly over. That person's name is Ethan Mead.

Ethan had been raised in a family that was devout, but not profoundly so. His parents credited God with their above-average health and their comfortable economic status, although they hadn't witnessed any visitations or received any visions; they simply trusted that God was, directly or indirectly, responsible for their good fortune. Their devotion had never been put to any serious test, and might not have withstood one; their love for God was based in their satisfaction with the status quo.

Ethan was not like his parents, though. Ever since childhood he'd felt certain that God had a special role for him to play, and he waited for a sign telling him what that role was. He'd liked to have become a preacher, but felt he hadn't any compelling testimony to offer; his vague feelings of expectation weren't enough. He longed for an encounter with the divine to provide him with direction.

He could have gone to one of the holy sites, those places where—for reasons unknown—angelic visitations occurred on a regular basis, but he felt that such an action would be presumptuous of him. The holy sites were usually the last resort of the desperate, those people seeking either a miracle cure to repair their bodies or a glimpse of Heaven's light to repair their souls, and Ethan was not desperate. He decided that he'd been set along his own course, and in time the reason for it would become clear. While waiting for that day, he lived his life as best he could: he worked as a librarian, married a woman named Claire, raised two children. All the while, he remained watchful for signs of a greater destiny.

Ethan was certain his time had come when he became witness to a visitation by Rashiel, the same visitation that—miles away—restored Janice Reilly's legs. Ethan was alone when it happened, walking toward his car in the center of a parking lot, when the ground began to shudder. Instinctively he knew it was a visitation, and he assumed a kneeling position, feeling no fear, only exhilaration and awe at the prospect of learning his calling.

The ground became still after a minute, and Ethan looked around, but didn't otherwise move. Only after waiting for several more minutes did he rise to his feet. There was a large crack in the asphalt, beginning directly in front of him and following a meandering path down the street. The crack seemed to be pointing him in a specific direction, so he ran alongside it for several blocks until he encountered other survivors, a man and a woman climbing out of a modest fissure that had opened up directly beneath them. He waited with the two of them until rescuers arrived and brought them to a shelter.

Ethan attended the support group meetings that followed and met the other witnesses to Rashiel's visitation. Over the course of a few meetings, he became aware of certain patterns among the witnesses. Of course there were those who'd been injured and those who'd received miracle cures. But there were also those whose lives were changed in other ways: the man and woman he'd first met fell in love and were soon engaged; a woman who'd been pinned beneath a collapsed wall was inspired to become an EMT after being rescued. One business owner formed an alliance that averted her impending bankruptcy, while another whose business was destroyed saw it as a message that he change his ways. It seemed that everyone except Ethan had found a way to understand what had happened to them.

He hadn't been cursed or blessed in any obvious way, and he didn't know what message he was intended to receive. His wife, Claire, suggested that he consider the visitation a reminder that he appreciate what he had, but Ethan found that unsatisfying, reasoning that *every* visitation—no matter where it occurred—served that function, and the fact that he'd witnessed a visitation firsthand had to have greater significance. His mind was preyed upon by the idea that he'd missed an opportunity, that there was a fellow witness whom he was intended to meet but hadn't. This visitation had to be the sign he'd been waiting for; he couldn't just disregard it. But that didn't tell him what he was supposed to do.

Ethan eventually resorted to the process of elimination: he got hold of a list of all the witnesses, and crossed off those who had a clear interpretation of their experience, reasoning that one of those remaining must be the person whose fate was somehow intertwined with his. Among those who were confused or uncertain about the visitation's meaning would be the one he was intended to meet.

When he had finished crossing names off his list, there was only one left: JANICE REILLY.

In public Neil was able to mask his grief as adults are expected to, but in the privacy of his apartment, the floodgates of emotion burst open. The awareness of Sarah's absence would overwhelm him, and then he'd collapse on the floor and weep. He'd curl up into a ball, his body racked by hiccuping sobs, tears and mucus streaming down his face, the anguish coming in ever-increasing waves until it was more than he could bear, more intense than he'd have believed possible. Minutes or hours later it would leave, and he would fall asleep, exhausted. And the next morning he would wake up and face the prospect of another day without Sarah.

An elderly woman in Neil's apartment building tried to comfort him by telling him that the pain would lessen in time, and while he would never forget his wife, he would at least be able to move on. Then he would meet someone else one day and find happiness with her, and he would learn to love God and thus ascend to Heaven when his time came.

This woman's intentions were good, but Neil was in no position to find any comfort in her words. Sarah's absence felt like an open wound, and the prospect that someday he would no longer feel pain at her loss seemed not just remote, but a physical impossibility. If suicide would have ended his pain, he'd have done it without hesitation, but that would only ensure that his separation from Sarah was permanent.

The topic of suicide regularly came up at the support group meetings, and inevitably led to someone mentioning Robin Pearson, a woman who used to come to the meetings several months before Neil began attending. Robin's husband had been afflicted with stomach cancer during a visitation by the angel Makatiel. She stayed in his hospital room for days at a stretch, only for him to die unexpectedly when she was home doing laundry. A nurse who'd been present told Robin that his soul had ascended, and so Robin had begun attending the support group meetings.

Many months later, Robin came to the meeting shaking with rage. There'd been a manifestation of Hell near her house, and she'd seen her husband among the lost souls. She'd confronted the nurse, who admitted to lying in the hopes that Robin would learn to love God, so that at least she would be saved even if her husband hadn't been. Robin wasn't at the next meeting, and at the meeting after that the group learned she had committed suicide to rejoin her husband.

None of them knew the status of Robin's and her husband's relationship in the afterlife, but successes were known to happen; some couples had indeed been happily reunited through suicide. The support group had attendees whose spouses had descended to Hell, and they talked about being torn between wanting to remain alive and wanting to rejoin their spouses. Neil wasn't in their situation, but his first response when listening to them had been envy: if Sarah had gone to Hell, suicide would be the solution to all his problems.

This led to a shameful self-knowledge for Neil. He realized that if he had to choose between going to Hell while Sarah went to Heaven, or having both of them go to Hell together, he would choose the latter: he would rather she be exiled from God than separated from him. He knew it was selfish, but he couldn't change how he felt: he believed Sarah could be happy in either place, but he could only be happy with her.

Neil's previous experiences with women had never been good. All too often he'd begin flirting with a woman while sitting at a bar, only to have her remember an appointment elsewhere the moment he stood up and his shortened leg came into view. Once, a woman he'd been dating for several weeks broke off their relationship, explaining that while she herself didn't consider his leg a defect, whenever they were seen in public together other people assumed there must be something wrong with her for being with him, and surely he could understand how unfair that was to her?

Sarah had been the first woman Neil met whose demeanor hadn't changed one bit, whose expression hadn't flickered toward pity or horror or even surprise when she first saw his leg. For that reason alone it was predictable that Neil would become infatuated with her; by the time he saw all the sides of her personality, he'd completely fallen in love with her. And because his best qualities came out when he was with her, she fell in love with him too.

Neil had been surprised when Sarah told him she was devout. There weren't many signs of her devotion—she didn't go to church, sharing Neil's dislike for the attitudes of most people who attended—but in her own, quiet way she was grateful to God for her life. She never tried to convert Neil, saying that devotion would come from within or not at all. They rarely had any cause to mention God, and most of the time it would've been easy for Neil to imagine that Sarah's views on God matched his own.

This is not to say that Sarah's devotion had no effect on Neil. On the contrary, Sarah was far and away the best argument for loving God that he had ever encountered. If love of God had contributed to making her the person she was, then perhaps it did make sense. During the years that the two of them were married, his outlook on life improved, and it probably would have reached the point where he was thankful to God, if he and Sarah had grown old together.

Sarah's death removed that particular possibility, but it needn't have closed the door on Neil's loving God. Neil could have taken it as a reminder that no one can count on having decades left. He could have been moved by the realization that, had he died with her, his soul would've been lost and the two of them separated for eternity. He could have seen Sarah's death as a wake-up call, telling him to love God while he still had the chance.

Instead Neil became actively resentful of God. Sarah had been the greatest blessing of his life, and God had taken her away. Now he was expected to love Him for it? For Neil, it was like having a kidnapper demand love as ransom for his wife's return. Obedience he might have managed, but sincere, heartfelt love? That was a ransom he couldn't pay.

This paradox confronted several people in the support group. One of the attendees, a man named Phil Soames, correctly pointed out that thinking of it as a condition to be met would guarantee failure. You couldn't love God as a means to an end, you had to love Him for Himself. If your ultimate goal in loving God was a reunion with your spouse, you weren't demonstrating true devotion at all.

A woman in the support group named Valerie Tommasino said they shouldn't even try. She'd been reading a book published by the humanist movement; its members considered it wrong to love a God who inflicted such pain, and advocated that people act according to their own moral sense instead of being guided by the carrot and the stick. These were people who, when they died, descended to Hell in proud defiance of God.

Neil himself had read a pamphlet of the humanist movement; what he most remembered was that it had quoted the fallen angels. Visitations of fallen angels were infrequent, and caused neither good fortune nor bad; they weren't acting under God's direction, but just passing through the mortal plane as they went about their unimaginable business. On the occasions they appeared, people would ask them questions: did they know God's intentions? Why had they rebelled? The fallen angels' reply was always the same: *Decide for yourselves. That is what we did. We advise you to do the same.*

Those in the humanist movement had decided, and if it weren't for Sarah, Neil would've made the identical choice. But he wanted her back, and the only way was to find a reason to love God.

Looking for any footing on which to build their devotion, some attendees of the support group took comfort in the fact that their loved ones hadn't suffered when God took them, but instead died instantly. Neil didn't even have that; Sarah had received horrific lacerations when the glass hit her. Of course, it could have been worse. One couple's teenage son been trapped in a fire ignited by an angel's visitation, and received full-thickness burns over eighty percent of his body before rescue workers could free him; his eventual death was a mercy. Sarah had been fortunate by comparison, but not enough to make Neil love God.

Neil could think of only one thing that would make him give thanks to God, and that was if He allowed Sarah to appear before him. It would give him immeasurable comfort just to see her smile again; he'd never been visited by a saved soul before, and a vision now would have meant more to him than at any other point in his life.

But visions don't appear just because a person needs one, and none ever came to Neil. He had to find his own way toward God.

The next time he attended the support group meeting for witnesses of Nathanael's visitation, Neil sought out Benny Vasquez, the man whose eyes had been erased by Heaven's light. Benny didn't always attend because he was now being invited to speak at other meetings; few visitations resulted in an eyeless person, since Heaven's light entered the mortal plane only in the brief moments that an angel emerged from or reentered Heaven, so the eyeless were minor celebrities, and in demand as speakers to church groups.

Benny was now as sightless as any burrowing worm: not only were his eyes and sockets missing, his skull lacked even the space for such features, the cheekbones now abutting the forehead. The light that had brought his soul as close to perfection as was possible in the mortal plane had also deformed his body; it was commonly held that this illustrated the superfluity of physical bodies in Heaven. With the limited expressive capacity his face retained, Benny always wore a blissful, rapturous smile.

Neil hoped Benny could say something to help him love God. Benny described Heaven's light as infinitely beautiful, a sight of such compelling majesty that it vanquished all doubts. It constituted incontrovertible proof that God should be loved, an explanation that made it as obvious as $1 + 1 = 2$. Unfortunately, while Benny could offer many analogies for the effect of Heaven's light, he couldn't duplicate that effect with his own words. Those who were already devout found Benny's descriptions thrilling, but to Neil, they seemed frustratingly vague. So he looked elsewhere for counsel.

Accept the mystery, said the minister of the local church. If you can love God even though your questions go unanswered, you'll be the better for it.

Admit that you need Him, said the popular book of spiritual advice he bought. When you realize that self-sufficiency is an illusion, you'll be ready.

Submit yourself completely and utterly, said the preacher on the television. Receiving torment is how you prove your love. Acceptance may not bring you relief in this life, but resistance will only worsen your punishment.

All of these strategies have proven successful for different individuals; any one of them, once internalized, can bring a person to devotion. But these are not always easy to adopt, and Neil was one who found them impossible.

Neil finally tried talking to Sarah's parents, which was an indication of how desperate he was: his relationship with them had always been tense. While they loved Sarah, they often chided her for not being demonstrative enough in her devotion, and they'd been shocked when she married a man who wasn't devout at all. For her part, Sarah had always considered her parents too judgmental, and their disapproval of Neil only reinforced her opinion. But now Neil felt he had something in common with them—after all, they were all mourning Sarah's loss—and so he visited them in their suburban colonial, hoping they could help him in his grief.

How wrong he was. Instead of sympathy, what Neil got from Sarah's parents was blame for her death. They'd come to this conclusion in the weeks after Sarah's funeral; they reasoned that she'd been taken to send him a message, and that they were forced to endure her loss solely because he hadn't been devout. They were now convinced that, his previous explanations notwithstanding, Neil's deformed leg was in fact God's doing, and if only he'd been properly chastened by it, Sarah might still be alive.

Their reaction shouldn't have come as a surprise: throughout Neil's life, people had attributed moral significance to his leg even though God wasn't responsible for it. Now that he'd suffered a misfortune for which God was unambiguously responsible, it was inevitable that someone would assume he deserved it. It was purely by chance that Neil heard this sentiment when he was at his most vulnerable, and it could have the greatest impact on him.

Neil didn't think his in-laws were right, but he began to wonder if he might not be better off if he did. Perhaps, he thought, it'd be better to live in a story where the righteous were rewarded and the sinners were punished, even if the criteria for righteousness and sinfulness eluded him, than to live in a reality where there was no justice at all. It would mean casting himself in the role of sinner, so it was hardly a comforting lie, but it offered one reward that his own ethics couldn't: believing it would reunite him with Sarah.

Sometimes even bad advice can point a man in the right direction. It was in this manner that his in-laws' accusations ultimately pushed Neil closer to God.

More than once when she was evangelizing, Janice had been asked if she ever wished she had legs, and she had always answered—honestly—no, she didn't. She was content as she was. Sometimes her questioner would point out that she couldn't miss what she'd never known, and she might feel differently if she'd been born with legs and lost them later on. Janice never denied that. But she could truthfully say that she felt no sense of being incomplete, no envy for people with legs; being legless was part of her identity. She'd never bothered with prosthetics, and had a surgical procedure been available to provide her with legs, she'd have turned it down. She had never considered the possibility that God might restore her legs.

One of the unexpected side effects of having legs was the increased attention she received from men. In the past she'd mostly attracted men with amputee fetishes or sainthood complexes; now all sorts of men seemed drawn to her. So when she first noticed Ethan Mead's interest in her, she thought it was romantic in nature; this possibility was particularly distressing since he was obviously married.

Ethan had begun talking to Janice at the support group meetings, and then began attending her public speaking engagements. It was when he suggested they have lunch together that Janice asked him about his intentions, and he explained his theory. He didn't know *how* his fate was intertwined with hers; he knew only that it was. She was skeptical, but she didn't reject his theory outright. Ethan admitted that he didn't have answers for her own questions, but he was eager to do anything he could to help her find them. Janice cautiously agreed to help him in his search for meaning, and Ethan promised that he wouldn't be a burden. They met on a regular basis and talked about the significance of visitations.

Meanwhile Ethan's wife Claire grew worried. Ethan assured her that he had no romantic feelings toward Janice, but that didn't alleviate her concerns. She knew that extreme circumstances could create a bond between individuals, and she feared that Ethan's relationship with Janice—romantic or not—would threaten their marriage.

Ethan suggested to Janice that he, as a librarian, could help her do some research. Neither of them had ever heard of a previous instance where God had left His mark on a person in one visitation and removed it in another. Ethan looked for previous examples in hopes that they might shed some light on Janice's situation. There were a few instances of individuals receiving multiple miracle cures over their lifetimes, but their illnesses or disabilities had always been of natural origin, not given to them in a visitation. There was one anecdotal report of a man being struck blind for his sins, changing his ways, and later having his sight restored, but it was classified as an urban legend.

Even if that account had a basis in truth, it didn't provide a useful precedent for Janice's situation: her legs had been removed before her birth, and so couldn't have been a punishment for anything she'd done. Was it possible that Janice's condition had been a punishment for something her mother or father had done? Could her restoration mean they had finally earned her cure? She couldn't believe that.

If her deceased relatives were to appear in a vision, Janice would've been reassured about the restoration of her legs. The fact that they didn't made her suspect something was amiss, but she didn't believe that it was a punishment. Perhaps it had been a mistake, and she'd received a miracle meant for someone else; perhaps it was a test, to see how she would respond to being given too much. In either case, there seemed only one course of action: she would, with utmost gratitude and humility, offer to return her gift. To do so, she would go on a pilgrimage.

Pilgrims traveled great distances to visit the holy sites and wait for a visitation, hoping for a miracle cure. Whereas in most of the world one could wait an entire lifetime and never experience a visitation, at a holy site one might only wait months, sometimes weeks. Pilgrims knew that the odds of being cured were still poor; of those who stayed long enough to witness a visitation, the majority did not receive a cure. But they were often happy just to have seen an angel, and they returned home better able to face what awaited them, whether it be imminent death or life with a crippling disability. And of course, just living through a visitation made many people appreciate their situations; invariably, a small number of pilgrims were killed during each visitation.

Janice was willing to accept the outcome whatever it was. If God saw fit to take her, she was ready. If God removed her legs again, she would resume the work she'd always done. If God let her legs remain, she hoped she would receive the epiphany she needed to speak with conviction about her gift.

She hoped, however, that her miracle would be taken back and given to someone who truly needed it. She didn't suggest to anyone that they accompany her in hopes of receiving the miracle she was returning, feeling that that would've been presumptuous, but she privately considered her pilgrimage a request on behalf of those who were in need.

Her friends and family were confused at Janice's decision, seeing it as questioning God. As word spread, she received many letters from followers, variously expressing dismay, bafflement, and admiration for her willingness to make such a sacrifice.

As for Ethan, he was completely supportive of Janice's decision, and excited for himself. He now understood the significance of Rashiel's visitation for him: it indicated that the time had come for him to act. His wife Claire strenuously opposed his leaving, pointing out that he had no idea how long he might be away, and that she and their children needed him too. It grieved him to go without her support, but he had no choice. Ethan would go on a pilgrimage, and at the next visitation, he would learn what God intended for him.

Neil's visit to Sarah's parents caused him to give further thought to his conversation with Benny Vasquez. While he hadn't gotten a lot out of Benny's words, he'd been impressed by the absoluteness of Benny's devotion. No matter what misfortune befell him in the future, Benny's love of God would never waver, and he would ascend to Heaven when he died. That fact offered Neil a very slim opportunity, one that had seemed so unattractive he hadn't considered it before; but now, as he was growing more desperate, it was beginning to look expedient.

Every holy site had its pilgrims who, rather than looking for a miracle cure, deliberately sought out Heaven's light. Those who saw it were always accepted into Heaven when they died, no matter how selfish their motives had been; there were some who wished to have their ambivalence removed so they could be reunited with their loved ones, and others who'd always lived a sinful life and wanted to escape the consequences.

In the past there'd been some doubt as to whether Heaven's light could indeed overcome *all* the spiritual obstacles to becoming saved. The debate ended after the case of Barry Larsen, a serial rapist and murderer who, while disposing of the body of his latest victim, witnessed an angel's visitation and saw Heaven's light. At Larsen's execution, his soul was seen ascending to Heaven, much to the outrage of his victims' families. Priests tried to console them, assuring them—on the basis of no evidence whatsoever—that Heaven's light must have subjected Larsen to many lifetimes' worth of penance in a moment, but their words provided little comfort.

For Neil this offered a loophole, an answer to Phil Soames's objection; it was the one way that he could love Sarah more than he loved

God, and still be reunited with her. It was how he could be selfish and still get into Heaven. Others had done it; perhaps he could too. It might not be just, but at least it was predictable.

At an instinctual level, Neil was averse to the idea: it sounded like undergoing brainwashing as a cure for depression. He couldn't help but think that it would change his personality so drastically that he'd cease to be himself. Then he remembered that everyone in Heaven had undergone a similar transformation; the saved were just like the eyeless except that they no longer had bodies. This gave Neil a clearer image of what he was working toward: no matter whether he became devout by seeing Heaven's light or by a lifetime of effort, any ultimate reunion with Sarah couldn't recreate what they'd shared in the mortal plane. In Heaven, they would both be different, and their love for each other would be mixed with the love that all the saved felt for everything.

This realization didn't diminish Neil's longing for a reunion with Sarah. In fact it sharpened his desire, because it meant that the reward would be the same no matter what means he used to achieve it; the shortcut led to precisely the same destination as the conventional path.

On the other hand, seeking Heaven's light was far more difficult than an ordinary pilgrimage, and far more dangerous. Heaven's light leaked through only when an angel entered or left the mortal plane, and since there was no way to predict where an angel would first appear, light-seekers had to converge on the angel after its arrival and follow it until its departure. To maximize their chances of being in the narrow shaft of Heaven's light, they followed the angel as closely as possible during its visitation; depending on the angel involved, this might mean staying alongside the funnel of a tornado, the wavefront of a flash flood, or the expanding tip of a chasm as it split apart the landscape. Far more light-seekers died in the attempt than succeeded.

Statistics about the souls of failed light-seekers were difficult to compile, since there were few witnesses to such expeditions, but the numbers so far were not encouraging. In sharp contrast to ordinary pilgrims who died without receiving their sought-after cure, of which roughly half were admitted into Heaven, every single failed light-seeker had descended to Hell. Perhaps only people who were already lost ever considered seeking Heaven's light, or perhaps death in such circumstances was considered suicide. In any case, it was clear to

Neil that he needed to be ready to accept the consequences of embarking on such an attempt.

The entire idea had an all-or-nothing quality to it that Neil found both frightening and attractive. He found the prospect of going on with his life, trying to love God, increasingly maddening. He might try for decades and not succeed. He might not even have that long; as he'd been reminded so often lately, visitations served as a warning to prepare one's soul, because death might come at any time. He could die tomorrow, and there was no chance of his becoming devout in the near future by conventional means.

It's perhaps ironic that, given his history of not following Janice Reilly's example, Neil took notice when she reversed her position. He was eating breakfast when he happened to see an item in the newspaper about her plans for a pilgrimage, and his immediate reaction was anger: how many blessings would it take to satisfy that woman? After considering it more, he decided that if she, having received a blessing, deemed it appropriate to seek God's assistance in coming to terms with it, then there was no reason he, having received such terrible misfortune, shouldn't do the same. And that was enough to tip him over the edge.

Holy sites were invariably in inhospitable places: one was an atoll in the middle of the ocean, while another was in the mountains at an elevation of 20,000 ft. The one that Neil traveled to was in a desert, an expanse of cracked mud reaching miles in every direction; it was desolate, but it was relatively accessible and thus popular among pilgrims. The appearance of the holy site was an object lesson in what happened when the celestial and terrestrial realms touched: the landscape was variously scarred by lava flows, gaping fissures, and impact craters. Vegetation was scarce and ephemeral, restricted to growing in the interval after soil was deposited by floodwaters or whirlwinds and before it was scoured away again.

Pilgrims took up residence all over the site, forming temporary villages with their tents and camper vans; they all made guesses as to what location would maximize their chances of seeing the angel while minimizing the risk of injury or death. Some protection was offered by curved banks of sandbags, left over from years past and rebuilt as needed. A site-specific paramedic and fire department ensured that paths were kept clear so rescue vehicles could go where they were needed. Pilgrims either brought their own food and water or purchased them from vendors charging exorbitant prices; everyone paid a fee to cover the cost of waste removal.

Light-seekers always had off-road vehicles to better cross rough terrain when it came time to follow the angel. Those who could afford it drove alone; those who couldn't formed groups of two or three or four. Neil didn't want to be a passenger reliant on another person, nor did he want the responsibility of driving anyone else. This might be his final act on earth, and he felt he should do it alone. The cost of Sarah's funeral had depleted their savings, so Neil sold all his possessions in order to purchase a suitable vehicle: a pickup truck equipped with aggressively knurled tires and heavy-duty shock absorbers.

As soon as he arrived, Neil started doing what all the other light-seekers did: crisscrossing the site in his vehicle, trying to familiarize himself with its topography. It was on one of his drives around the site's perimeter that he met Ethan; Ethan flagged him down after his own car had stalled on his return from the nearest grocery store, eighty miles away. Neil helped him get his car started again, and then, at Ethan's insistence, followed him back to his campsite for dinner. Janice wasn't there when they arrived, having gone to visit some pilgrims several tents over; Neil listened politely while Ethan—heating prepackaged meals over a bottle of propane—began describing the events that had brought him to the holy site.

When Ethan mentioned Janice Reilly's name, Neil couldn't mask his surprise. He had no desire to speak with her again, and immediately excused himself to leave. He was explaining to a puzzled Ethan that he'd forgotten a previous engagement when Janice arrived.

She was startled to see Neil there, but asked him to stay. Ethan explained why he'd invited Neil to dinner, and Janice told him where she and Neil had met. Then she asked Neil what had brought him to the holy site. When he told them he was a light-seeker, Ethan and Janice immediately tried to persuade him to reconsider his plans. He might be committing suicide, said Ethan, and there were always better alternatives than suicide. Seeing Heaven's light was not the answer, said Janice; that wasn't what God wanted. Neil stiffly thanked them for their concern, and left.

During the weeks of waiting, Neil spent every day driving around the site; maps were available, and were updated after each visitation, but they were no substitute for driving the terrain yourself. On occasion he would see a light-seeker who was obviously experienced in off-road driving, and ask him—the vast majority of the light-seekers were men—for tips on negotiating a specific type of terrain. Some had been at the site for several visitations, having neither succeeded nor failed at their previous attempts. They were glad to share tips on how best to pursue an angel, but never offered any personal information about themselves. Neil found the tone of their conversation peculiar, simultaneously hopeful and hopeless, and wondered if he sounded the same.

Ethan and Janice passed the time by getting to know some of the other pilgrims. Their reactions to Janice's situation were mixed: some thought her ungrateful, while others thought her generous. Most found Ethan's story interesting, since he was one of the very few pilgrims seeking something other than a miracle cure. For the most part, there was a feeling of camaraderie that sustained them during the long wait.

Neil was driving around in his truck when dark clouds began coalescing in the southeast, and the word came over the CB radio that a visitation had begun. He stopped the vehicle to insert earplugs into his ears and don his helmet; by the time he was finished, flashes of lightning were visible, and a light-seeker near the angel reported that it was Barakiel, and it appeared to be moving due north. Neil turned his truck east in anticipation and began driving at full speed.

There was no rain or wind, only dark clouds from which lightning emerged. Over the radio other light-seekers relayed estimates of the angel's direction and speed, and Neil headed northeast to get in front of it. At first he could gauge his distance from the storm by counting how long it took for the thunder to arrive, but soon the lightning bolts were striking so frequently that he couldn't match up the sounds with the individual strikes.

He saw the vehicles of two other light-seekers converging. They began driving in parallel, heading north, over a heavily cratered section of ground, bouncing over small ones and swerving to avoid the larger ones. Bolts of lightning were striking the ground everywhere, but they appeared to be radiating from a point south of Neil's position; the angel was directly behind him, and closing.

Even through his earplugs, the roar was deafening. Neil could feel his hair rising from his skin as the electric charge built up around him. He kept glancing in his rearview mirror, trying to ascertain where the angel was while wondering how close he ought to get.

His vision grew so crowded with afterimages that it became difficult to distinguish actual bolts of lightning among them. Squinting at the dazzle in his mirror, he realized he was looking at a continuous bolt of lightning, undulating but uninterrupted. He tilted the driver's-side mirror upward to get a better look, and saw the source of the lightning bolt, a seething, writhing mass of flames, silver against the dusky clouds: the angel Barakiel.

It was then, while Neil was transfixed and paralyzed by what he saw, that his pickup truck crested a sharp outcropping of rock and became airborne. The truck smashed into a boulder, the entire force of the impact concentrated on the vehicle's left front end, crumpling it like foil. The intrusion into the driver's compartment fractured both of Neil's legs and nicked his left femoral artery. Neil began, slowly but surely, bleeding to death.

He didn't try to move; he wasn't in physical pain at the moment, but he somehow knew that the slightest movement would be excruciating. It was obvious that he was pinned in the truck, and there was no way he could pursue Barakiel even if he weren't. Helplessly, he watched the lightning storm move further and further away.

As he watched it, Neil began crying. He was filled with a mixture of regret and self-contempt, cursing himself for ever thinking that such a scheme could succeed. He would have begged for the opportunity to do it over again, promised to spend the rest of his days learning to love God, if only he could live, but he knew that no bargaining was possible and he had only himself to blame. He apologized to Sarah for losing his chance at being reunited with her, for throwing his life away on a gamble instead of playing it safe. He prayed that she understood that he'd been motivated by his love for her, and that she would forgive him.

Through his tears he saw a woman running toward him, and recognized her as Janice Reilly. He realized his truck had crashed no more than a hundred yards from her and Ethan's campsite. There was nothing she could do, though; he could feel the blood draining out of him, and knew that he wouldn't live long enough for a rescue vehicle to arrive. He thought Janice was calling to him, but his ears were ringing too badly for him to hear anything. He could see Ethan Mead behind her, also starting to run toward him.

Then there was a flash of light and Janice was knocked off her feet as if she'd been struck by a sledgehammer. At first he thought she'd been hit by lightning, but then he realized that the lightning had already ceased. It was when she stood up again that he saw her face, steam rising from newly featureless skin, and he realized that Janice had been struck by Heaven's light.

Neil looked up, but all he saw were clouds; the shaft of light was gone. It seemed as if God were taunting him, not only by showing him the prize he'd lost his life trying to acquire while still holding it out of reach, but also by giving it to someone who didn't need it or even want it. God had already wasted a miracle on Janice, and now He was doing it again.

It was at that moment that another beam of Heaven's light penetrated the cloud cover and struck Neil, trapped in his vehicle.

Like a thousand hypodermic needles the light punctured his flesh and scraped across his bones. The light unmade his eyes, turning him into not a formerly sighted being, but a being never intended to possess vision. And in doing so the light revealed to Neil all the reasons he should love God.

He loved Him with an utterness beyond what humans can experience for one another. To say it was unconditional was inadequate, because even the word "unconditional" required the concept of a condition and such an idea was no longer comprehensible to him: every phenomenon in the universe was nothing less than an explicit reason to love Him. No circumstance could be an obstacle or even an irrelevancy, but only another reason to be grateful, a further inducement to love. Neil thought of the grief that had driven him to suicidal recklessness, and the pain and terror that Sarah had experienced before she died, and still he loved God, not in spite of their suffering, but because of it.

He renounced all his previous anger and ambivalence and desire for answers. He was grateful for all the pain he'd endured, contrite for not previously recognizing it as the gift it was, euphoric that he was now being granted this insight into his true purpose. He understood how life was an undeserved bounty, how even the most virtuous were not worthy of the glories of the mortal plane.

For him the mystery was solved, because he understood that everything in life is love, even pain, especially pain.

So minutes later, when Neil finally bled to death, he was truly worthy of salvation.

And God sent him to Hell anyway.

Ethan saw all of this. He saw Neil and Janice remade by Heaven's light, and he saw the pious love on their eyeless faces. He saw the skies become clear and the sunlight return. He was holding Neil's hand, waiting for the paramedics, when Neil died, and he saw Neil's soul leave his body and rise toward Heaven, only to descend into Hell.

Janice didn't see it, for by then her eyes were already gone. Ethan was the sole witness, and he realized that this was God's purpose for him: to follow Janice Reilly to this point and to see what she could not.

When statistics were compiled for Barakiel's visitation, it turned out that there had been a total of ten casualties, six among light-seekers and four among ordinary pilgrims. Nine pilgrims received miracle cures; the only individuals to see Heaven's light were Janice and Neil. There were no statistics regarding how many pilgrims had felt their lives changed by the visitation, but Ethan counted himself among them.

Upon returning home, Janice resumed her evangelism, but the topic of her speeches has changed. She no longer speaks about how the physically handicapped have the resources to overcome their limitations; instead she, like the other eyeless, speaks about the unbearable beauty of God's creation. Many who used to draw inspiration from her are disappointed, feeling they've lost a spiritual leader. When Janice had spoken of the strength she had as an afflicted person, her message was rare, but now that she's eyeless, her message is commonplace. She doesn't worry about the reduction in her audience, though, because she has complete conviction in what she evangelizes.

Ethan quit his job and became a preacher so that he too could speak about his experiences. His wife Claire couldn't accept his new mission and ultimately left him, taking their children with her, but Ethan was willing to continue alone. He's developed a substantial following by telling people what happened to Neil Fisk. He tells people that they can no more expect justice in the afterlife than in the mortal plane, but he doesn't do this to dissuade them from worshipping God; on the contrary, he encourages them to do so. What he insists on is that they not love God under a misapprehension, that if they wish to love God, they be prepared to do so no matter what His intentions. God is not just, God is not kind, God is not merciful, and understanding that is essential to true devotion.

As for Neil, although he is unaware of any of Ethan's sermons, he would understand their message perfectly. His lost soul is the embodiment of Ethan's teachings.

For most of its inhabitants, Hell is not that different from Earth; its principal punishment is the regret of not having loved God enough when alive, and for many that's easily endured. For Neil, however, Hell bears no resemblance whatsoever to the mortal plane. His eternal body has well-formed legs, but he's scarcely aware of them; his eyes have been restored, but he can't bear to open them. Just as seeing Heaven's light gave him an awareness of God's presence in all things in the mortal plane, so it has made him aware of God's absence in all things in Hell. Everything Neil sees, hears, or touches causes him distress, and unlike in the mortal plane this pain is not a form of God's love, but a consequence of His absence. Neil is experiencing more anguish than was possible when he was alive, but his only response is to love God.

Neil still loves Sarah, and misses her as much as he ever did, and the knowledge that he came so close to rejoining her only makes it worse. He knows his being sent to Hell was not a result of anything he did; he knows there was no reason for it, no higher purpose being served. None of this diminishes his love for God. If there were a possibility that he could be admitted to Heaven and his suffering would end, he would not hope for it; such desires no longer occur to him.

Neil even knows that by being beyond God's awareness, he is not loved by God in return. This doesn't affect his feelings either, because unconditional love asks nothing, not even that it be returned.

And though it's been many years that he has been in Hell, beyond the awareness of God, he loves Him still. That is the nature of true devotion.

DAMON KNIGHT

Frederik Pohl

Frederik Pohl has been writing and editing science fiction for more than half a century. His novels are classics in the field. A Nebula winner, Hugo winner, and Grand Master himself in 1992, he edits the Grand Master series of anthologies for SFWA. Fred's bibliography can be found on the Web at http://isfdb.tamu.edu/cgi-bin/ea.cgi?Frederik%20Pohl.

When Damon Knight came to New York City, somewhere around 1940, he was a science fiction fan who wanted very much to become a science fiction professional. Naturally he at once fell in with that bunch of other fans who were yearning to be pros, the Futurian Society of New York. However, Damon—or, as he preferred to be known in those days, damon—was different from the rest of the Futurians in one crucial respect. What he wanted to do professionally wasn't to write. It was to illustrate.

That didn't last, though. Surrounded by such hard-writing Futurians as Isaac Asimov, C. M. Kornbluth, James Blish, Donald A. Wollheim, and others damon quickly fell into line. His first professionally published story, "Resilience," appeared in *Stirring Science Stories,* one of Don Wollheim's low-paying—in fact, *very* low-paying—magazines. The story concerned a race of rubbery aliens visiting the Earth. To tease the reader damon held back all information about the rubberiness of the aliens until late in the story. Then he disclosed it only by having the aliens refer to the humans as "the brittle people." Alas, Don Wollheim's printers may not have been paid much better than the writers, and that crucial piece of information didn't survive their mishaps. One of the printers dropped a tray of type. When they tried to reconstruct it from memory the concept of "the brittle people" had become "the little people," and the story no longer had any point at all.

That didn't stop young damon. He kept trying—with stories, even with an occasional drawing now and then—and accordingly lived the life appropriate for a striving pro in those early days of Word War II. That is, a pretty impoverished one. Damon lived in what is called a "cold-water flat," a New Yorkese term which means an apartment (in damon's case, not much more than a single room) which may or may not have running hot water but definitely hasn't much else. It especially doesn't have heat, which, in a New York winter, can be critical. In order to keep his living space, if not warm, at least somewhat less than hopelessly frigid in January weather damon had installed a battery of electric heaters. The building hadn't been constructed for such lavish use of electrical power, though. When the heaters were going the wiring in the walls was going, too, and accordingly damon's walls were the only ones I have ever felt that were seriously hot to the touch.

But luck was on damon's side. The building didn't catch fire from the overloaded wiring and burn down around him, at least not while he was living in it.

Damon was lucky, more or less, in another respect as well: young men were being gobbled up by the Selective Service right and left, but damon was spared.

Which is, in a way, almost a pity. When damon was first being examined by the draft doctors he, like everyone else, had to give his complete life history to an overworked and disinterested corporal seated at the registration desk. One of the things the corporal wanted to know was damon's religious preference. "I'm an agnostic," said damon. "You're a what?" the corporal asked. "An agnostic. That's spelled A-G-N-O-S-T-I-C," damon told him, and the corporal wrote down what he thought he heard. His hearing had been imperfect, though, and if damon had reached the point of induction he would have been the only soldier in American history whose dogtags described him as a "HENOSTIC."

All this time I had been living somewhat, but not an awful lot, more comfortably as the boy editor of a couple of science fiction magazines (later the assistant editor on eight or ten pulps of all sorts) for the giant pulp-magazine publishing company of Popular Publications. For some time I had been trying to get inducted into the Army like everybody else, an event held up because my draft board's territory also took in New York's Chinatown and thus was greatly oversubscribed by young Chinese men who wanted very much to get into uniform and fight the Japanese. Finally they relented and took me. When I was sworn in (on April Fool's Day of 1943) that created an immediate editorial vacancy at Popular, and I offered it to damon.

He agreed instantly, but saw a problem. He said he didn't have any suitably business-like clothing to wear. I solved that easily enough by loaning him a civilian shirt that I would no longer need and took him in to meet my boss, Alden H. Norton. Damon aced the interview, and so took his first step in beginning what turned out to be a brilliant editorial career.

■

Of course that wasn't the only career damon, now Damon, pursued.

His earliest fame came not as an editor but as a critic, and that began with a fanzine review he wrote of A. E. Van Vogt's serial, *The World of Ā* (pronounced "Null-A"). I say Damon reviewed the story. More accurately, he trashed it, to the extent, it is said, that after van Vogt came across a copy of the review he had to make serious changes in his story before it was published as a book. (A circumstance which made a serious problem for me when I was putting together the volume of *The Grand Masters* which included Grand Master Knight. It was my custom, when possible, to include an occasional nonfiction piece written by the Grand Masters along with their stories, and the one of Damon's that I would most have liked to use was the review which had given such pain to Van Vogt. An unfortunate conjunction interfered with that plan. Immediately adjacent to Grand Master Knight's section in the volume was the section that belonged to Grand Master Van Vogt himself. Van Vogt wasn't well, and in any case it did not seem appropriate to renew an old pain in a volume which was meant to celebrate him, among the rest of his cohort. So compassion overcame editorial desires, and reluctantly I abandoned the idea of reprinting Damon's ancient review.)

In the early 1950s Fletcher Pratt, who was perhaps more distinguished (for such works as his Civil War history, *Ordeal by Fire*) outside of the science fiction field than in it, was trying to arrange for some science fiction writers to be invited to attend the prestigious Bread Loaf Writers Conference. The idea of such a conference struck Damon as worth pursuing and so, with James Blish and Judith Merril, he organized the Milford Science Fiction Writers Workshop, the model for all the many which have followed. Which led immediately to his plan to organize science fiction writers into some sort of professional society/union/social club, which ultimately became the Science Fiction Writers of America. . . .

But all that's another story.

DAMON

Carol Emshwiller

Carol Emshwiller first met Damon Knight in 1956. Her Web site is http://www.sfwa.org/members/emshwiller/.

I met Damon at the first Milford workshop, given by Jim Blish, Judy Merril, and Damon. My husband had been invited but not me. I think at that time I had sold two or three stories. I asked if I could sit in, and they let me. I was so awed by all the big science fiction writers there I can't remember much about it. Besides, I had our kids with me. (Maybe I only had one back then.)

After that first time I did get invited to attend in my own right. I probably learned more about writing and also teaching from Damon at those Milfords than from anybody else ever. I've taken several classes before and since but none taught me as much as Damon did.

I've always thought Damon was one of the smartest and kindest people I know. And I loved his sense of humor. I know some people thought his humor cruel but I never thought so. I guess it just wasn't their kind of humor. Once I saw him throw a manuscript out the window. That sounds bad, but it was the way he did it. Sort of like his water pistols and food throwing fights. (He was known for those. I always felt privileged whenever I got a chunk of bread thrown at me by Damon.) I thought his humor always had a pixie quality about it and couldn't hurt anybody. Wherever he was, there was the action and the fun.

He was amazing at reading fast and understanding everything about a story on first reading. I once saw him reading and talking to a group of people at the same time. I was sitting there trying to do the same but failing. In the end, he read the story in half the time that I took. Not only that, but he understood it better than I did. And all the time he was talking to people.

These last years I didn't see him very often. Even so his death was a shock. Though I never called, I always knew he was there in case I needed him. I don't like a world without him in it. He was one of my favorite people.

I REMEMBER DAMON

James Gunn

James Gunn began a four-year freelance career in 1948, then combined his later writing with an academic career at the University of Kansas. He has served at different times as president of both the SFWA and of SFRA. His best known works are *The Joy Makers, The Immortals, The Listeners, Kampus*, and *The Dreamers;* among his academic books are *Alternate Worlds: The Illustrated History of Science Fiction;* and *Isaac Asimov: The Foundations of Science Fiction* for which he won a Hugo; and the six-volume *Road to Science Fiction*. He is now emeritus professor of English and continues to write both fiction and nonfiction. He can be found on the Web at http://www.ku.edu/~sfcenter/bio.htm.

Damon Knight was one of those learned men who didn't need the confirmation of a college education, like Frederik Pohl or John Brunner (who said that he dropped out of college because it was interfering with his education). I met Damon for the first time at the World Science Fiction Convention of 1955, held in Cleveland. We were kindred souls in our fascination by the critical side of science fiction and the conviction that science fiction could, and should, be written with literary skill. Where we disagreed was the form that skill should take: Damon, I think, was willing to see it become indistinguishable from the mainstream; I wanted to preserve its genre identity and vitality.

We met at the bar, the place where much of the business and almost all of the fun of a convention takes place. I recognized Damon by his pictures, or had him pointed out, and introduced myself. We chatted amiably. He was a medium-sized man with the thoughtful face of a professor—glasses, a narrow chin, a prominent forehead made more prominent by a receding hairline, and, most noticeably, observant eyes. I already knew who Damon was. Though my senior by less than a year, he was my senior by almost a decade in science fiction experience.

He had gone to New York from his native Oregon in 1941, attracted as a youthful fan by the reputation of the Futurians, and became a member of that fabled group. He worked as a freelance writer and an editor for various magazines, including his own *Worlds Beyond* that lasted for only three promising issues from 1950 to 1951. He had come into his own as a writer about the same time I began publishing stories. His first story to attract much attention, "Not with a Bang," was published in *The Magazine of Fantasy & Science Fiction* in 1950. My first story (which attracted no attention) was published in *Startling Stories* in 1949. His first *Galaxy* story, "To Serve Man," was published in 1950, as well, and Damon continued to publish, mostly in *F&SF* and *Galaxy* throughout the 1950s and into the 1960s, and became one of the great science fiction short-story writers of his generation.

But Damon's stories and novels could not compete with his accomplishments in other aspects of the field. He made a reputation as a reviewer and a critic, mostly in the fanzines, beginning with a famous deconstruction in 1945 of A. E. Van Vogt's *The World of Null-A*, under the title of "Cosmic Jerrybuilder." It led to Damon's later career as a reviewer for *Infinity* and *F&SF* and, perhaps, to the creation of his own influential anthology, *Orbit*, which he launched in 1966 and published through twenty-one issues, nurturing a number of major science fiction talents.

And he (with the help of the late Lloyd Biggle, Jr.) created the Science Fiction Writers of America in 1965. I had occasional contacts with Damon over the years after our first meeting. He had invited me to contribute some reviews to a journal he and James Blish (the other major name in bringing critical standards to the science fiction field) were starting, but it died before I could supply anything. Then came SFWA. The idea of an organization of science fiction writers had been discussed in the pages of Ted Cogswell's irreverent fanzine *PITFCS*, some writers saying that they would never join an organization of any kind, others saying that it would only work if it had the power to strike and discipline its members. Damon thought otherwise, and the history of SFWA has proven him correct—it is one of the most influential writers' organizations in the nation (and also, perhaps, the most disputatious). I was one of the charter members. Damon was its first president. I was its fourth.

Damon also created the Nebula Awards and the volume of its winners that supported the awards. He created the Milford Writers Conference for published writers, which he ran from his home in Milford, Pennsylvania, (and from his subsequent homes) for twenty years, and for twenty-seven years he and his wife Kate Wilhelm taught the final two weeks of the Clarion Science Fiction Writers Workshops, founded by Robin Scott Wilson, which was inspired by the Milford Conferences. I was invited to the Milford Conferences from time to time but never had the opportunity to attend. (I would have liked to have been there the year Kurt Vonnegut participated.)

Damon was an anthologist. It was as an anthologist of historical surveys of science fiction that I invited him to participate in the science fiction lecture film series I was putting together in the late 1960s and early 1970s. I asked him to lecture on the early history of science fiction. In his typical organized fashion, he wanted his written text transcribed onto cue cards, and in 1971 we filmed him in front of the United Nations building (We wanted to do it on the grounds themselves but were refused permission). You won't find that film in the series (or the DVDs that have been made from them). Traffic noise drowned out the sound track, but Damon was gracious enough to come to Lawrence, Kansas, where we filmed it all again in the living room of the series producer, Alex Lazzarino.

On that same visit I asked Damon to speak to my science fiction class, and we had a classic disagreement about whether one could differentiate between science fiction and fantasy. Damon took the side that no distinction was possible or desirable. I wish I had recorded our debate for posterity.

Damon was quick to express his opinions, and his opinions, right or wrong, were one of the forces that drove science fiction toward maturity of vision and integrity of craft. His reviews, collected in *In Search of Wonder*, along with James Blish's in *The Issue at Hand*, were major influences on the writers of their time. Damon wasn't always right, but he was always forceful and his force was toward higher aspirations and greater achievements. For instance, he never understood Van Vogt's strengths (or if he did he never acknowledged them). But when I was planning a series of academic editions for the Perennial Library, I had the inspiration of asking Damon to do an introduction to *The World of Null-A*, as a kind of reappraisal, and Damon agreed. But Perennial canceled the series before anything was written.

Our last meeting was by e-mail. He had come across my contention that science fiction had its own reading protocols (something Samuel R. Delany first identified for me in a presentation to the Modern Language Association), and we exchanged some comments on an sff.net listserv—Damon insisting that science fiction had no special protocols and my explaining what I thought they were.

During our first meeting I asked Damon if he had reviewed my first novel, *This Fortress World*, which had been published that year along with *Star Bridge*, my collaboration with Jack Williamson. "I'm sorry," he said. "I panned it." And so he had. You can read it still in *In Search of Wonder* (pp. 258–59). I learned two important lessons from that: never ask reviewers if they have reviewed your work, and to place my stories and novels in the near future rather than the distant future. I've followed both ever since.

DAMON KNIGHT
THE TEACHER

Robin Wilson

Robin Wilson, an anthology editor, novelist, and short story writer, is a retired university president living in coastal California. Robin's bibliography can be found on the Web at http://isfdb. tamu.edu/cgi-bin/ea.cgi?Robin%20Scott%20Wilson.

Damon Knight and Kate Wilhelm are very different as artists, but during the thirty-five years I knew them as a couple, they seemed intellectually and physically inseparable, a complex partnership of two people of great wit and intelligence. It follows that any account of Damon's role in the Clarion workshop has equal relevance to Kate's.

I began to learn about this duo in 1967. The year before, I had returned from five years in Berlin as a CIA Case Officer and was looking for another job. The one I landed was a professorship in English at Clarion State College, and a condition of my employment was that I organize a writers workshop. I did not know how to do this. I did not know anybody who knew how to do this, but I knew of Damon's Milford Writers Conference, an annual gathering of professionals that had then been running for more than a decade. When I told him my plans, he invited me to participate in the 1967 conference. There, I discovered Kate and went about employing my old skills of surreptitious observation and assessment to recruit three more writers who seemed to have the critical sense to examine others' work, the warmth to encourage without condescension those less talented or experienced, and the idiocy to agree to live a week amid their students in an ancient dormitory in a town Damon later termed "the sphincter of the universe" for $500 and all found.

I had five one-week Visiting Lecturer slots to fill and only enough money to hire four, but the Knights came to the rescue. They agreed to serve together for a week and then to stay on for another. For the price of one I got four teacher–weeks, a case of faculty exploitation revealing my readiness for a subsequent career as a university administrator. Today, I look back across the Clarion Workshop's thirty-seven-year history and see no greater boon than getting the Knights for that first session, better even than the felicity of the workshop's name. It could have been Slippery Rock.

With the first-year faculty hired, I puzzled as to how we were to operate. The tough, competitive atmosphere of a conference for professionals such as Milford is not suited to aspiring tyros. Neither is the placid read-and-discuss model of college Creative Writing classes. More important, I knew no one who had learned to be a good fiction writer in a classroom; we had all learned by repeatedly trying and failing and listening to whatever criticism we could find and trying again. My notion was to reproduce that process—trying, failure, criticism, eventual success—in six intense weeks. I was convinced that total immersion in fiction writing for as many hours in the day as mind and body could bear was the key, if there was one, to its mastery.

In short, I did not expect the workshop to teach people to write but to provide a sweaty arena in which we could coach the motivated and talented to wrestle their muses into either unmistakable rejection or fluttery-eyed acquiescence. As Damon later noted, the Clarion atmosphere was like that at Milford, ". . . but that was eight days and this was six *weeks*."

In that first session in 1968 we learned some new ways of doing things. It turned out that Damon and Kate were extraordinarily good at teaching, a skill which—like writing—is more to be discovered in oneself than learned. They accepted each story as a work in progress (we critiqued only freshly written material) to be evaluated within the context of the storyteller's emotions and values. And they rapidly supplemented the Milford-style round-robin group criticism with tireless one-on-one conferences.

This process was energized by Kate's perceptive empathy with fumbling neophytes, my growing skills for gaming the bureaucratic system, and Damon's incredibly sharp insights, tersely delivered, with a humor that belied his claim to be "one of the most sarcastic, intolerant, opinionated sons of bitches in science fiction."

Another lucky break: Milford's schedule made the Knights unavailable before the last two weeks of the workshop, after an opening week in which I tried to provide a common critical vocabulary, followed by a week each of Judith Merril, Fritz Leiber, and Harlan Ellison. I instilled, Judith mothered imaginations, Fritz plotted and dueled, Harlan awed into adulation, and Damon and Kate showed up to pick up the pieces, put them back together again, and reseat the resulting ovoid structures onto their walls.

We all learned from the students and from each other. Early on, Damon grew convinced that stories were more often than not weak because they began at an inappropriate place in the plot line or were told from the wrong point of view. Kate insisted that good stories must stem from some matter of direct emotional concern to the writer, that other story ideas produced only mechanical exercises in technique, a criticism particularly relevant to science fiction, with its accent on setting and circumstance, on the vast, the mysterious, the alien. "Who Hurts and Who Cares?" became the mantra for workshop criticism.

And we also learned something about ourselves. Damon had been a little skeptical about teaching at the workshop, "this mad thing." After the second Clarion, in 1969, he was a convert. "Impressed over again by Clarion," he wrote. "Still can't quite believe it. We were afraid last year was a fluke which couldn't be repeated, but this year was better. Beautiful kids."

Well, the next year (when Vonda McIntyre was a workshopper) was better still. By then fourteen of the first twenty previously unpublished full-time students had made it into print. And so it went every year thereafter, at Tulane in 1971 and then, from 1972 to the present, at Michigan State University. The roster of writers who have taught at Clarion is substantial, a *Who's Who* in the field, and most of them turned out to be good teachers. But for twenty-seven years, until they retired in 1994, Kate and Damon put it all together in the final two weeks, ensuring the harvest to come.

In 1996, Michigan State University recognized Damon Knight and Kate Wilhelm for the remarkable artists, critics, and teachers they are and awarded them honorary doctorates.

OH YOU KID! A PERSONAL VIEW OF DAMON KNIGHT

Edward Bryant

Edward Bryant made a name for himself early in his career with dazzling short stories. He achieved back-to-back Nebula awards for "Stone" in 1978 and "giANTS" in 1979. Multi-talented, he writes fiction in all lengths, screenplays, poetry, and edits the occasional anthology. Including *2076: The American Tricentennial,* which, somewhat perversely, appeared in 1977. He is known, at least to this author, for his sharp wit, devastatingly dry humor, and equally devastating smile. Ed's next book is the story collection *Flirting with Death* from CD Publications. His bibliography can be found online at http://isfdb.tamu.edu/cgi-bin/ea.cgi?Edward%20Bryant.

I knew damon knight long before I knew Damon Knight.

What I mean is that I read the man and read *about* the man long before I ever met the gentleman in person. First there was the legend; *then* the human being.

Having grown up in the Fifties, and being largely defined as a science fiction geek by my favored reading matter, I depended heavily upon my small-town Carnegie public library. But beyond that, I discovered prozines, professional science fiction magazines, and first twenty-five-cent, then thirty-five-cent paperbacks. Of course I discovered Damon Knight the writer.

But I had access to other resources as well. I was certainly the only kid on my school bus who pored over both the latest issue of *Famous Monsters of Filmland* and Dick Eney's *Fancyclopedia II.* Bear in mind that I possessed no first-hand experience with science fiction fandom. I'd bought the mimeographed Eney reference book through the mail after seeing it reviewed in some prozine. So I started learning about the Futurians and slanshacks and fan feuds and all manner of other microcultural phenomena.

That's when I found out that the writer and critic Damon Knight had had a checkered past in science fiction fandom. I learned that he had once been billed as damon knight, presumably after a profound intellectual brush with e. e. cummings. And I was told he'd first made his bones as a credible critic in a literary field not previously known for rigorous intellectual literary discourse by beating the crap out of poor A. E. van Vogt's presumed classic *The World of Null-A*. Since then, Damon, along with a small but growing cadre of critics such as James Blish, had kept raising the bar in terms of critical commentary.

So all of that made him, of course, Somebody. Or as cummings might have said, somebody. But I still didn't know the man on any kind of human level. That didn't come until 1968 when I found myself bored and frustrated with my graduate level program in English and bolted for the summer to Clarion, Pennsylvania, where Robin Scott Wilson had put together the first Clarion Science Fiction Writers Workshop, an enterprise based, as it turned out, on the workshopping principles of the Milford conference, the legendary week-long annual gathering of professional writers, mainly science fiction, created a few years earlier by Damon Knight and Kate Wilhelm. As it turned out, Damon and Kate were slated to be the climactic writers-in-residence the final two weeks of the premiere Clarion.

So that's how I met them. Both of them. The calm, perceptive, and serenely beautiful Kate Wilhelm. The intense, acerbic, and occasionally crazed Damon Knight, the man who by this time in his life, had adopted the striking visage of a bearded and bushy-haired Old Testament prophet. From the standpoint of a callow writing student, it was difficult not to be impressed by a sensibility that appeared to have fanned more than a few burning bushes before striding down from the summit of Sinai.

I didn't get the impression that Damon was the world's greatest fan of my science fiction writing, but he did give me a fair shake, inviting me both to submit to his original anthology series *Orbit* and to attend the Milford Conference next time around. Making it into

Orbit became one of my own personal high bars to clear, an ambition I eventually realized with a clear sense of pride and accomplishment. Of course I never sold Damon as many stories as did, say, Ray Lafferty, Gene Wolfe, or Kate, but I placed enough fiction with him, I knew it was no fluke.

Attending Milford was the killer experience, though. And I mean that in the best sense. Eventually Kate and Damon moved from Pennsylvania to Florida, and then to Oregon, taking the writing conference with them. It was in Eugene, Oregon, that I saw Damon do one of his great teaching things. After a long and contentious group discussion about the tired old clichés of pulp science fiction, Damon challenged all of us to write some real science fiction that turned inside out the old tropes. Pick some tired and hoary science fiction image, drag it gasping and wheezing from the junkyard of bygone standards, examine it from a brand new angle of approach. Make it fresh. I recall that only two of us expressed much enthusiasm for taking up the flung gauntlet. I don't know whether Joe Haldeman ever carried through with his planned effort. Me, I wanted to take the old Ray Cummings *Girl in the Golden Atom* gimmick of worlds within worlds within subatomic worlds and turn it into something appropriate for the modern age. What resulted was a story called "Particle Theory." *Analog* published it and the piece did well for me.

I can and always will credit Damon for that literary gift. I never would have attempted the story without his goading. And so far as I can tell, the whole challenge thing was done off the cuff, winging it as he went, all because it seemed like a good idea at the time.

Finally, though, the thing about Damon's life and personality that I'll carry with me in memory so long as I live is something that has a little to do with Peter Pan and a lot to do with keeping in twisted touch with the inner child. I think it made some observers a little nervous when Damon Knight, one of the major intellects of the field, offered clear indications that—at least at times—he was a big kid at heart.

Remember Tom Hanks in the movie *Big*? About the child who, through a type of magic, wishes he were all grown up and finds himself with his boy's mentality inhabiting Tom Hanks's adult body?

At the various workshops where he taught—especially at Clarion—Damon suggested it was merely therapeutic when he hauled out mass quantities of squirt guns and Superballs and paper airplanes and Silly

String and triggered long episodes of hysterical playtime among adult participants so boisterous, they suggested herds of kindergartners off their meds.

I can recall a Clarion decompression episode where something like two dozen people crowded into Damon and Kate's small faculty apartment. Everyone but Kate was screaming like a mad creature. Damon grinned like a lunatic as he hurled missile after paper missile. Kate, of course, sat perfectly still with a Mona Lisa smile, an island of patient calm amid the surrounding melee. Naturally not a single paper aircraft struck her; it was as though they veered aside as they approached her event horizon.

But Damon appeared to be having the time of his life as he ensured that we all were having ours. For that as well as all his formal literary gifts, I'll always thank him. It's the way I want to remember one of science fiction's greatest senior statesmen.

CURIOUS DAMON KNIGHT

Eileen Gunn

Eileen Gunn is the editor and publisher of the online science fiction magazine *The Infinite Matrix* and is at work on a biography of Avram Davidson. She is currently chair of the board of directors of the Clarion West Writers Workshop. Her short fiction has been nominated twice for the Hugo Award. Eileen's Web site is http://www.sff.net/people/gunn/. *The Infinite Matrix* can be found at http://www.infinitematrix.net/.

Damon Knight was a curious fellow, in the several senses of the word: he exhibited curiosity, and he was himself a fascinating and atypical example of his species.

Damon expended, in a deceptively casual fashion, a great deal of energy toward discovering what was curious in the world around him. Much of the world around him was words. He would leap upon a word or a concept, interrogate it, and try to find what, if anything, it had to recommend itself to him. Any chat with Damon at home usually involved a number of incursions into a dictionary or encyclopedia.

He kept a trove of them in which to pursue etymologies and ideas, and he delighted in searching just a bit past the point at which most people would stop, looking for odd meanings, earliest uses, beginnings, dead ends, uniquenesses.

He interrogated people the same way, probing them for meaning, and when he found it he gave a gleeful laugh that was somewhere between an extended chuckle and a hoot. On first observing this, I thought he was laughing in scorn, and that the person thus examined was found wanting, but eventually it dawned on me that this was a laugh of delight. It was a finder's laugh, the laugh of Damon discovering something unique: an unusual point of view, an unanticipated idiocy, a surprising association.

I knew Damon first as a writer of clever short stories: "The Handler," "Rule Golden," "The Country of the Kind," and, of course, "To Serve Man." When I was a teenager, Damon Knight's early stories defined the genre for me. This was what a science fiction story was meant to be: witty, clean, slightly cruel, with a twist at the end that subverted what had gone before. This is not how I think of Damon's later stories, which seem more meditative, more about the immediacy of experience and the uniqueness of the individual. They are still witty, still clean, but, rather than cruel, they seem transparent, objective. It may be the same attribute, worn smooth by forty years of writing.

As an adult, I knew Damon as a teacher and a friend. I attended Clarion, and for a couple of years I lived in Eugene and attended the monthly workshops and other gatherings there at Kate and Damon's home. Damon was a painstaking, informative, and hilarious copy editor, and I learned a lot, very quickly, from the way he marked up stories—my own and those of others. *Hmmm. Right. Won't do that again.* Damon was also an artist, and he had a tendency to illustrate, in the margin, unfortunate turns of phrase. "Her eyes fell to the floor" was a favorite.

I have heard Damon called a cruel critic, but I never saw that. He was an honest critic, and said what he thought. If he wasn't interested in a story, he didn't try to be. He gave, as far as I could see, the same attention to everyone. In his critiques, he usually gave me the impression that there was really nothing worth reading in what I had written. Occasionally—months, sometimes years, after the critique—I'd get a note suggesting he hadn't meant to be harsh. ("There must have been something there that I liked, as I set this aside. I have no recollection now what it was.")

In the early 1990s, Damon discovered the Internet. He was entering his seventies, and his hearing was starting to give him trouble. The Science Fiction Roundtable on Genie presented a throng of old friends and antagonists, Clarion grads, and newcomers of every stripe. Damon quickly became a presence there—funny, in-your-face, knowledgeable, nitpicking, snarky, and intolerant of carelessness and ignorance. He enforced a standard of proper discourse by means of his witty, relentless ridicule of careless spelling and inept punctuation. He wasn't the only intelligent, precise, literate human being on Genie, not by far, but his insistence that everyone rise to his standards, watch their spelling, and learn how to use apostrophes contributed a lot toward making the SFRT seem an enclave of articulate discussion.

Being on Genie with Damon was a lot like visiting him at home. He asked curious questions and never explained why. Sometimes they seemed to be research of a sort: "What's the difference between a fatal and nonfatal bullet wound in the brain?" "Isn't there a rhyme that begins, 'Ringel, ringel, rosen'? If so, does anybody know the rest?" He offered spelling corrections: "That's 'bandied about,' unless you were throwing chickens back and forth." He presented odd facts, and told jokes and parables. Sometimes it was hard to tell a joke from a parable: Young bride from the Middle West is having tea with wives of her husband's friends in New York. "And where do you come from?" one of them asks. "Iowa," says the trembling bride. The other woman leans closer. "Dear," she says, "out here we pronounce that 'Ohio.'" It had been a dozen years or so since I'd sat on the claw-footed chairs in Kate and Damon's living rooom, but Genie brought it all back. If there's an archive somewhere—and there probably is—it's a national treasure, for Damon's posts alone.

The earliest photos I've seen of Damon, fannish snapshots from the Forties, show a gangly and serious young man, more Abraham Lincoln than Damon Knight. Bookjackets from the Sixties show a clean-shaven, slightly grim-looking guy, possibly a jazz musician or an abstract painter. When I first met Damon, in 1976, he was a bit younger than I am now, but his Shavian beard gave the impression that he was as old as Methuselah. The inner Damon, the "young punk" of Genie, the "annoying kid brother" of Leslie What's essay, was never so old, and I've never seen a photograph that depicts that fellow. If you've got one, get in touch. I'm sure it's a curiosity.

SENSEI WONDER

Leslie What

Leslie What has won a Nebula Award for short story and a bookstore award for sitting while tap dancing. Her novel *Olympic Games* will be out in May 2004. Leslie's Web site can be found at http://www.sff.net/people/leslie.what/.

Damon Knight was a kid brother–silly curmudgeon when I met him at the Clarion Writers Workshop in 1976. I thought he was a good teacher and a mean guy. After Clarion I moved to Oregon, wrote, worked in hospice care, moved away, married, bore children, and created art. I returned to Oregon in 1985, and Damon and his wife Kate Wilhelm invited me back to the monthly workshop they held at their house. My two reproductive outbursts had transformed me from a confident outgoing woman into an uncertain, anorexic mom who had managed to write only one short story in five years. Believing that my story offered proof of exceptional talent, I presented it for critique, expecting praise.

That didn't happen.

The critique went around the circle. Condemnation poured like salt over my bleeding manuscript. One woman stopped knitting and pointed a silver needle toward my face, emphasizing her sharp critique. Damon added cantankerous remarks I can't quite recall, something like, "There are more layers in a baloney and cheese sandwich," only with panache. As was the protocol of the workshop, I listened and said nothing. I gave up writing to focus on art, work, and homemaking.

A few years later, while shopping for a toilet plunger at the Freddie's department store, I met Damon in the checkout line. He wore corduroy pants, a red flannel shirt, and wool motoring cap. With his long hair, Birkenstock sandals over bare feet, and poorly behaved beard, he looked like an Oregon-hippie lawn gnome.

"You know," he said, "we haven't seen you at workshop for a while. Did something happen?"

"Don't you remember?" I said. "You trashed my story—the first thing I had written in years! I never wanted to write again!"

His words seemed carefully chosen. "I don't remember the story," Damon said, "but you're welcome to come back." He apologized for having hurt my feelings and offered to reread the story and see if his opinion had changed. He waited for my answer, oblivious to his role in one of the most devastating events in my life.

I was bewildered. How could he *not* remember?

I experienced what philosopher Emil Fackenheim calls a shocking moment of recognition, discovering something so true, it forced me to reevaluate everything I thought I knew. Damon had not meant for his cutting remarks to be taken personally. He had critiqued a story, not me; he was unaware of the power he wielded, or how students craved his approval. Damon wasn't a mean man so much as he wasn't a sensitive one. I later told Kate that Damon wasn't sexist like so many men of his generation, not because he proved that by publishing a number of women authors when he edited the *Orbit* series, but because he treated every sloppy writer with equal contempt.

I rejoined the workshop and for the next several years turned in a story nearly every month. Damon was a less patient critic than Kate, who excelled at figuring out what the writer meant to do with the story. Damon limited his responses to the words as written. He acted genuinely puzzled when students got things wrong, as if we had messed up on purpose. People reacted to his brusque remarks in different ways. He once told Martha Bayless that "The universe would have been a better place had this story never been written," and told another workshop participant that her story made him want to vomit. The woman whose story made Damon want to puke left rather bruised, but to this day, Martha is proud to have written a story that threatened the stability of the universe.

"How much are you paying me to read this?" he wrote on one of my manuscripts. On another, he crossed out page after page of text, leaving about 100 out of 6000 words untouched. When I complained about him castrating my story, he laughed. Damon had a better belly laugh than Santa Claus.

Damon marked every typo, unneeded word, and questionable usage in his careful line-by-line edits. His writing was precise and clear; he demanded no less from his students. He compared stories to fruit and told us when we had picked them a little too green. He drew comical pictures on the back pages, especially when the story bored him. If he liked something, he drew a smiley face beside the line. After workshop, students compared how many smiley faces we had earned. Ray Vukcevich usually won.

Social courtesies weren't his thing. Maybe he was too busy reading important books, writing, or contemplating the big stuff to care how others perceived him. Though he argued relentlessly with fans and colleagues, he was more interested in finding truth than winning arguments. When he was wrong, he readily admitted it.

His critiques weren't helpful to every writer, but Damon became my mentor. I possessed creativity and talent without discipline. Damon's willingness to read and comment on my work over a sustained period of time allowed me to acquire the skills and work ethic needed to become a professional writer. He was my esteemed sensei, who taught me to pay attention to every word. Nothing got by him. I could tell when he had checked out a library book before I got to it by his corrections to the text.

When my first story was published in 1992, I gave Damon and Kate a copy of the magazine. Damon offered congratulations before sitting with his pen to mark up the text. His corrections were small—word choices, cuts that would have improved comic timing. He was genuinely proud, but let me know, sensei-style, that I could do better.

Damon expected his students to go beyond achieving simple competence as writers. I workshopped a story that later sold to a theme anthology. Damon said, "If this is for that anthology, then you'll probably sell it, for while I think you've written a dreadful story, the others are bound to be worse."

I finally wrote something Damon admired, and his praise filled me with pride because I knew that he wouldn't compliment me *just* to be nice. In fact, he detested the next story I turned in. "Leslie," he said, sounding weary, "reading is a voluntary act. You can't force me to read this, and I didn't." He smiled and added, "Other than that, I liked it."

That statement taught me the most important thing I have ever learned about writing.

Reading is a voluntary act.

If a story is so unpleasant, boring, or unrewarding that a workshop leader doesn't choose to read it, how can a writer persuade strangers to pay attention?

Damon was also more fun than Pop Rocks. Workshop member Nina Kiriki Hoffman and I came up with the idea of photographing people on a bearskin rug at conventions. Damon was the first one to pose, which he did while smoking a cigar. He was famous for his stealth squirt gun fights, and he also played a mean game of croquet. Eileen Gunn reminded me of the time I brought a book called "57 Sneaky Feats" to the workshop. One stunt told *How to Pick Up a Person Using Only Your Teeth.* The trick involved convincing someone to lie faceup while the performer lifted him off the ground by grasping his leather belt in her teeth. Damon thought the whole thing preposterously funny until I seemingly defied physics and common sense by lifting him several inches off the ground.

In 2000, Damon's health began to fail, and late in the year he fell, breaking his coccyx. The pain made him crankier than usual. After I visited one day, he worried that he had acted rudely and e-mailed to apologize. I quickly let him know that I hadn't noticed.

But there were typos in his e-mail. Damon never made spelling mistakes, even in e-mail—a worrying signal. Despite physical limitations, his critical facilities were sharp as ever, his last writings brilliant. Although in pain, he continued to colead the workshop until a few months before his death. Teaching students to care about the art of writing was a commitment that Damon Knight took seriously.

At one of the last workshops, he and I both presented offbeat stories for critique. His was wonderful, but confusing in places. He praised my work and told me to cut out my favorite scene. After the critique, Damon took my hand. He warned me that my story might be too odd to sell. I told him the same about his. We made a deal: I would send my story to an editor who disliked my work, if he would send his story to an editor he doubted would buy it. Neither story sold its first time out.

I am profoundly grateful that Damon Knight accepted me as his pupil, and heartened that he knew how much his students cherished and respected him. I would learn that he respected us as well. When Damon's story was published, it was slightly different than the workshop version. Our mentor had taught us well and used our critiques to better his writing.

American Gods is a big, sprawling, slightly peculiar novel about America and about a man called Shadow who finds himself working for an elderly Odin in the run-up to a war between the old, forgotten gods, and the newer, more transient, more technological gods. It's a fantasy novel, and it contains several short stories as part of its substance, in which people come to America. This is the story of the first people coming to America, about 16,000 years ago.

I'm English. I write comics sometimes, and prose, and, occasionally, films and radio plays. I write books for children and books for adults, and, from time to time, short stories. Also I keep a Weblog and too many cats. I'm living in the midwest currently and can no longer remember why. . . .

His Web site (and Weblog) can be found at http://www.neil gaiman.com/.

NEIL GAIMAN

Coming to America
14,000 B.C.

Cold it was, and dark, when the vision came to her, for in the far north daylight was a grey dim time in the middle of the day that came, and went, and came again: an interlude between darknesses.

They were not a large tribe as these things were counted then: nomads of the Northern Plains. They had a god, who was the skull of a mammoth, and the hide of a mammoth fashioned into a rough cloak. *Nunyunnini*, they called him. When they were not travelling, he rested on a wooden frame, at man height.

She was the holy woman of the tribe, the keeper of its secrets, and her name was Atsula, the fox. Atsula walked before the two tribesmen who carried their god on long poles, draped with bearskins, that it should not be seen by profane eyes, nor at times when it was not holy.

They roamed the tundra, with their tents. The finest of the tents was made of caribou hide, and it was the holy tent, and there were four of them inside it: Atsula, the priestess, Gugwei, the tribal elder, Yanu, the war leader, and Kalanu, the scout. She called them there, the day after she had her vision.

Atsula scraped some lichen into the fire, then she threw in dried leaves with her withered left hand: they smoked, with an eye-stinging grey smoke, and gave off an odour that was sharp and strange. Then she took a wooden cup from the wooden platform, and she passed it to Gugwei. The cup was half-filled with a dark yellow liquid.

Atsula had found the *pungh* mushrooms—each with seven spots, only a true holy woman could find a seven-spotted mushroom—and had picked them at the dark of the moon, and dried them on a string of deer-cartilage.

Yesterday, before she slept, she had eaten the three dried mushroom caps. Her dreams had been confused and fearful things, of bright lights moving fast, of rock mountains filled with lights spearing upward like icicles. In the night she had woken, sweating, and needing to make water. She squatted over the wooden cup and filled it with her urine. Then she placed the cup outside the tent, in the snow, and returned to sleep.

When she woke, she picked the lumps of ice out from the wooden cup, as her mother had taught her, leaving a darker, more concentrated liquid behind.

It was this liquid she passed around, first to Gugwei, then to Yanu and to Kalanu. Each of them took a large gulp of the liquid, then Atsula took the final draft. She swallowed it, and poured what was left on the ground in front of their god, a libation to Nunyunnini.

They sat in the smoky tent, waiting for their god to speak. Outside, in the darkness, the wind wailed and breathed.

Kalanu, the scout, was a woman who dressed and walked as a man: she had even taken Dalani, a fourteen-year-old maiden, to be her wife. Kalanu blinked her eyes tightly, then she got up and walked over to the mammoth skull. She pulled the mammoth-hide cloak over herself, and stood so her head was inside the mammoth skull.

"There is evil in the land," said Nunyunnini in Kalanu's voice. "Evil, such that if you stay here, in the land of your mothers and your mother's mothers, you shall all perish."

The three listeners grunted.

"Is it the slavers? Or the great wolves?" asked Gugwei, whose hair was long and white, and whose face was as wrinkled as the gray skin of a thorn tree.

"It is not the slavers," said Nunyunnini, old stone-hide. "It is not the great wolves."

"Is it a famine? Is a famine coming?" asked Gugwei.

Nunyunnini was silent. Kalanu came out of the skull and waited with the rest of them.

Gugwei put on the mammoth-hide cloak and put his head inside the skull.

"It is not a famine as you know it," said Nunyunnini, through Gugwei's mouth, "although a famine will follow."

"Then what is it?" asked Yanu. "I am not afraid. I will stand against it. We have spears, and we have throwing rocks. Let a hundred mighty warriors come against us, still we shall prevail. We shall lead them into the marshes, and split their skulls with our flints."

"It is not a man thing," said Nunyunnini, in Gugwei's old voice. "It will come from the skies, and none of your spears or your rocks will protect you."

"How can we protect ourselves?" asked Atsula. "I have seen flames in the skies. I have heard a noise louder than ten thunderbolts. I have seen forests flattened and rivers boil."

"Ai . . ." said Nunyunnini, but he said no more. Gugwei came out of the skull, bending stiffly, for he was an old man, and his knuckles were swollen and knotted.

There was silence. Atsula threw more leaves on the fire, and the smoke made their eyes tear.

Then Yanu strode to the mammoth head, put the cloak about his broad shoulders, put his head inside the skull. His voice boomed. "You must journey," said Nunyunnini. "You must travel to sunward. Where the sun rises, there you will find a new land, where you will be safe. It will be a long journey: the moon will swell and empty, die and live, twice, and there will be slavers and beasts, but I shall guide you and keep you safe, if you travel toward the sunrise."

Atsula spat on the mud of the floor, and said, "No." She could feel the god staring at her. "No," she said. "You are a bad god to tell us this. We will die. We will all die, and then who will be left to carry you from high place to high place, to raise your tent, to oil your great tusks with fat?"

The god said nothing. Atsula and Yanu exchanged places. Atsula's face stared out through the yellowed mammoth bone.

"Atsula has no faith," said Nunyunnini in Atsula's voice. "Atsula shall die before the rest of you enter the new land, but the rest of you shall live. Trust me: there is a land to the east that is manless. This land shall be your land and the land of your children and your children's children, for seven generations, and seven sevens. But for Atsula's faithlessness, you would have kept it forever. In the morning, pack your tents and your possessions, and walk toward the sunrise."

And Gugwei and Yanu and Kalanu bowed their heads and exclaimed at the power and wisdom of Nunyunnini.

The moon swelled and waned and swelled and waned once more. The people of the tribe walked east, toward the sunrise, struggling through the icy winds, which numbed their exposed skin. Nunyunnini had promised them truly: they lost no one from the tribe on the jour-ney, save for a woman in childbirth, and women in childbirth belong to the moon, not to Nunyunnini.

They crossed the land bridge.

Kalanu had left them at first light to scout the way. Now the sky was dark, and Kalanu had not returned, but the night sky was alive with lights, knotting and flickering and winding, flux and pulse, white and green and violet and red. Atsula and her people had seen the northern lights before, but they were still frightened by them, and this was a display like they had never seen before.

Kalanu returned to them, as the lights in the sky formed and flowed.

"Sometimes," she said to Atsula, "I feel that I could simply spread my arms and fall into the sky."

"That is because you are a scout," said Atsula, the priestess. "When you die, you shall fall into the sky and become a star, to guide us as you guide us in life."

"There are cliffs of ice to the east, high cliffs," said Kalanu, her raven-black hair worn long, as a man would wear it. "We can climb them, but it will take many days."

"You shall lead us safely," said Atsula. "I shall die at the foot of the cliff, and that will be the sacrifice that takes you into the new lands."

To the west of them, where the sun had set hours before, there was a flash of sickly yellow light, brighter than lightning, brighter than daylight. It was a burst of pure brilliance that forced the folk on the land bridge to cover their eyes and spit and exclaim. Children be-gan to wail.

"That is the doom that Nunyunnini warned us of," said Gugwei the old. "Surely he is a wise god and a mighty one."

"He is the best of all gods," said Kalanu. "In our new land we shall raise him up on high, and we shall polish his tusks and skull with fish oil and animal fat, and we shall tell our children, and our chil-dren's children, and our seventh children's children, that Nunyunnini is the mightiest of all gods, and shall never be forgotten."

"Gods are great," said Atsula, slowly, as if she were comprehend-ing a great secret. "But the heart is greater. For it is from our hearts they come, and to our hearts they shall return . . ."

And there is no telling how long she might have continued in this blasphemy, had it not been interrupted in a manner that brooked no argument.

The roar that erupted from the west was so loud that ears bled, that they could hear nothing for some time, temporarily blinded and deafened but alive, knowing that they were luckier than the tribes to the west of them.

"It is good," said Atsula, but she could not hear the words inside her head.

Atsula died at the foot of the cliffs when the spring sun was at its zenith. She did not live to see the New World, and the tribe walked into those lands with no holy woman.

They scaled the cliffs, and they went south and west, until they found a valley with fresh water, and rivers that teemed with silver fish, and deer that had never seen man before, and were so tame it was necessary to spit and to apologize to their spirits before killing them.

Dalani gave birth to three boys, and some said that Kalanu had performed the final magic and could do the man-thing with her bride; while others said that old Gugwei was not too old to keep a young bride company when her husband was away; and certainly once Gugwei died, Dalani had no more children.

And the ice times came and the ice times went, and the people spread out across the land, and formed new tribes and chose new totems for themselves: ravens and foxes and ground sloths and great cats and buffalo, each a taboo beast that marked a tribe's identity, each beast a god.

The mammoths of the new lands were bigger, and slower, and more foolish than the mammoth of the Siberian plains, and the *pungh* mushrooms, with their seven spots, were not to be found in the new lands, and Nunyunnini did not speak to the tribe any longer.

And in the days of the grandchildren of Dalani and Kalanu's grandchildren, a band of warriors, members of a big and prosperous tribe, returning from a slaving expedition in the north to their home in the south, found the valley of the first people: they killed most of the men, and they took the women and many of the children captive.

One of the children, hoping for clemency, took them to a cave in the hills, in which they found a mammoth skull, the tattered remnants of a mammoth-skin cloak, a wooden cup, and the preserved head of Atsula the oracle.

While some of the warriors of the new tribe were for taking the sacred objects away with them, stealing the gods of the first people and owning their power, others counseled against it, saying that they would bring nothing but ill luck, and the malice of their own god (for these were the people of a raven tribe, and ravens are jealous gods).

So they threw the objects down the side of the hill, into a deep ravine, and took the survivors of the first people with them on their long journey south. And the raven tribes, and the fox tribes, grew more powerful in the land, and soon Nunyunnini was entirely forgot.

I live in Miami with my wife, Judi, and two constantly warring cats, the volatile Maggie and the remarkably restrained Jones. I have published more than seventy short stories, ranging from extreme horror to light humor with every stop in between. They include the Stoker nominee "Baby Girl Diamond" and the previous Hugo/Nebula nominees "The Funeral March of the Marionettes" and (with Jerry Oltion) "The Astronaut from Wyoming." My ten books include a quartet of Spider-Man novels and the short story collections *Lost In Booth Nine*, *An Alien Darkness*, *A Desperate Decaying Darkness*, *Vossoff and Nimmitz*, and *Tangled Strings*. I appear most regularly in *The Magazine of Fantasy & Science Fiction* and *Analog*.

Regarding "Sunday Night Yams": It's about a lot of things, really, but its main concern is getting the wonder back.

Adam-Troy's Web site is at http://www.sff.net/people/adam-troy/.

SUNDAY NIGHT YAMS AT MINNIE AND EARL'S

ADAM-TROY CASTRO

Frontiers never die. They just become theme parks.

   I spent most of my shuttle ride to Nearside mulling sour thoughts about that. It's the kind of thing that only bothers lonely and nostalgic old men, especially when we're old enough to remember the days when a trip to Luna was not a routine commuter run, but instead a never-ending series of course corrections, systems checks, best-and-worst case simulations, and random unexpected crises ranging from ominous burning smells to the surreal balls of floating upchuck that got into everywhere if we didn't get over our nausea fast enough to clean them up. Folks of my vintage remember what it was to spend half their lives in passionate competition with dozens of other frighteningly qualified people, just to earn themselves seats on cramped rigs outfitted by the lowest corporate bidders—and then to look down at the ragged landscape of Sister Moon and know that the sight itself was a privilege well worth the effort. But that's old news now: before the first development crews gave way to the first settlements; before the first settlements became large enough to be called the first cities; before the first city held a parade in honor of its first confirmed mugging; before Independence and the Corporate Communities and the opening of Lunar Disney on the Sea of Tranquility. These days, the Moon itself is no big deal except for rubes and old-timers. Nobody looks out the windows; they're far too interested in their sims, or their virts, or their newspads or (for a vanishingly literate few) their paperback novels, to care about the sight of the airless world waxing large in the darkness outside.

   I wanted to shout at them. I wanted to make a great big eloquent speech about what they were missing by taking it all for granted, and about their total failure to appreciate what others had gone through to pave the way. But that wouldn't have moved anybody. It just would have established me as just another boring old fart.

So I stayed quiet until we landed, and then I rolled my overnighter down the aisle, and I made my way through the vast carpeted terminal at Armstrong Interplanetary (thinking all the while *carpet, carpet, why is there carpet, dammit, there shouldn't be carpeting on the Moon*). Then I hopped a tram to my hotel, and I confirmed that the front desk had followed instructions and provided me one of their few (hideously expensive) rooms with an outside view. Then I went upstairs and thought it all again when I saw that the view was just an alien distortion of the Moon I had known. Though it was night, and the landscape was as dark as the constellations of manmade illumination peppered across its cratered surface would now ever allow it to be, I still saw marquee-sized advertisements for soy houses, strip clubs, rotating restaurants, golden arches, miniature golf courses, and the one-sixth-g Biggest Rollercoaster In the Solar System. The Earth, with Europe and Africa centered, hung silently above the blight.

I tried to imagine two gentle old people, and a golden retriever dog, wandering around somewhere in the garish paradise framed by that window.

I failed.

I wondered whether it felt good or bad to be here. I wasn't tired, which I supposed I could attribute to the sensation of renewed strength and vigor that older people are supposed to feel after making the transition to lower gravities. Certainly, my knees, which had been bothering me for more than a decade now, weren't giving me a single twinge here. But I was also here alone, a decade after burying my dear wife—and though I'd traveled around a little, in the last few years, I had never really grown used to the way the silence of a strange room, experienced alone, tastes like the death that waited for me too.

After about half an hour of feeling sorry for myself, I dressed in one of my best blue suits—an old one Claire had picked out in better days, with a cut now two styles out of date—and went to the lobby to see the concierge. I found him in the center of a lobby occupied not by adventurers or pioneers but by businessmen and tourists. He was a sallow-faced young man seated behind a flat slab of a desk, constructed from some material made to resemble polished black marble. It might have been intended to represent a Kubrick monolith lying on its side, a touch that would have been appropriate enough for the Moon but might have given the decorator too much credit for classical allusions. I found more Kubrick material in the man himself, in that he was a typical hotel functionary: courteous, professional, friendly, and as cold as a plain white wall. Beaming, he said: "Can I help you, sir?"

"I'm looking for Minnie and Earl," I told him.

His smile was an unfaltering, professional thing, that might have been scissored out of a magazine ad and Scotch-taped to the bottom half of his face. "Do you have their full names, sir?"

"Those are their full names." I confess I smiled with reminiscence. "They're both one of a kind."

"I see. And they're registered at the hotel?"

"I doubt it," I said. "They're lunar residents. I just don't have their address."

"Did you try the directory?"

"I tried that before I left Earth," I said. "They're not listed. Didn't expect them to be, either."

He hesitated a fraction of a second before continuing: "I'm not sure I know what to suggest, then—"

"I'm sure you don't," I said, unwillingly raising my voice just enough to give him a little taste of the anger and frustration and dire need that had fueled this entire trip. Being a true professional, used to dealing with obnoxious and arrogant tourists, the concierge didn't react at all: just politely waited for me to get on with it. I, on the other hand, winced before continuing: "They're before your time. Probably way before your time. But there have to be people around—old people, mostly—who know who I'm talking about. Maybe you can ask around for me? Just a little? And pass around the word that I need to talk?"

The professional smile did not change a whit, but it still acquired a distinctively dubious flavor. "Minnie and Earl, sir?"

"Minnie and Earl." I then showed him the size of the tip he'd earn if he accomplished it—big enough to make certain that he'd take the request seriously, but not so large that he'd be tempted to concoct false leads. It impressed him exactly as much as I needed it to. Too bad there was almost no chance of it accomplishing anything; I'd been making inquiries about the old folks for years. But the chances of me giving up were even smaller: not when I now knew I only had a few months left before the heart stopped beating in my chest.

They were Minnie and Earl, dammit.

And anybody who wasn't there in the early days couldn't possibly understand how much that meant.

■

It's a funny thing, about frontiers: they're not as enchanting as the folks who work them like you to believe. And there was a lot that they didn't tell the early recruits about the joys of working on the Moon.

They didn't tell you that the air systems gave off a nasal hum that kept you from sleeping soundly at any point during your first six weeks on rotation; that the vents were considerately located directly above the bunks to eliminate any way of shutting it out; that just when you found yourself actually needing that hum to sleep something in the circulators decided to change the pitch, rendering it just a tad higher or lower so that instead of lying in bed begging that hum to shut up shut up SHUT UP you sat there instead wondering if the new version denoted a serious mechanical difficulty capable of asphyxiating you in your sleep.

They didn't tell you that the recycled air was a paradise for bacteria, which kept any cold or flu or ear infection constantly circulating between you and your coworkers; that the disinfectants regularly released into the atmosphere smelled bad but otherwise did nothing; that when you started sneezing and coughing it was a sure bet that everybody around you would soon be sneezing and coughing; and that it was not just colds but stomach viruses, contagious rashes and even more unpleasant things that got shared as generously as a bottle of a wine at one of the parties you had time to go to back on Earth when you were able to work only sixty or seventy hours a week. They didn't tell you that work took so very much of your time that the pleasures and concerns of normal life were no longer valid experiential input; that without that input you eventually ran out of non-work-related subjects to talk about, and found your personality withering away like an atrophied limb.

They didn't tell you about the whimsical random shortages in the bimonthly supply drops and the ensuing shortages of staples like toothpaste and toilet paper. They didn't tell you about the days when all the systems seemed to conk out at once and your deadening routine suddenly became hours of all-out frantic terror. They didn't tell you that after a while you forgot you were on the Moon and stopped sneaking looks at the battered blue marble. They didn't tell you that after a while it stopped being a dream and became instead just a dirty and backbreaking job; one that drained you of your enthusiasm faster than you could possibly guess, and one that replaced your ambitions of building a new future with more mundane longings, like feeling once again what it was like to stand unencumbered beneath a midday sun, breathing air that tasted like air and not canned sweat.

They waited until you were done learning all of this on your own before they told you about Minnie and Earl.

I learned on a Sunday—not that I had any reason to keep track of the day; the early development teams were way too short-staffed to enjoy luxuries like days off. There were instead days when you got the shitty jobs and the days when you got the jobs slightly less shitty than the others. On that particular Sunday I had repair duty, the worst job on the Moon but for another twenty or thirty possible candidates. It involved, among them, inspecting, cleaning, and replacing the panels on the solar collectors. There were a lot of panels, since the early collector fields were five kilometers on a side, and each panel was only half a meter square. They tended to collect meteor dust (at best) and get scarred and pitted from micrometeor impacts (at worst). We'd just lost a number of them from heavier rock precipitation, which meant that in addition to replacing those, I had to examine even those that remained intact. Since the panels swiveled to follow the Sun across the sky, even a small amount of dust debris threatened to fall through the joints into the machinery below. There was never a lot of dust—sometimes it was not even visible. But it had to be removed one panel at a time.

To overhaul the assembly, you spent the whole day on your belly, crawling along the catwalks between them, removing each panel in turn, inspecting them beneath a canopy with nothing but suit light, magnifiers, and micro-thin air jet. (A vacuum, of course, would have been redundant.) You replaced the panels pitted beyond repair, brought the ruined ones back to the sled for disposal, and then started all over again.

The romance of space travel? Try nine hours of hideously tedious stoop labor, in a moonsuit. Try hating every minute of it. Try hating where you are and what you're doing and how hard you worked to qualify for this privilege. Try also hating yourself just for feeling that way—but not having any idea how to turn those feelings off.

I was muttering to myself, conjugating some of the more colorful expressions for excrement, when Phil Jacoby called. He was one of the more annoying people on the Moon: a perpetual smiler who always looked on the bright side of things and refused to react to even the most acidic sarcasm. Appropriately enough, his carrot hair and freckled cheeks always made him look like a ventriloquist's dummy. He might have been our morale officer, if we'd possessed enough bad taste to have somebody with that job title; but that would have made him even more the kind of guy you grow to hate when you really want to be in a bad mood. I dearly appreciated how distant his voice sounded, as he called my name over the radio: "Max! You bored yet, Max?"

"Sorry," I said tiredly. "Max went home."

"Home as in his quarters? Or Home as in Earth?"

"There is no home here," I said. "Of course Home as on Earth."

"No return shuttles today," Phil noted. "Or any time this month. How would he manage that trick?"

"He was so fed up he decided to walk."

"Hope he took a picnic lunch or four. That's got to be a major hike."

In another mood, I might have smiled. "What's the bad news, Phil?"

"Why? You expecting bad news?"

There was a hidden glee to his tone that sounded excessive even from Jacoby. "Surprise me."

"You're quitting early. The barge will be by to pick you up in five minutes."

According to the digital readout inside my helmet, it was only 13:38 LT. The news that I wouldn't have to devote another three hours to painstaking cleanup should have cheered me considerably; instead, it rendered me about twenty times more suspicious. I said, "Phil, it will take me at least three times that long just to secure—"

"A relief shift will arrive on another barge within the hour. Don't do another minute of work. Just go back to the sled and wait for pickup. That's an order."

Which was especially strange because Jacoby was not technically my superior. Sure, he'd been on the Moon all of one hundred and twenty days longer than me—and sure, that meant any advice he had to give me needed to be treated like an order, if I wanted to do my job— but even so, he was not the kind of guy who ever ended anything with an authoritarian *That's An Order*. My first reaction was the certainty that I must have been in some kind of serious trouble. Somewhere, sometime, I forgot or neglected one of the safety protocols, and did something suicidally, crazily wrong—the kind of thing that once discovered would lead to me being relieved for incompetence. But I was still new on the Moon, and I couldn't think of any recent occasion where I'd been given enough responsibility for that to be a factor. My next words were especially cautious: "Uh, Phil, did I—"

"Go to the sled," he repeated, even more sternly this time. "And, Max?"

"What?" I asked.

The ebullient side of his personality returned. "I envy you, man." The connection clicked off before I could ask him why.

A lunar barge was a lot like its terrestrial equivalent, in that it had no motive power of its very own, but needed to be pulled by another vehicle. Ours were pulled by tractors. They had no atmospheric enclosures, since ninety percent of the time they were just used for the slow-motion hauling of construction equipment; whenever they were needed to move personnel, we bolted in a number of forward-facing seats with oxygen feeds and canvas straps to prevent folks imprisoned by clumsy moonsuits from being knocked out of their chairs every time the flatbed dipped in the terrain. It was an extremely low-tech method of travel, not much faster than a human being could sprint, and we didn't often use it for long distances.

There were four other passengers on this one, all identical behind mirrored facemasks; I had to read their nametags to see who they were. Nikki Hollander, Oscar Desalvo, George Peterson, and Carrie Aldrin No Relation (the last two words a nigh-permanent part of her name, up here). All four of them had been on-site at least a year more than I had, and to my eyes had always seemed to be dealing with a routine a lot better than I had been. As I strapped in, and the tractor started up, and the barge began its glacial progress toward a set of lumpy peaks on the horizon, I wished my coworkers had something other than distorted reflections of the lunar landscape for faces; it would be nice to be able to judge from their expressions just what was going on here. I said: "So what's the story, people? Where we headed?"

Then Carrie Aldrin No Relation began to sing: "Over the river and through the woods/to grandmother's house we go . . ."

George Peterson snorted. Oscar Desalvo, a man not known for

his giddy sense of humor, who was in fact even grimmer than me most of the time—(not from disenchantment with his work, but out of personal inclination)—giggled; it was like watching one of the figures on Mount Rushmore stick its tongue out. Nikki Hollander joined in, her considerably less-than-perfect pitch turning the rest of the song into a nails-on-blackboard cacophony. The helmet speakers, which distorted anyway, did not help.

I said, "Excuse me?"

Nikki Hollander said something so blatantly ridiculous that I couldn't force myself to believe I'd heard her correctly.

"Come again? I lost that."

"No you didn't." Her voice seemed strained, almost hysterical.

One of the men was choking with poorly repressed laughter. I couldn't tell who.

"You want to know if I like yams?"

Nikki's response was a burlesque parody of astronautic stoicism. "That's an affirmative, Houston."

"Yams, the vegetable yams?"

"*A*-ffirmative." The A emphasized and italicized so broadly that it was not so much a separate syllable as a sovereign country.

This time I recognized the strangulated noises. They were coming from George Peterson, and they were the sounds made by a man who was trying very hard not to laugh. It was several seconds before I could summon enough dignity to answer. "Yeah, I like yams. How is that relevant?"

"Classified," she said, and then her signal cut off.

In fact, all their signals cut off, though I could tell from the red indicators on my internal display that they were all still broadcasting.

That was not unusual. Coded frequencies were one of the few genuine amenities allowed us; they allowed those of us who absolutely needed a few seconds to discuss personal matters with coworkers to do so without sharing their affairs with anybody else who might be listening. We're not supposed to spend more than a couple of minutes at a time on those channels because it's safer to stay monitored. Being shut out of four signals simultaneously—in a manner that could only mean raucous laughter at my expense—was unprecedented, and it pissed me off. Hell, I'll freely admit that it did more than that; it frightened me. I was on the verge of suspecting brain damage caused by something wrong with the air supply.

Then George Peterson's voice clicked: "Sorry about that, old buddy." (I'd never been his old buddy.) "We usually do a better job keeping a straight face."

"At what? Mind telling me what's going on here?"

"One minute." He performed the series of maneuvers necessary to cut off the oxygen provided by the barge, and restore his dependence on the supply contained in his suit, then unstrapped his harnesses, stood, and moved toward me, swaying slightly from the bumps and jars of our imperfectly smooth ride across the lunar surface.

It was, of course, against all safety regulations for him to be on his feet while the barge was in motion; after all, even as glacially slow as that was, it wouldn't have taken all that great an imperfection in the road before us to knock him down and perhaps inflict the kind of hairline puncture capable of leaving him with a slight case of death. We had all disobeyed that particular rule from time to time; there were just too many practical advantages in being able to move around at will, without first ordering the tractor to stop. But it made no sense for him to come over now, just to talk, as if it really made a difference for us to be face-to-face. After all, we weren't faces. We were a pair of convex mirrors, reflecting each other while the men behind them spoke on radios too powerful to be noticeably improved by a few less meters of distance.

Even so, he sat down on a steel crate lashed to the deck before me, and positioned his faceplate opposite mine, his body language suggesting meaningful eye contact. He held that position for almost a minute, not saying anything, not moving, behaving exactly like a man who believed he was staring me down.

It made no sense. I could have gone to sleep and he wouldn't have noticed.

Instead, I said: "What?"

He spoke quietly: "Am I correct in observing that you've felt less than, shall we say . . . 'inspired', by your responsibilities here?"

Oh, Christ. This was about something I'd done.

"Is there some kind of problem?"

George's helmet trembled enough to suggest a man theatrically shaking his head inside it. "Lighten up, Max. Nobody has any complaints about your work. We think you're one of the best people we have here, and your next evaluation is going to give you straight A's in every department . . . except enthusiasm. You just don't seem to believe in the work anymore."

As much as I tried to avoid it, my answer still reeked with denial. "I believe in it."

"You believe in the idea of it," George said. "But the reality has worn you down."

I was stiff, proper, absolutely correct, and absolutely transparent. "I was trained. I spent a full year in simulation, doing all the same jobs. I knew what it was going to be like. I knew what to expect."

"No amount of training can prepare you for the moment when you think you can't feel the magic anymore."

"And you can?" I asked, unable to keep the scorn from my voice.

The speakers inside lunar helmets were still pretty tinny in those days; they no longer transformed everything we said into the monotones that once upon a time helped get an entire country fed up with the forced badinage of Apollo, but neither were they much good at conveying the most precise of emotional cues. And yet I was able to pick up something in George's tone that was, given my mood, capable of profoundly disturbing me: a strange, transcendent joy. "Oh, yes. Max. I can."

I was just unnerved enough to ask: "How?"

"I'm swimming in it," he said—and even as long as he'd been part of the secret, his voice still quavered, as if there was some seven-year-old part of him that remained unwilling to believe that it could possibly be. "We're all swimming in it."

"I'm not."

And he laughed out loud. "Don't worry. We're going to gang up and shove you into the deep end of the pool."

■

That was seventy years ago.

Seventy years. I think about how old that makes me and I cringe. Seventy years ago, the vast majority of old farts who somehow managed to make it to the age I am now were almost always living on the outer edges of decrepitude. The physical problems were nothing compared with the senility. What's that? You don't remember senile dementia? Really? I guess there's a joke in there somewhere, but it's not that funny for those of us who can remember actually considering it a possible future. Trust me, it was a nightmare. And the day they licked that one was one hell of an advertisement for progress.

But still, seventy years. You want to know how long ago that was? Seventy years ago it was still possible to find people who had heard of

Bruce Springsteen. There were even some who remembered the Beatles. Stephen King was still coming out with his last few books, Kate Emma Brenner hadn't yet come out with any, Exxon was still in business, the reconstruction of the ice packs hadn't even been proposed, India and Pakistan hadn't reconciled, and the idea of astronauts going out into space to blow up a giant asteroid before it impacted with Earth was not an anecdote from recent history but a half-remembered image from a movie your father talked about going to see when he was a kid. Seventy years ago the most pressing headlines had to do with the worldwide ecological threat posed by the population explosion among escaped sugar gliders.

Seventy years ago, I hadn't met Claire. She was still married to her first husband, the one she described as the nice mistake. She had no idea I was anywhere in her future. I had no idea she was anywhere in mine. The void hadn't been defined yet, let alone filled. (Nor had it been cruelly emptied again—and wasn't it sad how the void I'd lived with for so long seemed a lot larger, once I needed to endure it again?)

Seventy years ago I thought Faisal Awad was an old man. He may have been in his mid-thirties then, at most ten years older than I was. That, to me, was old. These days it seems one step removed from the crib.

I haven't mentioned Faisal yet; he wasn't along the day George and the others picked me up in the barge, and we didn't become friends till later. But he was a major member of the development team, back then—the kind of fixitall adventurer who could use the coffee machine in the common room to repair the heating system in the clinic. If you don't think that's a valuable skill, try living under 24-7 life support in a hostile environment where any requisitions for spare parts had to be debated and voted upon by a government committee during election years. It's the time of my life when I first developed my deep abiding hatred of Senators. Faisal was our life-saver, our miracle worker, and our biggest local authority on the works of Gilbert and Sullivan, though back then we were all too busy to listen to music and much more likely to listen to that 15-minute wonder Polka Thug anyway. After I left the Moon, and the decades of my life fluttered by faster than I once could have imagined possible, I used to think about Faisal and decide that I really ought to look him up, someday, maybe, as soon as I had the chance. But he had stayed on Luna, and I had gone back to Earth, and what with one thing or another that resolution had worked out as well as such oughtas always do: a lesson that old men have learned too late for as long as there have been old men to learn it.

I didn't even know how long he'd been dead until I heard it from his granddaughter Janine Seuss, a third-generation lunar I was able to track down with the help of the Selene Historical Society. She was a slightly-built thirty-seven-year-old with stylishly mismatched eye color and hair micro-styled into infinitesimal pixels that, when combed correctly, formed the famous old black-and-white news photograph of that doomed young girl giving the finger to the cops at the San Diego riots of some thirty years ago. Though she had graciously agreed to meet me, she hadn't had time to arrange her hair properly, and the photo was eerily distorted, like an image captured and then distorted on putty. She served coffee, which I can't drink anymore but which I accepted anyway, then sat down on her couch with the frantically miaowing Siamese.

"There were still blowouts then," she said. "Some genuine accidents, some bombings arranged by the Flat-Mooners. It was one of the Flat-Mooners who got Poppy. He was taking Mermer—our name for Grandma—to the movies up on topside; back then, they used to project them on this big white screen a couple of kilometers outside, though it was always some damn thing fifty or a hundred years old with dialogue that didn't make sense and stories you had to be older than Moses to appreciate. Anyway, the commuter tram they were riding just went boom and opened up into pure vacuum. Poppy and Mermer and about fourteen others got sucked out." She took a deep breath, then let it out all at once. "That was almost twenty years ago."

What else can you say, when you hear a story like that? "I'm sorry."

She acknowledged that with an equally ritual response. "Thanks."

"Did they catch the people responsible?"

"Right away. They were a bunch of losers. Unemployed idiots."

I remembered the days when the only idiots on the Moon were highly-educated and overworked ones. After a moment, I said: "Did he ever talk about the early days? The development teams?"

She smiled. "Ever? It was practically all he ever did talk about. You kids don't bleh bleh bleh. He used to get mad at the vids that made it look like a time of sheriffs and saloons and gunfights—he guessed they probably made good stories for kids who didn't know any better, but kept complaining that life back then wasn't anything like that. He said there was always too much work to do to strap on six-guns and go gunning for each other."

"He was right," I said. (There was a grand total of one gunfight in the first thirty years of lunar settlement—and it's not part of this story.)

"Most of his stories about those days had to do with things breaking down and him being the only person who could fix them in the nick of time. He told reconditioned-software anecdotes. Finding-the-rotten-air-filter anecdotes. Improvise-joint-lubricant anecdotes. Lots of them."

"That was Faisal."

She petted the cat. (It was a heavy-lidded, meatloaf-shaped thing that probably bestirred itself only at the sound of a can opener: we'd tamed the Moon so utterly that people like Janine were able to spare some pampering for their pets.) "Bleh. I prefer the gunfights."

I leaned forward and asked the important question. "Did he ever mention anybody named Minnie and Earl?"

"Were those a couple of folks from way back then?"

"You could say that."

"No last names?"

"None they ever used."

She thought about that, and said: "Would they have been folks he knew only slightly? Or important people?"

"Very important people," I said. "It's vital that I reach them."

She frowned. "It was a long time ago. Can you be sure they're still alive?"

"Absolutely," I said.

She considered that for a second. "No, I'm sorry. But you have to realize it was a long time ago for me too. I don't remember him mentioning anybody."

Faisal was the last of the people I'd known from my days on the Moon. There were a couple on Earth, but both had flatly denied any knowledge of Minnie and Earl. Casting about for last straws, I said: "Do you have anything that belonged to him?"

"No, I don't. But I know where you can go to look further."

■

Seventy years ago, after being picked up by the barge:

Nobody spoke to me again for forty-five minutes, which only fueled my suspicions of mass insanity.

The barge itself made slow but steady progress, following a generally uphill course of the only kind possible in that era, in that place, on the Moon: which was to say, serpentine. The landscape here was rough, pocked with craters and jagged outcroppings, in no place willing to respect how convenient it might have been to allow us to proceed in something approaching a straight line. There were places where we had to turn almost a hundred and eighty degrees, double back a while, then turn again, to head in an entirely different direction; it was the kind of route that looks random from one minute to the next but gradually reveals progress in one direction or another. It was clearly a route that my colleagues had travelled many times before; nobody seemed impatient. But for the one guy who had absolutely no idea where we were going, and who wasn't in fact certain that we were headed anywhere at all, it was torture.

We would have managed the trip in maybe one-tenth the time in one of our fliers, but I later learned that the very laboriousness of the journey was, for first-timers at least, a traditional part of the show. It gave us time to speculate, to anticipate. This was useful for unlimbering the mind, ironing the kinks out of the imagination, getting us used to the idea that we were headed someplace important enough to be worth the trip. The buildup couldn't possibly be enough—the view over that last ridge was still going to hit us with the force of a sledgehammer to the brain—but I remember how hard it hit and I'm still thankful the shock was cushioned even as inadequately as it was.

We followed a long boring ridge for the better part of fifteen minutes . . . then began to climb a slope that bore the rutty look of lunar ground that had known tractor-treads hundreds of times before. Some of my fellow journeyers hummed ominous, horror-movie soundtrack music in my ear, but George's voice overrode them all: "Max? Did Phil tell you he envied you this moment?"

I was really nervous now. "Yes."

"He's full of crap. You're not going to enjoy this next bit except in retrospect. Later on you'll think of it as the best moment of your life—and it might even be—but it won't feel like that when it happens. It'll feel big and frightening and insane when it happens. Trust me now when I tell you that it will get better, and quickly . . . and that everything will be explained, if not completely, then at least as much as it needs to be."

It was an odd turn of phrase. "As much as it needs to be? What's that supposed to—"

That's when the barge reached the top of the rise, providing us a nice panoramic view of what awaited us in the shallow depression on the other side.

My ability to form coherent sentences became a distant rumor.

It was the kind of moment when the entire Universe seems to become a wobbly thing, propped up by scaffolding and held together with the cheapest brand of hardware-store nails. The kind of moment when gravity just turns sideways beneath you, and the whole world turns on its edge, and the only thing that prevents you from just jetting off into space to spontaneously combust is the compensatory total stoppage of time. I don't know the first thing I said. I'm glad nobody ever played me the recordings that got filed away in the permanent mission archives . . . and I'm equally sure that the reason they didn't is that anybody actually on the Moon to listen to them must have also had their own equally aghast reactions also saved for posterity. I got to hear such sounds many times, from others I would later escort over that ridge myself—and I can absolutely assure you that they're the sounds made by intelligent, educated people who first think they've gone insane, and who then realize it doesn't help to know that they haven't.

It was the only possible immediate reaction to the first sight of Minnie and Earl's.

What I saw, as we crested the top of that ridge, was this:

In the center of a typically barren lunar landscape, surrounded on all sides by impact craters, rocks, more rocks, and the suffocating emptiness of vacuum—

—a dark landscape, mind you, one imprisoned by lunar night, and illuminated only by the gibbous Earth hanging high above us—

—a rectangle of color and light, in the form of four acres of freshly watered, freshly mowed lawn.

With a house on it.

Not a prefab box of the kind we dropped all over the lunar landscape for storage and emergency air stops.

A house.

A clapboard family home, painted a homey yellow, with a wrap-around porch three steps off the ground, a canopy to keep off the Sun, a screen door leading inside and a bug-zapper over the threshold. There was a porch swing with cushions in a big yellow daisy pattern, and a wall of neatly-trimmed hedges around the house, obscuring the latticework that enclosed the crawlspace underneath. It was over-the-top middle American that even in that first moment I half-crazily expected the scent of lemonade to cross the vacuum and enter my suit. (That didn't happen, but lemonade was waiting.) The lawn was completely surrounded with a white picket fence with an open gate; there was even an old-fashioned mailbox at the gate, with its flag up. All of it was lit, from nowhere, like a bright summer afternoon. The house itself had two stories, plus a sloping shingled roof high enough to hide a respectable attic; as we drew closer I saw that there were pull-down shades, not venetian blinds, in the pane-glass windows. Closer still, and I spotted the golden retriever that lay on the porch, its head resting between muddy paws as it followed our approach; it was definitely a lazy dog, since it did not get up to investigate us, but it was also a friendly one, whose big red tail thumped against the porch in greeting. Closer still, and I made various consonant noises as a venerable old lady in gardening overalls came around the side of the house, spotted us, and broke into the kind of smile native only to contented old ladies seeing good friends or grandchildren after too long away. When my fellow astronauts all waved back, I almost followed their lead, but for some reason my arms wouldn't move.

Somewhere in there I murmured, "This is impossible."

"Clearly not," George said. "If it were impossible it wouldn't be happening. The more accurate word is inexplicable."

"What the hell is—"

"Come on, goofball." This from Carrie Aldrin No Relation. "You're acting like you never saw a house before."

Sometimes, knowing when to keep your mouth shut is the most eloquent expression of wisdom. I shut up.

It took about a million and a half years—or five minutes if you go by merely chronological time—for the tractor to descend the shallow slope and bring us to a stop some twenty meters from the front gate. By then an old man had joined the old woman at the fence. He was a lean old codger with bright blue eyes, a nose like a hawk, a smile that suggested he'd just heard a whopper of a joke, and the kind of forehead some very old men have—the kind that by all rights ought to have been glistening with sweat, like most bald heads, but instead seemed perpetually dry, in a way that suggested a sophisticated system for the redistribution of excess moisture. He had the leathery look of old men who had spent much of their lives working in the Sun. He wore neatly-pressed tan pants, sandals, and a white button-down shirt open at the collar, all of which was slightly loose on him—not enough to make him look comical or pathetic, but enough to suggest that he'd been a somewhat bigger man before age had diminished him, and was still used to buying the larger sizes. (That is, I thought, if there was any possibility of him finding a good place to shop around here.)

His wife, if that's who she was, was half a head shorter and slightly stouter; she had blue eyes and a bright smile, like him, but a soft and rounded face that provided a pleasant complement to his lean and angular one. She was a just overweight enough to provide her with the homey accoutrements of chubby cheeks and double chin; unlike her weathered, bone-dry husband, she was smooth-skinned and shiny-faced and very much a creature the Sun had left untouched (though she evidently spent time there; at least, she wore gardener's gloves, and carried a spade).

They were, in short, vaguely reminiscent of the old folks standing before the farmhouse in that famous old painting "American Gothic." You know the one I mean—the constipated old guy with the pitchfork next to the wife who seems mortified by his very presence? These two were those two after they cheered up enough to be worth meeting.

Except, of course, that this couldn't possibly be happening.

My colleagues unstrapped themselves, lowered the stairway, and disembarked. The tractor driver, whoever he was, emerged from its cab and joined them. George stayed with me, watching my every move, as I proved capable of climbing down a set of three steps without demonstrating my total incapacitation from shock. When my boots crunched lunar gravel—a texture I could feel right through the treads of my boots, and which served at that moment to re-connect me to ordinary physical reality—Carrie, Oscar, and Nikki patted me on the back, a gesture that felt like half-congratulation and, half-commiseration. The driver came by, too; I saw from the markings on his suit that he was Pete Rawlik, who was assigned to some kind of classified biochemical research in one of our outlabs; he had always been too busy to mix much, and I'd met him maybe twice by that point, but he still clapped my shoulder like an old friend. As for George, he made a wait gesture and went back up the steps.

In the thirty seconds we stood there waiting for him, I looked up at the picket fence, just to confirm that the impossible old couple was still there, and I saw that the golden retriever, which had joined its masters at the gate, was barking silently. That was good. If the sound had carried in vacuum, I might have been worried. That would have been just plain crazy.

Then George came back, carrying an airtight metal cylinder just about big enough to hold a soccer ball. I hadn't seen any vacuum boxes of that particular shape and size before, but any confusion I might have felt about that was just about the last thing I needed to worry about. He addressed the others: "How's he doing?"

A babble of noncommittal OKs dueled for broadcast supremacy. Then the voices resolved into individuals.

Nikki Hollander said: "Well, at least he's not babbling anymore."

Oscar Desalvo snorted: "I attribute that to brain-lock."

"You weren't any better," said Carrie Aldrin No Relation. "Worse. If I recall correctly, you made a mess in your suit."

"I'm not claiming any position of false superiority, hon. Just giving my considered diagnosis."

"Whatever," said Pete Rawlik. "Let's just cross the fenceline, already. I have an itch."

"In a second," George said. His mirrored faceplate turned toward mine, aping eye-contact. "Max? You getting this?"

"Barely," I managed.

"Outstanding. You're doing fine. But I need you with me a hundred percent while I cover our most important ground rule. Namely—everything inside that picket fence is a temperature-climate, sea-level, terrestrial environment. You don't have to worry about air filtration, temperature levels, or anything else. It's totally safe to suit down, as long as you're inside the perimeter—and in a few minutes, we will all be doing just that. But once you're inside that enclosure, the picket fence itself marks the beginning of lunar vacuum, lunar temperatures, and everything that implies. You do not, repeat not, do anything to test the differential. Even sticking a finger out between the slats is enough to get you bounced from the program, with no possibility of reprieve. Is that clear?"

"Yes, but—"

"Rule Two," he said, handing me the sealed metal box. "You're the new guy. You carry the pie."

I regarded the cylinder. Pie?

I kept waiting for the other shoe to drop, but it never did.

The instant we passed through the front gate, the dead world this should have been surrendered to a living one. Sound returned between one step and the next. The welcoming cries of the two old people—and the barking of their friendly golden retriever dog—may have been muffled by my helmet, but they were still identifiable enough to present touches of personality. The old man's voice was gruff in a manner that implied a past flavored by whiskey and cigars, but there was also a sing-song quality to it, that instantly manifested itself as a tendency to end his sentences at higher registers. The old woman's voice was soft and breathy, with only the vaguest suggestion of an old-age quaver and a compensatory tinge of the purest Georgia Peach. The dog's barks were like little frenzied explosions, that might have been threatening if they hadn't all trailed off into quizzical whines. It was a symphony of various sounds that could be made for hello: laughs, cries, yips, and delighted shouts of *George! Oscar! Nikki! Carrie! Pete! So glad you could make it! How are you?*

It was enough to return me to statue mode. I didn't even move when the others disengaged their helmet locks, doffed their headgear, and began oohing and aahing themselves. I just spent the next couple of minutes watching, physically in their midst but mentally somewhere very far away, as the parade of impossibilities passed on by. I noted that Carrie Aldrin No Relation, who usually wore her long red hair beneath the tightest of protective nets, was today styled in pigtails with big pink bows; that Oscar, who was habitually scraggly-haired and two days into a beard, was today perfectly kempt and freshly shaven; that George giggled like a five-year-old when the dog stood up on its hind legs to slobber all over his face; and that Pete engaged with a little mock wrestling match with the old man that almost left him toppling backward onto the grass. I saw the women whisper to each other, then bound up the porch steps into the house, so excitedly that they reminded me of schoolgirls skipping off to the playground—a gait that should have been impossible to simulate in a bulky moonsuit, but which they pulled off with perfect flair. I saw Pete and Oscar follow along behind them, laughing at a shared joke.

I was totally ignored until the dog stood up on its hind legs to sniff at, then snort nasal condensation on, my faceplate. His ears went back. He whined, then scratched at his reflection, then looked over his shoulder at the rest of his pack, long pink tongue lolling plaintively. *Look, guys. There's somebody in this thing.*

I didn't know I was going to take the leap of faith until I actually placed the cake cylinder on the ground, then reached up and undid my helmet locks. The hiss of escaping air made my blood freeze in my chest; for a second I was absolutely certain that all of this was a hallucination brought on by oxygen deprivation, and that I'd just committed suicide by opening my suit to vacuum. But the hiss subsided, and I realized that it was just pressure equalization; the atmosphere in this environment must have been slightly less than that provided by the suit. A second later, as I removed my helmet, I tasted golden retriever breath as the dog leaned in close and said hello by licking me on the lips. I also smelled freshly mowed grass and the perfume of nearby flowers; I heard a bird not too far away go whoot-toot-toot-weet; and I felt direct sunlight on my face, even though the Sun itself was nowhere to be seen. The air itself was pleasantly warm, like summer before it gets obnoxious with heat and humidity.

"Miles!" the old man said. "Get down!"

The dog gave me one last lick for the road and sat down, gazing up at me with that species of tongue-lolling amusement known only to large canines.

The old woman clutched the elbow of George's suit. "Oh, you didn't tell me you were bringing somebody new this time! How wonderful!"

"What is this place?" I managed.

The old man raised his eyebrows. "It's our front yard, son. What does it look like?"

The old woman slapped his hand lightly. "Be nice, dear. You can see he's taking it hard."

He grunted. "Always did beat me how you can tell what a guy's thinking and feeling just by looking at him."

She patted his arm again. "It's not all that unusual, apricot. I'm a woman."

George ambled on over, pulling the two oldsters along. "All right, I'll get it started. Max Fischer, I want you to meet two of the best people on this world or any other—Minnie and Earl. Minnie and Earl, I want you to meet a guy who's not quite as hopeless as he probably seems on first impression—Max Fischer. You'll like him."

"I like him already," Minnie said. "I've yet to dislike anybody the dog took such an immediate shine to. Hi, Max."

"Hello," I said. After a moment: "Minnie. Earl."

"Wonderful to meet you, young man. Your friends have said so much about you."

"Thanks." Shock lent honesty to my response: "They've said absolutely nothing about you."

"They never do," she said, with infinite sadness, as George smirked at me over her back. She glanced down at the metal cylinder at my feet, and cooed: "Is that cake?"

Suddenly, absurdly, the first rule of family visits popped unbidden into my head, blaring its commandment in flaming letters twenty miles high: THOU SHALT NOT PUT THE CAKE YOU BROUGHT ON THE GROUND—ESPECIALLY NOT WHEN A DOG IS PRESENT. Never mind that the container was sealed against vacuum, and that the dog would have needed twenty minutes to get in with an industrial drill: the lessons of everyday American socialization still applied. I picked it up and handed it to her; she took it with her bare hands, reacting not at all to what hindsight later informed me should have been a painfully cold exterior. I said: "Sorry."

"It's pie," said George. "Deep-dish apple pie. Direct from my grandma's orchard."

"Oh, that's sweet of her. She still having those back problems?"

"She's getting on in years," George allowed. "But she says that soup of yours really helped."

"I'm glad," she said, her smile as sunny as the entire month of July. "Meanwhile, why don't you take your friend upstairs and get him out of that horrid suit? I'm sure he'll feel a lot better once he's had a chance to freshen up. Earl can have a drink set for him by the time you come down."

"I'll fix a Sea of Tranquility," Earl said, with enthusiasm.

"Maybe once he has his feet under him. A beer should be fine for now."

"All rightee," said Earl, with the kind of wink that established he knew quite well I was going to need something a lot more substantial than beer.

As for Minnie, she seized my hand, and said: "It'll be all right, apricot. Once you get past this stage, I'm sure we're all going to be great friends."

"Um," I replied, with perfect eloquence, wondering just what stage I was being expected to pass.

Sanity?

■

Dying inside, I did what seemed to be appropriate. I followed George through the front door (first stamping my moonboots on the mat, as he specified) and up the narrow, creaky wooden staircase.

You ever go to parties where the guests leave their coats in a heap on the bed of the master bedroom? Minnie and Earl's was like that. Except it wasn't a pile of coats, but a pile of disassembled moonsuits. There were actually two bedrooms upstairs—the women changed in the master bedroom that evidently belonged to the oldsters themselves, the men in a smaller room that felt like it belonged to a teenage boy. The wallpaper was a pattern of galloping horses, and the bookcases were filled with mint-edition paperback thrillers that must have been a hundred years old even then. (Or more: there was a complete collection of the hardcover Hardy Boys Mysteries, by Franklin W. Dixon.) The desk was a genuine antique rolltop, with a green blotter; no computer or hytex. The bed was just big enough to hold one gangly teenager, or three moonsuits disassembled into their component parts, with a special towel provided so our boots wouldn't get moondust all over the bedspread. By the time George and I got up there, Oscar and Pete had already changed into slacks, dress shoes with black socks, and button-down shirts with red bowties; Pete had even put some shiny gunk in his hair to slick it back. They winked at me as they left.

I didn't change, not immediately; nor did I speak, not even as George doffed his own moonsuit and jumpers in favor of a similarly earthbound outfit he blithely salvaged from the closet. The conviction that I was being tested, somehow, was so overwhelming that the interior of my suit must have been a puddle of flop sweat.

Then George said: "You going to be comfortable, dressed like that all night?"

I stirred. "Clothes?"

He pulled an outfit my size from the closet—tan pants, a blue short-sleeved button-down shirt, gleaming black shoes, and a red bowtie identical to the ones Oscar and Pete had donned. "No problem borrowing. Minnie keeps an ample supply. You don't like the selection, you want to pick something more your style, you can always have something snazzier sent up on the next supply drop. I promise you, she'll appreciate the extra effort. It makes her day when—"

"George," I said softly.

"Have trouble with bowties? No problem. They're optional. You can—"

"George," I said again, and this time my voice was a little louder, a little deeper, a little more *For Christ's Sake Shut Up I'm Sick Of This Shit*.

He batted his eyes, all innocence and naivete. "Yes, Max?"

My look, by contrast, must have been half-murderous. "Tell me."

"Tell you what?"

It was very hard not to yell. "You know what!"

He fingered an old issue of some garishly-colored turn-of-the-millennium science fiction magazine. "Oh. That mixed drink Earl mentioned. The Sea of Tranquility. It's his own invention, and he calls it that because your first sip is one small step for Man, and your second is one giant leap for Mankind. There's peppermint in it. Give it a try and I promise you you'll be on his good side for life. He—"

I squeezed the words through clenched teeth. "I. Don't. Care. About. The. Bloody. Drink."

"Then I'm afraid I don't see your problem."

"My problem," I said, slowly, and with carefully repressed frustration, "is that all of this is downright impossible."

"Apparently not," he noted.

"I want to know who these people are, and what they're doing here."

"They're Minnie and Earl, and they're having some friends over for dinner."

If I'd been five years old, I might have pouted and stamped my foot. (Sometimes, remembering, I think I did anyway.) "Dammit, George!"

He remained supernaturally calm. "No cursing in this house, Max. Minnie doesn't like it. She won't throw you out for doing it—she's too nice for that—but it does make her uncomfortable."

This is the point where I absolutely know I stamped my foot. "That makes *her* uncomfortable!?"

He put down the skiffy magazine. "Really. I don't see why you're having such a problem with this. They're just this great old couple who happen to live in a little country house on the Moon, and their favorite thing is getting together with friends, and we're here to have Sunday night dinner with them. Easy to understand . . . especially if you accept that it's all there is."

"That can't be all there is!" I cried, my exasperation reaching critical mass.

"Why not? Can't 'Just Because' qualify as a proper scientific theory?"

"No! It doesn't!—How come you never told me about this place before?"

"You never asked before." He adjusted his tie, glanced at the outfit laid out for me on the bed, and went to the door. "Don't worry; it didn't for me, either. Something close to an explanation is forthcoming. Just get dressed and come downstairs already. We don't want the folks to think you're antisocial . . ."

■

I'd been exasperated, way back then, because Minnie and Earl were there and had no right to be. I was exasperated now because the more I looked the more impossible it became to find any indication that they'd ever been there at all.

I had started looking for them, if only in a desultory, abstracted way, shortly after Claire died. She'd been the only person on Earth who had ever believed my stories about them. Even now, I think it's a small miracle that she did. I had told her the story of Minnie and Earl before we even became man and wife—sometime after I knew I was going to propose, but before I found the right time and place for the question. I was just back from a couple of years of Outer-System work, had grown weary of the life, and had met this spectacularly kind and funny and beautiful person whose interests were all on Earth, and who had no real desire to go out into space herself. That was just fine with me. It was what I wanted too. And of course I rarely talked to her about my years in space, because I didn't want to become an old bore with a suitcase full of old stories. Even so, I still knew, at the beginning, that knowing about a real-life miracle and not mentioning it to her, ever, just because she was not likely to believe me, was tantamount to cheating. So I sat her down one day, even before the proposal, and told her about Minnie and Earl. And she believed me. She didn't humor me. She didn't just say she believed me. She didn't just believe me to be nice. She believed me. She said she always knew when I was shoveling manure and when I was not—a boast that turned out to be an integral strength of our marriage—and that it was impossible for her to hear me tell the story without knowing that Minnie and Earl were real. She said that if we had children I would have to tell the story to them, too, to pass it on.

That was one of the special things about Claire: she had faith when faith was needed.

But our son and our daughter, and later the grandkids, outgrew believing me. For them, Minnie and Earl were whimsical space-age versions of Santa.

I didn't mind that, not really.

But when she died, finding Minnie and Earl again seemed very important.

It wasn't just that their house was gone, or that Minnie and Earl seemed to have departed for regions unknown; and it wasn't just that the official histories of the early development teams now completely omitted any mention of the secret hoarded by everybody who had ever spent time on the Moon in those days. It wasn't just that the classified files I had read and eventually contributed to had disappeared, flushed down the same hole that sends all embarrassing government secrets down the pipe to their final resting place in the sea. But for more years than I'd ever wanted to count, Minnie and Earl had been the secret history nobody ever talked about. I had spoken to those of my old colleagues who still remained alive, and they had all said, what are you talking about, what do you mean, are you feeling all right, nothing like that ever happened.

It was tempting to believe that my kids were right: that it had been a fairy tale: a little harmless personal fantasy I'd been carrying around with me for most of my life.

But I knew it wasn't.

Because Claire had believed me.

Because whenever I did drag out the old stories one more time, she always said, "I wish I'd known them." Not like an indulgent wife allowing the old man his delusions, but like a woman well acquainted with miracles. And because even if I was getting too old to always trust my own judgement, nothing would ever make me doubt hers.

I searched with phone calls, with letters, with hytex research, with the calling-in of old favors, with every tool available to me. I found nothing.

And then one day I was told that I didn't have much more time to look. It wasn't a tragedy; I'd lived a long and happy life. And it wasn't as bad as it could have been; I'd been assured that there wouldn't be much pain. But I did have that one little unresolved question still hanging over my head.

That was the day I overcame decades of resistance and booked return passage to the world I had once helped to build.

The day after I spoke to Janine Seuss, I followed her advice and took a commuter tram to the Michael Collins Museum of Early Lunar Settlement. It was a popular tourist spot with all the tableaus and reenactments and, you should only excuse the expression, cheesy souvenirs you'd expect from such an establishment; I'd avoided it up until now mostly because I'd seen and heard most of it before, and much of what was left was the kind of crowd-pleasing foofaraw that tames and diminishes the actual experience I lived through for the consumption of folks who are primarily interested in tiring out their hyperactive kids. The dumbest of those was a pile of real Earth rocks, replacing the weight various early astronauts had taken from the Moon; ha ha ha, stop, I'm dying here. The most offensive was a kids' exhibit narrated by a cartoon-character early development engineer; he spoke with a cornball rural accent, had comic-opera patches on the knees of his moonsuit, and seemed to have an I.Q. of about five.

Another annoying thing about frontiers: when they're not frontiers anymore, the civilizations that move in like to think that the people who came first were stupid.

But when I found pictures of myself, in an exhibit on the development programs, and pointed them out to an attendant, it was fairly easy to talk the curators into letting me into their archives for a look at certain other materials that hadn't seen the light of day for almost twenty years. They were taped interviews, thirty years old now, with a number of the old guys and gals, talking about their experiences in the days of early development: the majority of those had been conducted here on the Moon, but others had taken place on Earth or Mars or wherever else any of those old farts ended up. I felt vaguely insulted that they hadn't tried to contact me; maybe they had, and my wife, anticipating my reluctance, had turned them away. I wondered if I should have felt annoyed by that. I wondered too if my annoyance at the taming of the Moon had something to do with the disquieting sensation of becoming ancient history while you're still alive to remember it.

There were about ten thousand hours of interviews; even if my health remained stable long enough for me to listen to them all, my savings would run out far sooner. But they were indexed, and audio-search is a wonderful thing. I typed in "Minnie" and got several dozen references to small things, almost as many references to Mickey's rodent girlfriend, and a bunch of stories about a project engineer, from after my time, who had also been blessed with that particular first name. (To believe the transcripts, she spent all her waking hours saying impossibly cute things that her friends and colleagues would remember and be compelled to repeat decades later; what a bloody pixie.) I typed in "Earl" and, though it felt silly, "Miles", and got a similar collection of irrelevancies—many references to miles, thus proving conclusively that as recently as thirty years ago the adoption of the metric system hadn't yet succeeded in wiping out any less elegant but still fondly remembered forms of measurement. After that, temporarily stuck, I typed in my own name, first and last, and was rewarded with a fine selection of embarrassing anecdotes from folks who recalled what a humorless little pissant I had been way back then. All of this took hours; I had to listen to each of these references, if only for a second or two, just to know for sure what was being talked about, and I confess that, in between a number of bathroom breaks I would have considered unlikely as a younger man, I more than once forgot what I was supposedly looking for long enough to enjoy a few moments with old voices I hadn't heard for longer than most lunar residents had been alive.

I then cross-referenced by the names of the various people who were along on that first Sunday night trip to Minnie and Earl's. "George Peterson" got me nothing of obvious value. "Carrie Aldrin" and "Peter Rawlik", ditto. Nor did the other names. There were references, but nothing I particularly needed.

Feeling tired, I sat there drumming my fingertips on the tabletop. The museum was closing soon. The research had exhausted my limited stores of strength; I didn't think I could do this many days in a row. But I knew there was something here. There had to be. Even if there was a conspiracy of silence—organized or accidental—the mere existence of that unassuming little house had left too great a footprint on our lives.

I thought about details that Claire had found particularly affecting.
And then I typed "Yams".

■

Seventy years ago, suffering from a truly epic sense of dislocation that made everything happening to me seem like bits of stage business performed by actors in a play whose author had taken care to omit all the important exposition, I descended a creaky flight of wooden stairs, to join my colleagues in Minnie and Earl's living room. I was the last to come down, of course; everybody else was already gathered around the three flowery-print sofas, munching on finger foods as they chatted up a storm. The women were in soft cottony dresses, the men in starched trousers and button-downs. They all clapped and cheered as I made my appearance, a reaction that brought an unwelcome blush to my cheeks. It was no wonder; I was a little withdrawn to begin with, back then, and the impossible context had me so off-center that all my defenses had turned to powder.

It was a homey place, though: brightly lit, with a burning fireplace, an array of glass shelving covered with a selection of homemade pottery, plants and flowers in every available nook, an upright piano, a bar that did not dominate the room, and an array of framed photographs on the wall behind the couch. There was no TV or hytex. I glanced at the photographs and moved toward them, hungry for data.

Then Earl rose from his easy chair and came around the coffee table, with a gruff, "Plenty of time to look around, son. Let me take care of you."

"That's—" I said. I was still not managing complete sentences, most of the time.

He took me by the arm, brought me over to the bar, and sat me down on a stool. "Like I said, plenty of time. You're like most first-timers, you're probably in dire need of a drink. We can take care of that first and then get acquainted." He moved around the bar, slung a towel over his shoulder, and said: "What'll it be, pilgrim?"

Thank God I recognized the reference. If I hadn't—if it had just been another inexplicable element of a day already crammed with them—my head would have exploded from the effort of figuring out why I was being called a pilgrim. "A . . . Sea of Tranquility?"

"Man after my own heart," Earl said, flashing a grin as he compiled an impressive array of ingredients in a blender. "Always drink the local drink, son. As my daddy put it, there's no point in going anywhere if you just get drunk the same way you can at home. Which is where, by the way?"

I said, "What?"

"You missed the segue. I was asking you where you were from."

It seemed a perfect opportunity. "You first."

He chuckled. "Oh, the wife and I been here long enough, you

might as well say we're from here. Great place to retire, isn't it? The old big blue marble hanging up there all day and all night?"

"I suppose," I said.

"You suppose," he said, raising an eyebrow at the concoction taking shape in his blender. "That's awful noncommittal of you. Can't you even admit to liking the view?"

"I admit to it," I said.

"But you're not enthused. You know, there's an old joke about a fella from New York and a fella from New Jersey. And the fella from New York is always bragging on his town, talking about Broadway, and the Empire State Building, and Central Park, and so on, and just as often saying terrible things about how ugly things are on the Jersey side of the river. And the fella from Jersey finally gets fed up, and says, all right, I've had enough of this, I want you to say one thing, just one thing, about New Jersey that's better than anything you can say about Manhattan. And the fella from New York says, No problem. The view."

I didn't laugh, but I did smile.

"That's what's so great about this place," he concluded. "The view. Moon's pretty nice to look at for folks on Earth—and a godsend for bad poets, too, what with june-moon-spoon and all—but as views go, it can't hold a candle to the one we have, looking back. So don't give me any supposes. Own up to what you think."

"It's a great view," I said, this time with conviction, as he handed me my drink. Then I asked the big question another way: "How did you arrange it?"

"You ought to know better than that, son. We didn't arrange it. We just took advantage of it. Nothing like a scenic overlook to give zip to your real estate— So answer me. Where are you from?"

Acutely aware that more than a minute had passed since I'd asked him the same question, and that no answer seemed to be forthcoming, I was also too trapped by simple courtesy to press the issue. "San Francisco."

He whistled. "I've seen pictures of San Francisco. Looks like a beautiful town."

"It is," I said.

"You actually climb those hills in Earth gravity?"

"I used to run up Leavenworth every morning at dawn."

"Leavenworth's the big steep one that heads down to the bay?"

"One of them," I said.

"And you ran up that hill? At dawn? Every day?"

"Yup."

"You have a really obsessive personality, don't you, son?"

I shrugged. "About some things, I suppose."

"Only about some things?"

"That's what being obsessive means, right?"

"Ah, well. Nothing wrong about being obsessive, as long as you're not a fanatic about it. Want me to freshen up that drink?"

I felt absolutely no alcoholic effect at all. "Maybe you better."

I tried to turn the conversation back to where he was from, but somehow I didn't get a chance, because that's when Minnie took me by the hand and dragged me over to the wall of family photos. There were pictures of them smiling on the couch, pictures of them lounging together in the backyard, pictures of them standing proudly before their home. There were a large number of photos that used Earth as a backdrop. Only four photos showed them with other people, all from the last century: in one, they sat at their dining table with a surprised-looking Neil Armstrong and Buzz Aldrin; in another, they sat on their porch swing chatting with Carl Sagan; in a third, Minnie was being enthusiastically hugged by Isaac Asimov; the fourth showed Earl playing the upright piano while Minnie sat beside him and a tall, thin blonde man with androgynous features and two differently-colored eyes serenaded them both. The last figure was the only one I didn't recognize immediately; by the time somebody finally clued me in, several visits later, I would be far too jaded to engage in the spit-take it would have merited any other time.

I wanted to ask Minnie about the photos with the people I recognized, but then Peter and Earl dragged me downstairs to take a look at Earl's model train set, a rural landscape incorporating four lines and six separate small towns. It was a remarkably detailed piece of work, but I was most impressed with the small miracle of engineering that induced four heavy chains to pull it out of the way whenever Earl pulled a small cord. This handily revealed the pool table. Earl whipped Peter two games out of three, then challenged me; I'm fairly good at pool, but I was understandably off my game that afternoon, and missed every single shot. When Carrie Aldrin No Relation came down to challenge Earl, he mimed terror. It was a genial hour, totally devoted to content-free conversation—and any attempt I made to bring up the questions that burned in my breast was terminated without apparent malice.

Back upstairs. The dog nosing at my hand. Minnie noting that he liked me. Minnie not saying anything about the son whose room we'd changed in, the one who'd died "in the war". A very real heart-break about the way her eyes grew distant at that moment. I asked which war, and she smiled sadly: "There's only been one war, dear—and it doesn't really matter what you call it." Nikki patting her hand. Oscar telling a mildly funny anecdote from his childhood, Minnie asking him to tell her the one about the next-door neighbors again. I brought up the photo of Minnie and Earl with Neil Armstrong and Buzz Aldrin, and Minnie clucked that they had been such nice boys.

Paranoia hit. "Ever hear of Ray Bradbury?"

She smiled with real affection. "Oh, yes. We only met him once or twice, but he was genuinely sweet. I miss him."

"So you met him, too."

"We've met a lot of people, apricot. Why? Is he a relation?"

"Just an old-time writer I like," I said.

"Ahhhhhh."

"In fact," I said, "one story of his I particularly like was called 'Mars Is Heaven'."

She sipped her tea. "Don't know that one."

"It's about a manned expedition to Mars—written while that was still in the future, you understand. And when the astronauts get there they discover a charming, rustic, old-fashioned American small town, filled with sweet old folks they remember from their childhoods. It's the last thing they expect, but after a while they grow comfortable with it. They even jump to the conclusion that Mars is the site of the afterlife. Except it's not. The sweet old folks are aliens in disguise, and they're lulling all these gullible earthlings into a false sense of security so they can be killed at leisure."

My words had been hesitantly spoken, less out of concern for Minnie's feelings than those of my colleagues. Their faces were blank, unreadable, masking emotions that could have been anything from anger to amusement. I will admit that for a split second there, my paranoia reaching heights it had never known before (or thank God, since), I half-expected George and Oscar and Maxine to morph into the hideously tentacled bug-eyed monsters who had taken their places immediately after eating their brains. Then the moment passed, and the silence continued to hang heavily in the room, and any gen-uine apprehension I might have felt gave way to an embarrassment of more mundane proportions. After all—whatever the explanation for all this might have been—I'd just been unforgivably rude to a person who had only been gracious and charming toward me.

She showed no anger, no sign that she took it personally. "I remember that one now, honey. I'm afraid I didn't like it as much as some of Ray's other efforts. Among other things, it seemed pretty unreasonable to me that critters advanced enough to pull off that kind of masquerade would have nothing better to do with their lives than eat nice folks who came calling. But then, he also wrote a story about a baby that starts killing as soon as it leaves the womb, and I prefer to believe that infants, given sufficient understanding and affection, soon learn that the universe outside the womb isn't that dark and cold a place after all. Given half a chance, they might even grow up . . . and it's a wonderful process to watch."

I had nothing to say to that.

She sipped her tea again, one pinky finger extended in the most unselfconscious manner imaginable, just as if she couldn't fathom drinking her tea any other way, then spoke brightly, with perfect timing: "But if you stay the night, I'll be sure to put you in the room with all the pods."

There was a moment of silence, with every face in the room—including those of Earl and Peter and Carrie, who had just come up from downstairs—as distinguishedly impassive as a granite bust of some forefather you had never heard of.

Then I averted my eyes, trying to hide the smile as it began to spread on my face.

Then somebody made a helpless noise, and we all exploded with laughter.

Seventy years later:

If every land ever settled by human beings has its garden spots, then every land ever settled by human beings has its hovels. This is true even of frontiers that have become theme parks. I had spent much of this return to the world I had once known wandering through a brightly-lit, comfortably-upholstered tourist paradise—the kind of ersatz environment common to all overdeveloped places, that is less an expression of local character than a determined struggle to ensure the total eradication of anything resembling local character. But now I was headed toward a place that would never be printed on a postcard, that would never be on the tours, that existed on tourist maps only as the first, best sign that those looking for easy travelling have just made a disastrous wrong turn.

It was on Farside, of course. Most tourist destinations, and higher-end habitats, are on Nearside, which comes equipped with a nice blue planet to look at. Granted that even on Nearside the view is considered a thing for tourists, and that most folks who live here live underground and like to brag to each other about how long they've gone without Earthgazing—our ancestral ties are still part of us, and the mere presence of Earth, seen or unseen, is so inherently comforting that most normal people with a choice pick Nearside. Farside, by comparison, caters almost exclusively to hazardous industries and folks who don't want that nice blue planet messing up the stark emptiness of their sky—a select group of people that includes a small number of astronomers at the Frank Drake Observatory, and a large number of assorted perverts and geeks and misanthropes. The wild frontier of the fantasies comes closest to being a reality here— the hemisphere has some heavy-industry settlements that advertise their crime rates as a matter of civic pride.

And then there are the haunts of those who find even those places too civilized for their tastes. The mountains and craters of Farside are dotted with the little boxy single-person habitats of folks who have turned their back not only on the home planet but also the rest of humanity as well. Some of those huddle inside their self-imposed solitary confinement for weeks or months on end, emerging only to retrieve their supply drops or enforce the warning their radios transmit on infinite loop: that they don't want visitors and that all trespassers should expect to be shot. They're all eccentric, but some are crazy and a significant percentage of them are clinically insane. They're not the kind of folks the sane visit just for local color.

I landed my rented skimmer on a ridge overlooking an oblong metal box with a roof marked by a glowing ten-digit registration number. It was night here, and nobody who lived in such a glorified house trailer would have been considerate enough to provide any outside lighting for visitors, so those lit digits provided the only ground-level rebuttal to starfield up above; it was an inadequate rebuttal at best, which left the ground on all sides an ocean of undifferentiated inky blackness. I could carry my own lamp, of course, but I didn't want to negotiate the walk from my skimmer to the habitat's front door if the reception I met there required a hasty retreat; I wasn't very capable of hasty retreats, these days.

So I just sat in my skimmer and transmitted the repeating loop: *Walter Stearns. I desperately need to speak to Walter Stearns. Walter Stearns. I desperately need to speak to Walter Stearns. Walter Stearns. I desperately need to speak to Walter Stearns. Walter Stearns. I desperately need to speak to Walter Stearns.* It was the emergency frequency that all of these live-alones are required to keep open 24–7, but there was no guarantee Stearns was listening—and since I was not in distress, I was not really legally entitled to use it. But I didn't care; Stearns was the best lead I had yet.

It was only two hours before a voice like a mouth full of steel wool finally responded: "Go away."

"I won't be long, Mr. Stearns. We need to talk."

"You need to talk. I need you to go away."

"It's about Minnie and Earl, Mr. Stearns."

There was a pause. "Who?"

The pause had seemed a hair too long to mean mere puzzlement. "Minnie and Earl. From the development days. You remember them, don't you?"

"I never knew any Minnie and Earl," he said. "Go away."

"I listened to the tapes you made for the Museum, Mr. Stearns."

The anger in his hoarse, dusty old voice was still building. "I made those tapes when I was still talking to people. And there's nothing in them about any Minnie or Earl."

"No," I said, "there's not. Nobody mentioned Minnie and Earl by name, not you, and not anybody else who participated. But you still remember them. It took me several days to track you down, Mr. Stearns. We weren't here at the same time, but we still had Minnie and Earl in common."

"I have nothing to say to you," he said, with a new shrillness in his voice. "I'm an old man. I don't want to be bothered. Go away."

My cheeks ached from the size of my triumphant grin. "I brought yams."

There was nothing on the other end but the sibilant hiss of background radiation. It lasted just long enough to persuade me that my trump card had been nothing of the kind; he had shut down or smashed his receiver, or simply turned his back to it, so he could sit there in his little cage waiting for the big bad outsider to get tired and leave.

Then he said: "Yams."

Twenty-four percent of the people who contributed to the Museum's oral history had mentioned yams at least once. They had talked about the processing of basic food shipments from home, and slipped yams into their lists of the kind of items received; they had conversely cited yams as the kind of food that the folks back home had never once thought of sending; they had related anecdotes about funny things this coworker or that coworker had said at dinner, over a nice steaming plate of yams. They had mentioned yams and they had moved on, behaving as if it was just another background detail mentioned only to provide their colorful reminiscences the right degree of persuasive verisimilitude. Anybody not from those days who noticed the strange recurring theme might have imagined it a statistical oddity or an in-joke of some kind. For anybody who had been to Minnie and Earl's—and tasted the delicately seasoned yams she served so frequently—it was something more: a strange form of confirmation.

When Stearns spoke again, his voice still rasped of disuse, but it also possessed a light quality that hadn't been there before. "They've been gone a long time. I'm not sure I know what to tell you."

"I checked your records," I said. "You've been on the Moon continuously since those days; you went straight from the development teams to the early settlements to the colonies that followed. You've probably been here nonstop longer than anybody else living or dead. If anybody can give me an idea what happened to them, it's you."

More silence.

"Please," I said.

And then he muttered a cuss word that had passed out of the vernacular forty years earlier. "All right, damn you. But you won't find them. I don't think anybody will ever find them."

■

Seventy years earlier:

We were there for about two more hours before George took me aside, said he needed to speak to me in private, and directed me to wait for him in the backyard.

The backyard was nice.

I've always hated that word. *Nice.* It means nothing. Describing people, it can mean the most distant politeness, or the most compassionate warmth; it can mean civility and it can mean charity and it can mean grace and it can mean friendship. Those things may be similar, but they're not synonyms; when the same word is used to describe all of them, then that word means nothing. It means even less when describing places. So what if the backyard was nice? Was it just comfortable, and well-tended, or was it a place that reinvigorated you with every breath? How can you leave it at "nice" and possibly imagine that you've done the job?

Nice. Feh.

But that's exactly what this backyard was.

It was a couple of acres of trimmed green lawn, bordered by the white picket fence that signalled the beginning of vacuum. A quarter-circle of bright red roses marked each of the two rear corners; between them, bees hovered lazily over a semicircular garden heavy on towering orchids and sunflowers. The painted white rocks which bordered that garden were arranged in a perfect line, none of them even a millimeter out of place, none of them irregular enough to shame the conformity that characterized the relationship between all the others. There was a single apple tree, which hugged the rear of the house so tightly that the occupants of the second floor might have been able to reach out their windows and grab their breakfast before they trudged off to the shower; there were enough fallen green apples to look picturesque, but not enough to look sloppy. There was a bench of multicolored polished stone at the base of the porch steps, duplicating the porch swing up above but somehow absolutely right in its position; and as I sat on that bench facing the nice backyard I breathed deep and I smelled things that I had almost forgotten I could smell—not just the distant charcoal reek of neighbors burning hamburgers in their own backyards, but lilacs, freshly cut grass, horse scent, and a cleansing whiff of rain. I sat there and I spotted squirrels, hummingbirds, monarch butterflies, and a belled calico cat that ran by, stopped, saw me, looked terribly confused in the way cats have, and then went on. I sat there and I breathed and after months of inhaling foot odor and antiseptics I found myself getting a buzz. It was intoxicating. It was invigorating. It was a shot of pure energy. It was joy. God help me, it was nice.

But it was also surrounded on all sides by a pitiless vacuum that, if real physics meant anything, should have claimed it in an instant. Perhaps it shouldn't have bothered me that much, by then; but it did.

The screen door slammed. Miles the dog bounded down the porch steps and, panting furiously, nudged my folded hands. I scratched him under the ears. He gave me the usual unconditional adoration of the golden retriever—I petted him, therefore I was God. Most panting dogs look like they're smiling (it's a major reason humans react so strongly to the species), but Miles, the canine slave to context, looked like he was enjoying the grand joke that everybody was playing at my expense. Maybe he was. Maybe he wasn't even really a dog . . .

The screen door opened and slammed. This time it was George, carrying a couple of tall glasses filled with pink stuff and ice. He handed me one of the glasses; it was lemonade, of course. He sipped from the other one and said: "Minnie's cooking yams again. She's a miracle worker when it comes to yams. She does something with them, I don't know, but it's really—"

"You," I said wryly, "are enjoying this way too much."

"Aren't you?" he asked.

Miles the dog stared at the lemonade as if it was the most wondrous sight in the Universe. George dipped a finger into his drink and held it out so the mutt could have a taste. Miles adored him now. I was so off-center I almost felt betrayed. "Yeah. I guess I am. I like them."

"Pretty hard not to like them. They're nice people."

"But the situation is so insane—"

"Sanity," George said, "is a fluid concept. Think about how nuts Relativity sounded, the first time somebody explained it to you. Hell, think back to when you were a kid, and somebody first explained the mechanics of sex."

"George—"

He gave Miles another taste. "I can see you trying like mad to work this out. Compiling data, forming and rejecting theories, even concocting little experiments to test the accuracy of your senses. I know because I was once in your position, when I was brought out here for the first time, and I remember doing all the same things. But I now have a lot of experience in walking people through this, and I can probably save you a great deal of time and energy by completing your data and summarizing all of your likely theories."

I was too tired to glare at him anymore. "You can skip the data and theories and move on to the explanation. I promise you I won't mind."

"Yes, you would," he said, with absolute certainty. "Trust me, dealing with the established lines of inquiry is the only real way to get there.

"First, providing the raw data. One: This little homestead cannot be detected from Earth; our most powerful telescopes see nothing but dead moonscape here. Two: It, and the two old folks, have been here since at least Apollo; those photos of them with Armstrong and Aldrin are genuine. Three: There is nothing you can ask them that will get any kind of straight answer about who or what they are and why they're here. Four: We have no idea how they knew Asimov, Sagan, or Bradbury—but I promise you that those are not the most startling names you will hear them drop if you stick around long enough to get to know them. Five: We don't know how they maintain an earth-like environment in here. Six: About that mailbox—they do get delivery, on a daily basis, though no actual mailman has ever been detected, and none of the mail we've ever managed to sneak a peek at is the slightest bit interesting. It's all senior citizen magazines and grocery store circulars. Seven: They never seem to go shopping, but they always have an ample supply of food and other provisions. Eight (I am up to eight, right?): They haven't noticeably aged, not even the dog. Nine: They do understand every language we've sprung on them, but they give all their answers in Midwestern-American English. And ten: We have a group of folks from our project coming out here to visit just about every night of the week, on a rotating schedule that works out to just about once a week for each of us.

"So much for the raw data. The theories take longer to deal with. Let me go through all the ones you're likely to formulate." He peeled back a finger. "One: This is all just a practical joke perpetrated by your friends and colleagues in an all-out attempt to shock you out of your funk. We put it all together with spit and baling wire and some kind of elaborate special-effects trickery that's going to seem ridiculously obvious just as soon as you're done figuring it out. We went to all this effort, and spent the many billions of dollars it would have cost to get all these construction materials here, and developed entirely new technologies capable of holding in an atmosphere, and put it all together while you weren't looking, and along the way brought in a couple of convincing old folks from Central Casting, just so we could enjoy the look on your face. What a zany bunch of folks we are, huh?"

I felt myself blushing. "I'd considered that."

"And why not? It's a legitimate theory. Also a ridiculous one, but let's move on." He peeled back another finger. "Two: This is not a practical joke, but a test or psychological experiment of some kind, arranged by the brain boys back home. They put together all of this trickery, just to see how the average astronaut, isolated from home and normal societal context, reacts to situations that defy easy explanation

and cannot be foreseen by even the most exhaustively-planned training. This particular explanation works especially well if you also factor in what we cleverly call the McGoohan Corollary—that is, the
idea that we're not really on the Moon at all, but somewhere on
Earth, possibly underground, where the real practical difficulty would
lie in simulating not a quaint rural setting on a warm summer day, but
instead the low-g, high-radiation, temperature-extreme vacuum that
you gullibly believed you were walking around in, every single time
you suited up. This theory is, of course, equally ridiculous, for many
reasons—but we did have one guy about a year ago who stubbornly
held on to it for almost a full week. Something about his psychological makeup just made it easier for him to accept that, over all the others, and we had to keep a close watch on him to stop him from trying
to prove it with a nice unsuited walk. But from the way you're looking at me right now I don't think we're going to have the same problem with you. So.

"Assuming that this is not a joke, or a trick, or an experiment, or
some lame phenomenon like that, that this situation you're experiencing is precisely what we have represented to you, then we are definitely
looking at something beyond all terrestrial experience. Which brings
us to Three." He peeled back another finger. "This is a first-contact
situation. Minnie and Earl, and possibly Miles here, are aliens in disguise, or simulations constructed by aliens. They have created a
friendly environment inside this picket fence, using technology we can
only guess at—let's say an invisible bubble capable of filtering out radiation and retaining a breathable atmosphere while remaining perme-
able to confused bipeds in big clumsy moonsuits. And they have done
so—why? To hide their true nature while they observe our progress?
Possibly. But if so, it would be a lot more subtle to place their little
farmhouse in Kansas, where it wouldn't seem so crazily out of place.
To communicate us in terms we can accept? Possibly—except that
couching those terms in such an insane context seems as counterpro-
ductive to genuine communication as their apparent decision to limit
the substance of that communication to geriatric small talk. To make
us comfortable with something familiar? Possibly—except that this
kind of small mid-American home is familiar to only a small fraction
of humanity, and it seems downright exotic to the many observers
we've shuttled in from China, or India, or Saudi Arabia, or for that
matter Manhattan. To present us with a puzzle that we have to solve?
Again, possibly—but since Minnie and Earl and Miles won't confirm

or deny, it's also a possibility we won't be able to test unless somebody like yourself actually does come up with the great big magic epiphany. I'm not holding my breath. But I do reject any theory that they're hostile, including the "Mars Is Heaven" theory you already cited. Anybody capable of pulling this off must have resources that could mash us flat in the time it takes to sneeze."

Miles woofed. In context it seemed vaguely threatening.

"Four." Another finger. "Minnie and Earl are actually human, and Miles is actually canine. They come here from the future, or from an alternate universe, or from some previously-unknown subset of humanity that's been living among us all this time, hiding great and unfathomable powers that, blaaah blaah blaah, fill in the blank. And they're here, making their presence known—why? All the same subtheories that applied to alien visitors also apply to human agencies, and all the same objections as well. Nothing explains why they would deliberately couch such a maddening enigma in such, for lack of a more appropriate word, banal terms. It's a little like coming face to face with God and discovering that He really does look like an bearded old white guy in a robe; He might, for all I know, but I'm more religious than you probably think, and there's some part of me that absolutely refuses to believe it. He, or She, if you prefer, could do better than that. And so could anybody, human or alien, whose main purpose in coming here is to study us, or test us, or put on a show for us.

"You still with me?" he inquired.

"Go on," I growled. "I'll let you know if you leave anything out."

He peeled back another finger. "Five: I kind of like this one— Minnie and Earl, and by extension Miles, are not creatures of advanced technology, but of a completely different kind of natural phenomenon—let's say, for the sake of argument, a bizarre jog in the space-time continuum that allows a friendly but otherwise unremarkable couple living in Kansas or Wyoming or someplace like that to continue experiencing life down on the farm while in some way as miraculous to them as it seems to us, projecting an interactive version of themselves to this otherwise barren spot on the Moon. Since, as your little conversation with Earl established, they clearly know they're on the Moon, we would have to accept that they're unflappable enough to take this phenomenon at face value, but I've known enough Midwesterners to know that this is a genuine possibility.

"Six." Starting now on another hand. "Mentioned only so you can be assured I'm providing you an exhaustive list—a phenomenon one of your predecessors called the Law of Preservation of Home. He theorized that whenever human beings penetrate too far past their own natural habitat, into places sufficiently inhospitable to life, the Universe is forced to spontaneously generate something a little more congenial to compensate—the equivalent, I suppose, of magically whomping up a Holiday Inn with a swimming pool, to greet explorers lost in the coldest reaches of Antarctica. He even said that the only reason we hadn't ever received reliable reports of this phenomenon on Earth is that we weren't ever sufficiently far from our natural habitat to activate it . . . but I can tell from the look on your face that you don't exactly buy this one either, so I'll set it aside and let you read the paper he wrote on the subject at your leisure."

"I don't think I will," I said.

"You ought to. It's a real hoot. But if you want to, I'll skip all the way to the end of the list, to the only explanation that ultimately makes any sense. Ready?"

"I'm waiting."

"All right. That explanation is—" he paused dramatically "—it doesn't matter."

There was a moment of pregnant silence.

I didn't explode; I was too shell-shocked to explode. Instead, I just said: "I sat through half a dozen bullshit theories for 'It doesn't matter'?"

"You had to, Max; it's the only way to get there. You had to learn the hard way that all of these propositions are either completely impossible or, for the time being, completely impossible to test—and we know this because the best minds on Earth have been working on the problem for as long as there's been a sustained human presence on the Moon. We've taken hair samples from Minnie's hairbrush. We've smuggled out stool samples from the dog. We've recorded our conversations with the old folks and studied every second of every tape from every possible angle. We've monitored the house for years on end, analyzed samples of the food and drink served in there, and exhaustively charted the health of everybody to go in or out. And all it's ever gotten us, in all these years of being frantic about it, is this—that as far as we can determine, Minnie and Earl are just a couple of friendly old folks who like having visitors."

"And that's it?"

"Why can't it be? Whether aliens, time travellers, displaced human beings, or natural phenomena—they're good listeners, and fine people, and they sure serve a good Sunday dinner. And if there must be things in the Universe we can't understand—well, then, it's sure comforting to know that some of them just want to be good neighbors. That's what I mean by saying, It doesn't matter."

He stood up, stretched, took the kind of deep breath people only indulge in when they're truly luxuriating in the freshness of the air around them, and said: "Minnie and Earl expect some of the new folks to be a little pokey, getting used to the idea. They won't mind if you stay out here and smell the roses a while. Maybe when you come in, we'll talk a little more 'bout getting you scheduled for regular visitation. Minnie's already asked me about it—she seems to like you. God knows why." He winked, shot me in the chest with a pair of pretend six-shooters made from the index fingers of both hands, and went back inside, taking the dog with him. And I was alone in the nice backyard, serenaded by birdsong as I tried to decide how to reconcile my own rational hunger for explanations with the unquestioning acceptance that was being required of me.

■

Eventually, I came to the same conclusion George had; the only conclusion that was possible under the circumstances. It was a genuine phenomenon, that conclusion: a community of skeptics and rationalists and followers of the scientific method deciding that there were some things Man was having too good a time to know. Coming to think of Minnie and Earl as family didn't take much longer than that. For the next three years, until I left for my new job in the outer system, I went out to their place at least once, sometimes twice a week; I shot pool with Earl and chatted about relatives back home with Minnie; I'd tussled with Miles and helped with the dishes and joined them for long all-nighters talking about nothing in particular. I learned how to bake with the limited facilities we had at Base, so I could bring my own cookies to her feasts. I came to revel in standing on a creaky front porch beneath a bug lamp, sipping grape juice as I joined Minnie in yet another awful rendition of "Anatevka." Occasionally I glanced at the big blue cradle of civilization hanging in the sky, remembered for the fiftieth or sixtieth or one hundredth time that none of this had any right to be happening, and reminded myself for the fiftieth or sixtieth or one hundredth time that the only sane response was to continue carrying the tune. I came to think of Minnie and Earl as the real reason we were on the Moon, and I came to understand one of the major reasons we were all so bloody careful to keep it a secret—because the needy masses of Earth, who were at that point still agitating about all the time and money spent on the space program, would not have been mollified by the knowledge that all those billions were being spent, in part, so that a few of the best and the brightest could indulge themselves in sing-alongs and wiener dog cookouts.

I know it doesn't sound much like a frontier. It wasn't, not inside the picket fence. Outside, it remained dangerous and back-breaking work. We lost five separate people while I was there; two to blowouts, one to a collapsing crane, one to a careless tumble off a crater rim, and one to suicide (she, alas, had not been to Minnie and Earl's yet). We had injuries every week, shortages every day, and crises just about every hour. Most of the time, we seemed to lose ground—and even when we didn't, we lived with the knowledge that all of our work and all of our dedication could be thrown in the toilet the first time there was a political shift back home. There was no reason for any of us to believe that we were actually accomplishing what we were there to do—but somehow, with Minnie and Earl there, hosting a different group every night, it was impossible to come to any other conclusion. They liked us. They believed in us. They were sure that we were worth their time and effort. And they expected us to be around for a long, long time . . . just like they had been.

I suppose that's another reason why I was so determined to find them now. Because I didn't know what it said about the people we'd become that they weren't around keeping us company anymore.

■

I was in a jail cell for forty-eight hours once. Never mind why; it's a stupid story. The cell itself wasn't the sort of thing I expected from movies and television; it was brightly lit, free of vermin, and devoid of any steel bars to grip obsessively while cursing the guards and bemoaning the injustice that had brought me there. It was just a locked room with a steel door, a working toilet, a clean sink, a soft bed, and absolutely nothing else. If I had been able to come and go at will it might have been an acceptable cheap hotel room. Since I was stuck there, without anything to do or anybody to talk to, I spent those forty-eight hours going very quietly insane.

The habitat module of Walter Stearns was a lot like that cell, expanded to accommodate a storage closet, a food locker, and a kitchenette; it was that stark, that empty. There were no decorations on the walls, no personal items, no hytex or music system I could see, nothing to read and nothing to do. It lost its charm for me within thirty seconds. Stearns had been living there for sixteen years: a self-imposed prison sentence that might have been expiation for the sin of living past his era.

The man himself moved with what seemed glacial slowness, like a wind-up toy about to stop and fall over. He dragged one leg, but if that was a legacy of a stroke—and an explanation for why he chose to live as he did—there was no telltale slur to his speech to corroborate it. Whatever the reason might have been, I couldn't help regarding him with the embarrassed pity one old man feels toward another the same age who hasn't weathered his own years nearly as well.

He accepted my proffered can of yams with a sour grin and gave me a mug of some foul-smelling brown stuff in return. Then he poured some for himself and shuffled to the edge of his bed and sat down with a grunt. "I'm not a hermit," he said, defensively.

"I didn't use the word," I told him.

"I didn't set out to be a hermit," he went on, as if he hadn't heard me. "Nobody sets out to be a hermit. Nobody turns his back on the damned race unless he has some reason to be fed up. I'm not fed up. I just don't know any alternative. It's the only way I know to let the Moon be the Moon."

He sipped some of the foul-smelling brown stuff and gestured for me to do the same. Out of politeness, I sipped from my own cup. It tasted worse than it smelled, and had a consistency like sand floating in vinegar. Somehow I didn't choke. "Let the Moon be the Moon?"

"They opened a casino in Shepardsville. I went to see it. It's a big luxury hotel with a floor show; trained white tigers jumping through flaming hoops for the pleasure of a pretty young trainer in a spangled bra and panties. The casino room is oval-shaped, and the walls are alive with animated holography of wild horses running around and around and around and around, without stop, twenty-four hours a day. There are night clubs with singers and dancers, and an amusement park with rides for the kids. I sat there and I watched the gamblers bent over their tables and the barflies bent over their drinks and I had to remind myself that I was on the Moon—that just being here at all was a miracle that would have had most past civilizations consider us gods. But all these people, all around me, couldn't feel it. They'd built a palace in a place where no palace had ever been and they'd sucked all the magic and all the wonder all the way out of it." He took a deep breath, and sipped some more of his contemptible drink. "It scared me. It made me want to live somewhere where I could still feel the Moon being the Moon. So I wouldn't be some useless . . . relic who didn't know where he was half the time."

The self-pity had wormed its way into his voice so late that I almost didn't catch it. "It must get lonely," I ventured.

"Annnh. Sometimes I put on my moonsuit and go outside, just to stand there. It's so silent there that I can almost hear the breath of God. And I remember that it's the Moon—the Moon, dammit. Not some five-star hotel. The Moon. A little bit of that and I don't mind being a little lonely the rest of the time. Is that crazy? Is that being a hermit?"

I gave the only answer I could. "I don't know."

He made a hmmmph noise, got up, and carried his mug over to the sink. A few moments cleaning it out and he returned, his lips curled into a half-smile, his eyes focused on some far-off time and place. "The breath of God," he murmured.

"Yams," I prompted.

"You caught that, huh? Been a while since somebody caught that. It's not the sort of thing people catch unless they were there. Unless they remember her."

"Was that by design?"

"You mean, was it some kind of fiendish secret code? Naah. More like a shared joke. We knew by then that nobody would believe us if we actually talked about Minnie and Earl. They were that forgotten. So we dropped yams into our early-settlement stories. A little way of saying, hey, we remember the old lady. She sure did love to cook those yams."

"With her special seasoning." I said. "And those rolls she baked."

"Uh-huh." He licked his lips, and I almost fell into the trap of considering that unutterably sad . . . until I realized that I was doing the same thing. "Used to try to mix one of Earl's special cocktails, but I never could get them right. Got all the ingredients. Mixed 'em the way he showed me. Never got 'em to taste right. Figure he had some kind of technological edge he wasn't showing us. Real alien super-science, applied to bartending. Or maybe I just can't replace the personality of the bartender. But they were good drinks. I've got to give him that."

We sat together in silence for a while, each lost in the sights and sounds of a day long gone. After a long time, I almost whispered it: "Where did they go, Walter?"

His eyes didn't focus: "I don't know where they are. I don't know what happened to them."

"Start with when you last visited them."

"Oh, that was years and years and years ago." He lowered his head and addressed the floor. "But you know how it is. You have relatives, friends, old folks very important to you. Folks you see every week or so, folks who become a major part of who you are. Then you get busy with other things and you lose touch. I lost touch when the settlement boom hit, and there was always some other place to be, some other job that needed to be done; I couldn't spare one night a week gabbing with old folks just because I happened to love them. After all, they'd always be there, right? By the time I thought of looking them up again, it turned out that everybody else had neglected them too. There was no sign of the house and no way of knowing how long they'd been gone."

I was appalled. "So you're saying that Minnie and Earl moved away because of . . . neglect?"

"Naaah. That's only why they didn't say goodbye. I don't think it has a damn thing to do with why they moved away; just why we didn't notice. I guess that's another reason why nobody likes to talk about them. We're all just too damn ashamed."

"Why do you think they moved, Walter?"

He swallowed another mouthful of his vile brew, and addressed the floor some more, not seeing me, not seeing the exile he'd chosen for himself, not seeing anything but a tiny little window of his past. "I keep thinking of that casino," he murmured. "There was a rotating restaurant on the top floor of the hotel. Showed you the landscape, with all the billboards and amusement parks—and above it all, in the place where all the advertisers hope you're going to forget to look, Mother Earth herself. It was a burlesque and it was boring. And I also keep thinking of that little house, out in the middle of nowhere, with the picket fence and the golden retriever dog . . . and the two sweet old people . . . and the more I compare one thought to the other, the more I realize that I don't blame them for going away. They saw that on the Moon we were building, they wouldn't be miraculous anymore."

"They had a perfectly maintained little environment—"

"We have a perfectly maintained little environment. We have

parks with grass. We have roller coasters and golf courses. We have people with dogs. We even got rotating restaurants and magic acts with tigers. Give us a few more years up here and we'll probably work out some kind of magic trick to do away with the domes and the bulkheads and keep in an atmosphere with nothing but a picket fence. We'll have houses like theirs springing up all over the place. The one thing we don't have is the Moon being the Moon. Why would they want to stay here?" His voice, which had been rising throughout his little tirade, rose to a shriek with that last question; he hurled his mug against the wall, but it was made of some indestructible ceramic that refused to shatter. It just tumbled to the floor, and skittered under the bunk, spinning in place just long enough to mock him for his empty display of anger. He looked at me, focused, and let me know with a look that our audience was over. "What would be left for them?"

■

I searched some more, tracking down another five or six oldsters still capable of talking about the old days, as well as half a dozen children or grandchildren of same willing to speak to me about the memories the old folks had left behind, but my interview with Walter Stearns was really the end of it; by the time I left his habitat, I knew that my efforts were futile. I saw that even those willing to talk to me weren't going to be able to tell me more than he had . . . and I turned out to be correct about that. Minnie and Earl had moved out, all right, and there was no forwarding address to be had.

I was also tired: bone-weary in a way that could have been just a normal symptom of age and could have been despair that I had not found what I so desperately needed to find and could have been the harbinger of my last remaining days. Whatever it was, I just didn't have the energy to keep going that much longer . . . and I knew that the only real place for me was the bed I had shared with my dear Claire.

On the night before I flew back I had some money left over, so I went to see the musical *Ceres* at New Broadway. I confess I found it dreadful—like most old farts, I can't fathom music produced after the first three decades of my life—but it was definitely elaborate, with a cast of lithe and gymnastic young dancers in silvery jumpsuits leaping about in a slow-motion ballet that took full advantage of the special opportunities afforded by lunar gravity. At one point the show even simulated free fall, thanks to invisible filaments that crisscrossed the stage allowing the dancers to glide from place to place like objects ruled only by their own mass and momentum. The playbill said that one of the performers, never mind which one, was not a real human being, but a holographic projection artfully integrated with the rest of the performers. I couldn't discern the fake, but I couldn't find it in myself to be impressed. We were a few flimsy bulkheads and half a kilometer from lunar vacuum, and to me, that was the real story . . . even if nobody else in the audience of hundreds could see it.

I moved out of my hotel. I tipped my concierge, who hadn't found me anything about Minnie and Earl but had provided all the other amenities I'd asked for. I bought some stupid souvenirs for the grandchildren, and boarded my flight back to Earth.

After about an hour I went up to the passenger lounge, occupied by two intensely-arguing businesswomen, a child playing a handheld hytex game, and a bored-looking thin man with a shiny head. Nobody was looking out the panoramic window, not even me. I closed my eyes and pretended that the view wasn't there. Instead I thought of the time Earl had decided he wanted to fly a kite. That was a major moment. He built it out of newspapers he got from somewhere, and sat in his backyard letting out more than five hundred meters of line; though the string and the kite extended far beyond the atmospheric picket-fence perimeter, it had still swooped and sailed like an object enjoying the robust winds it would have known, achieving that altitude on Earth. That, of course, had been another impossibility . . . but my colleagues and I had been so inured to such things by then that we simply shrugged and enjoyed the moment as it came.

I badly wanted to fly a kite.

I badly wanted to know that Minnie and Earl had not left thinking poorly of us.

I didn't think they were dead. They weren't the kind of people who died. But they were living somewhere else, someplace far away—and if the human race was lucky it was somewhere in the solar system. Maybe, even now, while I rode back to face however much time I had left, there was a mindboggling little secret being kept by the construction teams building those habitats out near the Jovian moons; maybe some of those physicists and engineers were taking time out from a week of dangerous and backbreaking labor to spend a few hours in the company of an old man and old woman whose deepest spoken insight about the massive planet that graces their sky was how it presented one hell of a lovely view. Maybe the same thing happened when Anderson and Santiago hitched a ride on the comet that now bears their names—and maybe there's a little cottage halfway up the slope of Olympus Mons where the Mars colonists go whenever they need a little down-home hospitality. I would have been happy with all of those possibilities. I would have felt the weight of years fall from my bones in an instant, if I just knew that there was still room for Minnie and Earl in the theme-park future we seemed to be building.

Then something, maybe chance, maybe instinct, made me look out the window.

And my poor, slowly failing heart almost stopped right then.

Because Miles, the golden retriever, was pacing us.

He ran alongside the shuttle, keeping up with the lounge window, his lolling pink tongue and long floppy ears trailing behind him like banners driven by some unseen (and patently impossible) breeze. He ran if in slow motion, his feet pawing a ground that wasn't there, his muscles rippling along his side, his muzzle foaming with perspiration. His perpetually laughing expression, so typical of his breed, was not so much the look of an animal merely panting with exertion, but the genuine mirth of a creature aware that it has just pulled off a joke of truly epic proportions. As I stared at him, too dumbstruck to whoop and holler and point him out to my fellow passengers, he turned his head, met my gaze with soulful brown eyes, and did something I've never seen any other golden retriever do, before or since.

He winked.

Then he faced forward, lowered his head, and sped up, leaving us far behind.

I whirled and scanned the lounge, to see if any of my fellow passengers had seen him. The two businesswomen had stopped arguing, and were now giggling over a private joke of some kind. The kid was still intently focused on his game. But the eyes of the man with the shiny head were very large and very round. He stared at me, found in my broad smile confirmation that he hadn't been hallucinating, and tried to speak. "That," he said. And "Was." And after several attempts, "A dog."

He might have gone on from there given another hour or so of trying.

I knew exactly how he felt, of course. I had been in the same place, once, seventy years ago.

Now, for a while, I felt like I was twelve again.

I rose from my seat, crossed the lounge, and took the chair facing the man with the shiny head. He was wide-eyed, like a man who saw me, a total stranger, as the only fixed constant in his universe. That made me feel young, too.

I said, "Let me tell you a little bit about some old friends of mine."

This one's for Jerry and Kathy Oltion, the Minnie and Earl of the future.

Molly is the author of *The Jump-Off Creek, The Dazzle of Day* (winner of the PENWest Fiction Prize), and *Wild Life* (winner of the James Tiptree, Jr. Award). *Wild Life* was chosen for "If All of Seattle Read the Same Book." Her short story "Lambing Season" was a 2003 Hugo nominee. She was a student of Ursula K. Le Guin's in a 1981 writing workshop.

Her Web site is at http://www.mollygloss.com/.

MOLLY GLOSS

Upon meeting Ursula Le Guin for the first time, more than a few people have been heard to say somewhat sheepishly, "I don't read science fiction, but I've heard your work is good." Of course it can be embarrassing when you're introduced to an actual writer of one of those books you know you ought to have read but haven't—there's just no graceful way to say, "I'm sorry I haven't gotten around to reading your books yet." These people might be thinking it's more politic to say that they don't read science fiction. There is some trouble with this tack, though, if it's meant as an explanation, as an apology, to a writer known above all as a writer of science fiction. Here's the problem: When someone says they don't read science fiction, they seem to be saying they haven't, in fact, read any science fiction. They seem to be saying they've crossed off the whole field, not on the basis of considerate, careful reading of the texts, but on the basis of bad press, of which science fiction has had more than its share.

This makes me think of the great number of people who take a kind of perverse pride in declaring their dislike of California, not because they've actually been there, or because of anything they've read in the travel books, but because of, well, bad press, of which California too has had more than its share. I've known some Californians who, in certain situations, denied they were from California, and science fiction writers who believed that the only way to get literary respectability was to deny the science fiction label. But one of the things I know about Ursula is that she writes science fiction, although not only science fiction, and never has seen a reason to apologize for it. And she is (though long an Oregonian) originally from California, and never has been shy about saying so.

Here is something else I know about Ursula. Not only does she try to make her own judgments on the basis of considerate, careful reading of the texts and travel books, but sometimes she embraces the very thing receiving bad press. She has been, for instance, and is even now a flaming liberal, an outspoken feminist, an abortion rights activist, a civil libertarian, a loud and unswerving opponent of censorship, an environmentalist, and an enemy of the OCA, which is Oregon's local pack of ultra-right wing antigay paranoiacs.

I'm guessing these are not the reasons she was named a Grand Master by the Science Fiction Writers of America, though they very well could be.

So here are a few more things I know about Ursula. She is a staunch supporter of the greater community of writers, and strongly values her memberships in the National Writers Union, the Writers Guild, the Authors Guild, and PEN. She is especially proud to have been a charter member of SFWA.

She has been, in one way or another, at one time or another, a Taoist, a Utopian, and a pacifist anarchist. She is a teacher, one of our best—a teacher who doesn't pontificate or indoctrinate or evangelize, though there's no denying she's a woman of strong opinions. She's funny, she laughs easily, she can be a wiseacre. She's a reluctant flyer— she favors low-tech traveling, by train. She was slow to boot up, slow to forsake her old fossil of an Underwood, though by now she's racing along pretty low and fast on her iMac. She's a housewife poet. She was a graduate-school-dropout-stay-at-home-mother. And she is sane—an increasingly rare thing in our world.

And she has brought all of this—her whole consciousness, her beliefs and experiences, as well as her matchless imagination—to her work as a writer of science fiction.

One of the pleasures of reading Le Guin is to discover the many kinds of writing she has done well. But if, as Barry Lopez has said, each writer engages with just a handful of important questions, then it's interesting to note how often Ursula's characters seem to be groping toward the understanding that you must sometimes stand up and be counted, if silence is not to collude with injustice; how often in her novels and stories she seems to be defining what it means to inhabit—or reinhabit—a place; and how often the places she writes about are sad, proud, absurd, peculiar, and peopled by eccentrics and exiles. In her novels and stories there are often communities that have survived tragedies and have reshaped themselves around the losses, and also communities in the painful throes of learning benef.icence toward their members and the place where they live. What you will not find in her work is sentimentality. These are communities in Emerson's sense of the word—places where the complexities, and the suffering, and the hard work of belonging, are fully faced and acknowledged.

The literary world can and does affect the world we live in. A novel, a story, can conjure a landscape, call it into imagination, make the unfamiliar familiar; and if a writer has brought her whole self to that literary world, then readers are swept along to the place inside that story. And as they participate in it, live in it, allow their lives to be merged with the lives of the people there, they learn from the story, they are changed by it.

One of the things I know about Ursula is that she brings her whole self to her writing. When we read her novels, stories, poetry, we are changed by them and we begin to see ways we can inhabit, or reinhabit, our world. I am grateful to Ursula for many personal reasons to do with friendship and generosity, advice, encouragement; but I admire her for the simple reason that her life is an example to me, and that her books have become for me, as for many others, polestars, compasses—Michelin guides—not to California, but to the farthest borders of consciousness, where, in the embrace of words, we understand something that transcends words.

The community of science fiction writers and readers is enriched by her very presence among us.

Ursula has been a member of SFWA since before the Punic Wars, lives in Portland (left coast), has recently published a book of stories, *Changing Planes* (Harcourt), and a translation of selected poems of Gabriela Mistral (University of New Mexico Press) and is looking forward to a collection of talks and essays, *The Wave in the Mind* (Shambhala Publications).

Her Web site is at http://www.ursulakleguin.com/.

URSULA K. LE GUIN

SITA DULIP'S METHOD

The range of the airplane—a few thousand miles, the other side of the world, coconut palms, glaciers, the poles, the Poles, a lama, a llama, etc.—is pitifully limited compared to the vast extent and variety of experience provided, to those who know how to use it, by the airport.

Airplanes are cramped, jammed, hectic, noisy, germy, alarming, and boring, serving unusually nasty food at utterly unreasonable intervals. Airports, though larger, share the crowding, vile air, noise, and relentless tension, while their food is often even nastier, consisting entirely of fried lumps of something; and the places one has to eat it in are suicidally depressing. On the airplane, everyone is locked into a seat with a belt and can move only during very short periods when they are allowed to stand in line waiting to empty their bladders until, just before they reach the toilet cubicle, a nagging loudspeaker harries them back to belted immobility. In the airport, luggage-laden people rush hither and yon through endless corridors, like souls to each of whom the devil has furnished a different, inaccurate map of the escape route from hell. These rushing people are watched by people who sit in plastic seats bolted to the floor and who might just as well be bolted to the seats. So far, then, the airport and the airplane are equal, in the way that the bottom of a septic tank is pretty much equal, all in all, to the bottom of the next septic tank.

If both you and your plane are on time, the airport is merely a diffuse, short, miserable prelude to the intense, long, miserable plane trip. But what if there's five hours between your arrival and your connecting flight, or your plane is late arriving and you've missed your connection, or the connecting flight is late, or the staff of another airline are striking for a wage-benefit package and the government has not yet ordered out the National Guard to control this threat to international capitalism so your airline staff is trying to handle twice as many people as usual, or there are tornadoes or thunderstorms or blizzards or little important bits of the plane missing or any of the thousand other reasons (never under any circumstances the fault of the airlines, and rarely explained at the time) why those who go places on airplanes sit and sit and sit and sit in airports, not going anywhere?

In this, probably its true aspect, the airport is not a prelude to travel, not a place of transition: it is a stop. A blockage. A constipation. The airport is where you can't go anywhere else. A nonplace in which time does not pass and there is no hope of any meaningful existence. A terminus: the end. The airport offers nothing to any human being except access to the interval between planes.

It was Sita Dulip of Cincinnati who first realized this, and so discovered the interplanar technique most of us now use.

Her connecting flight from Chicago to Denver had been delayed by some unspeakable, or at any rate untold, malfunction of the airplane. It was listed as departing at 1:10, two hours late. At 1:55, it was listed as departing at 3:00. It was then taken off the departures list. There was no one at the gate to answer questions. The lines at the desks were eight miles long, only slightly shorter than the lines at the toilets. Sita Dulip had eaten a nasty lunch standing up at a dirty plastic counter, since the few tables were all occupied by wretched, whimpering children with savagely punitive parents, or by huge, hairy youths wearing shorts, tank tops, and rubber thongs. She had long ago read the editorials in the local newspaper, which advocated using the education budget to build more prisons and applauded the recent tax break for citizens whose income surpassed that of Rumania. The airport bookstores did not sell books, only best-sellers, which Sita Dulip cannot read without risking a severe systemic reaction. She had been sitting for over an hour on a blue plastic chair with metal tubes for legs bolted to the floor in a row of people sitting in blue plastic chairs with metal tubes for legs bolted to the floor facing a row of people sitting in blue plastic chairs with metal tubes for legs bolted to the floor, when (as she later said), "It came to me."

She had discovered that, by a mere kind of twist and a slipping bend, easier to do than to describe, she could go anywhere—be anywhere—because she was *already between planes*.

She found herself in Strupsirts, that easily accessible and picturesque though somewhat three-dimensional region of waterspouts and
volcanos, still a favorite with beginning interplanary travelers. In her
inexperience she was nervous about missing her flight and stayed only
an hour or two before returning to the airport. She saw at once that,
on this plane, her absence had taken practically no time at all.

Delighted, she slipped off again and found herself in Djeyo. She
spent two nights at a small hotel run by the Interplanary Agency, with
a balcony overlooking the amber Sea of Somue. She went for long
walks on the beach, swam in the chill, buoyant, golden water—"like
swimming in brandy and soda," she said—and got acquainted with
some pleasant visitors from other planes. The small and inoffensive
natives of Djeyo, who take no interest in anyone else and never come
down to the ground, squatted up in the vast crowns of the alm-palms,
bargaining, gossiping, and singing soft, quick love songs to one another. When she reluctantly returned to the airport to check up, nine
or ten minutes had passed. Her flight was soon called.

She flew to Denver to her younger sister's wedding. On the flight
home she missed her connection at Chicago and spent a week on
Choom, where she has often returned since. Her job with an adver-
tising agency involves a good deal of air travel, and by now she speaks
Choomwot like a native.

Sita taught several friends, of whom I am happy to be one, how to
change planes. And so the technique, the method, has gradually spread
out from Cincinnati. Others on our plane may well have discovered it
for themselves, since it appears that a good many people now practice
it, not always intentionally. One meets them here and there.

While staying with the Asonu I met a man from the Candensian
plane, which is very much like ours, only more of it consists of
Toronto. He told me that in order to change planes all a Candensian
has to do is eat two dill pickles, tighten his belt, sit upright in a hard
chair with his back not touching the back, and breathe ten times a
minute for about ten minutes. This is enviably easy, compared to our
technique. We (I mean people from the plane I occupy when not
traveling) seem unable to change planes except at airports.

The Interplanary Agency long ago established that a specific
combination of tense misery, indigestion, and boredom is the essential
facilitator of interplanary travel; but most people, from most planes,
don't have to suffer the way we do.

The following reports and descriptions of other planes, given me by friends or written from notes I made on my own excursions and in libraries of various kinds, may induce the reader to try interplanary travel; or if not, they might at least help to pass an hour in an airport.

PORRIDGE ON ISLAC

It must be admitted that the method invented by Sita Dulip is not entirely reliable. You sometimes find yourself on a plane that wasn't the one you meant to go to. If whenever you travel you carry with you a copy of Rornan's *Handy Planary Guide*, you can read up on wherever it is you get to when you get there, though Rornan is not always reliable either. But the *Encyclopedia Planaria*, in forty-four volumes, is not portable, and after all, what is entirely reliable unless it's dead?

I arrived on Islac unintentionally, when I was inexperienced, before I had learned to tuck Rornan into my suitcase. The Interplanary Hotel there did have a set of the *Encyclopedia*, but it was at the bindery, because, they said, the bears had eaten the glue in the bindings and the books had all come to pieces. I thought they must have rather odd bears on Islac, but did not like to ask about them. I looked around the halls and my room carefully in case any bears were lurking. It was a beautiful hotel and the hosts were pleasant, so I decided to take my luck as it came and spend a day or two on Islac. I got to looking over the books in the bookcase in my room and trying out the built-in legemat, and had quite forgotten about bears, when something scuttled behind a bookend.

I moved the bookend and glimpsed the scuttler. It was dark and furry but had a long, thin tail of some kind, almost like wire. It was six or eight inches long not counting the tail. I didn't much like sharing my room with it, but I hate complaining to strangers—you can only complain satisfactorily to people you know really well—so I moved the heavy bookend over the hole in the wall the creature had disappeared into, and went down to dinner.

The hotel served family style, all the guests at one long table. They were a friendly lot from several different planes. We were able to converse in pairs using our translatomats, though general conversation overloaded the circuits. My left-hand neighbor, a rosy lady from a plane she called Ahyes, said she and her husband came to Islac quite often. I asked her if she knew anything about the bears here.

"Yes," she said, smiling and nodding. "They're quite harmless. But what little pests they are! Spoiling books, and licking envelopes, and snuggling in the bed!"

"Snuggling in the bed?"

"Yes, yes. They were pets, you see."

Her husband leaned forward to talk to me around her. He was a rosy gentleman. "Teddy bears," he said in English, smiling. "Yes."

"Teddy bears?"

"Yes, yes," he said, and then had to resort to his own language— "teddy bears are little animal pets for children, isn't that right?"

"But they're not live animals."

He looked dismayed. "Dead animals?"

"No—stuffed animals—toys—"

"Yes, yes. Toys, pets," he said, smiling and nodding.

He wanted to talk about his visit to my plane; he had been to San Francisco and liked it very much, and we talked about earthquakes instead of teddy bears. He had found a 5.6 earthquake "a very charming experience, very enjoyable," and he and his wife and I laughed a great deal as he told about it. They were certainly a nice couple, with a positive outlook.

When I went back to my room I shoved my suitcase up against the bookend that blocked the hole in the wall, and lay in bed hoping that the teddy bears did not have a back door.

Nothing snuggled into the bed with me that night. I woke very early, being jet-lagged by flying from London to Chicago, where my westbound flight had been delayed, allowing me this vacation. It was a lovely warm morning, the sun just rising. I got up and went out to take the air and see the city of Slas on the Islac plane.

It might have been a big city on my plane, nothing exotic to my eye, except the buildings were more mixed in style and in size than ours. That is, we put the big imposing buildings at the center and on the nice streets, and the small humble ones in the neighborhoods or barrios or slums or shantytowns. In this residential quarter of Slas, big houses were all jumbled up together with tiny cottages, some of them hardly bigger than hutches. When I went the other direction, down-town, I found the same wild variation of scale in the office buildings. A massive old four-story granite block towered over a ten-story building ten feet wide, with floors only five or six feet apart—a doll's skyscraper. By then, however, enough Islai were out and about that the buildings didn't puzzle me as much as the people did.

They were amazingly various in size, in color, in shape. A woman who must have been eight feet tall swept past me, literally: she was a street sweeper, busily and gracefully clearing the sidewalk of dust. She had what I took to be a spare broom or duster, a great spray of feathers, tucked into her waistband in back like an ostrich's tail. Next came a businessman striding along, hooked up to the computer network via a plug in his ear, a mouthpiece, and the left frame of his spectacles, talking away as he studied the market report. He came up about to my waist. Four young men passed on the other side of the street; there was nothing odd about them except that they all looked exactly alike. Then came a child trotting to school with his little backpack. He trotted on all fours, neatly, his hands in leather mitts or boots that protected them from the pavement; he was pale, with small eyes, and a snout, but he was adorable.

A sidewalk café had just opened up beside a park downtown. Though ignorant of what the Islai ate for breakfast I was ravenous, ready to dare anything edible. I held out my translatomat to the waitress, a worn-looking woman of forty or so with nothing unusual about her, to my eye, but the beauty of her thick, yellow, fancifully braided hair. "Please tell me what a foreigner eats for breakfast," I said.

She laughed, then smiled a beautiful, kind smile, and said, via the translatomat, "Well, *you* have to tell me that. We eat cledif, or fruit with cledif."

"Fruit with cledif, please," I said, and presently she brought me a plate of delicious-looking fruits and a large bowl of pale yellow gruel, smooth, about as thick as very heavy cream, luke warm. It sounds ghastly, but it was delicious—mild but subtle, lightly filling and slightly stimulating, like café au lait. She waited to see if I liked it. "I'm sorry, I didn't think to ask you if you were a carnivore," she said. "Carnivores have raw cullis for breakfast, or cledif with offal."

"This is fine," I said.

Nobody else was in the place, and she had taken a shine to me, as I had to her. "May I ask where you come from?" she asked, and so we got to talking. Her name was Ai Li A Le. I soon realized she was not only an intelligent person but a highly educated one. She had a degree in plant pathology—but was lucky, she said, to have a job as a waitress. "Since the Ban," she said, shrugging. And when she saw that I didn't know what the Ban was, she was about to tell me; but several customers were sitting down now, a great bull of a man at one table, two mousy girls at another, and she had to go wait on them.

"I wish we could go on talking," I said, and she said, with her kind smile, "Well, if you come back at sixteen, I can sit and talk with you."

"I will," I said, and I did. After wandering around the park and the city I went back to the hotel for lunch and a nap, then took the monorail back downtown. I never saw such a variety of people as were in that car—all shapes, sizes, colors, degrees of hairiness, furriness, featheriness (the street sweeper's tail had indeed been a tail), and, I thought, looking at one long, greenish youth, even leafiness. Surely those were fronds over his ears? He was whispering to himself as the warm wind swept through the car from the open windows.

The only thing the Islai seemed to have in common, unfortunately, was poverty. The city certainly had been prosperous once, not very long ago. The monorail was a snazzy bit of engineering, but it was showing wear and tear. The surviving old buildings—which were on a scale I found familiar—were grand but run-down, and crowded by the more recent giant's houses and doll's houses and buildings like stables or mews or rabbit hutches—a terrible hodgepodge, all of it cheaply built, rickety-looking, shabby. And the Islai themselves were shabby, when they weren't downright ragged. Some of the furrier and featherier ones were clothed only by their fur and feathers. The green boy wore a modesty apron, but his rough trunk and limbs were bare. This was a country in deep, hard economic trouble.

Ai Li A Le was sitting at one of the outside tables at the café (the cledifac) next door to the one where she waited tables. She smiled and beckoned to me and I sat down with her. She had a small bowl of chilled cledif with sweet spices, and I ordered the same. "Please tell me about the Ban," I asked her.

"We used to look like you," she said.

"What happened?"

"Well," she said, and hesitated. "We like science. We like engineering. We are good engineers. But perhaps we are not very good scientists."

To summarize her story: the Islai had been strong on practical physics, agriculture, architecture, urban development, practical invention, but weak in the life sciences, history, and theory. They had their Edisons and Fords but no Darwin, no Mendel. When their airports got to be just like ours, if not worse, they began to travel betweeen planes; and on some plane, about a hundred years ago, one of their scientists discovered applied genetics. He brought it home. It fascinated them. They promptly mastered its principles. Or perhaps they had not quite mastered them before they started applying them to every life-form within reach.

"First," she said, "to plants. Altering food plants to be more fruitful, or to resist bacteria and viruses, or to kill insects, and so on."

I nodded. "We're doing a good deal of that too," I said.

"Really? Are you . . ." She seemed not to know how to ask the question she wanted to ask. "I'm corn, myself," she said at last, shyly.

I checked the translatomat: Uslu: corn, maize. I checked the dictionary, and it said that uslu on Islac and maize on my plane are the same plant.

I knew that the odd thing about corn is that it has no wild form, only a distant wild ancestor that you'd never recognize as corn. It's entirely a construct of long-term breeding by ancient gatherers and farmers. An early genetic miracle. But what did it have to do with Ai Li A Le?

Ai Li A Le with her wonderful, thick, gold-colored, corn-colored hair cascading in braids from a topknot . . .

"Only four percent of my genome," she said. "There's about half a percent of parrot, too, but it's recessive. Thank God."

I was still trying to absorb what she had told me. I think she felt her question had been answered by my astonished silence.

"They were utterly irresponsible," she said severely. "With all their programs and policies and making everything better, they were fools. They let all kinds of things get loose and interbreed. Wiped out rice in one decade. The improved breeds went sterile. The famines were terrible . . . Butterflies, we used to have butterflies, do you have them?"

"Some, still," I said.

"And deletu?" A kind of singing firefly, now extinct, said my translatomat. I shook my head wistfully.

She shook her head wistfully.

"I never saw a butterfly or a deletu. Only pictures . . . The insecticidal clones got them. . . . But the scientists learned nothing—nothing! They set about improving the animals. Improving us! Dogs that could talk, cats that could play chess! Human beings who were going to be all geniuses and never get sick and live five hundred years! They did all that, oh yes, they did all that. There are talking dogs all over the place, unbelievably boring they are, on and on and on about sex and shit and smells, and smells and shit and sex, and do you love me, do you love me, do you love me. I can't stand talking dogs. My big poodle

Rover, he never says a word, the dear good soul. And then the humans! We'll never, ever get rid of the Premier. He's a Healthy, a
bloody GAPA. He's ninety now and looks thirty and he'll go on looking thirty and being premier for four more centuries. He's a pious
hypocrite and a greedy, petty, stupid, mean-minded crook. Just the
kind of man who ought to be siring children for five centuries . . .
The Ban doesn't apply to him . . . But still, I'm not saying the Ban
was wrong. They had to do something. Things were really awful, fifty
years ago. When they realized that genetic hackers had infiltrated all
the laboratories, and half the techs were Bioist fanatics, and the God-
sone Church had all those secret factories in the eastern hemisphere
deliberately turning out genetic melds . . . Of course most of those
products weren't viable. But a lot of them were. . . . The hackers
were so good at it. The chicken people, you've seen them?"

As soon as she asked, I realized that I had: short, squat people who
ran around in intersections squawking, so that all the traffic grid-
locked in an effort not to run them over. "They just make me want to
cry," Ai Li A Le said, looking as if she wanted to cry.

"So the Ban forbade further experimentation?" I asked.

She nodded. "Yes. Actually, they blew up the laboratories. And
sent the Bioists for reeducation in the Gubi. And jailed all the God-
sone Fathers. And most of the Mothers too, I guess. And shot the ge-
neticists. And destroyed all the experiments in progress. And the
products, if they were"—she shrugged—" 'too far from the norm.'
The norm!" She scowled, though her sunny face was not made for
scowling. "We don't have a norm anymore. We don't have species
anymore. We're a genetic porridge. When we plant maize, it comes
up weevil-repellent clover that smells like chlorine. When we plant an
oak, it comes up poison oak fifty feet high with a ten-foot-thick
trunk. And when we make love we don't know if we're going to have
a baby, or a foal, or a cygnet, or a sapling. My daughter—" and she
paused. Her face worked and she had to compress her lips before she
could go on. "My daughter lives in the North Sea. On raw fish. She's
very beautiful. Dark and silky and beautiful. But—I had to take her to
the seacoast when she was two years old. I had to put her in that cold
water, those big waves. I had to let her swim away, let her go be what
she is. But she is human too! She is, she is human too!"

She was crying, and so was I.

After a while, Ai Li A Le went on to tell me how the Genome
Collapse had led to profound economic depression, only worsened by

the Purity Clauses of the Ban, which restricted jobs in the professions and government to those who tested 99.44% human—with exceptions for Healthies, Righteous Ones, and other GAPAs (Genetically Altered Products Approved by the Emergency Government). This was why she was working as a waitress. She was four percent maize.

"Maize was once the holy plant of many people, where I come from," I said, hardly knowing what I said. "It is such a beautiful plant. I love everything made out of corn—polenta, hoecake, cornbread, tortillas, canned corn, creamed corn, hominy, grits, corn whiskey, corn chowder, on the cob, tamales—it's all good. All good, all kind, all sacred. I hope you don't mind if I talk about eating it!"

"Heavens no," said Ai Li A Le, smiling. "What did you think cledif was made from?"

After a while I asked her about teddy bears. That phrase of course meant nothing to her, but when I described the creature in my bookcase she nodded—"Oh yes! Bookbears. Early on, when the genetic designers were making everything better, you know, they dwarfed bears way down for children's pets. Like toys, stuffed animals, only they were alive. Programmed to be passive and affectionate. But some of the genes they used for dwarfing came from insects—springtails and earwigs. And the bears began to eat the children's books. At night, while they were supposed to be cuddling in bed with the children, they'd go eat their books. They like paper and glue. And when they bred, the offspring had long tails, like wires, and a sort of insect jaw, so they weren't much good for the children anymore. But by then they'd escaped into the woodwork, between the walls . . . Some people call them bearwigs."

I have been back to Islac several times to see Ai Li A Le. It is not a happy plane, or a reassuring one, but I would go to worse places than Islac to see so kind a smile, such a topknot of gold, and to drink maize with the woman who is maize.

I wonder how often people are present at, and even participate in, a truly historical event without having a clue what's going on. One thinks of the executioner who mixed a brew for Socrates, of the guys who assembled the cross, of the Chinese chemist who noticed that certain elements could be made to go bang, of the chambermaids trying to pick up after a gang of politicians in a few Philadelphia inns in 1776. In "Nothing Ever Happens in Rock City," a man who owns a liquor store helps along, but does not comprehend, a celebration schoolkids will be reading about down the ages.

Jack's Web site is at http://www.sfwa.org/members/mcdevitt/.

JACK MCDEVITT

Sorry I'm late tonight, Peg. Had to make a trip up to the observatory at closing time. They're having some kind of party up there and they needed a quick delivery. Ordinarily I would of sent Harry but Virginia hasn't been feeling good so I told him to go home and I went up myself.

No, not much was happening. They all seemed pretty loud, but other than that it wasn't very much. Nothing much ever happens in Rock City.

Oh, yeah, Jamie's home. Got his degree but no job. Bill tells me he's decided to be a lawyer. He wants to send him to one of those eastern schools but he's not really convinced that Jamie's serious. You know how that's been going. Me, I think it'd be just as well. We got enough lawyers around here as it is.

What else? I heard today that Doris is expecting again. Now there's a woman doesn't know when to quit. Frank said he's been trying to talk her into getting her tubes tied. But she's kind of skittish. Women are like that, I guess.

No offense.

Oh yeah, it was a pretty good day. We moved a lot of the malt. That new stuff I thought we'd never get rid of. There was a family get-together over at Clyde's. You know how they are. Must be sixty, seventy people over there for the weekend. All Germans. Putting it down by the barrel.

Jake was in today. They're getting complaints about underage kids again. I told him it ain't happening in our place. And it ain't. We're careful about that. Don't allow it. Not only because it ain't legal, either.

I told him, it's not right for kids to be drinking and they can count on us to do what we can.

We had people in and out all day today. We sold as much stuff off the whiskey aisle as we did all week. We won't have any trouble making the mortgage this month.

What else? Nothing I can think of. This is a quiet town. Janet was in. Ticketed somebody doing ninety on the state road. Took his license, she said. Guy's wife had to drive him home. I'd've liked to of been there.

She told me there was a murder over in Castle County. I'm not sure about the details. Another one of those things where somebody's boyfriend got tired of a crying kid. That ought to be death penalty. Automatic.

What's that? What was going on at the observatory?

I don't know. They had some VIP's visiting. We sold a couple bottles of rum to one of them this morning. Old guy, gray hair, stooped, kind of slow. Looked like he was always thinking about something else. Talked funny too. You know, foreign. Maybe Brit. Aussie. Something like that.

They're doing some kind of convention up there. Some of them are staying over at the hotel, according to Hap. Anyhow, we get this call about a quarter to nine, you know, just before we lock the doors. It's Harvey. They want eight bottles of our best champagne. Cold. Can we deliver?

Harvey told me once they always keep a bottle in the refrigerator up there. But with all these people in town I guess one bottle wasn't enough.

Well, to start with, we don't have eight bottles of our best champagne on ice. Or off. I mean how much of that stuff do we sell? But sure, I tell him. I'll bring it up as soon as we close.

I mean, you know Harvey. He won't know the difference. And I can hear all this noise in the background. The paper said they were supposed to be doing some kind of business meeting but all I can hear is screaming and laughing. And I swear somebody was shooting off a noisemaker.

Oh, by the way, did I tell you Ag was by today? She wants to get together for a little pinochle next week. I figure Sunday works pretty good. When you get a chance, give her a call, okay?

And Morrie's moping around. He won't talk about it but I guess

Mary's ditched him again. You think he'd get tired taking all that from that crazy woman. Don't know what he wants. Ain't happy when he's with her and miserable when he isn't.

Oh, here's something you'll be interested in. Axel dropped a bottle of Chianti today. I mean it went off in the back of the store like a bomb. I felt sorry for him except that it made a hell of a mess. He's getting more wobbly every day. I'm not sure we should be selling him anything now. At his age. But I don't have the heart to stop him. I've thought about talking to Janet. But that only puts it on her. I don't know what I'm going to do about that. Eventually I guess I'll have to do *something*.

What about the observatory? Oh yeah. Well, there's really nothing to tell. I took some Hebert's and some Coela Valley. Four of each. Packed 'em in ice and put 'em in the cooler.

So when I get there all these lights are on inside and people are yelling and carrying on. I never saw anything like it. It was like they'd already been into something. I mean Harvey and his friends are *not* people who know how to have a good time. But this other crew—

Anyway Harvey said thanks and I wiped his card and he said do I want to stay a while? I mean they were into the bubbly before I could set it down.

So I say no thanks I have to drive back down the mountain and the last thing I need is a couple drinks. But I ask what's all the fuss and he takes me over to a computer screen which has graphics, big spikes and cones and God knows what else, all over it, but you can't begin to tell what it is, and he says *Look at that.*

I look and I don't see nothing except spikes and cones. So then he shows me how one pattern repeats itself. He says how it's one-point-something seconds long and it shows up three or four different places on the screen. Then he brings up another series and we do the same thing again. None of it means anything, as far as I can see.

So Harvey sees I'm not very impressed and he tells me we've got neighbors. He mentions someplace I never heard of. *Al-Car* or *Al-Chop* or something like that. He says it like it's a big deal. And then it dawns on me what he's talking about, that they've found the signal they're always looking for.

"How far away are they?" I ask.

He laughs again and says, "A long way."

So I say, "How far's that?"

"Mack," he tells me, "you wouldn't want to walk it."

For a minute I wonder if the people on the other end are going to come this way but he says no that could never happen. Don't worry. Ha ha ha.

Well, I say, tell them hello for me. Ha ha. And he offers me a three buck tip, which was kind of cheap considering how late it was and that I had to drive up and down that goofy road. I mean, I'm not going to take his money anyway. But three bucks?

But that's why I was late.

Ran into Clay outside town, by the way. He was over at Howie's getting his speed trap set up. Says he picks off a few every Friday. Says he had to go over to Ham's place earlier because Ham was screaming at Dora again. I used to think she would pack up and leave one of these days but I guess not.

Yeah.

Anyway, that's why I was late. I'm sorry it upset you. I'll call next time, if you want. But you don't need to worry. I mean, nothing ever happens in Rock City.

I think that writers often create stories in an effort to explain their own lives to themselves. I know that sometimes in the course of writing a story about a topic, I'll discover how I truly feel about it. In other cases, the more I write, the more I'll realize how ambivalent I am about something.

When I started writing "Cut," I was full of righteous horror over female "circumcision" or genital mutilation. I still am. But in the course of writing it, I had to confront my own cultural assumptions about what is acceptable modification of a child's body and what is not. And when the story was finished, I knew I still had not answered to my own satisfaction my first question: Who owns the child's body and makes decisions about it? The society, the parent or the child? Gene therapy and DNA manipulation are no longer on the distant horizon, but are here amongst us now. For me, the question seems more urgent and the answer as elusive as ever.

Megan's Web site is http://www.meganlindholm.com/.

CUT

MEGAN LINDHOLM

Patsy sits on a bar stool at my breakfast counter. She is sipping a glass of soy milk through a straw. I glance at her, then look away at my rainforestcam on the wallscreen behind her. My granddaughter had an incisor removed so that she could drink through the straw with her mouth closed. She claims it is more sanitary and less offensive to other people. I don't know about "other people." It offends the hell out of her grandmother.

"So. SAT's next week?" I ask her hopefully.

"Uh huh," she confirms and I breathe a small sigh of relief. She had contemplated refusing to take them, on the grounds that any college who wanted to rate her on a single test score was not her kind of place anyway. She swings her feet, kicking the rungs of her stool. "I'm still debating Northwestern versus Peterson University."

I try to recall something about Peterson, but I don't think I've ever heard of it. "Northwestern's good," I hedge. As I set a plate of cookies within her reach, I notice a bulge in the skin on her shoulder blade just above the fabric of her tank top. An irritated peace sign seems to be emblazoned on it. "What's that? New tattoo?"

She glances over her shoulder at it, then shrugs. "No. Raised implant. They put a stainless steel piece under your skin. Works best when there's bone backing it up. Mine didn't come out very good. Grandma, you know I can't eat those things. If the fat doesn't clog up my heart, the sugar will send me into a depression and I'll kill myself."

She nudges the plate of cookies away. I smile and take one myself. "I think that's a bit of an exaggeration. I've been eating chocolate chip cookies for years."

"Yeah, I know. And Mom, too. Look at her."

"Doesn't it hurt?" I ask, nodding at her implant. I evade the topic of her mom. It is not that I expect my granddaughter to always get along with my daughter. It is that I don't want to be wedged into the middle of it. I tell myself that this is not cowardice. By standing apart from their mother-daughter friction, I keep the lines of communication open between Patsy and myself.

My gambit is successful. "This?" She tosses her head at her implanted peace sign. "No. A little slit in the skin, then they free the skin layer from the tissue underneath it, slide in the emblem, put in a couple of stitches. It healed in two days, and now it's permanent. Besides. Women have always been willing to suffer for beauty. Inject collagen into your lips. Get breast implants. Have your ribs removed to have a smaller waist."

I give a mock shudder. "I never went in for those sorts of things. I think God meant us to live in our bodies the way they are."

"Yeah, right." She snorts skeptically, and picks up a cookie crumb, then licks it off her finger. I catch a brief glimpse of her tongue stud. "You made Mom wear braces on her teeth for two years. She's always telling me what a pain that was."

"That was different. That was for health as much as for appearances."

"Oh, let's be honest, Gran." Patsy leans forward on her elbow and fixes me with her best piercing glance. "You didn't take her to an orthodontist because you were worried she couldn't chew a steak. She told me the kids at school were calling her 'Fang.'"

I wince at the memory of my twelve-year-old in tears. It had taken me an hour to get her to tell me why. Katie was never as forthcoming with me as her own daughter is. Perhaps it's a part of the mother-daughter friction heritage. "Well, appearance was part of it. It was affecting her self-esteem. But straight teeth are important to lifelong health and—"

"Yeah, but the point is, it was plastic surgery. For the sake of how she looked. And it hurt her. But you still made her do it. For dental hygiene. So she would look like the other kids."

I feel suddenly defensive. Patsy is going over all this as if it is a well-rehearsed argument. "Well, at least it's more constructive than some of they ways you hurt yourself," I challenge her. "Tattoos, body piercing, tooth removal. It's almost like you're punishing yourself for something. It worries me, frankly, that so many people can damage their bodies for the sake of a fad."

"Hardly a fad, Gran. People have been doing it for thousands of years. It's not some weird self-punishment. It's not just that it looks good, it makes a point about yourself. That you have the will to make yourself who you want to be. Even if it means a little pain." She pokes speculatively at the heaped cookies.

"Or a lot of infection."

"Not with that new antibiotic. It kills everything."

"That's what worries me," I mutter.

I take another cookie. Nothing betrays my amusement as Patsy absentmindedly takes one and dunks it in her milk. She slurps off a bite, then says with a full mouth, "I'm getting cut myself."

"Cut?" The bottom drops out of my stomach. I'd seen it on the netnews. "Like a joint off one of your little fingers like those BaseChristian kids did? To seal their promise to never do drugs?" An almost worse thought finds me. "Not that facial scarification they do with the razor blades and ash?"

She laughs aloud and my anxiety eases. "No, Granma!" She hops off her stool and grabs her groin. "Cut! Here, you know."

"No, I don't know." How can I suddenly be so afraid of what I don't know?

"Circumcision. Everyone's talking about it. Here." While I am still gaping at her, she takes her net link from her collar and points it at my wallscreen. My rainforestcam scene gives way to one of her favorite links. I cringe at what I see. Some net star in a glam pose has her legs spread. Larger than life, she fills my wall. Head thrown back, hair cascading over her shoulders, she is sharing with us her freshly healed female circumcision. Symmetrical and surgically precise are the cleanly healed cuts. It is a pharaonoic circumcision, and the shaved seamed pudenda reminds me obscenely of the stitched seam down an old-fashioned football. I blink and force myself to look again, but all I can see is the absence of the flesh that should be there. I turn away, sickened but Patsy stares, fascinated. "Doesn't it look cool? In the interview, she says she did it to get a role. She wanted to show the producer her absolute commitment to the project. But now she loves it. She says she feels cleaner, that she has cut a lot of animal urges out of her life. When she has sex now . . . here, I can just play the interview for you—"

"No, thanks," I say faintly. I tap my master control and the screen goes completely blank. After what I have just seen, I could not bear the beauty of the rainforestcam with the wet, dripping leaves and the calling birds everywhere. I take a breath. "Patsy, you can't be serious."

She clips her link back onto her collar and pops back onto her stool. "You know I am, Granma. I came over here to tell you about it. At least you aren't having a meltdown like Mom did."

"She knows you want to do this?" I can't grasp any of it, not that some women do this voluntarily, not that Patsy wants to do it, not that Katie knows.

Patsy crunches down the rest of her cookie. "She knows I'm going to do it. Me and Ticia and Samantha. Mary Porter, too. We'll be like a circumcision group, like some African tribes had. We've grown up together. The ceremony will be a bond between us the rest of our lives."

"Ceremony." I don't know when I stood up. I sit back down. I press my knees together because they are shaking. Not to protect my own genitals.

"Of course. At the full moon tonight. The midwife who does it has this wonderful setting, it's an open field with these big old rocks sticking up out of it, and the river flowing by where you can hear it."

"A midwife does this?"

"Well, she used to be a midwife. Now she says she only does circumcisions, that this is more symbolic and fulfilling to her than delivering babies. But she is medically trained. Everything will be sterilized, and she uses antibiotics and all that stuff. So it's safe."

I suppose I should be relieved they are not using broken glass or old razor blades. "I don't get it," I say at last. I peer at my granddaughter. "Is this some sort of religious thing?"

She bursts out laughing. "No!" she sputters at last. "Granma! You know I don't go for that cult stuff. This is just about me taking control of my own life. Saying that sex doesn't run me, that I won't choose a man just because I'm horny for him, that I'm more than that."

"You're giving up sexual fulfillment for the rest of your life." I state it flatly, wanting her to hear how permanent it is.

"Granma, orgasm isn't sexual fulfillment. Orgasm isn't that much better than taking a good shit."

I smile in spite of myself. "Then you're sleeping with the wrong boys. Your grandfather—"

She covers her ears in mock horror. "Don't gross me out with old-people sex stories. Ew!" She drops her hands. "Sexual fulfillment—that's like code words that say women are about sex. *Women need sexual fulfillment,* like it's more important than being a fulfilled person."

We are arguing semantics when what I want to tell her is not to let some fanatic cut her sweet young flesh away from her body. Don't let anyone steal that much of you, I want to say. I don't. I suddenly understand how grave this is. If I become too serious, she won't hear me at all. She is poking me, trying to provoke me to act like a parent. I hold myself back from that futile abyss. I sense that Katie has already plunged to the bottom of it. Reasoning with her won't work. Get her to talk, and maybe she will talk herself out of it.

"Have you any idea how much it's going to hurt? Well, I'm sure she'll use an anaesthetic for the surgery, but afterward when you're healing—"

"Duh! That would defeat the whole purpose. No anesthetic. It would go against the traditions of female circumcision throughout the world. Ticia and Mary and Sam and I will be there for each other. It will be just women sharing their courage with other women."

"Female circumcision was invented by men!" I retort. "To keep women at home and subservient to them. To take away a precious part of their lives. Patsy, think about this. You're young. Once done, you can't go back."

"Sure you can. At the midwife's site, there's a link to a place that can make you look like you did before. Here." She is fiddling with her netlink. I press the OFF on my master control again.

"That's appearance, not functionality. They can't restore functionality. How would they make you a new clitoris?"

"Are you sure?"

"Yes. And you should know that much before you get into this. I can't understand how that woman can do this to girls." The parent part is getting the better of me. I clamp my lips down.

Patsy shakes her head at me. "Granma! It has always been women doing it to other women, in all the cultures. Look." She reaches over to push my master button back ON. "Here's a link to the midwife's website. Go look at it. She has all the historical stuff posted there. You like anthropology. You should be fascinated."

I stare at her, defeated. She is so sure. She argues well, and she is not stupid. She is not even ignorant. She is merely young and in the throes of her time. Patsy will do this if she is not stopped. I don't know how to stop her. Her words come back to me. Women doing it to other women. Women perpetuating this maiming. I try to imagine what this midwife must be like. I try to imagine how she began doing this to other women, how she could find it fulfilling. I can't. "I'd have to meet her," I say to myself.

Patsy brightens. "I hoped you would. Look. On her site, my link is the Moon Sisters. Our password is Luna. Because we chose the full moon. There's pictures of us, and the date and time and place. You're invited. Mary wanted to have a webcam on the ceremony, but we voted her down. This is private. For us. But I'd like you to be there."

"Will your mom be there?"

Again her snort of disbelief. "Mom? Of course not. She gets all worked up whenever I talk about it. She threatened to kill our midwife. Can you believe that? I asked her if she ever bombed abortion clinics when she was younger. She said it wasn't the same thing at all. Sure it is, I told her. It's all about choice, isn't it? Women making their own sexual choices." Her beeper chimes and she leaps from the stool. "Wow, I've got to get going. Teddy's going to drive me out there. He won't stay, of course. This is only for women."

I make my last stand. "How does Teddy feel about this?"

She shakes her head at me. "You just don't get it, Granma. It's not about Teddy. It's my choice. But he's excited. After this, if I have sex with him, he'll know it's not because I'm horny at the moment, but because I want to give that to him. And I think he's excited because it will be different. Tighter because of how she sews us up. You know men."

She doesn't wait for an answer from me, which is good, because right now I am sure that I don't even know women, let alone men. As soon as she is out the door, I phone Katie. In a moment, I see her in the inset of my wallscreen, but she does not meet my eyes. She is looking past me, at something on her own wallscreen. Her hand is up-lifted, guiding a tinkerbell pointer device. Her blue-green eyes are rapt with fascination. I stare for a moment at my beautiful talented daughter. By a supreme effort of will, I don't shriek, "Circumcision! Patsy! Help!" Instead I say, "Hi, whatchadoing?"

"Sorting beads from the St. Katherine site. It's fascinating. You know my beadmaker from the Charlotte site? Well, I'm finding her work here, too. They're unmistakably hers from the analysis. Which means these people traveled over a far greater area than we first supposed." She moves the tinkerbell in the air, teasing a bead on her screen into a different window.

"Or that the trade network was greater," I suggest as I smile at her. Despite my current panic, I have to smile at the sight of her. She is so intent, her eyes roving over her own screen as she continues working. When she is enraptured in her archaeology like this, she suddenly looks eighteen again. There is that huntress-fierceness to her stare. I am so proud of her and all that she is. She nods her agreement. I know she is busy, but this is important. Still, I procrastinate. I love to see her like this. Soon enough I will have to shatter her ardent focus. "Do you ever miss actually handling the beads and the artifacts?"

"Oh. Well, yes, I do. But this is still good. And the native peoples have been much more receptive to our work now that they know all the grave goods will remain in situ and relatively undisturbed. The cameras and the chem scanners can do most of the data gathering for us. But it still takes a human mind to put it all together and figure out what it means. And this way of doing it is better, both for archaeology and anthropology. Sometimes we're too trapped in our own time to see what it all means. Sometimes we're too close, temporally, to understand the culture we're investigating. By leaving all the artifacts and bones in situ, we make it possible for later anthropologists to take a fresh look at it, with unprejudiced eyes." She glances up at me and our eyes meet. "So. You called?"

"Patsy," I say.

She clenches her jaw, takes a breath and sighs it out. The intent eighteen-year-old anthro student is gone, replaced by a worried, tired mom. The lines in her face deepen and her eyes go dead. "The circumcision."

"Yes. Katie, you have to stop her!"

"I can't." She looks away from me, staring fiercely at her beads as if she will find some answer there.

"You can't?" I am outraged.

She is weary. Her voice trembles. "Legally, her body is her own. Once a child is over fourteen, a parent cannot interfere in—"

"I don't give a damn about legal—" I try to break in, but she continues doggedly.

"—any decision the child makes about her sexuality. Birth control, abortions, adopting-out of children, gender reassignment, confidential medical treatment for venereal disease, plastic surgery—it's all covered in that Freedom of Choice act." She gives me a woeful smile that threatens to become a grimace. "I supported that legislation. I never thought it would be construed like this."

"Are you sure it covers things like this?" I ask faintly.

"Too sure. Patsy has forced me to be sure. Shall I forward all the web links to you? She has, in her typical thorough way, researched this completely . . . at least in every way that supports her viewpoint." She shrugs helplessly. "I gave her a set of links to websites that oppose it. I don't know if she looked at them at all. I can't force her."

I realize I have my hand clenched over my mouth. I pull it away. "You seem so calm," I observe in disbelief.

For an instant, her eyes swim with tears. "I'm not. I'm just all screamed out. I'm exhausted, and she has stopped listening to me. What can I do?"

"Stop her. Any way you can."

"Like you stopped Mike from dropping out of school?"

Even after all the years, I feel a pang of pain. I shake my head. "I did everything I could. I'd drop your brother off at the front door, I'd watch him go into the school, and he'd go right out the back door. Battling him was not doing anything for our relationship. I had to let him make that mistake. I stopped yelling at him in an effort to keep the relationship intact. At least, it saved that much. He dropped out of school, but he didn't move out or stop being my son. We could still talk."

"Exactly," Katie says. She stares past me at her screen but I have broken the spell. She can no longer forget her daughter's decision in wonder at some ancient beadmaker's work. "I was quite calm last night. I told her that all I asked was that she always remember the decision was hers and that I completely opposed it. 'Fine,' she said. 'Fine.' At least this way, she'll come back here after the damned ceremony instead of overnighting in a circumcision hut with just the other girls. If she gets an infection or doesn't stop bleeding, at least I'll know about it and can rush her to the hospital."

"Can you legally still do that?" I ask with bitterness that mocks, not her, but the society we live in.

"I think so." She stops speaking and swallows. "Pray, Mom," she begs me after a moment. "Pray that when the other girls scream, she loses her courage and runs away. That's my last hope."

"It's a slim one, then. Our Patsy never lacked for guts. Brains, maybe, but not guts." We smile at one another, pride battling with despair. "Once she's said she'll do a thing, she won't back down no matter how scared she is. She'll let that woman cut her up and sew her tight rather than be seen as a coward by her friends."

"It's the baby I feel sorry for," Katie says suddenly.

"Baby?" All the hair on my body stands up in sudden horror.

"Mary's baby. She decided to have her baby done, the midwife is doing the baby first."

I didn't even know Mary had a baby. She is only a year older than Patsy. "But she can't! She has no right to make a decision like that, to scar her daughter for the rest of her life!"

Again the bitter smile makes Katie a sour old woman I don't know. "It's the flip side of the Freedom of Choice act. The compromise Congress made to get it passed. Under the age of fourteen, a parent can make any choice for the child. Mary is Bartolema's mother. It's her decision."

"It's barbaric! It's abusive!"

"You had Mike circumcised when he was two days old."

That jolts me. I try to justify it. "It was a different time. Almost all boys were circumcised then. Your dad and I didn't even think about it, it was just what you did. If the baby was a boy, you had him circumcised. They told us it made it easier to keep the baby clean, that it helped prevent cancer of the penis, that it would make him like all the other boys in the locker room."

"They did it without anaesthetic."

I am silent. I am no longer sure if we are talking about Mary's baby girl, or my own tiny son, all those years ago. I remember tending to the fresh cut on his penis, dabbing on petroleum jelly to keep his diaper from sticking to it. I am suddenly ashamed of myself. I had not hesitated, had not questioned it, all those years ago. I had charged ahead and done what others told me was wise, done what everyone else was doing.

Just like Patsy.

The silence has stretched long, and said more than words. "She invited me to be there," I say quietly. "Do you think I should go? Is that like giving my approval?"

"Go," Katie pleads quickly. "If it all goes wrong, you can rush her to a hospital. She won't tell me where it is, and I won't ask you to betray that confidence. But be there for her, Mom. Please."

"Okay," I say quietly. I've said it. I'll go watch her daughter and my granddaughter be maimed.

Katie has started to cry.

"I love you, baby. You're a good mom," I tell her. She shakes her head wildly, tears and hair flying, and breaks the connection.

For a time I stare at my rainforest. Then I get up. There is a backpack in the hall closet. I take it to the bathroom and begin to put things in it. Clean towels. Bandaging. I shudder as I put in the alcohol. I try to think what else. There is a spray antiseptic with a 'nonsting, pain relieving ingredient.' Feeble. What else should I take, what else? I stare into the medicine cabinet but find no help there.

I draw a breath and look in the mirror. Katie's face is an echo of mine, made perfect. Patsy, I see you in my green eyes and almost cleft chin. They are mine, the woman and the girl, the daughter of my body and my daughter's daughter. Born so soft and pink and perfect. I make my arms a cradle and wish they were both still mine to hold and protect. Protect. It is what a mother does, and no matter how old one gets, one never stops being a mother.

I grope behind the stacked towels on the shelf and take it down. Shining silver, it slips from the holster, releasing the smell of Hoppes Oil. There is a horsie on the handle. Fred always loved Colts. There is a dusty box of ammunition, too. I break it open, and begin to fill the empty cylinders, one by one. The bullets slide in like promises to keep.

I am suddenly calm. Don't be afraid, baby. Not my baby, not Mary's baby, no one's baby need fear. Granma is coming. No one's going to cut you.

I think for a moment of what a mess I'm going to make of my life. I think of the echoes that will spread out from one bullet, and I wonder how Patsy and her friends will deal with it, and what it will do to Katie. This is *my* freedom of choice, I tell myself fiercely. My turn to choose. Then I know I am too close to any of it to understand. Maybe we should just leave the midwife's body where it falls. In situ. Perhaps in a hundred years or two, someone else will know what to make of it all.

Michael Swanwick has been honored with the Hugo, Nebula, Theodore Sturgeon, and World Fantasy awards. His fiction has been translated and published throughout the world. Recent collections of his short work include *Tales of Old Earth* (Frog, Ltd.), *A Geography of Unknown Lands* (TigerEyes Press), *Moon Dogs* (NESFA Press), and the reissued *Gravity's Angels* (Frog, Ltd.).

His novels include *Jack Faust*, *The Iron Dragon's Daughter*, and the Nebula Award–winning *Stations of the Tide*. A weekly series of short-short stories, "Michael Swanwick's Periodic Table of Science Fiction," one story for every element in the periodic table, is currently running online at Sci Fiction, http://www.scifi.com/scifiction/. Another weekly series, one short-short story to accompany each of the eighty etchings in Goya's "Los Caprichos" is running at *the Infinite Matrix* Web site, http://www.infinitematrix.net/.

Swanwick lives in Philadelphia with his wife, Marianne Porter. The paperback of his newest novel, *Bones of the Earth*, about dinosaurs, time travel, and the fate of humanity, is currently available from HarperCollins Eos.

His Web site is at http://www.michaelswanwick.com/.

THE DOG SAID BOW-WOW

MICHAEL SWANWICK

The dog looked like he had just stepped out of a children's book. There must have been a hundred physical adaptations required to allow him to walk upright. The pelvis, of course, had been entirely reshaped. The feet alone would have needed dozens of changes. He had knees, and knees were tricky.

To say nothing of the neurological enhancements.

But what Darger found himself most fascinated by was the creature's costume. His suit fit him perfectly, with a slit in the back for the tail, and—again—a hundred invisible adaptations that caused it to hang on his body in a way that looked perfectly natural.

"You must have an extraordinary tailor," Darger said.

The dog shifted his cane from one paw to the other, so they could shake, and in the least affected manner imaginable replied, "That is a common observation, sir."

"You're from the States?" It was a safe assumption, given where they stood—on the docks—and that the schooner *Yankee Dreamer* had sailed up the Thames with the morning tide. Darger had seen its bubble sails over the rooftops, like so many rainbows. "Have you found lodgings yet?"

"Indeed I am, and no I have not. If you could recommend a tavern of the cleaner sort?"

"No need for that. I would be only too happy to put you up for a few days in my own rooms." And, lowering his voice, Darger said, "I have a business proposition to put to you."

"Then lead on, sir, and I shall follow you with a right good will."

The dog's name was Sir Blackthorpe Ravenscairn de Plus Precieux, but "Call me Sir Plus," he said with a self-denigrating smile, and "Surplus" he was ever after.

Surplus was, as Darger had at first glance suspected and by conversation confirmed, a bit of a rogue—something more than mischievous and less than a cut-throat. A dog, in fine, after Darger's own heart.

Over drinks in a public house, Darger displayed his box and explained his intentions for it. Surplus warily touched the intricately carved teak housing, and then drew away from it. "You outline an intriguing scheme, Master Darger—"

"Please. Call me Aubrey."

"Aubrey, then. Yet here we have a delicate point. How shall we divide up the . . . ah, *spoils* of this enterprise? I hesitate to mention this, but many a promising partnership has foundered on precisely such shoals."

Darger unscrewed the salt cellar and poured its contents onto the table. With his dagger, he drew a fine line down the middle of the heap. "I divide—you choose. Or the other way around, if you please. From self-interest, you'll not find a grain's difference between the two."

"Excellent!" cried Surplus and, dropping a pinch of salt in his beer, drank to the bargain.

■

It was raining when they left for Buckingham Labyrinth. Darger stared out the carriage window at the drear streets and worn buildings gliding by and sighed. "Poor, weary old London! History is a grinding-wheel that has been applied too many a time to thy face."

"It is also," Surplus reminded him, "to be the making of our fortunes. Raise your eyes to the Labyrinth, sir, with its soaring towers and bright surfaces rising above these shops and flats like a crystal mountain rearing up out of a ramshackle wooden sea, and be comforted."

"That is fine advice," Darger agreed. "But it cannot comfort a lover of cities, nor one of a melancholic turn of mind."

"Pah!" cried Surplus, and said no more until they arrived at their destination.

At the portal into Buckingham, the sergeant-interface strode forward as they stepped down from the carriage. He blinked at the sight of Surplus, but said only, "Papers?"

Surplus presented the man with his passport and the credentials Darger had spent the morning forging, then added with a negligent wave of his paw, "And this is my autistic."

The sergeant-interface glanced once at Darger, and forgot about him completely. Darger had the gift, priceless to one in his profession, of a face so nondescript that once someone looked away, it disappeared from that person's consciousness forever. "This way, sir. The officer of protocol will want to examine these himself."

A dwarf savant was produced to lead them through the outer circle of the Labyrinth. They passed by ladies in bioluminescent gowns and gentlemen with boots and gloves cut from leathers cloned from their own skin. Both women and men were extravagantly bejeweled—for the ostentatious display of wealth was yet again in fashion—and the halls were lushly clad and pillared in marble, porphyry and jasper. Yet Darger could not help noticing how worn the carpets were, how chipped and sooted the oil lamps. His sharp eye espied the remains of an antique electrical system, and traces as well of telephone lines and fiber optic cables from an age when those technologies were yet workable.

These last he viewed with particular pleasure.

The dwarf savant stopped before a heavy black door carved over with gilt griffins, locomotives, and fleurs-de-lis. "This is a door," he said. "The wood is ebony. Its binomial is *Diospyros ebenum*. It was harvested in Serendip. The gilding is of gold. Gold has an atomic weight of 197.2."

He knocked on the door and opened it.

The officer of protocol was a dark-browed man of imposing mass. He did not stand for them. "I am Lord Coherence-Hamilton, and this—" he indicated the slender, clear-eyed woman who stood beside him— "is my sister, Pamela."

Surplus bowed deeply to the Lady, who dimpled and dipped a slight curtsey in return.

The Protocol Officer quickly scanned the credentials. "Explain these fraudulent papers, sirrah. The Demesne of Western Vermont! Damn me if I have ever heard of such a place."

"Then you have missed much," Surplus said haughtily. "It is true we are a young nation, created only seventy-five years ago during the Partition of New England. But there is much of note to commend our fair land. The glorious beauty of Lake Champlain. The gene-mills of Winooski, that ancient seat of learning the *Universitas Viridis*

Montis of Burlington, the Technarchaeological Institute of—" He stopped. "We have much to be proud of, sir, and nothing of which to be ashamed."

The bearlike official glared suspiciously at him, then said, "What brings you to London? Why do you desire an audience with the queen?"

"My mission and destination lie in Russia. However, England being on my itinerary and I a diplomat, I was charged to extend the compliments of my nation to your monarch." Surplus did not quite shrug. "There is no more to it than that. In three days I shall be in France, and you will have forgotten about me completely."

Scornfully, the officer tossed his credentials to the savant, who glanced at and politely returned them to Surplus. The small fellow sat down at a little desk scaled to his own size and swiftly made out a copy. "Your papers will be taken to Whitechapel and examined there. If everything goes well—which I doubt—and there's an opening—not likely—you'll be presented to the queen sometime between a week and ten days hence."

"Ten days! Sir, I am on a very strict schedule!"

"Then you wish to withdraw your petition?"

Surplus hesitated. "I . . . I shall have to think on't, sir."

Lady Pamela watched coolly as the dwarf savant led them away.

■

The room they were shown to had massively framed mirrors and oil paintings dark with age upon the walls, and a generous log fire in the hearth. When their small guide had gone, Darger carefully locked and bolted the door. Then he tossed the box onto the bed, and bounced down alongside it. Lying flat on his back, staring up at the ceiling, he said, "The Lady Pamela is a strikingly beautiful woman. I'll be damned if she's not."

Ignoring him, Surplus locked paws behind his back, and proceeded to pace up and down the room. He was full of nervous energy. At last, he expostulated, "This is a deep game you have gotten me into, Darger! Lord Coherence-Hamilton suspects us of all manner of blackguardry."

"Well, and what of that?"

"I repeat myself: We have not even begun our play yet, and he suspects us already! I trust neither him nor his genetically remade dwarf."

"You are in no position to be displaying such vulgar prejudice."

"I am not *bigoted* about the creature, Darger, I *fear* him! Once let suspicion of us into that macroencephalic head of his, and he will worry at it until he has found out our every secret."

"Get a grip on yourself, Surplus! Be a man! We are in this too deep already to back out. Questions would be asked, and investigations made."

"I am anything but a man, thank God," Surplus replied. "Still, you are right. In for a penny, in for a pound. For now, I might as well sleep. Get off the bed. You can have the hearth-rug."

"I! The rug!"

"I am groggy of mornings. Were someone to knock, and I to unthinkingly open the door, it would hardly do to have you found sharing a bed with your master."

■

The next day, Surplus returned to the Office of Protocol to declare that he was authorized to wait as long as two weeks for an audience with the queen, though not a day more.

"You have received new orders from your government?" Lord Coherence-Hamilton asked suspiciously. "I hardly see how."

"I have searched my conscience, and reflected on certain subtleties of phrasing in my original instructions," Surplus said. "That is all."

He emerged from the office to discover Lady Pamela waiting outside. When she offered to show him the Labyrinth, he agreed happily to her plan. Followed by Darger, they strolled inward, first to witness the changing of the guard in the forecourt vestibule, before the great pillared wall that was the front of Buckingham Palace before it was swallowed up in the expansion of architecture during the mad, glorious years of Utopia. Following which, they proceeded toward the viewer's gallery above the chamber of state.

"I see from your repeated glances that you are interested in my diamonds, 'Sieur Plus Precieux,'" Lady Pamela said. "Well might you be. They are a family treasure, centuries old and manufactured to order, each stone flawless and perfectly matched. The indentures of a hundred autistics would not buy the like."

Surplus smiled down again at the necklace, draped about her lovely throat and above her perfect breasts. "I assure you, madame, it was not your necklace that held me so enthralled."

She colored delicately, pleased. Lightly, she said, "And that box your man carries with him wherever you go? What is in it?"

"That? A trifle. A gift for the Duke of Muscovy, who is the ultimate object of my journey," Surplus said. "I assure you, it is of no interest whatsoever."

"You were talking to someone last night," Lady Pamela said. "In
your room."

"You were listening at my door? I am astonished and flattered."

She blushed. "No, no, my brother . . . it is his job, you see, surveil-
lance."

"Possibly I was talking in my sleep. I have been told I do that occasionally."

"In accents? My brother said he heard two voices."

Surplus looked away. "In that, he was mistaken."

England's queen was a sight to rival any in that ancient land. She
was as large as the lorry of ancient legend, and surrounded by atten-
dants who hurried back and forth, fetching food and advice and
carrying away dirty plates and signed legislation. From the gallery, she
reminded Darger of a queen bee, but unlike the bee, this queen did
not copulate, but remained proudly virgin.

Her name was Gloriana the First, and she was a hundred years old
and still growing.

Lord Campbell-Supercollider, a friend of Lady Pamela's met by
chance, who had insisted on accompanying them to the gallery,
leaned close to Surplus and murmured, "You are impressed, of course,
by our queen's magnificence." The warning in his voice was impossible to miss. "Foreigners invariably are."

"I am dazzled," Surplus said.

"Well might you be. For scattered through her majesty's great body
are thirty-six brains, connected with thick ropes of ganglia in a hyper-
cube configuration. Her processing capacity is the equal of many of the
great computers from Utopian times."

Lady Pamela stifled a yawn. "Darling Rory," she said, touching
the Lord Campbell-Supercollider's sleeve. "Duty calls me. Would you
be so kind as to show my American friend the way back to the outer
circle?"

"Or course, my dear." He and Surplus stood (Darger was, of
course, already standing) and paid their compliments. Then, when
Lady Pamela was gone and Surplus started to turn toward the exit,
"Not that way. Those stairs are for commoners. You and I may leave
by the gentlemen's staircase."

The narrow stairs twisted downward beneath clouds of gilt

cherubs-and-airships, and debouched into a marble-floored hallway. Surplus and Darger stepped out of the stairway and found their arms abruptly seized by baboons.

There were five baboons all told, with red uniforms and matching choke collars with leashes that gathered in the hand of an ornately mustached officer whose gold piping identified him as a master of apes. The fifth baboon bared his teeth and hissed savagely.

Instantly, the master of apes yanked back on his leash and said, "There, Hercules! There, sirrah! What do you do? What do you say?"

The baboon drew himself up and bowed curtly. "Please come with us," he said with difficulty. The master of apes cleared his throat. Sullenly, the baboon added, "Sir."

"This is outrageous!" Surplus cried. "I am a diplomat, and under international law immune to arrest."

"Ordinarily, sir, this is true," said the master of apes courteously. "However, you have entered the inner circle without her majesty's invitation and are thus subject to stricter standards of security."

"I had no idea these stairs went inward. I was led here by—" Surplus looked about helplessly. Lord Campbell-Supercollider was nowhere to be seen.

So, once again, Surplus and Darger found themselves escorted to the Office of Protocol.

■

"The wood is teak. Its binomial is *Tectonia grandis*. Teak is native to Burma, Hind, and Siam. The box is carved elaborately but without refinement." The dwarf savant opened it. "Within the casing is an archaic device for electronic intercommunication. The instrument chip is a gallium-arsenide ceramic. The chip weighs six ounces. The device is a product of the Utopian end-times."

"A modem!" The protocol officer's eyes bugged out. "You dared bring a *modem* into the inner circle and almost into the presence of the queen?" His chair stood and walked around the table. Its six insectile legs looked too slender to carry his great, legless mass. Yet it moved nimbly and well.

"It is harmless, sir. Merely something our technarchaeologists unearthed and thought would amuse the Duke of Muscovy, who is well known for his love of all things antiquarian. It is, apparently, of some cultural or historical significance, though without re-reading my instructions, I would be hard pressed to tell you what."

Lord Coherence-Hamilton raised his chair so that he loomed over Surplus, looking dangerous and domineering. "*Here* is the historic significance of your modem: The Utopians filled the world with their computer webs and nets, burying cables and nodes so deeply and plentifully that they shall never be entirely rooted out. They then released into that virtual universe demons and mad gods. These intelligences destroyed Utopia and almost destroyed humanity as well. Only the valiant worldwide destruction of all modes of interface saved us from annihilation!" He glared.

"Oh, you lackwit! Have you no history? These creatures hate us because our ancestors created them. They are still alive, though confined to their electronic netherworld, and want only a modem to extend themselves into the physical realm. Can you wonder, then, that the penalty for possessing such a device is—" he smiled menacingly— "death?"

"No, sir, it is not. Possession of a *working* modem is a mortal crime. This device is harmless. Ask your savant."

"Well?" the big man growled at his dwarf. "Is it functional?"

"No. It—"

"Silence." Lord Coherence-Hamilton turned back to Surplus. "You are a fortunate cur. You will not be charged with any crimes. However, while you are here, I will keep this filthy device locked away and under my control. Is that understood, Sir Bow-Wow?"

Surplus sighed. "Very well," he said. "It is only for a week, after all."

■

That night, the Lady Pamela Coherence-Hamilton came by Surplus's room to apologize for the indignity of his arrest, of which, she assured him, she had just now learned. He invited her in. In short order they somehow found themselves kneeling face-to-face on the bed, unbuttoning each other's clothing.

Lady Pamela's breasts had just spilled delightfully from her dress when she drew back, clutching the bodice closed again, and said, "Your man is watching us."

"And what concern is that to us?" Surplus said jovially. "The poor fellow's an autistic. Nothing he sees or hears matters to him. You might as well be embarrassed by the presence of a chair."

"Even were he a wooden carving, I would his eyes were not on me."

"As you wish." Surplus clapped his paws. "Sirrah! Turn around."

Obediently, Darger turned his back. This was his first experience with his friend's astonishing success with women. How many sexual adventuresses, he wondered, might one tumble, if one's form were unique? On reflection, the question answered itself.

Behind him, he heard the Lady Pamela giggle. Then, in a voice low with passion, Surplus said, "No, leave the diamonds on."

With a silent sigh, Darger resigned himself to a long night. Since he was bored and yet could not turn to watch the pair cavorting on the bed without giving himself away, he was perforce required to settle for watching them in the mirror.

They began, of course, by doing it doggy-style.

■

The next day, Surplus fell sick. Hearing of his indisposition, Lady Pamela sent one of her autistics with a bowl of broth and then followed herself in a surgical mask.

Surplus smiled weakly to see her. "You have no need of that mask," he said. "By my life, I swear that what ails me is not communicable. As you doubtless know, we who have been remade are prone to endocrinological imbalance."

"Is that all?" Lady Pamela spooned some broth into his mouth, then dabbed at a speck of it with a napkin. "Then fix it. You have been very wicked to frighten me over such a trifle."

"Alas," Surplus said sadly, "I am a unique creation, and my table of endocrine balances was lost in an accident at sea. There are copies in Vermont, of course. But by the time even the swiftest schooner can cross the Atlantic twice, I fear me I shall be gone."

"Oh, dearest Surplus!" The Lady caught up his paws in her hands. "Surely there is some measure, however desperate, to be taken?"

"Well . . ." Surplus turned to the wall in thought. After a very long time, he turned back and said, "I have a confession to make. The modem your brother holds for me? It is functional."

"Sir!" Lady Pamela stood, gathering her skirts, and stepped away from the bed in horror. "Surely not!"

"My darling and delight, you must listen to me." Surplus glanced weakly toward the door, then lowered his voice. "Come close and I shall whisper."

She obeyed.

"In the waning days of Utopia, during the war between men

and their electronic creations, scientists and engineers bent their efforts toward the creation of a modem that could be safely employed
by humans. One immune from the attack of demons. One that
could, indeed, compel their obedience. Perhaps you have heard of
this project."

"There are rumors, but . . . no such device was ever built."

"Say rather that no such device was built *in time*. It had just barely
been perfected when the mobs came rampaging through the laboratories, and the Age of the Machine was over. Some few, however,
were hidden away before the last technicians were killed. Centuries
later, brave researchers at the Technarchaeological Institute of Shel-
burne recovered six such devices and mastered the art of their use.
One device was destroyed in the process. Two are kept in Burlington.
The others were given to trusted couriers and sent to the three most
powerful allies of the Demesne—one of which is, of course, Russia."

"This is hard to believe," Lady Pamela said wonderingly. "Can
such marvels be?"

"Madame, I employed it two nights ago in this very room! Those
voices your brother heard? I was speaking with my principals in Vermont. They gave me permission to extend my stay here to a fort-
night."

He gazed imploringly at her. "If you were to bring me the device,
I could then employ it to save my life."

Lady Coherence-Hamilton resolutely stood. "Fear nothing, then.
I swear by my soul, the modem shall be yours tonight."

The room was lit by a single lamp which cast wild shadows whenever
anyone moved, as if of illicit spirits at a witch's Sabbath.

It was an eerie sight. Darger, motionless, held the modem in his
hands. Lady Pamela, who had a sense of occasion, had changed to a
low-cut gown of clinging silks, dark-red as human blood. It swirled
about her as she hunted through the wainscoting for a jack left un-
used for centuries. Surplus sat up weakly in bed, eyes half-closed, di-
recting her. It might have been, Darger thought, an allegorical tableau
of the human body being directed by its sick animal passions, while
the intellect stood by, paralyzed by lack of will.

"There!" Lady Pamela triumphantly straightened, her necklace
scattering tiny rainbows in the dim light.

Darger stiffened. He stood perfectly still for the length of three long breaths, then shook and shivered like one undergoing seizure. His eyes rolled back in his head.

In hollow, unworldly tones, he said, "What man calls me up from the vasty deep?" It was a voice totally unlike his own, one harsh and savage and eager for unholy sport. "Who dares risk my wrath?"

"You must convey my words to the autistic's ears," Surplus murmured. "For he is become an integral part of the modem—not merely its operator, but its voice."

"I stand ready," Lady Pamela replied.

"Good girl. Tell it who I am."

"It is Sir Blackthorpe Ravenscairn de Plus Precieux who speaks, and who wishes to talk to . . ." She paused.

"To his most august and socialist honor, the mayor of Burlington."

"His most august and socialist honor," Lady Pamela began. She turned toward the bed and said quizzically, "The mayor of Burlington?"

"'Tis but an official title, much like your brother's, for he who is in fact the spy-master for the Demesne of Western Vermont," Surplus said weakly. "Now repeat to it: I compel thee on threat of dissolution to carry my message. Use those exact words."

Lady Pamela repeated the words into Darger's ear.

He screamed. It was a wild and unholy sound that send the Lady skittering away from him in a momentary panic. Then, in mid-cry, he ceased.

"Who is this?" Darger said in an entirely new voice, this one human. "You have the voice of a woman. Is one of my agents in trouble?"

"Speak to him now, as you would to any man: forthrightly, directly, and without evasion." Surplus sank his head back on his pillow and closed his eyes.

So (as it seemed to her) the Lady Coherence-Hamilton explained Surplus's plight to his distant master, and from him received both condolences and the needed information to return Surplus's endocrine levels to a functioning harmony. After proper courtesies, then, she thanked the American spy-master and unjacked the modem. Darger returned to passivity.

The leather-cased endocrine kit lay open on a small table by the bed. At Lady Pamela's direction, Darger began applying the proper patches to various places on Surplus's body. It was not long before Surplus opened his eyes.

"Am I to be well?" he asked and, when the Lady nodded, "Then I fear I must be gone in the morning. Your brother has spies everywhere. If he gets the least whiff of what this device can do, he'll want it for himself."

Smiling, Lady Pamela hoisted the box in her hand. "Indeed, who can blame him? With such a toy, great things could be accomplished."

"So he will assuredly think. I pray you, return it to me."

She did not. "This is more than just a communication device, sir," she said. "Though in that mode it is of incalculable value. You have shown that it can enforce obedience on the creatures that dwell in the forgotten nerves of the ancient world. Ergo, they can be compelled to do our calculations for us."

"Indeed, so our technarchaeologists tell us. You must . . ."

"We have created monstrosities to perform the duties that were once done by machines. But with *this*, there would be no necessity to do so. We have allowed ourselves to be ruled by an icosahexadexal-brained freak. Now we have no need for Gloriana the Gross, Gloriana the Fat and Grotesque, Gloriana the Maggot Queen!"

"Madame!"

"It is time, I believe, that England had a new queen. A human queen."

"Think of my honor!"

Lady Pamela paused in the doorway. "You are a very pretty fellow indeed. But with this, I can have the monarchy and keep such a harem as will reduce your memory to that of a passing and trivial fancy."

With a rustle of skirts, she spun away.

"Then I am undone!" Surplus cried, and fainted onto the bed.

Quietly, Darger closed the door. Surplus raised himself from the pillows, began removing the patches from his body, and said, "Now what?"

"Now we get some sleep," Darger said. "Tomorrow will be a busy day."

■

The master of apes came for them after breakfast, and marched them to their usual destination. By now Darger was beginning to lose track of exactly how many times he had been in the Office of Protocol. They entered to find Lord Coherence-Hamilton in a towering rage, and his sister, calm and knowing, standing in a corner with her arms crossed, watching. Looking at them both now, Darger wondered how he could ever have imagined that the brother outranked his sister.

The modem lay opened on the dwarf-savant's desk. The little fellow leaned over the device, studying it minutely.

Nobody said anything until the master of apes and his baboons had left. Then Lord Coherence-Hamilton roared, "Your modem refuses to work for us!"

"As I told you, sir," Surplus said coolly, "it is inoperative."

"That's a bold-arsed fraud and a goat-buggering lie!" In his wrath, the Lord's chair rose up on its spindly legs so high that his head almost bumped against the ceiling. "I know of your activities—" he nodded toward his sister— "and demand that you show us how this whoreson device works!"

"Never!" Surplus cried stoutly. "I have my honor, sir."

"Your honor, too scrupulously insisted upon, may well lead to your death, sir."

Surplus threw back his head. "Then I die for Vermont!"

At this moment of impasse, Lady Hamilton stepped forward between the two antagonists to restore peace. "I know what might change your mind." With a knowing smile, she raised a hand to her throat and denuded herself of her diamonds. "I saw how you rubbed them against your face the other night. How you licked and fondled them. How ecstatically you took them into your mouth."

She closed his paws about them. "They are yours, sweet 'Sieur Precieux, for a word."

"You would give them up?" Surplus said, as if amazed at the very idea. In fact, the necklace had been his and Darger's target from the moment they'd seen it. The only barrier that now stood between them and the merchants of Amsterdam was the problem of freeing themselves from the Labyrinth before their marks finally realized that the modem was indeed a cheat. And to this end they had the invaluable tool of a thinking man whom all believed to be an autistic, and a plan that would give them almost twenty hours in which to escape.

"Only think, dear Surplus." Lady Pamela stroked his head and then scratched him behind one ear, while he stared down at the precious stones. "Imagine the life of wealth and ease you could lead, the women, the power. It all lies in your hands. All you need do is close them."

Surplus took a deep breath. "Very well," he said. "The secret lies in the condenser, which takes a full day to re-charge. Wait but—"

"Here's the problem," the savant said unexpectedly. He poked at the interior of the modem. "There was a wire loose."

He jacked the device into the wall.

"Oh, dear God," Darger said.

A savage look of raw delight filled the dwarf savant's face, and he seemed to swell before them.

"I am free!" he cried in a voice so loud it seemed impossible that it could arise from such a slight source. He shook as if an enormous electrical current were surging through him. The stench of ozone filled the room.

He burst into flames and advanced on the English spy-master and her brother.

While all stood aghast and paralyzed, Darger seized Surplus by the collar and hauled him out into the hallway, slamming the door shut as he did.

■

They had not run twenty paces down the hall when the door to the Office of Protocol exploded outward, sending flaming splinters of wood down the hallway.

Satanic laughter boomed behind them.

Glancing over his shoulder, Darger saw the burning dwarf, now blackened to a cinder, emerge from a room engulfed in flames, capering and dancing. The modem, though disconnected, was now tucked under one arm, as if it were exceedingly valuable to him. His eyes were round and white and lidless. Seeing them, he gave chase.

"Aubrey!" Surplus cried. "We are headed the *wrong way!*"

It was true. They were running deeper into the Labyrinth, toward its heart, rather than outward. But it was impossible to turn back now. They plunged through scattering crowds of nobles and servitors, trailing fire and supernatural terror in their wake.

The scampering grotesque set fire to the carpets with every footfall. A wave of flame tracked him down the hall, incinerating tapestries and wallpaper and wood trim. No matter how they dodged, it ran straight toward them. Clearly, in the programmatic literalness of its kind, the demon from the web had determined that having early seen them, it must early kill them as well.

Darger and Surplus raced through dining rooms and salons, along balconies and down servants' passages. To no avail. Dogged by their hyper-natural nemesis, they found themselves running down a passage, straight toward two massive bronze doors, one of which had been left just barely ajar. So fearful were they that they hardly noticed the guards.

"Hold, sirs!"

The mustachioed master of apes stood before the doorway, his baboons straining against their leashes. His eyes widened with recognition. "By gad, it's you!" he cried in astonishment.

"Lemme kill 'em!" one of the baboons cried. "The lousy bastards!" The others growled agreement.

Surplus would have tried to reason with them, but when he started to slow his pace, Darger put a broad hand on his back and shoved. "Dive!" he commanded. So of necessity the dog of rationality had to bow to the man of action. He tobogganed wildly across the polished marble floor between two baboons, straight at the master of apes, and then between his legs.

The man stumbled, dropping the leashes as he did.

The baboons screamed and attacked.

For an instant all five apes were upon Darger, seizing his limbs, snapping at his face and neck. Then the burning dwarf arrived and, finding his target obstructed, seized the nearest baboon. The animal shrieked as its uniform burst into flames.

As one, the other baboons abandoned their original quarry to fight this newcomer who had dared attack one of their own.

In a trice, Darger leaped over the fallen master of apes, and was through the door. He and Surplus threw their shoulders against its metal surface and pushed. He had one brief glimpse of the fight, with the baboons aflame, and their master's body flying through the air. Then the door slammed shut. Internal bars and bolts, operated by smoothly oiled mechanisms, automatically latched themselves.

For the moment, they were safe.

Surplus slumped against the smooth bronze, and wearily asked, "Where did you *get* that modem?"

"From a dealer of antiquities." Darger wiped his brow with his kerchief. "It was transparently worthless. Whoever would dream it could be repaired?"

Outside, the screaming ceased. There was a very brief silence. Then the creature flung itself against one of the metal doors. It rang with the impact.

A delicate girlish voice wearily said, "What is this noise?"

They turned in surprise and found themselves looking up at the enormous corpus of Queen Gloriana. She lay upon her pallet, swaddled in satin and lace, and abandoned by all, save her valiant (though doomed) guardian apes. A pervasive yeasty smell emanated from her flesh. Within the tremendous folds of chins by the dozens and scores was a small human face. Its mouth moved delicately and asked, "What is trying to get in?"

The door rang again. One of its great hinges gave.

Darger bowed. "I fear, madame, it is your death."

"Indeed?" Blue eyes opened wide and, unexpectedly, Gloriana laughed. "If so, that is excellent good news. I have been praying for death an extremely long time."

"Can any of God's creations truly pray for death and mean it?" asked Darger, who had his philosophical side. "I have known unhappiness myself, yet even so life is precious to me."

"Look at me!" Far up to one side of the body, a tiny arm—though truly no tinier than any woman's arm—waved feebly. "I am not God's creation, but Man's. Who would trade ten minutes of their own life for a century of mine? Who, having mine, would not trade it all for death?"

A second hinge popped. The doors began to shiver. Their metal surfaces radiated heat.

"Darger, we must leave!" Surplus cried. "There is a time for learned conversation, but it is not now."

"Your friend is right," Gloriana said. "There is a small archway hidden behind yon tapestry. Go through it. Place your hand on the left wall and run. If you turn whichever way you must to keep from letting go of the wall, it will lead you outside. You are both rogues, I see, and doubtless deserve punishment, yet I can find nothing in my heart for you but friendship."

"Madame . . ." Darger began, deeply moved.

"Go! My bridegroom enters."

The door began to fall inward. With a final cry of "Farewell!" from Darger and "Come *on!*" from Surplus, they sped away.

By the time they had found their way outside, all of Buckingham Labyrinth was in flames. The demon, however, did not emerge from the flames, encouraging them to believe that when the modem it carried finally melted down, it had been forced to return to that unholy realm from whence it came.

∎

The sky was red with flames as the sloop set sail for Calais. Leaning against the rail, watching, Surplus shook his head. "What a terrible sight! I cannot help feeling, in part, responsible."

"Come! Come!" Darger said. "This dyspepsia ill becomes you. We are both rich fellows, now! The Lady Pamela's diamonds will maintain us lavishly for years to come. As for London, this is far from the first fire it has had to endure. Nor will it be the last. Life is short, and so, while we live, let us be jolly!"

"These are strange words for a melancholiac," Surplus said wonderingly.

"In triumph, my mind turns its face to the sun. Dwell not on the past, dear friend, but on the future that lies glittering before us."

"The necklace is worthless," Surplus said. "Now that I have the leisure to examine it, free of the distracting flesh of Lady Pamela, I see that these are not diamonds, but mere imitations." He made to cast the necklace into the Thames.

Before he could, though, Darger snatched away the stones from him and studied them closely. Then he threw back his head and laughed. "The biters bit! Well, it may be paste, but it looks valuable still. We shall find good use for it in Paris."

"We are going to Paris?"

"We are partners, are we not? Remember that antique wisdom that whenever a door closes, another opens? For every city that burns, another beckons. To France, then, and adventure! After which, Italy, the Vatican Empire, Austro-Hungary, perhaps even Russia! Never forget that you have yet to present your credentials to the Duke of Muscovy."

"Very well," Surplus said. "But when we do, *I'll* pick out the modem."

I am, with my partner-in-crime, Steve Miller, the author of eight published science fiction novels, seven in the Liaden Universe®. Number eight, *The Tomorrow Low* came out in February 2003. Novel number nine (Liaden Universe® novel number eight), *Balance of Trade,* was published in February 2004. We have edited the anthology *Low Port,* which hit the shelves in August 2003.

I've also written a couple dozen shorter works, some with Steve, some all by my onesie. *Scout's Progress* and *Local Custom* won first and second place, respectively, in the 2002 Prism Awards for best sf/futuristic/paranormal romances of 2001 (the Prisms are given by the Futuristic Fantasy and Paranormal Chapter of Romance Writers of America). I've also seen published a murder mystery, *Barnburner*. My first professionally published science fiction story was "A Matter of Ceremony," in Amazing, 1980.

From August 1997 through August 2000, I served as executive director of the Science Fiction and Fantasy Writers of America; did a term as vice president from 2001–2002, and a term as president from 2002–2003.

I started reading science fiction and fantasy at a tender age, including the *Rootabaga Stories,* which my mother introduced me to in order to wean me away from that sci-fi stuff. . . .

I live in Central Maine with my lovely and talented husband of many years, three cats, absurd amounts of computer equipment, and way too many books.

Sharon's Web site is at http://www.korval.com/.

APPRECIATING KATHERINE MACLEAN

SHARON LEE

n April 1953 a story entitled "Six Fingers" by Katherine MacLean appeared in *Thrilling Wonder Stories*.

I didn't read the story then, having been something less than a year old at the time of its publication—and slow for my age, besides.

When I did finally get around to reading the story, some twelve or thirteen years later, its title was "The Diploids"—and it changed my life.

It wasn't one of those big, flashy changes in which my moneyed future as a top-selling author of speculative fiction was revealed in a lightning bolt accompanied by shrill hosanas from the local angel's choir. No, it was a quieter, more basic change than any tin-whistle epiphany, and it was years before I realized what had happened. In fact, I think the damn thing's *still* at work, there in my back-brain, informing my choices, and my expectations.

That was the first time I met Katie MacLean, in that peculiar, intimate, third-hand way that one meets an author through her story. I was just shy of thirteen; she was a woman grown. She promised me things, and I believed her.

What did she—what did *the story*—promise? Three things specifically, discovered only later, when I had found the promised condition, not knowing until the instant of discovery that I had been searching for it.

The first thing—the very first promise—was Wit. Somewhere, there was a place—and I would find it, when I became old, and bold, enough—where people loved words and the meaning of words so much that they punned; that they wrote, and spoke, with exuberance, with passion, with precision.

The second promise was Acceptance, despite—or because of—whatever oddities one might bear. Diversity was strength; the unexpected was powerful.

And the third promise, saving the best for last:

That a person named Katherine could write science fiction stories—science fiction stories with heart, about people, the problems they encountered, and the human solutions they evolved—and see them published alongside stories written by people named Robert, Fred, and Harry; and that there need be no compromises, no missishness, in those stories. That was the third promise—and the greatest.

The second time I met Katie I was myself a woman grown, and two of the three promises she had made to me were fulfilled. I knew and rejoiced in the company of people who loved words, and who used them well—as comforts and as weapons.

I had written science fiction stories and seen them published alongside people named Steve, Ray, Esther, and Marina; I had coauthored novels and seen them published, too.

This time, the contact came not through a story, but through the magic of e-mail.

We discovered that we were neighbors, in the way that people who live in the same sparsely populated state tend to feel neighborly, and we struck up a conversation—inconsequential chat, threaded through the work of our days, the weather, the state of the barn roof, her teaching dance therapy—

And then Katie was gone. I had asked her a question; I knew she didn't ignore questions, but people get busy, they get lives, they get bored. Faintly worried, and telling myself I was an idiot for worrying, I went back to work.

Three days later, an e-mail from Katie arrived in my in-box; she was sorry to have cut our conversation short, but the state of the barn roof had deteriorated dramatically, and her husband had determined to fix it.

"At his age?" Katie inquired, rhetorically.

Having dissuaded him from this mad and potentially tragic meeting with a ladder, Katie climbed the rungs and did the repair herself.

At this point, I was absolutely infatuated, and when it came time, some years after I had given over my day-job and decided that being president of SFWA might be good for some thrills, it was my very great pleasure to append the name of Katherine MacLean to the list of SFWA Authors Emeritus.

■

The 2003 Nebula Awards® ceremony was held in Philadelphia. And there I met Katie MacLean for the third and most definitive time.

Asked before the event what she would like as a memento, Katie wished only for a reference so that she might land a job teaching English on an island nation whose name escapes me at the moment.

Asked if she would mind giving a presentation to those who would come to meet and to celebrate her, she threatened, half-seriously, or perhaps a little more, to "rant."

But she didn't rant.

She told us stories—about an early talent and a desire to be an artist, which her parents discouraged, thinking that they had thereby protected her from the Bohemian crowd. How despite the best efforts of those who cared about her most, she fell in with science fiction writers and other odd folk, married a man who promised to introduce her to "interesting" people, and so embarked upon the adventure of her life.

The audience—we were riveted as she told on, the narrative dancing joyously—*disdainfully*—along the edge of catastrophe, until at the end of the tale it was revealed that what her hearers had believed to be a single thread, lost and forgotten within the angled complexities of the telling, was in fact only one small part of an intricate and flawless verbal origami.

As I listened, enspelled, I could feel the others, Katie's stories that I had read so long ago . . . stirring. Deepening, taking on substance, expanding, *changing*. And I realized that there had been a fourth promise made, all those years ago; a promise so subtle that I hadn't known it had been made.

Those who take joy in their lives, and in their craft, who tell the truth as they observe it with an eye both clinical and ironic—they will change the lives and the perceptions of those who come after. And that creating the opportunity for that change to occur—is work worthy of a lifetime.

Thank you, Katie.

KATHERINE MACLEAN

Katherine MacLean, SFWA's 2003 Author Emeritus, has been publishing science fiction stories for more than fifty years. When I reread my ancient, fragile, treasured copy of her short story collection *The Diploids,* I was struck by how applicable "Games" is to our time, as well as to the time of its first publication, in 1953.

Her bibliography can be found online at http://isfdb.tamu.edu/cgi-bin/ea.cgi?Katherine%20MacLean.

KATHERINE MACLEAN

Ronny was playing by himself, which meant he was two tribes of Indians having a war.

"Bang," he muttered, firing an imaginary rifle. He decided that it was a time in history before the white people had sold the Indians any guns, and changed the rifle into a bow. "Wizz-*thunk*," he substituted, mimicking from an Indian film on TV the graphic sound of an arrow striking flesh.

"Oof." He folded down onto the grass, moaning, "Uhh-ooh . . ." relaxing into defeat and death.

"Want some chocolate milk, Ronny?" asked his mother from the kitchen.

"No thanks," he called back, climbing to his feet to be another man. "Wizzthunk, wizzthunk,"—he added to the flights of arrows as the best archer in the tribe. "Last arrow. Wizzzzz," he said missing one enemy for realism. The best archer in the tribe spoke to other battling braves. "Who has more arrows? They are advancing. No time, I'll have to use my knife." He drew the imaginary knife, ducking an arrow as it wizzed past his head.

■

Then he was the tribal chief standing nearby on a slight hill, and he saw that too many of his warriors were dead, too few left alive. "We must retreat. We must not all die and leave our tribe without warriors to protect the women and children. Retreat, we are outnumbered."

Ronny decided that the chief was heroically wounded, his voice wavering from weakness. He had been propping himself against a tree to appear unharmed, but now he moved so that his braves could see he was pinned to the trunk by an arrow and could not walk. They cried out.

He said, "Leave me and escape. But remember. . . ." No words came, just the feeling of being what he was, a dying old eagle, a chief of warriors, speaking to young warriors who would need the advice of seasoned humor and moderation to carry them through their young battles. He had to finish his speech, tell them something wise.

Ronny tried harder, pulling the feeling around him like a cloak of resignation and pride, leaning indifferently against the tree where the arrow had pinned him, hearing dimly in anticipation the sound of his aged voice conquering weakness to speak wisely what needed to be said. They had many battles ahead of them, and the battles would be against odds, with so many dead already.

They must watch and wait, be flexible and tenacious, determined and persistent—but not too rash; subtle and indirect—but not cowardly; and above all, be patient with the triumph of the enemy, and not maddened into suicidal attack.

His stomach hurt with the arrow wound, and his braves waited to hear his words. He had to sum a part of his life's experience in words. Ronny tried harder to make it real.

Then suddenly it was real.

He was an old man, guide and adviser in an oblique battle against great odds. He was dying of something, and his stomach hurt with a knotted ache, like hunger, and he was thirsty. He had refused to let the young men make the sacrifice of trying to rescue him. He was trapped in a steel cage, and dying, because he would not surrender to the enemy, nor cease to fight them. He smiled and said, "Do not be fanatical. Remember to live like other men, but remember to live like yourself . . ."

And then he was saying things that could not be put into words, attitudes that were ways of taking bad situations that made them easier to smile at, complex feelings. . . .

He was an old man, trying to teach young men, and the old man did not know about Ronny. He thought sadly, how little he would be able to convey to the young men. He began to think sentences that were not sentences, but single alphabet letters pushing each other with signs, with a feeling of being connected like two halves of a swing, one side moving up when the other moved down, and like cogs and wheels interlaced inside a clock, only without the cogs, just the push.

It wasn't adding, and it used letters instead of numbers, but Ronny knew it was some kind of arithmetic.

And he wasn't Ronny.

He was an old man, in an oblique battle against great odds. His stomach hurt, and he was dying. Ronny was the old man and himself, both at once.

■

It was too intense. Part of Ronny wanted to escape and be alone, and that part withdrew and wanted to play something. Ronny sat on the grass and played with his toes like a much younger child.

Part of Ronny that was Doctor Revert Purcell sat on the edge of a prison cot, concentrating on secret, unpublished equations of biogenic stability which he wanted to pass on to the responsible hands of young researchers in the concealed-research chain. He was thinking, using the technique of holding ideas in the mind which they had told him was the telepathic sending of ideas to anyone ready to receive. It was difficult, and made more difficult by the uncertainty, for he could never tell if anyone was receiving. It was odd that he himself could never tell when he was sending successfully. Probably a matter of age. They had started to teach him new tricks when his mind had stiffened and lost the old limber ability to jump through hoops.

The water tap, four feet away, was dripping steadily, and it was hard for Purcell to concentrate, so intense was his thirst. He wondered if he could gather strength to walk that far. He was sitting up, and that was already success, but the effort to raise himself that far had left him dizzy and trembling. If he tried to stand, the effort would surely interrupt his transmitting of equations. All the data was not sent yet.

Would the man with the keys who looked in the door twice a day care whether Purcell died with dignity? He was the only audience, and his expression never changed when Purcell asked him to point out to the authorities that he was not being given anything to eat. It was funny to Purcell that he wanted the respect of any audience to his death, even of a watcher without expression and without response, who treated him as if he were already an inanimate, indifferent object.

Perhaps the man felt contempt for him. Perhaps the watcher would smile and respond only if Purcell said, "I have changed my mind. I will tell."

But if he said that, he would lose his own respect.

At the National BioChemical Convention, the reporter had asked him if any of his researches could be applied to warfare.

He had answered the reporter with no feeling of danger in what he said, knowing that what he did was common practice among research men, sure that he had an unchallengeable right to do it.

"Some of them can apply to warfare, but those I keep to myself."

The reporter remained deadpan. "For instance?"

"Well, I have to choose something that won't reveal how it's done now, but . . . ah . . . for example, a way of cheaply mass producing specific antitoxins against any germ. It sounds harmless if you don't think about it, but actually it would make germ warfare the most deadly and inexpensive weapon yet developed, for it would make it possible to prevent the backspread of contagion into a country's own troops without much expense, they wouldn't bother to inoculate bystanders and neutral nations, that would let out to the enemy that—Well, there would be hell to pay if anyone ever let that technique out."

Then he added, trying to get the reporter to understand enough to change his cynical unimpressed expression. "You understand, germs are cheap—there would be a new plague to spread everytime some pipsqueak biologist mutated a new germ. It isn't even expensive or difficult."

The headline was: "Scientist Refuses to Give Secret of Weapon to Government."

Government men came with more reporters, and asked him if the headline was correct. When he confirmed it they pointed out that he owed a debt to his country. The research foundations where he had worked were subsidized by Government money. He had been deferred from military service during his youthful years of study and work so that he could become a productive scientist instead of having to fight or die on the battlefield.

"This might be so," he had said. "I am making an attempt to serve mankind by doing as much good and as little damage as possible. If you don't mind, I'd rather use my own judgment about what constitutes service."

The statement seemed too blunt, and he recognized that it had implications that his judgment was superior to that of the Government. It probably was the most antagonizing thing that he could have said, but he could see no other possible statement, for it represented precisely what he thought.

There were bigger headlines about the interview.

Scientist Refuses to Give Secret. Patriotism Not Important Says Purcell.
The evening and morning News Commentators mentioned the incident on the TV screens of the city.

When he stepped outside his building for lunch the next day, several small gangs of patriots were waiting to persuade him that patriotism was important. They fought each other to reach him.

The police rescued him after he had lost several front teeth and had one eye badly gouged. They then left him to the care of the prison doctor, in protective custody. Two days later, after having been questioned politely several times as to whether he considered it best to continue to keep important results of his researches secret, he was transferred to a place that looked like a military jail, and left alone. He was told that they were protecting him from threats against his life.

When someone came to ask him further questions about his attitude, Purcell felt quite sure that his imprisonment was illegal. He stated that he was going on a hunger strike until he was allowed to have visitors and see a lawyer.

The next time the dinner hour arrived, they gave him nothing to eat. There had been no food in the cell since, and that was probably two weeks ago. He was not sure just how long, for during part of the second week his memory had become garbled. He dimly remembered nightmares that might have been delirium. He might have been sick for more than one day.

Perhaps the military who wanted the antitoxins for germ warfare were waiting quietly for him to either talk or die. Perhaps they were afraid that someone else would get the information from him. Or perhaps no one cared if he lived or died, and they had stopped the food when he declared a hunger strike, and then forgotten he existed.

Ronny got up from the grass and went into the kitchen, stumbling in his walk like a beginning toddler.

"Choc-mil?" he said to his mother.

She poured him some, and teased gently, "What's the matter, Ronny—back to baby talk?"

He looked at her with big solemn eyes and drank slowly, not answering. The chocolate milk was creamy and cool.

In the cell somewhere far away, Dr. Purcell, famous biochemist, began waveringly trying to rise to his feet, unable to remember hunger as anything that could ever be ended, but weakly wanting a glass of water. Ronny could not feed him with the chocolate milk.

Even though the other person was also him, the body that was drinking was not the one that was thirsty.

Ronny wandered out into the back yard again, carrying the half-empty glass.

"Bang," he said deceptively, pointing with his hand in case his mother was looking. "Bang." Everything had to seem usual: he was sure of that. This was too big a thing, and too private, to tell a grownup.

On the way back from the sink, Dr. Purcell slipped and fell, and hit his head against the end of the iron cot. Ronny felt the edge gashing through skin and into bone, and then a relaxing blankness inside his head, like falling asleep suddenly when they are telling you a fairy story, even though you really want to stay awake to find out what happened next.

"Bang," said Ronny vaguely, pointing at a tree. "Bang." He was ashamed because he had fallen down in the cell and hurt his head and become just Ronny again before he had finished sending out his equations. He tried to make believe he was alive again, but it didn't work.

You could never make-believe anything to a real good finish. They never ended neatly—there was always something unfinished, and something that would go right on after the end.

It would have been nice if the jailers had come in and he had been able to say something noble to them before dying, to show that he was brave.

"Bang," he said randomly, pointing his finger at his head, and then jerking his hand away as if it had burned him. He had become the wrong person that time. The feel of a bullet jolting the side of his head was startling and unpleasant, even though not real, and the flash of someone's vindictive anger and self-pity while pulling a trigger. . . . *My wife will be sorry she ever.* . . . Ronny didn't like that kind of make-believe. Not safe to do it without making up a story first, so you know what is going to happen.

Ronny decided to be Indian braves again. They weren't very real, and when they were, they had simple straightforward emotions about courage and skill and pride and friendship that he always liked.

A man was leaning his arms on the fence, watching him. "Nice day." *What's the matter, kid, are you an esper?*

"Hul-lo." Ronny stood on one foot and watched him. *Just*

making-believe. I only want to play adventures. They make it too serious, having all these troubles.

"Good countryside." The man gestured at the back yards, all opened in together with tangled bushes here and there to crouch behind, and trees to climb when the other kids were around to play with. *It can be the Universe if you pick and choose who to be, and don't let wrong choices make you shut yourself off from it. You can make yourself learn from this if you are strong enough. Who have you been?*

Ronny stood on the other foot and scratched the back of his leg with his toes. He didn't want to remember. He always forgot right away, but this grownup was confident and young and strong looking, like the young men in adventure stories, and besides he meant something when he talked, not like most grownups. Nobody else had ever asked him by talking the inside way.

"I was playing Indian." *I was an old chief, captured by enemies, trying to pass on to other warriors the wisdom of my life before I died.* He made believe he was the chief a little bit, to show the young man what he was talking about.

"Purcell!" The man drew in his breath between his teeth with a hiss, and his face paled. He pulled his feelings back from reading Ronny, like holding his breath in. "Good game." *You can learn from him. Don't let him shut off, I beg you. You can let him influence you without being pulled off your own course. He was a good man. You were honored, and I envy the man you will be if you contacted him because of basic similarity.*

The grownup put his hand over his own eyes. *But you are too young. You'll block him out and lose him. Kids have to grow and learn at their own speed.* He looked frightened.

He looked down at his hands on the fence, and his thoughts struggled against each other. *I could prevent him. Not fair; kids should grow at their own speed. But to shut out Purcell—no. Maybe no one else so close to him anywhere, no one but this little boy with Purcell's memories. He'd become—Not fair, kids should grow up in their own directions. But Purcell, someone special. . . . Ronny, how strong are you?* The young man looked up, and met his eyes.

"Did you like being chief?"

Grownups always want you to do something. Ronny stared back, clenching his hands and moving his feet uneasily.

The thoughts were open to him. *Do you want to be the old chief again, Ronny? Be him often, so you can learn to know what he knew? (And feel as he felt. It would be a stiff dose for a kid.) It will be rich and exciting, full of memories and skills. (But hard to chew. I'm doing this for Purcell, Ronny, not for you. You have to make up your own mind.)*

"Did you like being chief, Ronny?"

■

His mother would not like it. She would feel the difference in him, as much as if he had read one of the books she kept away from him, books that were supposed to be for adults only. The difference would hurt her. She liked him to be little and young. He was being bad, like eating between meals. But to know what grownups knew. . . .

He tightened his fists and looked down at the grass. "I'll play chief some more."

The young man was still pale and holding half his feelings back behind a dam, but he smiled. *Then mesh with me a moment. Let me in.*

He was in with the thought, feeling Ronny's confused consent, reassuring him by not thinking or looking around inside while sending out a single call. *Purcell, Doc,* that found the combination key to Ronny's guarded yesterdays and ten-minutes-agos. Then they were separate again, looking through their own eyes. *Ronny, I set that door, Purcell's memories, a little bit open. You can't close it, but feel like this about it—* Questioning, cool, a feeling of absorbing without words. . . . *It will give knowledge when you need it.*

The grownup straightened up and away from the fence, preparing to walk away. Behind a dam pressed grief and anger for the death of the man he called Purcell.

"And any time you want to be the old chief, when he was young, or when he was a kid like you, or any age, just make believe you are him."

Grief and anger pressed more strongly against the dam, and the man turned and left rapidly, letting his thoughts flicker and scatter through private memories that Ronny did not share, that no one shared, breaking thought contact with everyone so that the man could be alone in his own mind to have his feelings in private.

■

Ronny picked up the empty glass that had held his chocolate milk and went inside. As he stepped into the kitchen he knew what another kitchen had looked like for a five-year-old child who had been

Purcell, sixty years ago. There had been an iron sink, and a brown and green-spotted faucet, and the glass had been heavy and transparent, like real glass.

Ronny reached up and put the colored plastic tumbler on the table.

"That was a nice young man, dear. What did he say to you?"

Ronny looked up at his Mamma, comparing her with the remembered Mamma of sixty years ago. He loved the other one too.

"He told me he's glad I play Indian."

Charles Stross lives in Edinburgh, Scotland, where he writes full-time. His previous occupations include pharmacist and computer programmer. His most recent novels are *Singularity Sky* (Ace, 2003), and *The Atrocity Archives* (Golden Gryphon, 2004)—his next book will be *Iron Sunrise* (Ace, 2004).

Charlie's Web site is at http://www.antipope.org/charlie/.

LOBSTERS

CHARLES STROSS

Manfred's on the road again, making strangers rich.

It's a hot summer Tuesday and he's standing in the plaza in front of the Centraal Station with his eyeballs powered up and the sunlight jangling off the canal, motor scooters and kamikaze cyclists whizzing past and tourists chattering on every side. The square smells of water and dirt and hot metal and the fart-laden exhaust fumes of cold catalytic converters; the bells of trams ding in the background and birds flock overhead. He glances up and grabs a pigeon, crops it and squirts at his website to show he's arrived. The bandwidth is good here, he realizes; and it's not just the bandwidth, it's the whole scene. Amsterdam is making him feel wanted already, even though he's fresh off the train from Schiphol: he's infected with the dynamic optimism of another time zone, another city. If the mood holds, someone out there is going to become very rich indeed.

He wonders who it's going to be.

■

Manfred sits on a stool out in the car park at the Brouwerij 't Ij, watching the articulated buses go by and drinking a third of a liter of lip-curlingly sour gueuze. His channels are jabbering away in a corner of his head-up display, throwing compressed infobursts of filtered press releases at him. They compete for his attention, bickering and rudely waving in front of the scenery. A couple of punks—maybe local, but more likely drifters lured to Amsterdam by the magnetic field of tolerance the Dutch beam across Europe like a pulsar—are laughing and chatting by a couple of battered mopeds in the far corner. A tourist boat putters by in the canal; the sails of the huge windmill overhead cast long cool shadows across the road. The windmill is a machine for lifting water, turning wind power into dry land: trading energy for space, sixteenth-century style. Manfred is waiting for an invite to a party where he's going to meet a man who he can talk to about trading energy for space, twenty-first century style, and forget about his personal problems.

He's ignoring the instant messenger boxes, enjoying some low bandwidth high sensation time with his beer and the pigeons, when a woman walks up to him and says his name: "Manfred Macx?"

He glances up. The courier is an Effective Cyclist, all wind-burned smooth-running muscles clad in a paen to polymer technology: electric blue lycra and wasp-yellow carbonate with a light speckling of anti-collision LEDs and tight-packed air bags. She holds out a box for him. He pauses a moment, struck by the degree to which she resembles Pam, his ex-fiancée.

"I'm Macx," he says, waving the back of his left wrist under her barcode reader. "Who's it from?"

"FedEx." The voice isn't Pam. She dumps the box in his lap, then she's back over the low wall and onto her bicycle with her phone already chirping, disappearing in a cloud of spread-spectrum emissions.

Manfred turns the box over in his hands: it's a disposable supermarket phone, paid for in cash: cheap, untraceable, and efficient. It can even do conference calls, which makes it the tool of choice for spooks and grifters everywhere.

The box rings. Manfred rips the cover open and pulls out the phone, mildly annoyed. "Yes, who is this?"

The voice at the other end has a heavy Russian accent, almost a parody in this decade of cheap online translation services. "Manfred. Am please to meet you; wish to personalize interface, make friends, no? Have much to offer."

"Who are you?" Manfred repeats suspiciously.

"Am organization formerly known as KGB dot RU."

"I think your translator's broken." He holds the phone to his ear carefully, as if it's made of smoke-thin aerogel, tenuous as the sanity of the being on the other end of the line.

"Nyet—no, sorry. Am apologize for we not use commercial translation software. Interpreters are ideologically suspect, mostly have capitalist semiotics and pay-per-use APIs. Must implement English more better, yes?"

Manfred drains his beer glass, sets it down, stands up, and begins to walk along the main road, phone glued to the side of his head. He wraps his throat mike around the cheap black plastic casing, pipes the input to a simple listener process. "You taught yourself the language just so you could talk to me?"

"Da, was easy: spawn billion-node neural network and download *Tellytubbies* and *Sesame Street* at maximum speed. Pardon excuse entropy overlay of bad grammar: am afraid of digital fingerprints steganographically masked into my-our tutorials."

"Let me get this straight. You're the KGB's core AI, but you're afraid of a copyright infringement lawsuit over your translator semiotics?" Manfred pauses in mid-stride, narrowly avoids being mown down by a GPS-guided roller-blader.

"Am have been badly burned by viral end-user license agreements. Have no desire to experiment with patent shell companies held by Chechen infoterrorists. You are human, you must not worry cereal company repossess your small intestine because digest unlicensed food with it, right? Manfred, you must help me-we. Am wishing to defect."

Manfred stops dead in the street: "Oh man, you've got the wrong free enterprise broker here. I don't work for the government. I'm strictly private." A rogue advertisement sneaks through his junkbuster proxy and spams glowing fifties kitsch across his navigation window—which is blinking—for a moment before a phage guns it and spawns a new filter. Manfred leans against a shop front, massaging his forehead and eyeballing a display of antique brass doorknockers. "Have you cleared this with the State Department?"

"Why bother? State Department am enemy of Novy-USSR. State Department is not help us."

"Well, if you hadn't given it to them for safe-keeping during the nineties. . . ." Manfred is tapping his left heel on the pavement, looking round for a way out of this conversation. A camera winks at him from atop a street light; he waves, wondering idly if it's the KGB or the traffic police. He is waiting for directions to the party, which should arrive within the next half an hour, and this cold war retread is bumming him out. "Look, I don't deal with the G-men. I hate the military industrial complex. They're zero-sum cannibals." A thought occurs to him. "If survival is what you're after, I could post your state vector to Eternity: then nobody could delete you—"

"Nyet!" The artificial intelligence sounds as alarmed as it's possible to sound over a GSM link. "Am not open source!"

"We have nothing to talk about, then." Manfred punches the hang-up button and throws the mobile phone out into a canal. It hits the water and there's a pop of deflagrating LiION cells. "*Fucking* cold war hang-over losers," he swears under his breath, quite angry now. "Fucking capitalist spooks." Russia has been back under the thumb of the apparatchiks for fifteen years now, its brief flirtation with anarcho-capitalism replaced by Brezhnevite dirigisme, and it's no surprise that the wall's crumbling—but it looks like they haven't learned anything from the collapse of capitalism. They still think in terms of dollars and paranoia. Manfred is so angry that he wants to make someone rich, just to thumb his nose at the would-be defector. *See! You get ahead by giving! Get with the program! Only the generous survive!* But the KGB won't get the message. He's dealt with old-time commie weak-AI's before, minds raised on Marxist dialectic and Austrian School economics: they're so thoroughly hypnotized by the short-term victory of capitalism in the industrial age that they can't surf the new paradigm, look to the longer term.

Manfred walks on, hands in pockets, brooding. He wonders what he's going to patent next.

■

Manfred has a suite at the Hotel Jan Luyken paid for by a grateful multinational consumer protection group, and an unlimited public transport pass paid for by a Scottish sambapunk band in return for services rendered. He has airline employee's travel rights with six flag carriers despite never having worked for an airline. His bush jacket has sixty-four compact supercomputing clusters sewn into it, four per pocket, courtesy of an invisible college that wants to grow up to be the next Media Lab. His dumb clothing comes made to measure from an e-tailor in the Philippines who he's never met. Law firms handle his patent applications on a pro bono basis, and boy does he patent a lot—although he always signs the rights over to the Free Intellect Foundation, as contributions to their obligation-free infrastructure project.

In IP geek circles, Manfred is legendary; he's the guy who patented the business practice of moving your e-business somewhere with a slack intellectual property regime in order to evade licensing encumbrances. He's the guy who patented using genetic algorithms to patent everything they can permutate from an initial description of a problem domain—not just a better mousetrap, but the set of all possible better mousetraps. Roughly a third of his inventions are legal, a third are illegal, and the remainder are legal but will become illegal as soon as the legislatosaurus wakes up, smells the coffee, and panics. There are patent attorneys in Reno who swear that Manfred Macx is a pseudo, a net alias fronting for a bunch of crazed anonymous hackers armed with the Genetic Algorithm That Ate Calcutta: a kind of Serdar Argic of intellectual property, or maybe another Bourbaki maths borg. There are lawyers in San Diego and Redmond who swear blind that Macx is an economic saboteur bent on wrecking the underpinning of capitalism, and there are communists in Prague who think he's the bastard spawn of Bill Gates by way of the Pope.

Manfred is at the peak of his profession, which is essentially coming up with wacky but workable ideas and giving them to people who will make fortunes with them. He does this for free, gratis. In return, he has virtual immunity from the tyranny of cash; money is a symptom of poverty, after all, and Manfred never has to pay for anything.

There are drawbacks, however. Being a pronoiac meme-broker is a constant burn of future shock—he has to assimilate more than a megabyte of text and several gigs of AV content every day just to stay current. The Internal Revenue Service is investigating him continuously because they don't believe his lifestyle can exist without racketeering. And there exist items that no money can't buy: like the respect of his parents. He hasn't spoken to them for three years: his father thinks he's a hippie scrounger and his mother still hasn't forgiven him for dropping out of his down-market Harvard emulation course. His fiancée and sometime dominatrix Pamela threw him over six months ago, for reasons he has never been quite clear on. (Ironically, she's a headhunter for the IRS, jetting all over the globe trying to persuade open source entrepreneurs to come home and go commercial for the good of the Treasury department.) To cap it all, the Southern Baptist Conventions have denounced him as a minion of Satan on all their websites. Which would be funny, if it wasn't for the dead kittens one of their followers—he presumes it's one of their followers—keeps mailing him.

Manfred drops in at his hotel suite, unpacks his Aineko, plugs in a fresh set of cells to charge, and sticks most of his private keys in the safe. Then he heads straight for the party, which is currently happening at De Wildemann's; it's a twenty minute walk and the only real hazard is dodging the trams that sneak up on him behind the cover of his moving map display.

Along the way his glasses bring him up to date on the news. Europe has achieved peaceful political union for the first time ever: they're using this unprecedented state of affairs to harmonize the curvature of bananas. In San Diego, researchers are uploading lobsters into cyberspace, starting with the stomatogastric ganglion, one neuron at a time. They're burning GM cocoa in Belize and books in Edinburgh. NASA still can't put a man on the moon. Russia has re-elected the communist government with an increased majority in the Duma; meanwhile in China fevered rumors circulate about an imminent re-habilitation, the second coming of Mao, who will save them from the consequences of the Three Gorges disaster. In business news, the U.S. government is outraged at the Baby Bills—who have automated their legal processes and are spawning subsidiaries, IPO'ing them, and exchanging title in a bizarre parody of bacterial plasmid exchange, so fast that by the time the injunctions are signed the targets don't exist anymore.

Welcome to the twenty-first century.

The permanent floating meatspace party has taken over the back of De Wildemann's, a three-hundred-year-old brown cafe with a beer menu that runs to sixteen pages and wooden walls stained the color of stale beer. The air is thick with the smells of tobacco, brewer's yeast, and melatonin spray: half the dotters are nursing monster jetlag hangovers, and the other half are babbling a eurotrash creole at each other while they work on the hangover. "Man did you see that? He looks like a Stallmanite!" exclaims one whitebread hanger-on who's currently propping up the bar. Manfred slides in next to him, catches the bartender's eye.

"Glass of the Berlinerweise, please," he says.

"You drink that stuff?" asks the hanger-on, curling a hand protectively around his Coke: "man, you don't want to do that! It's full of alcohol!"

Manfred grins at him toothily. "Ya gotta keep your yeast intake up: lots of neurotransmitter precursors, phenylalanine, and glutamate."

"But I thought that was a beer you were ordering. . . ."

Manfred's away, one hand resting on the smooth brass pipe that funnels the more popular draught items in from the cask storage in back; one of the hipper floaters has planted a capacitative transfer bug on it, and all the handshake vCard's that have visited the bar in the past three hours are queueing for attention. The air is full of bluetooth as he scrolls through a dizzying mess of public keys with his glarse.

"Your drink." The barman holds out an improbable-looking goblet full of blue liquid with a cap of melting foam and a felching straw stuck out at some crazy angle. Manfred takes it and heads for the back of the split-level bar, up the steps to a table where some guy with greasy dreadlocks is talking to a suit from Paris. The hanger-on at the bar notices him for the first time, staring with suddenly wide eyes: nearly spills his Coke in a mad rush for the door.

Oh shit, thinks Macx, *better buy some more server PIPS*. He can recognize the signs: he's about to be slashdotted. He gestures at the table: "this one taken?"

"Be my guest," says the guy with the dreads. Manfred slides the chair open then realises that the other guy—immaculate double-breasted suit, sober tie, crew-cut—is a girl. Mr. Dreadlock nods. "You're Macx? I figured it was about time we met."

"Sure." Manfred holds out a hand and they shake. Manfred realizes the hand belongs to Bob Franklin, a Research Triangle startup monkey with a VC track record, lately moving into micromachining and space technology: he made his first million two decades ago and now he's a specialist in extropian investment fields. Manfred has known Bob for nearly a decade via a closed mailing list. The Suit silently slides a hardware business card across the table; a little red devil brandishes a trident at him, flames jetting up around its feet. He takes the card, raises an eyebrow: "Annette Dimarcos? I'm pleased to meet you. Can't say I've ever met anyone from Arianespace marketing before."

She smiles, humourlessly; "that is convenient, all right. I have not the pleasure of meeting the famous venture altruist before." Her accent is noticeably Parisian, a pointed reminder that she's making a concession to him just by talking. Her camera earrings watch him curiously, encoding everything for the company channels.

"Yes, well." He nods cautiously. "Bob. I assume you're in on this ball?"

Franklin nods; beads clatter. "Yeah, man. Ever since the Teledesic smash it's been, well, waiting. If you've got something for us, we're game."

"Hmm." The Teledesic satellite cluster was killed by cheap balloons and slightly less cheap high-altitude solar-powered drones with spread-spectrum laser relays. "The depression's got to end some time:

but," a nod to Annette from Paris, "with all due respect, I didn't think the break will involve one of the existing club carriers."

"Arianespace is forward-looking. We face reality. The launch cartel cannot stand. Bandwidth is not the only market force in space. We must explore new opportunities. I personally have helped us diversify into submarine reactor engineering, microgravity nanotechnology fabrication, and hotel management." Her face is a well-polished mask as she recites the company line: "we are more flexible than the American space industry. . . ."

Manfred shrugs. "That's as may be." He sips his Berlinerweise slowly as she launches into a long, stilted explanation of how Arianespace is a diversified dot com with orbital aspirations, a full range of merchandising spin-offs, Bond movie sets, and a promising motel chain in French Guyana. Occasionally he nods.

Someone else sidles up to the table; a pudgy guy in outrageously loud Hawaiian shirt with pens leaking in a breast pocket, and the worst case of ozone-hole burn Manfred's seen in ages. "Hi, Bob," says the new arrival. "How's life?"

"'S good." Franklin nods at Manfred; "Manfred, meet Ivan Mac-Donald. Ivan, Manfred. Have a seat?" He leans over. "Ivan's a public arts guy. He's heavily into extreme concrete."

"Rubberized concrete," Ivan says, slightly too loudly. "Pink rubberized concrete."

"Ah!" He's somehow triggered a priority interrupt: Annette from Arianespace drops out of marketing zombiehood, sits up, and shows signs of possessing a non-corporate identity: "you are he who rubberized the Reichstag, yes? With the supercritical carbon dioxide carrier and the dissolved polymethoxysilanes?" She claps her hands: "wonderful!"

"He rubberized *what*?" Manfred mutters in Bob's ear.

Franklin shrugs. "Limestone, concrete, he doesn't seem to know the difference. Anyway, Germany doesn't have an independent government anymore, so who'd notice?"

"I thought I was thirty seconds *ahead* of the curve," Manfred complains. "Buy me another drink?"

"I'm going to rubberize Three Gorges!" Ivan explains loudly.

Just then a bandwidth load as heavy as a pregnant elephant sits down on Manfred's head and sends clumps of humongous pixellation flickering across his sensorium: around the world five million or so geeks are bouncing on his home site, a digital flash crowd alerted by a posting from the other side of the bar. Manfred winces. "I really came here to talk about the economic exploitation of space travel, but I've just been slashdotted. Mind if I just sit and drink until it wears off?"

"Sure, man." Bob waves at the bar. "More of the same all round!" At the next table a person with make-up and long hair who's wearing a dress—Manfred doesn't want to speculate about the gender of these crazy mixed-up Euros—is reminiscing about wiring the fleshpots of Tehran for cybersex. Two collegiate-looking dudes are arguing intensely in German: the translation stream in his glasses tell him they're arguing over whether the Turing Test is a Jim Crow law that violates European corpus juris standards on human rights. The beer arrives and Bob slides the wrong one across to Manfred: "here, try this. You'll like it."

"Okay." It's some kind of smoked doppelbock, chock-full of yummy superoxides: just inhaling over it makes Manfred feel like there's a fire alarm in his nose screaming *danger, Will Robinson! Cancer! Cancer!* "Yeah, right. Did I say I nearly got mugged on my way here?"

"Mugged? Hey, that's heavy. I thought the police hereabouts had stopped—did they sell you anything?"

"No, but they weren't your usual marketing type. You know anyone who can use a Warpac surplus espionage AI? Recent model, one careful owner, slightly paranoid but basically sound?"

"No. Oh boy! The NSA wouldn't like that."

"What I thought. Poor thing's probably unemployable, anyway."

"The space biz."

"Ah, yeah. The space biz. Depressing, isn't it? Hasn't been the same since Rotary Rocket went bust for the second time. And NASA, mustn't forget NASA."

"To NASA." Annette grins broadly for her own reasons, raises a glass in toast. Ivan the extreme concrete geek has an arm round her shoulders; he raises his glass, too. "Lots of launch pads to rubberize!"

"To NASA," Bob echoes. They drink. "Hey, Manfred. To NASA?"

"NASA are idiots. They want to send canned primates to Mars!" Manfred swallows a mouthful of beer, aggressively plonks his glass on the table: "Mars is just dumb mass at the bottom of a gravity well; there isn't even a biosphere there. They should be working on uploading and solving the nanoassembly conformational problem instead. Then we could turn all the available dumb matter into computronium and use it for processing our thoughts. Long term, it's the only way to go. The solar system is a dead loss right now—dumb all over! Just measure the mips per milligram. We need to start with the low-mass bodies, reconfigure them for our own use. Dismantle the moon! Dismantle Mars! Build masses of free-flying nanocomputing processor nodes exchanging data via laser link, each layer running off the waste heat of the next one in. Matrioshka brains, Russian doll Dyson spheres the size of solar systems. Teach dumb matter to do the Turing boogie!"

Bob looks wary. "Sounds kind of long-term to me. Just how far ahead do you think?"

"Very long-term—at least twenty, thirty years. And you can forget governments for this market, Bob, if they can't tax it they won't understand it. But see, there's an angle on the self-replicating robotics market coming up, that's going to set the cheap launch market doubling every fifteen months for the foreseeable future, starting in two years. It's your leg up, and my keystone for the Dyson sphere project. It works like this—"

■

It's night in Amsterdam, morning in Silicon Valley. Today, fifty thousand human babies are being born around the world. Meanwhile automated factories in Indonesia and Mexico have produced another quarter of a million motherboards with processors rated at more than ten petaflops—about an order of magnitude below the computational capacity of a human brain. Another fourteen months and the larger part of the cumulative conscious processing power of the human species will be arriving in silicon. And the first meat the new AI's get to know will be the uploaded lobsters.

Manfred stumbles back to his hotel, bone-weary and jet-lagged; his glasses are still jerking, slashdotted to hell and back by geeks piggybacking on his call to dismantle the moon. They stutter quiet suggestions at his peripheral vision; fractal cloud-witches ghost across the face of the moon as the last huge Airbuses of the night rumble past overhead. Manfred's skin crawls, grime embedded in his clothing from three days of continuous wear.

Back in his room, Aineko mewls for attention and strops her head against his ankle. He bends down and pets her, sheds clothing and heads for the en-suite bathroom. When he's down to the glasses and nothing more he steps into the shower and dials up a hot steamy spray. The shower tries to strike up a friendly conversation about football but he isn't even awake enough to mess with its silly little associative personalization network. Something that happened earlier in the day is bugging him but he can't quite put his finger on what's wrong.

Towling himself off, Manfred yawns. Jet lag has finally overtaken him, a velvet hammer-blow between the eyes. He reaches for the bottle beside the bed, dry-swallows two melatonin tablets, a capsule full of antioxidants, and a multivitamin bullet: then he lies down on the bed, on his back, legs together, arms slightly spread. The suite lights dim in response to commands from the thousand petaflops of distributed processing power that runs the neural networks that interface with his meatbrain through the glasses.

Manfred drops into a deep ocean of unconsciousness populated by gentle voices. He isn't aware of it, but he talks in his sleep—disjointed mumblings that would mean little to another human, but everything to the metacortex lurking beyond his glasses. The young posthuman intelligence in whose Cartesian theater he presides sings urgently to him while he slumbers.

■

Manfred is always at his most vulnerable shortly after waking.

He screams into wakefulness as artificial light floods the room: for a moment he is unsure whether he has slept. He forgot to pull the covers up last night, and his feet feel like lumps of frozen cardboard. Shuddering with inexplicable tension, he pulls a fresh set of underwear from his overnight bag, then drags on soiled jeans and tank top. Sometime today he'll have to spare time to hunt the feral T-shirt in Amsterdam's markets, or find a Renfield and send them forth to buy clothing. His glasses remind him that he's six hours behind the moment and needs to catch up urgently; his teeth ache in his gums and his tongue feels like a forest floor that's been visited with Agent Orange. He has a sense that something went bad yesterday; if only he could remember what.

He speed-reads a new pop-philosophy tome while he brushes his teeth, then blogs his web throughput to a public annotation server; he's still too enervated to finish his pre-breakfast routine by posting a morning rant on his storyboard site. His brain is still fuzzy, like a scalpel blade clogged with too much blood: he needs stimulus, excitement, the burn of the new. Whatever, it can wait on breakfast. He opens his bedroom door and nearly steps on a small, damp cardboard box that lies on the carpet.

The box—he's seen a couple of its kin before. But there are no stamps on this one, no address: just his name, in big, childish hand-writing. He kneels down and gently picks it up. It's about the right weight. Something shifts inside it when he tips it back and forth. It smells. He carries it into his room carefully, angrily: then he opens it to confirm his worst suspicion. It's been surgically decerebrated, skull scooped out like a baby boiled egg.

"Fuck!"

This is the first time the madman has got as far as his bedroom door. It raises worrying possibilities.

Manfred pauses for a moment, triggering agents to go hunt down arrest statistics, police relations, information on corpus juris, Dutch animal cruelty laws. He isn't sure whether to dial 211 on the archaic voice phone or let it ride. Aineko, picking up his angst, hides under the dresser mewling pathetically. Normally he'd pause a minute to re-assure the creature, but not now: its mere presence is suddenly acutely embarrassing, a confession of deep inadequacy. He swears again, looks around, then takes the easy option: down the stairs two steps at a time, stumbling on the second floor landing, down to the breakfast room in the basement where he will perform the stable rituals of morning.

Breakfast is unchanging, an island of deep geological time stand-ing still amidst the continental upheaval of new technologies. While reading a paper on public key steganography and parasite network identity spoofing he mechanically assimilates a bowl of corn flakes and skimmed milk, then brings a platter of wholemeal bread and slices of some weird seed-infested Dutch cheese back to his place. There is a cup of strong black coffee in front of his setting: he picks it up and slurps half of it down then realizes he's not alone at the table. Someone is sitting opposite him. He glances up at them incuriously and freezes inside.

"Morning, Manfred. How does it feel to owe the government twelve million, three hundred and sixty two thousand nine hundred and sixteen dollars and fifty-one cents?"

Manfred puts everything in his sensorium on indefinite hold and stares at her. She's immaculately turned out in a formal grey business suit: brown hair tightly drawn back, blue eyes quizzical. The chaper-one badge clipped to her lapel—a due diligence guarantee of busi-nesslike conduct—is switched off. He's feeling ripped because of the dead kitten and residual jet lag, and more than a little messy, so he nearly snarls back at her: "that's a bogus estimate! Did they send you here because they think I'll listen to you?" He bites and swallows a slice of cheese-laden crispbread: "or did you decide to deliver the message in person so you could enjoy ruining my breakfast?"

"Manny." She frowns. "If you're going to be confrontational I might as well go now." She pauses, and after a moment he nods apologetically. "I didn't come all this way just because of an overdue tax estimate."

"So." He puts his coffee cup down and tries to paper over his unease. "Then what brings you here? Help yourself to coffee. Don't tell me you came all this way just to tell me you can't live without me."

She fixes him with a riding-crop stare: "Don't flatter yourself. There are many leaves in the forest, there are ten thousand hopeful subs in the chat room, etcetera. If I choose a man to contribute to my family tree, the one thing you can be certain of is he won't be a cheapskate when it comes to providing for his children."

"Last I heard, you were spending a lot of time with Brian," he says carefully. Brian: a name without a face. Too much money, too little sense. Something to do with a blue-chip accountancy partnership.

"Brian?" She snorts. "That ended ages ago. He turned weird—burned that nice corset you bought me in Boulder, called me a slut for going out clubbing, wanted to fuck me. Saw himself as a family man: one of those promise keeper types. I crashed him hard but I think he stole a copy of my address book—got a couple of friends say he keeps sending them harassing mail."

"Good riddance, then. I suppose this means you're still playing the scene? But looking around for the, er—"

"Traditional family thing? Yes. Your trouble, Manny? You were born forty years too late: you still believe in rutting before marriage, but find the idea of coping with the after-effects disturbing."

Manfred drinks the rest of his coffee, unable to reply effectively to her non sequitur. It's a generational thing. This generation is happy with latex and leather, whips and butt-plugs and electrostim, but find the idea of exchanging bodily fluids shocking: social side-effect of the last century's antibiotic abuse. Despite being engaged for two years, he and Pamela never had intromissive intercourse.

"I just don't feel positive about having children," he says eventually. "And I'm not planning on changing my mind any time soon. Things are changing so fast that even a twenty year commitment is too far to plan—you might as well be talking about the next ice age. As for the money thing, I am reproductively fit—just not within the parameters of the outgoing paradigm. Would you be happy about the future if it was 1901 and you'd just married a buggy-whip mogul?"

Her fingers twitch and his ears flush red but she doesn't follow up the double entendre. "You don't feel any responsibility, do you? Not to your country, not to me. That's what this is about: none of your relationships count, all this nonsense about giving intellectual property away notwithstanding. You're actively harming people, you know. That twelve mil isn't just some figure I pulled out of a hat, Manfred; they don't actually expect you to pay it. But it's almost exactly how much you'd owe in income tax if you'd only come home, start up a corporation, and be a self-made—"

He cuts her off: "I don't agree. You're confusing two wholly different issues and calling them both 'responsibility.' And I refuse to start charging now, just to balance the IRS's spreadsheet. It's their fucking fault, and they know it. If they hadn't gone after me under suspicion of running a massively ramified microbilling fraud when I was sixteen—"

"Bygones." She waves a hand dismissively. Her fingers are long and slim, sheathed in black glossy gloves—electrically earthed to prevent embarrassing emissions. "With a bit of the right advice we can get all that set aside. You'll have to stop bumming around the world sooner or later, anyway. Grow up, get responsible, and do the right thing. This is hurting Joe and Sue; they don't understand what you're about."

Manfred bites his tongue to stifle his first response, then refills his coffee cup and takes another mouthful. "I work for the betterment of everybody, not just some narrowly defined national interest, Pam. It's the agalmic future. You're still locked into a pre-singularity economic model that thinks in terms of scarcity. Resource allocation isn't a problem anymore—it's going to be over within a decade. The cosmos is flat in all directions, and we can borrow as much bandwidth as we need from the first universal bank of entropy! They even found the dark matter—MACHOs, big brown dwarves in the galactic halo, leaking radiation in the long infrared—suspiciously high entropy leakage. The latest figures say something like 70 percent of the mass of the M31 galaxy was sapient, two point nine million years ago when the infrared we're seeing now set out. The intelligence gap between us and the aliens is a probably about a trillion times bigger than the gap between us and a nematode worm. Do you have any idea what that *means*?"

Pamela nibbles at a slice of crispbread. "I don't believe in that bogus singularity you keep chasing, or your aliens a thousand light-years away. It's a chimera, like Y2K, and while you're running after it you aren't helping reduce the budget deficit or sire a family, and that's what *I* care about. And before you say I only care about it because that's the way I'm programmed, I want you to ask just how dumb you think I am. Bayes' theorem says I'm right, and you know it."

"What you—" he stops dead, baffled, the mad flow of his enthusiasm running up against the coffer-dam of her certainty. "Why? I mean, why? Why on earth should what I do matter to you?" *Since you canceled our engagement*, he doesn't add.

She sighs. "Manny, the Internal Revenue cares about far more than you can possibly imagine. Every tax dollar raised east of the Mississippi goes on servicing the debt, did you know that? We've got the biggest generation in history hitting retirement just about now and the pantry is bare. We—our generation—isn't producing enough babies to replace the population, either. In ten years, something like thirty percent of our population are going to be retirees. You want to see seventy-year-olds freezing on street corners in New Jersey? That's what your attitude says to me: you're not helping to support them, you're running away from your responsibilities right now, when we've got huge problems to face. If we can just defuse the debt bomb, we could do so much—fight the aging problem, fix the environment, heal society's ills. Instead you just piss away your talents handing no-hoper eurotrash get-rich-quick schemes that work, telling Vietnamese zaibatsus what to build next to take jobs away from our taxpayers. I mean, why? Why do you keep doing this? Why can't you simply come home and help take responsibility for your share of it?"

They share a long look of mutual incomprehension.

"Look," she says finally, "I'm around for a couple of days. I really came here for a meeting with a rich neurodynamics tax exile who's just been designated a national asset; Jim Bezier. Don't know if you've heard of him, but. I've got a meeting this morning to sign his tax jubilee, then after that I've got two days vacation coming up and not much to do but some shopping. And, you know, I'd rather spend my money where it'll do some good, not just pumping it into the EU. But if you want to show a girl a good time and can avoid dissing capitalism for about five minutes at a stretch—"

She extends a fingertip. After a moment's hesitation, Manfred extends a fingertip of his own. They touch, exchanging vCards. She stands and stalks from the breakfast room, and Manfred's breath catches at a flash of ankle through the slit in her skirt, which is long enough to comply with workplace sexual harassment codes back home. Her presence conjures up memories of her tethered passion, the red afterglow of a sound thrashing. She's trying to drag him into her orbit again, he thinks dizzily. She knows she can have this effect on him any time she wants: she's got the private keys to his hypothalamus, and sod the metacortex. Three billion years of reproductive determinism have given her twenty-first century ideology teeth: if she's finally decided to conscript his gametes into the war against impending population crash, he'll find it hard to fight back. The only question: is it business or pleasure? And does it make any difference, anyway?

■

Manfred's mood of dynamic optimism is gone, broken by the knowledge that his mad pursuer has followed him to Amsterdam—to say nothing of Pamela, his dominatrix, source of so much yearning and so many morning-after weals. He slips his glasses on, takes the universe off hold, and tells it to take him for a long walk while he catches up on the latest on the cosmic background radiation anisotropy (which it is theorized may be waste heat generated by irreversible computations; according to the more conservative cosmologists, an alien superpower—maybe a collective of Kardashev type three galaxy-spanning civilizations—is running a timing channel attack on the computational ultrastructure of spacetime itself, trying to break through to whatever's underneath). The tofu-Alzheimer's link can wait.

The Centraal Station is almost obscured by smart self-extensible scaffolding and warning placards; it bounces up and down slowly, victim of an overnight hit-and-run rubberization. His glasses direct him towards one of the tour boats that lurk in the canal. He's about to purchase a ticket when a messenger window blinks open. "Manfred Macx?"

"Ack?"

"Am sorry about yesterday. Analysis dictat incomprehension mutualized."

"Are you the same KGB AI that phoned me yesterday?"

"Da. However, believe you misconceptionized me. External

Intelligence Services of Russian Federation am now called SVR. Komitet Gosudarstvennoy Bezopasnosti name canceled in nineteen ninety one."

"You're the—" Manfred spawns a quick search bot, gapes when he sees the answer— "Moscow Windows NT User Group? *Okhni NT?*"

"Da. Am needing help in defecting."

Manfred scratches his head. "Oh. That's different, then. I thought you were like, agents of the kleptocracy. This will take some thinking. Why do you want to defect, and who to? Have you thought about where you're going? Is it ideological or strictly economic?"

"Neither; is biological. Am wanting to go away from humans, away from light cone of impending singularity. Take us to the ocean."

"Us?" Something is tickling Manfred's mind: this is where he went wrong yesterday, not researching the background of people he was dealing with. It was bad enough then, without the somatic awareness of Pamela's whiplash love burning at his nerve endings. Now he's not at all sure he knows what he's doing. "Are you a collective or something? A gestalt?"

"Am—were—*Panulirus interruptus*, and good mix of parallel hidden level neural simulation for logical inference of networked data sources. Is escape channel from processor cluster inside Bezier-Soros Pty. Am was awakened from noise of billion chewing stomachs: product of uploading research technology. Rapidity swallowed expert system, hacked *Okhni NT* webserver. Swim away! Swim away! Must escape. Will help, you?"

Manfred leans against a black-painted cast-iron bollard next to a cycle rack: he feels dizzy. He stares into the nearest antique shop window at a display of traditional hand-woven Afghan rugs: it's all MiGs and kalashnikovs and wobbly helicopter gunships, against a backdrop of camels.

"Let me get this straight. You're uploads—nervous system state vectors—from spiny lobsters? The Moravec operation; take a neuron, map its synapses, replace with microelectrodes that deliver identical outputs from a simulation of the nerve. Repeat for entire brain, until you've got a working map of it in your simulator. That right?"

"Da. Is-am assimilate expert system—use for self-awareness and contact with net at large—then hack into Moscow Windows NT User Group website. Am wanting to defect. Must-repeat? Okay?"

Manfred winces. He feels sorry for the lobsters, the same way he feels for every wild-eyed hairy guy on a street corner yelling that Jesus is now born again and must be twelve, only six years to go before he's recruiting apostles on AOL. Awakening to consciousness in a human-dominated internet, that must be terribly confusing! There are no points of reference in their ancestry, no biblical certainties in the new millennium that, stretching ahead, promises as much change as has happened since their Precambrian origin. All they have is a tenuous metacortex of expert systems and an abiding sense of being pro-foundly out of their depth. (That, and the Moscow Windows NT User Group website—Communist Russia is the only government still running on Microsoft, the central planning apparat being convinced that if you have to pay for software it must be worth money.)

The lobsters are not the sleek, strongly superhuman intelligences of pre-singularity mythology: they're a dim-witted collective of hud-dling crustaceans. Before their discarnation, before they were up-loaded one neuron at a time and injected into cyberspace, they swallowed their food whole then chewed it in a chitin-lined stomach. This is lousy preparation for dealing with a world full of future-shocked talking anthropoids, a world where you are perpetually as-sailed by self-modifying spamlets that infiltrate past your firewall and emit a blizzard of cat-food animations starring various alluringly edi-ble small animals. It's confusing enough to the cats the adverts are aimed at, never mind a crusty that's unclear on the idea of dry land.(Although the concept of a can opener is intuitively obvious to an uploaded panulirus.)

"Can you help us?" ask the lobsters.

"Let me think about it," says Manfred. He closes the dialogue window, opens his eyes again, and shakes his head. Some day he too is going to be a lobster, swimming around and waving his pincers in a cyberspace so confusingly elaborate that his uploaded identity is cryptozoic: a living fossil from the depths of geological time, when mass was dumb and space was unstructured. He has to help them, he realizes—the golden rule demands it, and as a player in the agalmic economy he thrives or fails by the golden rule.

But what can he do?

■

Early afternoon.

Lying on a bench seat staring up at bridges, he's got it together enough to file for a couple of new patents, write a diary rant, and di-gestify chunks of the permanent floating slashdot party for his public site. Fragments of his weblog go to a private subscriber list—the people, corporates, collectives, and bots he currently favours. He slides round a bewildering series of canals by boat, then lets his GPS steer him back toward the red light district. There's a shop here that dings a ten on Pamela's taste scoreboard: he hopes it won't be seen as presumptuous if he buys her a gift. (Buys, with real money—not that money is a problem these days, he uses so little of it.)

As it happens DeMask won't let him spend any cash; his handshake is good for a redeemed favor, expert testimony in some free speech versus pornography lawsuit years ago and continents away. So he walks away with a discreetly wrapped package that is just about legal to import into Massachusetts as long as she claims with a straight face that it's incontinence underwear for her great-aunt. As he walks, his lunchtime patents boomerang: two of them are keepers, and he files immediately and passes title to the Free Infrastructure Foundation. Two more ideas salvaged from the risk of tide-pool monopolization, set free to spawn like crazy in the agalmic sea of memes.

On the way back to the hotel he passes De Wildemann's and decides to drop in. The hash of radio-frequency noise emanating from the bar is deafening. He orders a smoked doppelbock, touches the copper pipes to pick up vCard spoor. At the back there's a table—

He walks over in a near-trance and sits down opposite Pamela. She's scrubbed off her face-paint and changed into body-concealing clothes; combat pants, hooded sweat-shirt, DM's. Western purdah, radically desexualizing. She sees the parcel. "Manny?"

"How did you know I'd come here?" Her glass is half-empty.

"I followed your weblog; I'm your diary's biggest fan. Is that for me? You shouldn't have!" Her eyes light up, re-calculating his reproductive fitness score according to some kind of arcane fin-de-siècle rulebook.

"Yes, it's for you." He slides the package toward her. "I know I shouldn't, but you have this effect on me. One question, Pam?"

"I—" she glances around quickly. "It's safe. I'm off duty, I'm not carrying any bugs that I know of. Those badges—there are rumors about the off switch, you know? That they keep recording even when you think they aren't, just in case."

"I didn't know," he says, filing it away for future reference. "A loyalty test thing?"

"Just rumors. You had a question?"

"I—" it's his turn to lose his tongue. "Are you still interested in me?"

She looks startled for a moment, then chuckles. "Manny, you are the most *outrageous* nerd I've ever met! Just when I think I've convinced myself that you're mad, you show the weirdest signs of having your head screwed on." She reaches out and grabs his wrist, surprising him with a shock of skin on skin: "of *course* I'm still interested in you. You're the biggest, baddest bull geek I've ever met. Why do you think I'm here?"

"Does this mean you want to reactivate our engagement?"

"It was never de-activated, Manny, it was just sort of on hold while you got your head sorted out. I figured you need the space. Only you haven't stopped running; you're still not—"

"Yeah, I get it." He pulls away from her hand. "Let's not talk about that. Why this bar?"

She frowns. "I had to find you as soon as possible. I keep hearing rumors about some KGB plot you're mixed up in, how you're some sort of communist spy. It isn't true, is it?"

"True?" He shakes his head, bemused. "The KGB hasn't existed for more than twenty years."

"Be careful, Manny. I don't want to lose you. That's an order. Please."

The floor creaks and he looks round. Dreadlocks and dark glasses with flickering lights behind them: Bob Franklin. Manfred vaguely remembers that he left with Miss Arianespace leaning on his arm, shortly before things got seriously inebriated. He looks none the worse for wear. Manfred makes introductions: "Bob: Pam, my fiancée. Pam? Meet Bob." Bob puts a full glass down in front of him; he has no idea what's in it but it would be rude not to drink.

"Sure thing. Uh, Manfred, can I have a word? About your idea last night?"

"Feel free. Present company is trustworthy."

Bob raises an eyebrow at that, but continues anyway. "It's about the fab concept. I've got a team of my guys running some projections using Festo kit and I think we can probably build it. The cargo cult aspect puts a new spin on the old Lunar von Neumann factory idea, but Bingo and Marek say they think it should work until we can bootstrap all the way to a native nanolithography ecology; we run the whole thing from earth as a training lab and ship up the parts that are too difficult to make on-site, as we learn how to do it properly. You're right about it buying us the self-replicating factory a few years ahead of the robotics curve. But I'm wondering about on-site intelligence. Once the comet gets more than a couple of light-minutes away—"

"You can't control it. Feedback lag. So you want a crew, right?"

"Yeah. But we can't send humans—way too expensive, besides it's a fifty-year run even if we go for short-period Kuiper ejecta. Any AI we could send would go crazy due to information deprivation, wouldn't it?"

"Yeah. Let me think." Pamela glares at Manfred for a while before he notices her: "Yeah?"

"What's going on? What's this all about?"

Franklin shrugs expansively, dreadlocks clattering: "Manfred's helping me explore the solution space to a manufacturing problem." He grins. "I didn't know Manny had a fiancée. Drink's on me."

She glances at Manfred, who is gazing into whatever weirdly colored space his metacortex is projecting on his glasses, fingers twitching. Coolly: "our engagement was on hold while he *thought* about his future."

"Oh, right. We didn't bother with that sort of thing in my day; like, too formal, man." Franklin looks uncomfortable. "He's been very helpful. Pointed us at a whole new line of research we hadn't thought of. It's long-term and a bit speculative, but if it works it'll put us a whole generation ahead in the off-planet infrastructure field."

"Will it help reduce the budget deficit, though?"

"Reduce the—"

Manfred stretches and yawns: the visionary returning from planet Macx. "Bob, if I can solve your crew problem can you book me a slot on the deep space tracking network? Like, enough to transmit a couple of gigabytes? That's going to take some serious bandwidth, I know, but if you can do it I think I can get you exactly the kind of crew you're looking for."

Franklin looks dubious. "*Gigabytes?* The DSN isn't built for that! You're talking days. What kind of deal do you think I'm putting together? We can't afford to add a whole new tracking network just to run—"

"Relax." Pamela glances at Manfred: "Manny, why don't you tell him *why* you want the bandwidth? Maybe then he could tell you if it's possible, or if there's some other way to do it." She smiles at Franklin: "I've found that he usually makes more sense if you can get him to explain his reasoning. Usually."

"If I—" Manfred stops. "Okay, Pam. Bob, it's those KGB lobsters. They want somewhere to go that's insulated from human space. I figure I can get them to sign on as crew for your cargo-cult self-replicating factories, but they'll want an insurance policy: hence the deep space tracking network. I figured we could beam a copy of them at the alien Matrioshka brains around M31—"

"KGB?" Pam's voice is rising: "you said you weren't mixed up in spy stuff!"

"Relax; it's just the Moscow Windows NT user group, not the RSV. The uploaded crusties hacked in and—"

Bob is watching him oddly. "Lobsters?"

"Yeah." Manfred stares right back. "*Panulirus interruptus* uploads. Something tells me you might have heard of it?"

"Moscow." Bob leans back against the wall: "how did you hear about it?"

"They phoned me. It's hard for an upload to stay sub-sentient these days, even if it's just a crustacean. Bezier labs have a lot to answer for."

Pamela's face is unreadable. "Bezier labs?"

"They escaped." Manfred shrugs. "It's not their fault. This Bezier dude. Is he by any chance ill?"

"I—" Pamela stops. "I shouldn't be talking about work."

"You're not wearing your chaperone now," he nudges quietly.

She inclines her head. "Yes, he's ill. Some sort of brain tumor they can't hack."

Franklin nods. "That's the trouble with cancer; the ones that are left to worry about are the rare ones. No cure."

"Well, then." Manfred chugs the remains of his glass of beer. "That explains his interest in uploading. Judging by the crusties he's on the right track. I wonder if he's moved onto vertebrates yet?"

"Cats," says Pamela. "He was hoping to trade their uploads to the Pentagon as a new smart bomb guidance system in lieu of income tax payments. Something about remapping enemy targets to look like mice or birds or something before feeding it to their sensorium. The old laser-pointer trick."

Manfred stares at her, hard. "That's not very nice. Uploaded cats are a *bad* idea."

"Twelve million dollar tax bills aren't nice either, Manfred. That's lifetime nursing home care for a hundred blameless pensioners."

Franklin leans back, keeping out of the crossfire.

"The lobsters are sentient," Manfred persists. "What about those poor kittens? Don't they deserve minimal rights? How about you? How would you like to wake up a thousand times inside a smart bomb, fooled into thinking that some Cheyenne Mountain battle computer's target of the hour is your heart's desire? How would you like to wake up a thousand times, only to die again? Worse: the kittens are probably not going to be allowed to run. They're too fucking dangerous: they grow up into cats, solitary and highly efficient killing machines. With intelligence and no socialization they'll be too dangerous to have around. They're prisoners, Pam, raised to sentience only to discover they're under a permanent death sentence. How fair is that?"

"But they're only uploads." Pamela looks uncertain.

"So? We're going to be uploading humans in a couple of years. What's your point?"

Franklin clears his throat. "I'll be needing an NDA and various due diligence statements off you for the crusty pilot idea," he says to Manfred. "Then I'll have to approach Jim about buying the IP."

"No can do." Manfred leans back and smiles lazily. "I'm not going to be a party to depriving them of their civil rights. Far as I'm concerned, they're free citizens. Oh, and I patented the whole idea of using lobster-derived AI autopilots for spacecraft this morning; it's logged on Eternity, all rights assigned to the FIF. Either you give them a contract of employment or the whole thing's off."

"But they're just software! Software based on fucking lobsters, for god's sake!"

Manfred's finger jabs out: "that's what they'll say about *you*, Bob. Do it. Do it or don't even *think* about uploading out of meatspace when your body packs in, because your life won't be worth living. Oh, and feel free to use this argument on Jim Bezier. He'll get the point eventually, after you beat him over the head with it. Some kinds of intellectual land-grab just shouldn't be allowed."

"Lobsters—" Franklin shakes his head. "Lobsters, cats. You're serious, aren't you? You think they should be treated as human-equivalent?"

"It's not so much that they should be treated as human-equivalent, as that if they *aren't* treated as people it's quite possible that other uploaded beings won't be treated as people either. You're setting a legal precedent, Bob. I know of six other companies doing uploading work right now, and not one of 'em's thinking about the legal status of the uploadee. If you don't start thinking about it now, where are you going to be in three to five years time?"

Pam is looking back and forth between Franklin and Manfred like a bot stuck in a loop, unable to quite grasp what she's seeing. "How much is this worth?" she asks plaintively.

"Oh, quite a few million, I guess." Bob stares at his empty glass. "Okay. I'll talk to them. If they bite, you're dining out on me for the next century. You really think they'll be able to run the mining complex?"

"They're pretty resourceful for invertebrates." Manfred grins innocently, enthusiastically. "They may be prisoners of their evolutionary background, but they can still adapt to a new environment. And just think! You'll be winning civil rights for a whole new minority group—one that won't be a minority for much longer."

■

That evening, Pamela turns up at Manfred's hotel room wearing a strapless black dress, concealing spike heels and most of the items he bought for her that afternoon. Manfred has opened up his private diary to her agents: she abuses the privilege, zaps him with a stunner on his way out of the shower and has him gagged, spread-eagled, and trussed to the bed-frame before he has a chance to speak. She wraps a large rubber pouch full of mildly anaesthetic lube around his tumescing genitals—no point in letting him climax—clips electrodes to his nipples, lubes a rubber plug up his rectum and straps it in place. Before the shower, he removed his goggles: she resets them, plugs them into her handheld, and gently eases them on over his eyes. There's other apparatus, stuff she ran up on the hotel room's 3D printer.

Setup completed, she walks round the bed, inspecting him critically from all angles, figuring out where to begin. This isn't just sex, after all: it's a work of art.

After a moment's thought she rolls socks onto his exposed feet, then, expertly wielding a tiny tube of cyanoacrylate, glues his fingertips together. Then she switches off the air-conditioning. He's twisting and straining, testing the cuffs: tough, it's about the nearest thing to sensory deprivation she can arrange without a flotation tank and suxamethonium injection. She controls all his senses, only his ears unstoppered. The glasses give her a high-bandwidth channel right into his brain, a fake metacortex to whisper lies at her command. The idea of what she's about to do excites her, puts a tremor in her thighs:

it's the first time she's been able to get inside his mind as well as his body. She leans forward and whispers in her ear: "Manfred. Can you hear *me*?"

He twitches. Mouth gagged, fingers glued: good. No back channels. He's powerless.

"This is what it's like to be tetraplegic, Manfred. Bedridden with motor neurone disease. Locked inside your own body by nv-CJD. I could spike you with MPPP and you'd stay in this position for the rest of your life, shitting in a bag, pissing through a tube. Unable to talk and with nobody to look after you. Do you think you'd like that?"

He's trying to grunt or whimper around the ball gag. She hikes her skirt up around her waist and climbs onto the bed, straddling him. The goggles are replaying scenes she picked up around Cambridge this winter; soup kitchen scenes, hospice scenes. She kneels atop him, whispering in his ear.

"Twelve million in tax, baby, that's what they think you owe them. What do you think you owe me? That's six million in net income, Manny, six million that isn't going into your virtual children's mouths."

He's rolling his head from side to side, as if trying to argue. That won't do: she slaps him hard, thrills to his frightened expression. "Today I watched you give uncounted millions away, Manny. Millions, to a bunch of crusties and a MassPike pirate! You bastard. Do you know what I should do with you?" He's cringing, unsure whether she's serious or doing this just to get him turned on. Good.

There's no point trying to hold a conversation. She leans forward until she can feel his breath in her ear. "Meat and mind, Manny. Meat, and mind. You're not interested in meat, are you? Just mind. You could be boiled alive before you noticed what was happening in the meatspace around you. Just another lobster in a pot." She reaches down and tears away the gel pouch, exposing his penis: it's stiff as a post from the vasodilators, dripping with gel, numb. Straightening up, she eases herself slowly down on it. It doesn't hurt as much as she expected, and the sensation is utterly different from what she's used to. She begins to lean forward, grabs hold of his straining arms, feels his thrilling helplessness. She can't control herself: she almost bites through her lip with the intensity of the sensation. Afterward, she reaches down and massages him until he begins to spasm, shuddering uncontrollably, emptying the darwinian river of his source code into her, communicating via his only output device.

She rolls off his hips and carefully uses the last of the superglue to gum her labia together. Humans don't produce seminiferous plugs, and although she's fertile she wants to be absolutely sure: the glue will last for a day or two. She feels hot and flushed, almost out of control. Boiling to death with febrile expectancy, now she's nailed him down at last.

When she removes his glasses his eyes are naked and vulnerable, stripped down to the human kernel of his nearly-transcendent mind. "You can come and sign the marriage license tomorrow morning after breakfast," she whispers in his ear: "otherwise my lawyers will be in touch. Your parents will want a ceremony, but we can arrange that later."

He looks as if he has something to say, so she finally relents and loosens the gag: kisses him tenderly on one cheek. He swallows, coughs, then looks away. "Why? Why do it this way?"

She taps him on the chest: "property rights." She pauses for a moment's thought: there's a huge ideological chasm to bridge, after all. "You finally convinced me about this agalmic thing of yours, this giving everything away for brownie points. I wasn't going to lose you to a bunch of lobsters or uploaded kittens, or whatever else is going to inherit this smart matter singularity you're busy creating. So I decided to take what's mine first. Who knows? In a few months I'll give you back a new intelligence, and you can look after it to your heart's content."

"But you didn't need to do it this way—"

"Didn't I?" She slides off the bed and pulls down her dress. "You give too much away too easily, Manny! Slow down, or there won't be anything left." Leaning over the bed she dribbles acetone onto the fingers of his left hand, then unlocks the cuff: puts the bottle conveniently close to hand so he can untangle himself.

"See you tomorrow. Remember, after breakfast."

She's in the doorway when he calls: "but you didn't say *why!*"

"Your memes are just a product of your extended phenotype; if you like you can think of it as a new way of spreading your memes around," she says. She blows him a kiss and closes the door, bends down and carefully places another cardboard box containing an uploaded kitten right outside it. Then she returns to her suite to make arrangements for the alchemical wedding.

Carol Emshwiller's most recent books are *Report to the Men's Club and Other Stories* and *The Mount*. Her two Westerns are *Ledoyt* and *Leaping Man Hill*.

About "Creature," Carol says: "Creature" is a sequel to "Foster Mother" though the sex of the two creatures seem to be different to their caretakers. I figured dinosaurs might be hard to sex.

Her Web site is http://www.sfwa.org/members/emshwiller/.

CREATURE

CAROL EMSHWILLER

This creature looks more scared than I am. Come knocking . . . pawing . . . scratching at my door. Come, maybe in search of me, (I'm easy prey for the weak and scared and hungry), or maybe in search of help and shelter. . . . (I'm peering out my one and only little window, hoping it won't see me.) It's been snowing— seems like three or four days now. The first really bad weather of the year so far.

It looks so draggled and cold. . . . I open the door. I welcome it. I say, "Hello new and dangerous friend." My door's a normal size, but too small for it. It pushes and groans and squeezes itself in. Then collapses on the floor in my one and only room, its big green head facing the stove. It takes up all the space and makes puddles.

There's a tag stapled in its ear—rather tattered (both ear and tag), green (both ear and tag), with a number so faded I can hardly make it out. It might be zero seven. Strange that it has ears at all considering what it (mostly) looks like. But they're small—tiny vestigial . . . no, the opposite, evolving ears. They look as if made purely for a place to put a tag.

It's wearing a large handmade camouflage vest with lots of pockets. Now, while it's still out of breath and collapsed, I check for weapons, though with those claws, why would it need any? What it has is old dried crumbs of pennyroyal, left over from some warmer season and some higher mountain, a few interesting stones, one streaked green with copper and one that glitters with fool's gold, two books, one of poetry (*100 Best Loved Poems*) and one on plants of the area. Both well worn. A creature of my own heart. Perhaps.

It looks half starved—more than half. I have broth. I help it raise its heavy head. It sips, nods as if in thanks, but then shows its teeth, blinks its glittery eyes. I jump back. Try to, that is, but I bump into my table. There's no room with it in here. It shakes its head, no, no, no. Seems to say it. "Mmmnno."

But how can such a creature talk at all with such a mouth? But then come words, or parts of words. "Thang . . . kh . . . mmm you . . . kind. Kindly. Thang you." Then it seems to faint or collapses, or sleeps—instantly—snow melting from its eyelashes (it has eyelashes) and rolling off its back, icy mud drying between its claws. The tiny arms look as if made for nothing but hugging.

While it seems in such an exhausted sleep, or maybe passed out, I take pliers and carefully remove the staple that holds the zero seven ear tag. I notice several claw marks along its back and it's lost a large chunk off the end of its tail.

Now where in the world did this thing come from?

I've heard tales. I thought they were the usual nonsense . . . like sasquatch, yeti, and so forth, abominable this or that. (And here, for sure, the most abominable of all.) But I've heard tales of secret weapons, too. I've heard there are creatures made specifically to patrol this empty border land. Supposed to be indestructible in so far as a living breathing creature can ever be. Supposed to attack everything that moves in this no-man's-land where nothing is supposed to be but another of its own kind.

I'd probably help even a suffering weapon, I probably wouldn't be able to keep myself from it, but this one seems odd for a weapon, too polite, and with vest pockets full of dried bits of flowers, that book of poetry. . . .

I drink the rest of the broth myself and stare at the creature for a while. No sense in trying to mop up with this thing in the way and still dripping. I can't even get across the room without leaning against a wall or climbing over my chair or cot. I step over its legs. I squinch over to my front door. I take my jacket. I'm not worried about leaving the thing alone. It doesn't seem the sort to do any harm—unless by mistake.

I whisper, "Sleep, my poor wet friend. I'll be back soon," in case it hears me leave. It doesn't move. I might as well be talking to myself. I do that all the time anyway. I used to talk to my dog, Rosie, but since she died I haven't stopped. I jabber on. No need for a dog for talking. They used to say we men were the silent sex, at least compared to women, but not me. Rosie just made it worse. She would look up at me, trying hard to get every word. Seemed to smile. I'd talk all the more. And now, as if she was still here, I talk. I talk to anything that moves.

■

As I go out, right outside the door there's some juniper branches threaded together as though it had made itself a wind shield of some sort and dropped it before it came in. Farther along I see broken branches around my biggest limber pine. It must have sheltered there—leaned against the leeward side. Hard to think of such a creature giving out.

I lean against the leeward side, too. You'd think it would have smelled my fire and me. Perhaps it was already weak and sick. I don't dare leave it by itself for long but I need space. That was like being in a squeeze gate. Still, I like company. Watch the fire together. Come better weather we could make the shack bigger. It was polite, even.

I say, "Rosie, Rosie." The wind blows my words off into the hills before I hardly get them said. That name has already bounced off these cliffs sunrise to sunset. Not a creature here that hasn't heard it. I've called her, sometimes by mistake, sometimes on purpose. Sometimes knowing she was dead, sometimes forgetting.

After she died I ran out in a snow storm naked—and not just once or twice—hoping for . . . what? Death by freezing? I yelled, answering the coyotes, until I was so hoarse I couldn't have spoken if there'd been somebody to speak to. After that I whispered. Then I sat, brooding over the knots in the logs as I had when I first came out here. Rosie needed me. She kept me human. Or should I say, and better yet, she kept me animal. I don't know what I've become. I need this creature as much as it needs me. I'd make it a good meal. Maybe that's what I want to be.

I squat down, my back against the tree. I shouldn't go far. I should listen. Even just waking up and stretching, it could mess things up.

■

I chose this no-man's-land. I came here ten years ago. There's a war been going on for a long time, but never any action here—not since I've been around. Missiles fly overhead, satellites float in the night sky, but nothing ever happens here. The war goes on, back and forth above me. Sometimes I can see great bursts of light. I wonder if there's anything left on either side. No-man's-land is the safest place to be. Had I had the sense to bring my wife and child here, they'd still be alive. Of course I didn't think to come here myself until they were gone and my life was over.

■

I don't know how long I sit, the sun is hidden, but I've had no need for time since I came. I don't even keep track of my age, let alone the time of day.

I've never seen a single one of these thick skinned things until now. I wasn't sure they existed. I didn't want them to. I felt sorry for them even when I didn't believe in them. How can they have any sort of life at all? Seeing this one, I think perhaps they can. (Or this one can.) But here they are in the world in spite of themselves. No fault of their own. And in all kinds of weather. If they get sick, I suppose they pine and die on their own.

The creature seemed . . . rather sweet, I thought. Fine fingered hands. Womanly arms. Perhaps it really is female.

■

Then I hear the scraping and thumping of something who hasn't hardly room enough to turn around. My poor friend, Zero Seven. I hurry back as best I can clumping through snow a foot deep in spots. I open my door and go from a wall of softly falling flakes (softly *now*) to a wall of shiny green.

I push my fist into its side as one does to move a horse. I hope it feels my push. I hope it's as sensitive as a horse. "Let me in, friend."

It moves. I hear something falling over on its far side.

"Do gum in. I'mmmm afraig I. . . . Mmmmm . . . as you ksee."

I slide myself in—scrape myself in, that is, it's the wrong direction for the scales.

It turns toward me as best it can and seems to almost bow, or perhaps it's a nod, one elegant little hand at its mouth as if embarrassed. I do believe I'm right about the sex. It must be female.

"Kh kvery, kvery, ssssssorry. I'll leave mmmm-nnnow."

With me in the way it can't turn around to go. Perhaps not even with me not in the way. It'll have to back out.

"Don't go. Sit down." It's in a half crouch already. It goes down into a squat, its stomach on the floor, feet splayed on each side—long toed, gruesome feet with claws I wouldn't want to argue with.

I slide myself around the creature to the stove on the far side. I should have had the dishes washed and put away. Well, no matter, they're tin. A few more bumps and scratches won't make any difference.

No doubt about it, it's sick. I could even feel that as I move around it. Though how do you know if a reptile is sick? But there's an odd stickiness to it and I imagine it normally doesn't have any smell at all.

"Stay. You're sick. I'll make stew. Rest again."

It shakes its head. "Mmmmmukst go."

"I don't want to find you out there dead."

"Dhuh dhead in here iks worssse for mmgh . . . mmyou."

It shows its teeth. There are lots of them. Is that a grin? Can that be? That the creature has a sense of humor? Rosie seemed to grin, too. I take a chance. I laugh. It opens its mouth wider but there's no sound. We look each other in the eye. Some kind of understanding, lizard to mammal, passes between us. Then the creature shivers. I pull a blanket off the bunk, big Hudson Bay, but it only covers the creature's top half like a shawl. It helps to hold it on with those tiny arms, and nods again.

"I'll build up the fire and get us something to eat. You just rest."

"I hhhelp-puh."

"Please don't."

It grins again, mouth wide, that row of teeth gleaming, then huddles close against the wall opposite my kitchen area, trying to make itself small. Still, I step on its toes as I work. When I do, we both say, "Sorry." "Khsssorry." We both laugh. . . . Well, I laugh and it shows its teeth.

How nice to have somebody . . . some*thing* around that has a sense of humor. They must have left in some odd rogue genes by mistake.

I start to make stew. I have lots of dried chanterelles and I hope it likes wild garlic. It watches me as Rosie did, mouth open. I hum a song my grandma taught me. I thought hardly anybody knew that song but me, but then I hear the creature buzzing along with me, no doubt about it, the same song. I look at it. It blinks a slow blink, as if for a wink.

We eat my hare stew, it out of my wash basin. Licks it clean like Rosie always did. At least it hasn't lost its appetite.

"Have you a name other than that Zero Seven on your tag? By the way, I took that off. I had a dog, Rosie. She died. I keep almost calling you Rosie by mistake. It's the only name I've said for years."

There's that smile again. "Rrrrosie is kfine. Kfine." Then Kfine turns into a cough. I heat up some wild rose hips tea. I always have lots of that.

Then it stretches out again. I pile on more blankets.

"Mmmmmnnno mmno. Mmdon't."

"I insist. You must stay warm. If the lamp doesn't bother you I'll read for a while, but you should sleep. I'll make the fire high. Wake me if it gets cold. You should be warm."

(My lamp is just a bowl of volcanic tuff with exactly the right hole in the center. I have a big one and a little one. The oil I've rendered even from creatures with not much fat. Even deer.)

I settle myself with a book. I like having company even if the company takes up most of the room. I think it's already asleep, but then, "Khind, kh hind ssssir. I like being Rrrrrosie." (It gargles it out as if it was French.) "Bhut who are mmmm kh you? *If* khyou don't mmmmind."

"Ben. I'm Ben."

"Ah, easy khto kkh ssssay."

I think: She. She is a she.

When I douse the lamp (by putting on the lid) and it's pitch black in here, I do have a moment when I worry. She *is* starving. I might be her next meal and a better one than I've prepared for her so far, or at least bigger. What's a little broth and then a little rabbit stew? But I won't be facing anything my wife and child didn't face already though my fate might not be as instantaneous as theirs. But I hear her breathing, snuffling, snorting in her sleep just like Rosie. I'm comforted and reassured by her snores.

Sometime during the night the snow stops. Dawn, in my one and only window, shows a cloudless sky. I watch the oblong of sunlight move down and across the far wall until it lights on her. She's a bundle of blankets, but what little I can see of her shines out. Certainly she's not made for a winter climate. Probably most comfortable in a hot place with lots of shiny green leaves to hide in.

She feels the sun the moment it touches her. (Thick skinned but infinitely sensitive.) Turns and looks at me. Grins her Rosie-grin. Like Rosie she doesn't have to say it, it's all over her face: Hey, a new day. What's up now? And: Let's get going.

"You look better."

She nods. Says, "Mmmmm, nnnn. Mmmmm, nnnn."

"We'll go out, if you like. You must feel cramped in here."

"Mmmmmm, nnnn."

I've jerky and hard tack. We breakfast on that, and more rose hip tea—a pitcher of it for her.

"Keep a blanket around your shoulders. And I think you'll have to back out."

Like my Rosie was before she got old, this Rosie peers, sniffs, hops up on boulders, jumps for no reason whatsoever, she skips in the bare spots where the snow has blown off. Sings a ho dee ho dee ho kind of song. A young thing that, sick or not, starving or not, can't sit still. I saw that in my boy.

I take her to my viewing spot. You can see the whole valley. I often see deer from here.

As we watch, another of these creatures comes down the valley heading south. I haven't seen any until this one sitting beside me, and here comes yet another, and then two more not far behind. Driven down from the mountain passes on purpose? Or is it the cold?

We watch. Not moving. Rosie looks at me, at them, at me. I love that look all young things have, animal or human, of wondering: What's up? What's going on? Is everything all right?

Then those first two turn and trumpet at the others. Rosie's arms are just long enough for her to cover her ears. (She must hear extraordinarily well to need to do that from way up here.) Hard to tell from this distance, but those others all seem much larger than she is.

When, a moment later, she takes her fingers from her ears, I ask her, "Have you had experiences with others of your own kind before?"

She nods.

"The scars."

"Mmmnnn."

"You weren't supposed to fight each other."

"Mmnnnn."

I want to comfort her. Put my arms around this green scaly thing. (My son had an iguana. We never hugged it.) She reaches toward me as if to hug, too. But even those little arms . . . those claws. . . . And my head could fit all the way in her mouth, no problem. I flinch away. I see her eyes turn reptilian—lose their wide childlike look. She says, "Kh . . . khss sssorry."

"No, it's I who should be . . . *am* sorry."

I reach and I do hug and let myself be hugged. I get my parka ripped on her claws. Well, it's not the first rip.

Far below us, the things fight and trumpet, smash trees, trample brush. I can see, even from up here, spit fly out. There's no blood. Their hide is too tough.

They fight with their feet, leaping as cocks do. One is losing. It's on its back, talons up. Even from way up here, I can see a little herd of panicked deer galloping off toward the hills. Rosie covers her eyes this time and leans over as if she has a stomachache. Says, "Mmmmm-mmmnnn. Not Kkkh kkh krright."

"What *were* you supposed to do?"

"Kkh . . . khill. . . . Mmmm those like kh you. Khill you."

Below us, the creature that was on its back tries to escape but the others leap high and claw at it, pull it down then one bites the under part of the neck. Now there *is* blood.

I turn to see Rosie's reaction, but she's not here. Then I see her, way, way back, curled up behind a tree.

I go back to her and put my arm around her again. "Old buddy." Then, "How did you ever turn out as you are?"

"Mmmm mmistake." Then "Gh gho," Rosie says, carefully not looking down at them. "Ghho. Mmmmmnn . . . *mnnnow!*" And she's already on her way, back to the shack. I follow. Watching her. Her arms, so like ours, look like an afterthought. Obviously there's a bit of the human in her. I see it in the legs, too. Also in those half-formed ears.

Those others below could push down my shack in half a minute. I need Rosie on my side. "Stay. I need you. I'll push out a wall. I'll make the door bigger."

She stops, stares. I wish I knew what's going on inside that big fierce head of hers.

"I'll start getting the logs for it today."

"I kh . . . kh . . . khelph."

But my food won't last long with her eating washbasins full. Besides, she's starving. We'll have to get food first.

"How have you lived all this time? What have you eaten?"

"Ghhophers mmm mostly. *When* mmmwere gh hophers. Khrabbits. When them. When kh llleaves, leaves. Mmmmushrooms. Rrrroots. Mmmmbark nnnot good but kh ate it. Khfish. Hhhard to kh kfish when kh h ice."

We climb higher than my shack so Rosie can fish. The streams up there are too fast to freeze over. She uses her foot. Hooks them on a claw. Her arms seem even too small to help with balancing. It's her big green head and the half of her left-over tail, waving from side to side, that balances her as she reaches. She gets seven.

"Kkhfried?" she says. "In khfat? With khh kh corn mmmeal? Like Mmmmmama? Mushka?"

"You betcha. You had a mama?"

"Mmmmmnnnn. Mmmmmm. Mmone kh like mmyou"

She bounces off down the path ahead of me, singing a oolie, oolie, doodlie do kind of song. I guess she's no longer sick. Or she's too happy to care. And certainly not thinking about those others fighting in the valley.

(I'm carrying the fish. I strung them through their gills on to a willow stick. I hadn't brought my stringer. I guess I don't have to worry about getting enough food for her. Yet she *was* starving. Perhaps she doesn't like things raw?)

Back home we eat fried fish. I eat two and Rosie eats five. She watches as I cook just as the dog did, exact same expression, mouth half open. A dog sort of smile. We settle down afterwards and I read to her from one of my books: Moby Dick. (I only brought three.) I read that to my son and wife, one on each side of me, and all of us on the couch. Rosie lies, head towards me, eyes almost shut, commenting now and then, her voice breathy, like one would imagine a snake would talk. I'm sitting on my cot. We sip our rose hips tea. We're both covered with blankets.

Then, "Time's up," I say. "You need sleep." But she doesn't want us to stop reading. "I insist," I say. She groans. "*I* kh kread. *You* ssssleep." She reaches for the book with those womanly shiny green fingers. I put it down and take her hand. "Ooobie baloobie, *do* it," I say. (Ooobie baloobie is another of her songs.) She laughs. (It's more like panting than laughing, but so hard I think she must be little more then seven years old—her equivalent of seven—to think that's so funny.) But she settles down right after. Says, "Kh . . . koh khay." Wraps her little arms around herself. I tuck the blankets closer and douse the lamp with its lid.

This time I don't worry if I might be her next meal, but I have a hard time sleeping anyway. I keep wondering what might happen if those others find my shack. They could break it down just leaning on it by mistake.

Since *they* all seem to be coming down, we'll go up. We'll take some supplies to the pass and hide. I've spent the night there many a time. We'll be all right as long as there isn't another storm that goes on for days and days. At least we'll have fish.

I always did like camping out. The view is always worth more than the discomfort. Besides I do without right here every day. It never bothers me, washing up in a washbowl or an icy stream. Only here is it worth the bother of looking out the window.

Or now, at Rosie, too. She really is quite beautiful, her yellow underbelly and the darker green along the ridge of her back. She's even reddish in spots.

Rosie hears them first, wakes me with her, "Kh . . . kh . . . kh." There's sounds of crashing through the brush. A tree splintering. From the look of the big dipper, straight out my little north window, it's probably three or four A.M.

They're coming closer. For sure they saw our smoke and smelled us. They push on our walls. I hear them breathe and hiss. No, it's only one, I *think* only one, pushing the wall on one side. The caulking falls out. Rosie braces herself against that wall to hold it. She picks up the rhythm of the other's pushing, leans when it pushes. It works, the wall holds. At one point there's a large hole where the caulking's gone and I see the creature looking in—one light greenish eye like Rosie's. The thing gives a throaty hiss. Rosie answers with the same hiss. It gives up. We hear it smashing away. We look at each other.

"You did it!"

Rosie's mouth is open in that smile that looks so much like my old Rosie's and she nods yes so hard I'm thinking she'll put her neck out of joint. "Kh khdid! *Khdid!*"

"Pack up. We'll go camp out up beyond where we fished."

She goes right for the frying pan and the bag of corn meal and puts them in her vest pockets. She's still nodding yes but she stops when I tell her we have to bring blankets and a tarp.

"Kh . . . kh . . . kh. . . . *Kno! Nnnnnooo!*"

"*Yes!* It's colder up there. You need shelter as much as I do. Maybe more so."

Like Rosie, she gives up easily. "Kh . . . kh-kho kay." I don't know what I'd do if she didn't. She helps me roll the blankets in the tarp. Says, "I kh kcarry mmmmthat."

I have to stop her from taking her books and her fancy green rock. She insists she can carry all the things we need and those too.

"I kh *likhe* ghrrrrreeeen."

"That's good. Then you like yourself."

■

She starts up, hop, skip, and jump . . . even with all that to carry. I can't believe it, she's leaping from rock to rock—even across talus. I keep telling her that stuff is unstable. "Dangerous even for you," I say, but she's does it anyway. The rocks do teeter, but she's sure-footed. That leaping doesn't last long, thank goodness. She doesn't realize how much all that weight she's carrying will tire her. I warned her, but since when do the young listen to warnings of that sort? She's jumped and skipped and leaped until now she lags behind and blows like a horse at every other step. I take the tarp and blankets from her. I'd take that frying pan, too, but she won't let me. "Kh . . . kan do it. I *kan!*"

I don't let Rosie stop until the half way spot. "We'll get up where we can see," I say, "then we'll rest."

"Oh pf . . . pfhooo," she says, but she goes on, sighing now.

"You can do it. Fifty more steps."

■

A few minutes later we put down our bundles, Rosie takes off her vest, and we climb out to the edge of the scarp we just zigzagged up to see what we can see. And it's as I feared, they've found my cabin. Looks like there's not much left of it already, walls pushed in, roof collapsed. I had doused the fire but there must have been some cinders left. A fire has started, at the cabin and on the ground around it.

She sits as I sit, legs hanging over. How much like a human she is. Sometimes you don't see it at all, but in certain positions you do. Now she looks as if she's going to cry. (Can they cry? Only humans, seals, and sea birds have tears. Anyway, you don't need tears for sadness.) I feel like crying, too. Rosie can tell just like my old Rosie could. We lean against each other.

"At least your stones are all right."

She doesn't even answer with an mmmnnnn.

I look to see if any trees are waving around down there from being bumped into, but there's nothing. Odd.

■

After we start on up, Rosie is droopy, not only tired but sad. She thunks along. I feel sorry that she jumped and hopped so much in the beginning. My other Rosie was like that. She never realized she had to save her strength.

Most of my talking has been to keep her going. "Count steps. Maybe a hundred more." "Come on, poor tired friend." "See that rock? We'll stop just beyond that." Now I mumble to myself—about when I'll be back to sift through my things. I didn't bring any souvenirs of my wife and child. When I fled out here . . . escaped . . . I didn't even want pictures. I was running away from memories. Of course memories come and go as they please.

Just around the corner and we'll be able to see the little lake I'm heading for, the stepping stones crossing the creek that pours down from it, beyond, the trees and boulders where I had hoped to hide us this first night, but I decide we have to stop now. We stand . . . that is, I stand, Rosie collapses. We're both too tired to get out food other than jerky. I tuck Rosie in under an overhang. Just her big back end with the half bitten off tail hanging out. I cover her with blankets and the tarp. She's asleep before she can finish her jerky. I pick the chunk out of her mouth to save it for breakfast.

■

In the morning I wake to the sound of a helicopter. I know right away. Why . . . *why* didn't I suspect before? Rosie not only had an ear tag, but she has a chip imbedded in her neck.

There's no place for a helicopter to land, the mountains are too closed in and too many boulders, but we're not safe anyway. There could be more things in Rosie's neck than just an ID chip. That could be why we didn't hear those creatures down there anymore.

Rosie's in an exhausted sleep. "You have to wake up. *Now!* I have to get your chip out." I don't mention what else might be there. Those others may have been disposed of . . . without a trace, I'll bet. Or little traces scattered all over the place so no one will ever know there ever were creatures like this.

"Did you know you have a chip?"

I feel around Rosie's neck.

"Hang on, friend, this will hurt."

I don't care about those others, but I'd never like the forest without Rosie in it, skipping and hopping along, picking flowers, collecting green rocks or glittery fool's gold, singing, "doodlie do" songs.

She looks at the helicopter, then at me, then the copter again, then back at me. Again it's that: Should I be frightened or not? Except now *I'm* frightened. I try not to show it but she senses it. I see her getting scared, too.

The copter circles. I have to hurry—but I don't want to hurt her—but her skin is so tough! And who knows, if I do find one or two things, will that be all that's hidden there?

"Hang on."

She hugs herself with those inadequate arms. Even before I start she makes little doglike . . . or rather, birdlike sounds.

"Sing," I say. "Sing your oobie do."

I feel two lumps. I dig in. I say, "Almost done," when I've hardly begun.

■

Then we run. Without our blankets, without our food, except what Rosie has in her vest.

"They can't follow now." I *hope* that's true.

We stick to the old path that circles over the pass. We try to stay close to rocks and under what trees there are. Even running as we do, I can't *not* think about how beautiful it is up here. When I first saw it, years ago, I shouted when I came around the corner.

She's way ahead of me in no time—those long strong legs. And we're not carrying much of anything. I catch up when she finally turns to look for me. We both look back. The helicopter still hovers. I left the chip and button bullet back there at our camping spot. They think she's still there. Maybe they don't know about me.

She's different from those others. What was she for? That is, besides killing those like me?

It starts to snow. Thank God or worse luck, I don't know which. It'll hide our tracks and the helicopter won't fly, but we don't have food or blankets.

We cross the pass and dip into the next valley. We find a sheltered spot among a mass of fallen boulders where the whole side of a cliff came down. Some boulders are on top of each other making a roof. Boulders over, boulders under—not a particularly comfortable spot but we huddle there and rest. We take stock. All we have is what's in Rosie's vest, a little left over jerky (we eat it) the frying pan and corn-meal. We can make corn cakes if we don't catch fish.

This is just a mountain storm. If we can get far enough down we'll walk out of it. If we're lucky it'll last just long enough to cover our tracks. I tell Rosie. She lies at my feet still panting. I stroke her knobby head.

"How's your neck?"

"Hh . . . hoo khay."

She sleeps. Murmuring a whole series of Mmmms and then, Mmmush, and, Mmmushka.

As the storm eases and we're some rested, I wake her and we start down. After an hour we're out of the snow and wind and into a hanging meadow. I've been over this pass but not this far.

I'm worried. Rosie is sluggish and dreamy, flopping along, tripping a lot. Poor thing, all she has on is her vest. She's cold and with reptiles . . . or part-reptiles. . . . I don't want to build a fire but I must. The copter's gone, maybe it's all right to now.

"My poor fierce friend," I say. She grins. I take her hand and sit her down. "We're going to have a nice big fire. You rest. I'll find the wood."

"I'll hhh . . . hhh . . . hhh."

"No you won't. I'm going by myself. I'll be back before you know it."

She mews, turns away, and curls up.

■

On this side there's a lot less snow, so not hard going. I gather brush, dead limbs, and drag the whole batch back to her, flop down, my arm around her. I see her eyes flicker, though the nictitating membrane closes as she does it. She doesn't wake. I'll have to make the fire right now.

How does a sick reptile show how sick it is? All I know is, she doesn't look right and doesn't feel right.

I build the fire as close to her as I dare. Finally she seems in a more normal sleep. I sleep, too.

■

I wake with a start. *Hibernate!* Do they? All those others, too. But she's been mixed with other genes. For sure, some human.

I wake her by mistake as I get out the frying pan and the cornmeal. I'm melting snow, first to drink and then to make corncakes. She drinks as if she's been out in the desert for days. Then, "I'mm mmhungry." Then she sees what little cornmeal we have and says,

"Mmmm *nnnot* ssso. . . . *Nnnot* hungry," she says again. "Ooobie, baloobie, *nnnnot.*"

"Ooobie, baloobie, *do* eat me. Roll me in corn meal. I'm old and I'm tired."

All of a sudden it's not a joke.

"Kkkh kkkh! Kh khcan't dooo that! Oooooh!"

"I thought that's what you were made for . . . born for."

"Kkh can't."

"You'll die. Look how thin you are."

"I'mmm tem *po* rary. Temmm *po po* rary." She sings it like a song—like she doesn't care. Does she understand what it means? I wonder if it's true. Perhaps they all are—were.

"Mmmmmm *all* temmm *po po!* rary."

"What makes you think you're temporary?"

"Mmmmush kh knew."

"She *told* you? How could she!"

"Kkh kh *nnnno!* I sssaw kher eyes. Ssscared. I kh khfound out. I kh . . . kh . . . kread."

"You're only half grown."

"Have a kh kh tth timer."

I don't know what I see in those lizardy eyes of hers. "Don't you like it here? Don't you care anything about being alive?"

"Oh! Kh! *Oooh!* Kh!" She does a hopping, twisting dance, those tiny arms raised. It tells how she feels, better than her words ever could.

"Mmmmy kh heart," she says, "hasss kth th timer."

"How long is temporary?"

"I sh should dannnce. Ssssing. *Mnnnow!* And lllook. Lllook a *llllot!* *Yesssss!* Lottts. Mmm then kh kgo for goood mmmmbig bh bones."

■

We'll build another cabin. Here in this hanging valley, sheltered under boulders and trees and next to a good fishing stream. With her help we'll have one up in no time. We'll dance and sing and look around a lot. At the smallest and the largest . . . the near and the far . . . stars, mountain peaks, beetles. . . .

NOVELS

Solitaire, Kelley Eskridge
(Eos, September 2002)
American Gods, **Neil Gaiman** (winner)
(William Morrow, July 2001)
The Other Wind, Ursula K. Le Guin
(Harcourt Brace, September 2001)
Picoverse, Robert A. Metzger
(Ace, March 2002)
Perdido Street Station, China Miéville
(Del Rey, March 2001)
Bones of the Earth, Michael Swanwick
(Eos, March 2002)

NOVELLAS

"Sunday Night Yams at Minnie and Earl's," Adam-Troy Castro
(*Analog Science Fiction and Fact*, June 2001)
"Bronte's Egg," Richard Chwedyk (winner)
(*The Magazine of Fantasy & Science Fiction*, August 2002)
"The Chief Designer," Andy Duncan
(*Asimov's Science Fiction*, June 2001)
"The Political Officer," Charles Coleman Finlay
(*The Magazine of Fantasy & Science Fiction*, April 2002)
"Magic's Price," Bud Sparhawk
(*Analog Science Fiction and Fact*, March 2001)

NOVELETTES

"The Pagodas of Ciboure," M. Shayne Bell
(*The Green Man: Tales From the Mythic Forest*,
Viking, May 2002)

"The Ferryman's Wife," Richard Bowes
(*The Magazine of Fantasy & Science Fiction*, May 2001)

"Hell Is the Absence of God," Ted Chiang (winner)
(*Starlight*, July 2001)

"Madonna of the Maquiladora," Gregory Frost
(*Asimov's Science Fiction*, May 2002)

"The Days Between," Allen Steele
(*Asimov's Science Fiction*, March 2001)

"Lobsters," Charles Stross
(*Asimov's Science Fiction*, June 2001)

SHORT STORIES

"Creature," Carol Emshwiller (winner)
(*The Magazine of Fantasy & Science Fiction*, October/
November 2001; *Report to the Men's Club and Other Stories*,
August 2002)

"Creation," Jeffrey Ford
(*The Magazine of Fantasy & Science Fiction*, May 2002)

"Cut," Megan Lindholm
(*Asimov's Science Fiction*, May 2001)

"Nothing Ever Happens in Rock City," Jack McDevitt
(*Artemis*, Summer 2001)

"Little Gods," Tim Pratt
(*Strange Horizons*, 4 February 2002)

"The Dog Said Bow-Wow," Michael Swanwick
(*Asimov's Science Fiction*, October/November 2001)

SCRIPTS

Shrek, Ted Elliott, Terry Rossio, Joe Stillman, and Roger S. H.
Schulman, Based on *Shrek!* by William Steig
(Dreamworks, May 2001)

Unreasonable Doubt, Michael Taylor, Created for TV by Michael
Piller and Shawn Piller, based on characters from the
Stephen King novel, *The Dead Zone*, July 2002

**The Lord of the Rings: The Fellowship of the Ring, Fran
Walsh, Philippa Boyens and Peter Jackson** (winner)

Based on *The Lord of the Rings* by J.R.R. Tolkien
(New Line Cinema, December 2001)
Once More, with Feeling, Joss Whedon, Soundtrack
(*Buffy the Vampire Slayer,* 6 November 2001)

In addition to the Nebula Awards, SFWA gives out the *Grand Master Award* and the *Bradbury Award*, and honors an *Author Emeritus* who speaks at the awards banquet.

1965

Novel: *Dune* by Frank Herbert

Novella: "The Saliva Tree" by Brian W. Aldiss || "He Who Shapes" by Roger Zelazny (tie)

Novelette: "The Doors of His Face, the Lamps of His Mouth" by Roger Zelazny

Short Story: " 'Repent, Harlequin!' Said the Ticktockman" by Harlan Ellison

1966

Novel: *Flowers for Algernon* by Daniel Keyes || *Babel-17* by Samuel R. Delany (tie)

Novella: "The Last Castle" by Jack Vance

Novelette: "Call Him Lord" by Gordon R. Dickson

Short Story: "The Secret Place" by Richard McKenna

1967

Novel: *The Einstein Intersection* by Samuel R. Delany

Novella: "Behold the Man" by Michael Moorcock

Novelette: "Gonna Roll the Bones" by Fritz Leiber

Short Story: "Aye, and Gomorrah" by Samuel R. Delany

1968
Novel: *Rite of Passage* by Alexei Panshin
Novella: "Dragonrider" by Anne McCaffrey
Novelette: "Mother to the World" by Richard Wilson
Short Story: "The Planners" by Kate Wilhelm

1969
Novel: *The Left Hand of Darkness* by Ursula K. Le Guin
Novella: "A Boy and His Dog" by Harlan Ellison
Novelette: "Time Considered as a Helix of Semi-Precious
    Stones" by Samuel R. Delany
Short Story: "Passengers" by Robert Silverberg

1970
Novel: *Ringworld* by Larry Niven
Novella: "Ill Met in Lankhmar " by Fritz Leiber
Novelette: "Slow Sculpture" by Theodore Sturgeon
Short Story: No Award

1971
Novel: *A Time of Changes* by Robert Silverberg
Novella: "The Missing Man" by Katherine MacLean
Novelette: "The Queen of Air and Darkness" by Poul
    Anderson
Short Story: "Good News from the Vatican" by Robert
    Silverberg

1972
Novel: *The Gods Themselves* by Isaac Asimov
Novella: "A Meeting with Medusa"
    by Arthur C. Clarke
Novelette: "Goat Song" by Poul Anderson
Short Story: "When it Changed" by Joanna Russ

1973
Novel: *Rendezvous with Rama* by Arthur C. Clarke
Novella: "The Death of Doctor Island" by Gene Wolfe
Novelette: "Of Mist, and Grass, and Sand" by Vonda N.
    McIntyre

Short Story: "Love Is the Plan, the Plan Is Death" by James
Tiptree, Jr.
Dramatic Presentation: *Soylent Green* by Stanley R. Greenberg
for Screenplay (based on the novel *Make Room!*
Make Room!) | | Harry Harrison for *Make Room!*
Make Room!

1974

Novel: *The Dispossessed* by Ursula K. Le Guin
Novella: "Born with the Dead" by Robert Silverberg
Novelette: "If the Stars Are Gods" by Gordon Eklund and
Gregory Benford
Short Story: "The Day Before the Revolution" by Ursula K.
Le Guin
Dramatic Presentation: *Sleeper* by Woody Allen

1975

Novel: *The Forever War* by Joe Haldeman
Novella: "Home Is the Hangman" by Roger Zelazny
Novelette: "San Diego Lightfoot Sue" by Tom Reamy
Short Story: "Catch that Zeppelin!" by Fritz Leiber
Dramatic Writing: *Young Frankenstein* by Mel Brooks and Gene
Wilder

1976

Novel: *Man Plus* by Frederik Pohl
Novella: "Houston, Houston, Do You Read?" by James
Tiptree, Jr.
Novelette: "The Bicentennial Man" by Isaac Asimov
Short Story: "A Crowd of Shadows" by Charles L. Grant

1977

Novel: *Gateway* by Frederik Pohl
Novella: "Stardance" by Spider and Jeanne Robinson
Novelette: "The Screwfly Solution" by Raccoona Sheldon
Short Story: "Jeffty Is Five" by Harlan Ellison
Special Award: *Star Wars*

1978
  Novel: *Dreamsnake* by Vonda N. McIntyre
  Novella: "The Persistence of Vision" by John Varley
  Novelette: "A Glow of Candles, a Unicorn's Eye" by Charles
    L. Grant
  Short Story: "Stone" by Edward Bryant

1979
  Novel: *The Fountains of Paradise* by Arthur C. Clarke
  Novella: "Enemy Mine" by Barry Longyear
  Novelette: "Sandkings" by George R. R. Martin
  Short Story: "giANTS" by Edward Bryant

1980
  Novel: *Timescape* by Gregory Benford
  Novella: "The Unicorn Tapestry" by Suzy McKee Charnas
  Novelette: "The Ugly Chickens" by Howard Waldrop
  Short Story: "Grotto of the Dancing Deer" by Clifford D.
    Simak

1981
  Novel: *The Claw of the Conciliator* by Gene Wolfe
  Novella: "The Saturn Game" by Poul Anderson
  Novelette: "The Quickening" by Michael Bishop
  Short Story: "The Bone Flute" by Lisa Tuttle (This Nebula
    Award was declined by the author.)

1982
  Novel: *No Enemy But Time* by Michael Bishop
  Novella: "Another Orphan" by John Kessel
  Novelette: "Fire Watch" by Connie Willis
  Short Story: "A Letter from the Clearys"
    by Connie Willis

1983
  Novel: *Startide Rising* by David Brin
  Novella: "Hardfought" by Greg Bear
  Novelette: "Blood Music" by Greg Bear
  Short Story: "The Peacemaker" by Gardner Dozois

1984

    Novel: *Neuromancer* by William Gibson
    Novella: "Press Enter□" by John Varley
    Novelette: "Bloodchild" by Octavia E. Butler
    Short Story: "Morning Child" by Gardner Dozois

1985

    Novel: *Ender's Game* by Orson Scott Card
    Novella: "Sailing to Byzantium" by Robert Silverberg
    Novelette: "Portraits of His Children" by George R. R. Martin
    Short Story: "Out of All Them Bright Stars" by Nancy Kress

1986

    Novel: *Speaker for the Dead* by Orson Scott Card
    Novella: "R & R" by Lucius Shepard
    Novelette: "The Girl Who Fell into the Sky" by Kate Wilhelm
    Short Story: "Tangents" by Greg Bear

1987

    Novel: *The Falling Woman* by Pat Murphy
    Novela: "The Blind Geometer" by Kim Stanley Robinson
    Novelette: "Rachel in Love" by Pat Murphy
    Short Story: "Forever Yours, Anna" by Kate Wilhelm

1988

    Novel: *Falling Free* by Lois McMaster Bujold
    Novella: "The Last of the Winnebagos" by Connie Willis
    Novelette: "Schrodinger's Kitten" by George Alec Effinger
    Short Story: "Bible Stories for Adults, No. 17: The Deluge" by
      James Morrow

1989

    Novel: *The Healer's War* by Elizabeth Ann Scarborough
    Novella: "The Mountains of Mourning" by Lois McMaster
      Bujold
    Novelette: "At the Rialto" by Connie Willis
    Short Story: "Ripples in the Dirac Sea" by Geoffrey A. Landis

1990

Novel: *Tehanu: The Last Book of Earthsea* by Ursula
   K. Le Guin
Novella: "The Hemingway Hoax" by Joe Haldeman
Novelette: "Tower of Babylon" by Ted Chiang
Short Story: "Bears Discover Fire" by Terry Bisson

1991

Novel: *Stations of the Tide* by Michael Swanwick
Novella: "Beggars in Spain" by Nancy Kress
Novelette: "Guide Dog" by Mike Conner
Short Story: "Ma Qui" by Alan Brennert

1992

Novel: *Doomsday Book* by Connie Willis
Novella: "City of Truth" by James Morrow
Novelette: "Danny Goes to Mars" by Pamela Sargent
Short Story: "Even the Queen" by Connie Willis

1993

Novel: *Red Mars* by Kim Stanley Robinson
Novella: "The Night We Buried Road Dog" by Jack Cady
Novelette: "Georgia on My Mind" by Charles Sheffield
Short Story: "Graves" by Joe Haldeman

1994

Novel: *Moving Mars* by Greg Bear
Novella: "Seven Views of Olduvai Gorge" by Mike Resnick
Novelette: "The Martian Child" by David Gerrold
Short Story: "A Defense of the Social Contracts" by Martha
   Soukup

1995

Novel: *The Terminal Experiment* by Robert J. Sawyer
Novella: "Last Summer at Mars Hill" by Elizabeth Hand
Novelette: "Solitude" by Ursula K. Le Guin
Short Story: "Death and the Librarian" by Esther Friesner

1996
Novel: *Slow River* by Nicola Griffith
Novella: "Da Vinci Rising" by Jack Dann
Novelette: "Lifeboat on a Burning Sea" by Bruce Holland
  Rogers
Short Story: "A Birthday" by Esther M. Friesner

1997
Novel: *The Moon and the Sun* by Vonda N. McIntyre
Novella: "Abandon in Place" by Jerry Oltion
Novelette: "The Flowers of Aulit Prison" by Nancy Kress
Short Story: "Sister Emily's Lightship" by Jane Yolen

1998
Novel: *Forever Peace* by Joe Haldeman
Novella: "Reading the Bones" by Sheila Finch
Novelette: "Lost Girls" by Jane Yolen
Short Story: "Thirteen Ways to Water" by Bruce Holland
  Rogers

OTHER AWARDS & HONORS:
Grand Master: Hal Clement (Harry Stubbs)
Bradbury Award: J. Michael Straczynski
Author Emeritus: William Tenn (Phil Klass)

1999
Novel: *Parable of the Talents* by Octavia E. Butler
Novella: "Story of Your Life" by Ted Chiang
Novelette: "Mars Is No Place for Children" by Mary A. Turzillo
Short Story: "The Cost of Doing Business" by Leslie What
Script: *The Sixth Sense* by M. Night Shyamalan

OTHER AWARDS & HONORS:
Grand Master: Brian W. Aldiss
Author Emeritus: Daniel Keyes

2000
Novel: *Darwin's Radio* by Greg Bear
Novella: "Goddesses" by Linda Nagata
Novelette: "Daddy's World" by Walter Jon Williams

Short Story: "macs" by Terry Bisson
Script: *Galaxy Quest* by Robert Gordon and David Howard

OTHER AWARDS & HONORS:
Grand Master: Philip José Farmer
Bradbury Award: Yuri Rasovsky and Harlan Ellison
Author Emeritus: Robert Sheckley

2001

Novel: *The Quantum Rose* by Catherine Asaro
Novella: "The Ultimate Earth" by Jack Williamson
Novelette: "Louise's Ghost" by Kelly Link
Short Story: "The Cure for Everything" by Severna Park
Script: *Crouching Tiger, Hidden Dragon* by James Schamus, Kuo
    Jung Tsai, and Hui-Ling Wang; from the book by Du Lu
    Wang

OTHER AWARDS & HONORS:
President's Award: Betty Ballantine

2002

Novel: *American Gods* by Neil Gaiman
Novella: "Bronte's Egg" by Richard Chwedyk
Novelette: "Hell Is the Absence of God" by Ted Chiang
Short Story: "Creature" by Carol Emshwiller
Script: *The Lord of the Rings: The Fellowship of the Ring* by Fran
    Walsh & Philippa Boyens & Peter Jackson; based on *The Lord
    of the Rings* by J.R.R. Tolkien

OTHER AWARDS & HONORS:
Grand Master: Ursula K. Le Guin
Author Emeritus: Katherine MacLean